Immaculate Misconceptions

Lynn Peters was born and brought up in Croydon. She read English at Cardiff University and now works as a freelance writer. She was a regular contributor of humorous and raunchy verse to *Cosmopolitan* from 1984, and replaced Dr Ruth as contributing editor for the American magazine, *Redbook*. She writes regularly for *She* and *Woman's Journal*, and her articles appear in magazines all over the world. Lynn has also written for several TV comedy series, including *The Real McCoy*. She lives in Surrey with her husband and two children.

Immaculate Misconceptions

LYNN PETERS

Lynn Peters (signature)

LONDON · SYDNEY · NEW YORK · TOKYO · SINGAPORE · TORONTO

First published in Great Britain by Simon & Schuster, 1995
This paperback edition first published by Pocket Books, 1997

An imprint of Simon & Schuster Ltd
A Viacom Company

Copyright © Lynn Peters, 1995

This book is copyright under the Berne Convention
No reproduction without permission
All rights reserved

The right of Lynn Peters to be identified as author of this work has been asserted in accordance with sections 77 and 78 of the Copyright, Designs and Patents Act, 1988.

Simon & Schuster Ltd
West Garden Place
Kendal Street
London
W2 2AQ

Simon & Schuster of Australia Pty Ltd
Sydney

A CIP catalogue record for this book is available from the British Library.

ISBN 0 671 85360 0

Printed and bound in Great Britain by Cox & Wyman, Reading

To John, with love

Prologue

When I was fourteen my friend wrote 'Having Sex: An Instruction Manual'. It had one page with two matchstick people lying face to face. One had a skirt on. Under the diagram were two arrows pointing in opposite directions, and the caption read: 'Insert and repeat as necessary'.

We read it under our desk lids in maths, passing it along, and I thought it was the funniest thing I'd ever read, cutting out as it did all the heavy breathing, the soul-searching and heartache that, according to novels like *Peyton Place*, which we sneaked from our parents' cupboards, were crucial to the sexual act. Now I wonder what was so funny. If only relationships could be that simple.

Chapter 1

God, it's hot in here. You'd think they were trying to breed germs, not kill them. I've asked to have a window open but they say the other patients might not like it. Actually, we'd all like it, only the others just moan about it to each other and are scared to ask the nurses in case they take umbrage and withhold their right to a bedpan. I'm the only one who says anything. And it's so aggravating. You'd think the one chance you get to lie in bed for a couple of weeks without being poked and probed awake at 3 a.m. by a horny husband, or jumped on at the crack of dawn by a six year old wanting you to search for a video, you could snooze and doze and enjoy the comfort, but I just lie here sweating and tortured by the urge to kick all the covers on to the floor and lie on the bed stark naked.

Of course, that's the other strange thing. I've not worn nightdresses in two decades, well, except when I was in having the children. These are the same nightdresses too, front opening, of course, for the breastfeeding. Robert said he would get me something new, but I like to think that by wearing these old ones I'm letting everyone know that I'm not the sort of woman who usually wears anything in bed at all (though what they probably think is that

I'm a poor pathetic creature who has had to wear the same old nightdresses since her children were born). But it's important to feel you're making statements of individualism and sexuality in a place like this, even if they're misunderstood. Even though you know they'll go on thinking of you as just a recipient of pills and blanket baths. But I suppose that's why.

These beds are strange too; so hard, not like ours, or any bed I've ever been in. The mattress doesn't let you nestle down, it holds you on the surface, as though it's rejecting you, reminding you that they want you out of here at the earliest opportunity. (If you don't take the hint, meals show up regularly to reinforce the point.) And it's disconcerting to lie in a bed that has nothing to do with sex. Which has never had anything to do with sex. Except indirectly. With it being the reason we're all in here, I mean.

I've just finished eating (or more precisely, not eating) lunch when they bring a hysterectomy back from theatre and pull the screens round. This is how they speak. 'This is the hysterectomy.' 'She's the cone biopsy.' It's demoralizing to realise our chief significance to them is as a combination of symptoms. Do they suspect the internal struggles that haunt my waking moments? Are they aware of the sparky intelligence and lively character that flutter beneath my ragged nightie and drugged surface? No, all the nurses see is nil by mouth or total bed rest; they're blind to the complex and fascinating personalities we know ourselves to be. Well, maybe not the hysterectomy: she looks like that probably is the most interesting thing about her.

The curtains they're pulling round her bed are bright orange with huge golden sunflowers splashed across, so that when you wake up you're immediately dazzled. I guess they intend it to be cheering but it's very disorientating. I came round thinking I'd passed out in a meadow; either that, or I'd been reborn as part of a psychedelic record cover left over from the seventies. And jollity is depressing. Why don't they drop the pretence and just paint everywhere grey? At least that would match our mood and their mashed potato. These colours just show up how ill we look. I saw her face, the hysterectomy, before the screens went round: the texture of parchment, the mottled cream of Basildon Bond notepaper. She's on a drip, of course, and her mouth was open as she lay flat on her back. She didn't move at all, as though even in sleep she knew that any sudden movement would stretch the newly placed stitches, or pull the hand with the drip, bringing that raw dragging pain you get when the needle pulls against the taut skin. (When the nurse put my drip up I said, 'It hurts.' She said, 'Well it would, wouldn't it? You've got a needle sticking in your hand.')

There are five of us on this ward. Jamila, the Asian woman in the corner, is in with a threatened miscarriage; next to her is Millie, then Jean. Opposite Jean is an empty bed, then there's the woman with the hysterectomy, then me. Jamila doesn't speak much English. She has a tiny face like a doll's. Her husband is small too, with a thin reedy moustache, but he's a bully for all his lack of size and resemblance to Charlie Chaplin (or perhaps because of it). Jamila is frightened of him, she cowers down in her bed when he walks in. The nurse told me it's because Jamila's husband thinks she won't bleed again if she stays lying flat, and he has threatened her that there'll be trouble if she loses the baby. I smile across at Jamila and try to look encouraging. She smiles back but her eyes seem full of tears.

Robert didn't come tonight. He's in Coventry, and it's too far for his mother to bring the children on the bus.

Robert would have liked more children, but if I had to go through the Miracle That Is Childbirth again my eyes would be as full of tears as Jamila's. When he suggested we have another baby, I told him I was all for it, just as soon as they'd found a way for the man to do the pushing and get the labour pains while the woman mops his brow and tells him to keep breathing. It's criminal, I said, that science isn't seeking a way to let men experience the full majesty of motherhood which you only get by having a pair of forceps shoved up your nether regions. Since then the subject has been closed. Of course, now it's closed for good.

Jean is concerned that I won't have visitors tonight but I don't mind being on my own. I need time to get things in perspective.

You'd think there'd be plenty of time to think in here, but in fact even the nights are taken up with activity. In some ways it's like being at home — I'm still getting poked and probed awake at 3 a.m. Only in here it's to take my temperature and give me more medication. At home I roll over to the furthest extremity of the bed and feign a deeper sleep, but here the drip stops me rolling anywhere and they just plug a thermometer in my mouth. On my first night, before the operation, I told the nurse I wouldn't need any sleeping pills, I never had trouble sleeping. She said, 'You will in here.'

Those first few nights it was Bertha's team. Bertha is a giant of a woman, black and cheery with a booming laugh. You hear her coming long before she gets to the ward. She calls to nurses in other rooms, and the trolley rattles with her laughter as she clangs it against the skirting board and door frame. When she enters our ward, she puts the centre light on. I remember learning about Florence Nightingale at school and how she passed silently among the sick carrying her lamp. Bertha doesn't know those stories. She seems to resent the fact that we're asleep when she is up and working, as though our being here were evidence of our laziness. She knocks the trolley against the foot of my bed as she comes to me, and tugs roughly at my arm feeling for the pulse. I flinch because she always chooses the arm with the drip but she is oblivious of me, calling over her shoulder to the other nurse. They are discussing last year's holidays. And then they go clanking on their way down the corridor and it seems that I have barely begun to doze again when the nurse brings round tea at six (which is also like being at home, only better because there I have to make my own tea).

Despite the obvious drawbacks, to be honest, I like being in hospital. The nights may be filled with turmoil, but in the daytime you can lie and stare at the ceiling and there is absolutely nothing that you ought to be doing instead. No washing, no ironing, no one to take to cubs or brownies, no PTA meetings, no excuses to make for why you can't stay late at work, no house to hoover, no ornaments to dust, no dinners to cook, no orgasms to fake, no lies to tell.

You have time to think in here, and I've been thinking about growing up. What it was like. Because you wonder sometimes, 'how did I get from there to here?' When I was at school, reading my friend's sex manual, I thought the world was full of good things and they could all be mine. When did I find out it wasn't like that? What happened to that fourteen year old that turned her from a bright, hopeful, romantic adolescent into — into me? It isn't your parents who fuck you up, that's just one of the things we went around quoting at university which sounded so good and turned out not to be true at all — or at least, not for me. I know who it was, and I know what it was. It was Max. I was all right until I met him.

Josie came to visit this afternoon. Josie is small and fair and pretty and fills me with moral ambiguity. She lives next door. We were friends immediately she moved in, which is years ago now, but I can't see why she likes me. I don't think I like her. She's always happy, which is intensely irritating, and then there's the small matter of her affair. I know very well that the reason she comes is not for my benefit but because she wants to talk about it, and I'm the only one she can tell. It's been going on for three years now and I've disapproved since the beginning, though I've never told her. At the outset I didn't think it was my place to give an opinion, and now I've earned the right it's too late. I think she should finish with him partly because, although Josie has no children, he has three and it's unfair to his wife, but mainly because I can no longer look Josie's husband David in the eye. When we go there to dinner, he hugs me hello and I think, 'Do I owe it to you to tell you? Or do I owe it to you to protect you from knowing?' Of course, I say nothing but look guilty, so that no doubt David thinks not that Josie is having an affair but that I am.

You probably think I'm just jealous of Josie because my own sex life is such a shambles, but you'd be entirely wrong.

'Ellie, darling, how are you?' Josie is in high spirits today. She spent the weekend with her lover, and I appreciate her self-control in putting off telling me about it until she has at least asked me how I am. She has brought me some grapes and immediately begins to pick at them. Her hair is in a short sleek bob and she wears a brightly coloured mohair jumper with black leggings. She looks both sporty and stylish. I begin to regret my stance on the old nightdresses.

'I'm fine,' I say, which is all anyone wants to hear, though if she really wants to know what is concerning me, it's the impossibility of ever passing a motion on a bedpan.

'You're looking a bit pale,' she says, looking concerned and leaning closer to peer at my face. 'Would you like me to put some make-up on for you?'

I thank her and tell her that it is one of the things I should like least. A small consolation of being in hospital is that no one — except for Josie, evidently — expects you to look your best. Besides, I have made an effort, did she but know it. Only yesterday the nurse washed the vomit out of my hair, and I have combed it today in preparation for Josie's visit.

She glances round the ward, and I understand as never before just how accurate the phrase 'looking down your nose' is.

'Did you think about going private?' she asks.

I had thought about it, actually. In the way you think you'd like to own a Rolls Royce or live in the Bahamas. 'We aren't in BUPA, Josie.'

'Ah.' She has obviously never considered this possibility, but in any case I don't agree with private medicine. I don't want to be operated on at a hospital that thinks it's a five-star hotel and where I have to worry about how they'll get the stains out if I bleed on the fitted carpet.

'Well, there's no danger of this place thinking it's a hotel, is there?' she says genially, as Millie calls for a bedpan. She asks a few questions about the other patients and then there is a pause, after which she begins in the way I know she surely will: 'I saw Greg yesterday.'

When you're fourteen, an opening like that is a cause for high excitement. What did he say? What did he do? But when you're thirty-eight you know those things. He will have done what they all do, said what they all say. Of course I don't say this. Instead I say, 'What happened?'

'We had the most incredible time. Just by chance his work meant he actually had to be in Tunbridge Wells on Friday, so it gave us an extra day! Wasn't that just incredible?'

I agree that it was.

'And the sex just gets better all the time. It was never like this with David.' She has told me this before but I don't believe her. I think that the vividness of sexual experience fades, like pain, so that in latter years you can't believe it was ever so intense as it is now.

'What does he do that's different?' I don't want to ask this but the question comes out anyway, and she would be disappointed if it didn't. All the same, I'm sorry I haven't better self control.

'He can go on for hours,' she says, 'and then when you come, he's ready to start again almost straight away. He can go on practically all night.'

Mercifully, Glad arrives then with the tea trolley, and I wonder afresh if there's some law which demands you must be called Glad or Ida to do this sort of work. Ida wheels round the display of ladies' razors and soap. Visitors aren't allowed tea, but Glad gives Josie a cup anyway. Josie has that effect on people.

When Glad has gone, lumbering off to the next bed, I say, just to be awkward, 'Suppose you don't want to go on all night? Suppose you want to go to sleep, like normal people?'

Josie laughs. 'You don't want to sleep when you're with Greg.'

I pull a grape off its stem and crunch into the pip.

'So anyway,' she goes on, 'that's how it is. I mean, it isn't *just* the sex, but it is pretty unimprovable. And he looks gorgeous with his clothes off. Not like David . . .'

This is more interesting and will need considering later — not concerning Greg, but David. I used to have a fantasy about Josie's David, and in my fantasies he looked very gorgeous with his clothes off. The sex was pretty unimprovable too, although there wasn't a lot of sex in that particular fantasy, it being one of those where the main thing is that he adores you and follows you round the shops buying you things.

She continues, 'Greg won't say he loves me but I know he does.' I wonder if she is trying to convince herself or me. 'He sort of feels that if he puts it into words it's more of a betrayal of his wife.'

'You mean, more than actually screwing you is?'

She ignores my sarcasm. 'It's as though, as long as he can go on not saying it, then it might not be true, and we can all go on like this. But we can't; he'll leave her in the end, I know he will.'

'But how would you manage?' Josie doesn't work and Greg runs a small landscape gardening business: very small — it's just him. I don't see him being able to keep her in quite the way her solicitor husband does.

'I know. Awful isn't it?' She shrugs but also smiles because we both know that actually this situation suits her perfectly.

It must be nice to be Josie: confident, attractive, and so certain everything will always work out in your favour. She's only ever had one operation and that was the cosmetic removal of a mole. Time to take that smile off Josie's face.

'Don't you ever feel guilty?'

She frowns. I try making her frown a bit more.

'Because I just don't know how you can do it, Josie, making love with one man then coming home and making love with another.'

She opens her bag to take out her cigarettes, remembers where she is and snaps it shut. When she looks at me again her eyes look watery. 'It's all very well for you, Ellie, you have the perfect relationship with Robert. But it's not like that for everyone, you know.' She's upset now, which is a greater reaction than I'd intended, and I'm mad at myself. She doesn't have to visit me, after all.

'I'm sorry, I only meant . . .' I meant what I said, is the truth of it, but she accepts the apology.

'You don't know what it's like. I can't bear David to touch me. I lay there and he just does it.'

'You don't do anything?'

'I can't help it. Admittedly it's worse now there's Greg, but it's been pretty awful for years. We never had much of a sex life really, but I thought that's what sex was like.' Now the habitual smile has gone from her face, and with it the jaunty turn of her head. She looks older; I can see fine lines on the outer corners of her eyes. We are the same age, though she always looks a good five years younger, but now it strikes me that it is partly her demeanour that creates this impression.

'Doesn't David say anything?'

'Because I just lie there? I suppose he's used to it. And quite honestly, he's glad when I let him have it at all.' And then the spark returns. 'And so he should be, because when you compare what he can do with what Greg can do—'

'But it must have been good with David once,' I insist. For some reason, it's important for me to believe that this is so.

'These grapes are nice,' she says.

Wednesday today. They don't give you any rest in here. They've got Rita (the hysterectomy) up already, and she only had it done yesterday. She looks drawn, and her face is the sort of beige that fashion pundits advise middle-aged women against wearing, but they do anyway. She seems too small for her dressing gown, and her hair is flat at the back and sticking up on the crown. (We all wear it like that here.) She can hardly move and of course she's still strapped to the drip, but even she has to sit in a day chair for the requisite number of hours. That suits me though, it gives me someone else to talk to. The last woman in that bed was deaf and though we nodded and smiled and pointed, you couldn't call it a proper conversation.

'How are you feeling?' I can guess but it's polite to ask.

'A bit queasy. They want me to eat but I can't face it.' Well, you don't need to be ill to feel like that about the damp toast that congeals in the mouth like chewed up paper, or the milk they bring for cereal, which is neither cold nor truly warm.

'What have you had done?' It's protocol not to refer to a person's condition until they've told you themselves what it is.

'Hysterectomy,' answers Rita, breathing the word out on a sigh. She pulls a wry face and adjusts her position in the chair. She has moved barely an inch but still she lays back with her eyes closed for a moment before she continues: 'I had it done yesterday.' New patients, because they've been unconscious and not known what's going on, always imagine that you have too.

They can also tend to imagine that some medical knowledge will have rubbed off on you: 'I shouldn't be in too long should I?'

I have no idea but I don't let that stand in my way. 'They won't keep you long. That's why the food's so awful — so you won't linger.' She laughs at that. She has barely tried it yet but must have noticed that cooked cabbage smell that reminds me of the shade my little boy ends up with when he mixes together all the colours in his paintbox.

'Have you got children?' Rita wants me to take her mind off her discomfort.

'Yes. Two. Rebecca and Simon.'

'One of each, that's nice.'

I nod and smile. 'Have you got children, Rita?' We must learn to be friends, at least while we share the same few feet of breathing space.

'Six.'

'Six? No wonder you want a hysterectomy!' She laughs at my joke. 'But it must be nice to have a big family.'

'No one wants that big a family. It just happens to you.' She eases herself in her seat and her face looks grey.

'Are you a Catholic?' I ask when she recovers.

'Not Catholic. Just careless.'

There's a pause and she looks anxious.

'I wonder if I'll have to use a bedpan.'

'What are you in for then?'

I am glad Rita has finally asked me. One of the few pleasures of being in hospital is the chance to recount your medical history to an interested audience. Healthy people never really want to know. 'A hysterectomy, same as you. I had a tumour.'

Rita nods understandingly. 'Women's troubles.' Then she says, 'Got a husband?' It comes out *got-husband?* I guess Rita has lived all her life around London, she has that way of running the words together. It's a strange question to ask; I thought our discussion of children had implied they had a father.

'Yes. And presumably you've got a husband too, with all those kids.'

She nods and laughs a laugh which turns into a cough, the result of the anaesthetic. 'I had a husband all right. Left me the day my eldest was born. He came to see me in hospital, brought me a bunch of tulips and a box of Black Magic and said he was off. Couldn't face the responsibility.'

I can't see what's funny, and I can't see why she wants to tell me about it either. Except that in hospital we seem to be telling complete strangers our deepest secrets all the time. Maybe it's the feeling that you could die at any minute, so you want to review your memories while you still have the chance — and if you can find a listener, so much the better. Maybe it's because, in the event you should live, a stranger won't be around to embarrass you with your confessions in years to come. Besides, in hospital there's no time for building up relationships gradually.

Rita interrupts my reverie. 'He was all right. He'd come home for a few months then go off again. Mostly working abroad on building sites. It didn't bother me; he sent the money back.' Perhaps she senses the question I'm too tactful to ask.

'He's dead now. Got drunk and fell down a trench they'd been digging. We got a bit of compensation. It weren't his fault, it should've been lit, and a man's entitled to a drink now and then isn't he?'

'Rita, that's terrible. I'm so sorry.'

She looks surprised to see me upset by it, and smiles fondly to herself. 'He was the only one, ever. All the kids are his.'

'But didn't you mind him going off like that?' It was a tactless question but I couldn't help it. How could you keep having children in a situation like that?

She laughs again. 'Stupid, isn't it? But he did always come back, so he was reliable in his own way. And I always loved him, and that means you're stuck with it.' She looks out of the window, smiling at some memory which after all she decides not to share.

Later she resumes the subject. 'Good to you, is he, your hubby?' I wonder what constitutes 'good' in her reckoning. Probably someone who doesn't desert every time you get pregnant.

'Robert does his share around the house.' His share being to eat, sleep and live in it, while mine is to cook, clean, hoover and polish.

'How long you been married?'

'Sixteen years. There's never been anyone else.' Now why do I say that? It sounds like I'm trying to hide something.

'It's all right,' she says, sensing the defensive tone in my voice. 'Thirty years it would've been with my old man. There's Janice, she's a new age traveller, don't hear much from her. Poor old Alan, he was killed in Northern Ireland. Bernie, he's still in the army. Steven's eighteen, Darren's sixteen, and Gina's fourteen. You'll see Steven, he'll be in later.'

I can't think of anything further to say and pick up a

Immaculate Misconceptions

copy of *Woman's Journal* that Josie left for me, but Rita goes on, 'Got a good job, has he, your husband?'

'He's an architect.'

I always feel embarrassed about telling people. When we first met it was a prestigious thing to be, but now people see architects as the cause of modern monstrosities and the reason that every shopping centre resembles every other shopping centre. Robert isn't responsible for any of that but I often sense a veiled hostility when I mention what he does. But Rita just says: 'You should be comfortable, then.'

Robert says architects are the poor relations of the professional world, but we live in a Victorian semi and Robert gets a company car so we'd certainly seem 'comfortable' to someone who has brought up six children virtually single-handed. I wonder what she does for a living.

'Cleaning. At the local comprehensive. There's some dirty bleeders down that school.' Then she smiles fondly again. 'But my Steven went there and he turned out all right.'

There is a pause in which it becomes evident that Rita isn't going to ask if I work.

'I'm lucky,' I say, 'I've been able to do a job I really like.'

'I'd have thought you didn't need to work.'

I let that pass. 'I like working. I write for the *Guardian*.'

She's interested now. I like people to know about that early on, it makes them see me differently.

'What, one of them posh papers?'

'It's the local *Guardian*,' I explain. 'I write for the women's page.'

She looks disappointed and picks up my *Woman's Journal* from the bedside cabinet where I have placed it. I'm irritated that I left it within her reach, and depression closes in swiftly. She should have said, 'What's your name? I know you! You did that piece on . . .' But she has reminded me that I am thirty-eight years old and all I do is write the odd column on a freesheet.

'My Steven's got a good job. He's in the building trade. Got an apprenticeship straight from school, never looked back. He could have his own company one day.'

I begin to form a joke in my head about someone with his own window cleaning company — got his own mop and bucket — but realise the tactlessness of this in time. 'He sounds ambitious,' I say.

'Oh he is,' she says proudly.

'Mummy! Look what I've brought you!' Simon has made me a get well card and Rebecca is carrying a bag of oranges. I don't like oranges but Robert has forgotten that; his mother will have recommended them to help with my bowels.

'Feeling better?' Robert kisses me briefly, looking at me with concern. 'When do you think they'll let you come home?'

'Yes, when Mummy?' Rebecca and Simon chorus and Simon adds, 'Because then Nanny can go home. She won't let us watch *EastEnders*.' His concern is touching. I smile. 'Another day or so, I expect.'

The children begin squabbling over who can sit on the one chair, and Robert perches on the bed next to me. We have a few brief words while the children are occupied.

'Seriously, how do you feel?'

'Not too bad at all.'

He takes my hand. 'You're going to be so pleased when you see what I've done at home.'

Against my better judgement I feel hope forming 'Pleased about what?'

IMMACULATE MISCONCEPTIONS

'No, I want it to be a surprise.'

'Oh, go on.'

'It won't be a surprise then.' He demurs some more but I force him. I know Robert and surprises. Once he came home from work, alight with pleasure that he'd won a prize in the raffle. First prize was a weekend in Amsterdam, second was a portable colour television, third was a meal at a swish restaurant. Lesser prizes included bottles of brandy, whisky and wine. He made me guess what he'd won. It was eau de toilette, some unknown make in a suspiciously large bottle. I forget what it was called but Midnight in Potter's Bar wouldn't have been inappropriate. I never did understand why he was so pleased with his winnings. And he never understood why I was so disappointed.

'Please, just tell me. I want to be surprised now.' The surprise is that he's mended the lock on the wardrobe door and painted the hall ceiling. Of course, put like that, it is surprising. I've only been waiting for those jobs to be done for two years.

After my surprise we sit in silence while I practise looking pleased and try to think of something to talk about.

Robert comes up with a topic first. 'Did you ask when we can have sex?' He has asked this every day and I've been putting off giving an answer.

'Hard to say. Probably about three months,' I venture and then add, 'minimum.'

'Three *months*?' He looks horrified. And then he looks suspicious. 'Have you actually asked?'

I shrug and he assumes I haven't, but actually I asked the consultant only yesterday. He came round with a team of students, so after he had examined me I asked for a quiet word out of their earshot. 'When can you have sex?' he repeated loudly, for the benefit of the students. 'Entirely up to you, my dear, but I should wait till you get home, it embarrasses Sister.' Give me a doctor without a sense of humour any day. I don't want to be exchanging sexual innuendo with someone who's seen me with my legs up in stirrups.

I don't tell Robert the consultant's joke though, because if it's really up to me when I have sex, then I won't ever have it. 'Is everything all right at home?' His mother is staying to look after the children.

Robert sighs. 'Yes. But she thinks they should be in bed by seven.'

'I thought that's what you thought.'

'They don't like it.'

'Well, they'll have to put up with it.'

He nods morosely. He seemed such a strong, independent character when we met, but now I feel the weight of his reliance on me. Sometimes he makes me feel responsible for him and I don't like it.

Suddenly the doors at the end of the ward swing open and I see, striding down the ward, a figure I know instinctively to be Rita's son Steven. This may be partly because his presence, along with two other adolescents, seems to fill the room and Rita's description of her six kids had somehow made it sound as though there were dozens of them. But mainly because no one else in this ward but Rita looks as though they could be related to him. He is tall, with a well-developed neck and shoulders for his eighteen years, and he has the confidence and swagger that men in the building trade seem to develop. He wears battered trainers and jeans marked with paint, and there is at tear in the shoulder of his ancient suede bomber jacket. He sports a baseball cap at a jaunty angle and has three earrings in the lobe of one ear. At first glance he looks the type you wouldn't want to push up against in a pub, but his amiable expression and air of affability give the lie to that.

'Hello mum!' he calls out from half way down our six-bed ward. 'All right then?' There's no need to shout but his voice booms out. He's accompanied by a boy of about sixteen and a girl who, from her tight skirt, dangly earrings and mascara, could pass for twenty-five. But when the girl pushes past Jamila's husband, who has just arrived, and rushes up to Rita, stopping sharp at Rita's bark to 'Slow down, it's not a bleeding racetrack', I guess she must be fourteen-year-old Gina.

The sombre atmosphere of the ward is at once dispelled. A nurse appears at the entrance to investigate the commotion, and the room is suddenly alive with vigour and activity as Steven's voice fills the room: 'Bernie's been on the phone, says you're not to worry. Darren's been doing his homework. I done the ironing . . .'

Robert looks at me, bemused. 'What the hell—'

Irrationally, I feel suddenly protective towards Rita's pride and joy. 'For goodness sake,' I snap. 'It's only Steven.'

Chapter 2

The consultant came round this morning. He said, 'How are we doing today?' I said, 'I'm fine, I can't speak for you.' He raised one eyebrow and began discussing the chart at the end of my bed with the nurse. I felt like saying, 'I'm not stupid. I could have been a doctor myself, you know, only I'm allergic to stethoscopes,' but then I remembered I had to ask him about something. I switched to reverent patient mode and my heart started to beat faster. I tried sounding casual.

'I was wondering about the test results—'

'Test results? Haven't you had them yet? It's probably a bit early, I'll chase them up.' He patted my leg and moved on to Jamila, and my spirits drooped because I should have made him tell me. I should have grasped his hand and dragged out an answer to what is in the back of my mind, or mostly in the front of my mind unless I can push it out, and which is the reason I lie awake in the night listening to the drugs trolley, and have no appetite for the meals even if they're edible, and why I am so resentful of Josie and her happiness – of *everyone* and their happiness – please, please tell me, am I going to die?

* * *

'You know the worst thing about being in hospital?'

Rita is still confined to a chair for most of the day so she makes a captive audience for my philosophising. 'Not having sex,' she fires back.

'I said the worst thing, not the best,' I retort, making Rita laugh so that she clutches her side. She has combed her hair this morning but her pale complexion speaks of a vulnerability which I suspect we all share, even Millie across the room, with her low-cut négligé and ever-made-up face, though she hides it better than we do. She is in with a threatened miscarriage, the same as Jamila. Millie's boyfriend, the father, is only twenty-two, eight years younger than Millie. I suppose she feels obliged to make an effort.

'What's the worst thing then?'

'The worst thing is you have too much time to think. You start to worry what will happen if you die. Or what will happen if you don't die, and how long it will be before you're really well again, or if you ever will be really well again, or whether it will all come back. Once you get one thing, you're suddenly aware of all the other illnesses out there waiting to get you. You wonder how any of us survives.'

'Have a polo, dear,' says Rita.

'And the other thing,' I continue later, as we peruse the beef and Yorkshire pudding that is placed before us in a thick gravy already beginning to congeal, 'is that as soon as you realise you won't live forever, you start to worry about all the things you haven't done.'

'That's how I look at it,' Rita concurs. 'If I die tomorrow, just think of all the beds I'll never make, and all the meals I'll never cook and all the loos I'll never clean. Let some other bleeder take a turn.' She laughs to herself, separating a greasy ribbon of fat from the meat and popping the fat, not the meat, into her mouth.

'No,' I say, 'that isn't what I mean. Just think of all the places you've never been to, or all the things you haven't learned about. I want to travel, I want to have a career. I want to . . .' Unexpectedly I discover that if I say what I want to do I will cry. I want to see my children grow up. And I want to fall in love again.

'There, there, sweetheart.' Rita hears the break in my voice and looks up from attacking her meat. She can't move to comfort me but I feel waves of sympathy emanating from her, and her voice has a tender note that I have only heard before when she talked about her son Steven. 'You're young and you're strong. You've got nothing to worry about. And you got a good husband.'

Crying has made my mouth salivate and now the meat I am chewing feels pappy and full of sinews. I swallow it with an effort and wipe my eyes, feeling guilty because Rita has so much more to complain of, but doesn't.

'You want to forget about it when you get out of here and enjoy yourself. Get that husband of yours to take you on holiday or something. Do something to cheer yourself up.'

She's right, of course, but a holiday with Robert is not the answer. He'd think it was a chance to review our love life.

Rita is rooting in her handbag and produces a packet of cigarettes which she handles fondly. 'Wheel me down to the dayroom, will you darlin'?' she says, wheedling. 'I'll die if I don't have a puff soon.'

They all leave you with something, your old loves. Even Robert has, though he is still current. What Robert has left me with is a lack of interest in sex. It was different when we met, of course. We were at university. I walked into the student's union one night with my flatmate Carol, and she introduced us. Afterwards I remembered that this was the guy she had been talking about when she told me she fancied someone. But by then it was too late. Robert liked me.

Robert is tall, with fair hair that flops across his eyes as he moves. He is constantly having to toss it back from his face, and it was that simple movement that made me first fall in love with him. Isn't that stupid? As if the slope of a cheek or timbre of a voice makes any difference spread over a lifetime. But then, perhaps it is as reliable a guide as anything else. Maybe it is a good thing to be delighted a dozen times a day by a mannerism, so that your feelings of love are constantly being reinforced. I didn't eat for three days after we first went to bed. I had to go out to the local Spar to buy a bar of Fruit and Nut just so I wouldn't die of starvation. The sun was out that day, and I thought: Now it will be out for ever, and this strange sweet sickness in my stomach must be what all the songs are about. I'd always imagined it as a cerebral thing; I'd thought that you felt love in the mind, and that sex was its expression in the body. I didn't realise that love has its physical manifestations too, quite separate from sex. When you're young you don't know just how much you don't know.

We went to bed on the second date. Not that there was anything strange in that — this was the early seventies, and most of us thought that having sex was what a university education was for. When else would it be so easy to slip away in the afternoon and insert and repeat as necessary?

But in any case, our second date wasn't the second time we had met. Robert lived in the flat next door, and one of his flatmates was engaged to one of mine, so we had seen each other around even before Carol introduced us. And after the introduction we still didn't date immediately. He was going out with a humanities student, and things were a bit rocky with Max; when were they ever otherwise? In fact, that's how I got so friendly with Robert, now I come to think about it, because he provided a sympathetic and patient ear, as well as the odd glass of wine, when I needed to talk. It was easy to tell Robert, who didn't know Max and brought no preconceptions. I couldn't have told Carol those things. She would just have said, 'How can you stand that jerk?' even more often than she did already.

But Robert was entirely different from Max — everyone liked him. He always looked sexy. He still does, with his long legs and neat bum. I don't know what's the matter with me.

Millie likes Robert. I have seen her eyeing him when he arrives. This afternoon I have a book open on my lap and wish to be thought to be reading, but this doesn't deter Millie. 'Ellie,' she calls, 'come and talk to me.'

I feel sorry for Millie, on total bed rest. She could be using a bedpan for the next three months. But she thinks if she can keep this baby then she will keep her boyfriend. She should know better; she surely sees his glances straying around the room when he comes to visit her. And he never stays long.

'How long have you been married?' Millie has a romantic view of marriage which strikes me as quaintly old-fashioned. She gives a gasp of admiration when I tell her. 'So long! That's what I want. It must be lovely.' I tell her it is, seeing as that's what she wants to hear, and she grins conspiratorially. 'Don't you ever fancy doing it with someone else?'

I remind her of my stitched and sanitary-towelled state and we start to laugh at the idea of *fancying* it, let alone *doing* it. I think that you get to an age when you just feel tired of all that. Sex is only like eating, isn't it? You're hungry, you eat, you get hungry again, you eat again. It's no big deal.

I tell her this and Millie looks saddened. 'I don't ever want to feel like that. If that's what being married and having children does, maybe I better steer clear.' I have put her in a bad mood and now I feel depressed myself. I go back to my bed and lie down.

My first boyfriend, Stuart. I am fourteen and so pleased someone is finally taking me out — and not a silly schoolboy, like the other girls are dating. Stuart has a job, he is a postman.

I thought that everyone else in the class was already having intense and meaningful relationships, but as soon as I met Stuart I realised I was wrong. In fact there were only about four of us with partners, and only one of them was serious. When you're not doing something you desperately want to, it always seems like everyone but you is doing it.

Stuart was nineteen and I was proud of going out with someone so mature. It gave me some kudos in the other girls' eyes, and more importantly in my own. There was only one slight drawback — I didn't really like Stuart. He wore lace-up shoes, which nobody did then, a brown tweed jacket, and trousers with knife-edge creases. I'd have liked him to wear jeans but they weren't universal the way they are now. If you wore jeans then you were what my mother called 'a certain type'. She meant rebellious, bad. Max, who'd been expelled at fifteen for smoking dope, didn't wear jeans either. But I didn't mind what Max wore.

Stuart had strange hobbies: plane-spotting and predicting the weather. I used to predict the opposite of whatever he had said just to be bloody-minded, and I was right as often as he was. We would spend afternoons at Gatwick watching planes take off to exotic destinations while he explained the minute differences between seemingly identical aircraft. But he was interesting if you could get him on to the idiosyncrasies of the householders where he delivered his letters. One elderly lady often tried to persuade him to go inside for a cuddle. I thought she sounded lonely but Stuart found her overtures disturbing.

He didn't like any of the things I did. He wasn't interested in pop music, even less in the groups that played it. He didn't like fashion, he didn't watch television ... I wonder what we used to talk about, on those long afternoons walking through woods or travelling to Gatwick Airport, when we'd exhausted the latest tale of Miss Overton's overtures.

But I remember what we talked about once. We were sitting on a 68 bus coming home from an afternoon's shopping in Croydon. I had no money but I liked to browse, but he had been tedious about not liking the pop music playing in the boutiques. Soon we would be getting off the bus and walking home. And then I would have to kiss him goodbye.

'Why are you staring at my mouth?' he said. He had been looking out of the window; I didn't realise he could see me.

'I'm not.'

'What's wrong with my mouth?'

'Nothing. I wasn't staring.'

'You were.'

'You imagined it.' I stared past him, gazing out of the window, trying to give the impression that I'd been doing that all along.

'You don't like me much, do you?' The question dropped like a stone into a deep pond. A dull splosh and then silence.

'I'm going out with you, aren't I?' Somehow I couldn't bring myself to tell a direct lie.

'You don't like kissing me, do you?' he said.

'This is our stop,' I said, getting up.

The truth is, he was right but I couldn't help it. The important thing was to have a boyfriend, someone who liked you – whether you liked him was incidental. But you can't not kiss your boyfriend. Stuart's mouth was wide with pink fleshy lips, and his jaw was already shaped with the jowls that would surely be his distinguishing feature in his later years. There was the suggestion of stubble on his chin and a tiny froth of saliva at the corner of his mouth. Or do I imagine that?

As we walked home, not hand in hand today, he said, not looking at me, 'We don't have to kiss if you don't want to.'

Oh Stuart, you were so thoughtful, why did I care so little for you? But I had such high expectations. I wanted to feel how they did in the pages of *Jackie*. But I didn't ache, or yearn, or catch my breath. What I used to feel was this: the date's nearly over and now I have to kiss him.

The first boyfriend; the first date; the first kiss. We were standing on the porch, we'd been to the pictures, a James Bond film during which I'd sat woodenly through what seemed uncomfortably explicit sex scenes. He must have noticed my embarrassment because he asked at one point if I wanted to leave. He was always protective of me and aware of the age difference between us. Perhaps that's why, standing on the porch, he began to take his leave without mentioning it. What I'd been waiting for. So that the suggestion for it had to come from me.

'Don't you want to kiss me, Stuart?' I said. So his mouth hadn't put me off then, I suppose. He stepped toward me uncertainly, and put his arm round my shoulders. He closed his eyes but didn't turn his head to one side as I knew you should, but I did, so that was all right, and our noses didn't bump, which would have been embarrassing. He was a lot taller than me so he had to lean down. The tweed of his jacket was rough against my cheek. I parted my lips and his mouth met mine.

And nothing happened. We stood, transfixed, lips glued, and felt nothing. And not only that, but his lips were pursed, as though he was kissing a visiting relative. Except that it wasn't like that at all, because my mouth covered his in a strangely unpleasant way. I could feel the puckered skin of his lips between mine.

'Do you always kiss with your lips apart?' he said. I'd never kissed anyone before but we all know to kiss like that, don't we, we've seen the films. We'd just been watching James Bond make an art of it, for goodness' sake.

'Yes,' I said, 'don't you?'

So we kissed again and this time he parted his lips and it felt more comfortable but not exciting or stimulating in any way, and neither of us knew about tongues, so we just stood there, with our lips pressed against each other's for maybe thirty seconds, and then he drew back. I imagined it showed a want of passion to be the first to draw out of a kiss. He smiled at me with satisfaction and with what, it occurs to me now, was tenderness. 'Till next Friday,' he said.

Poor Stuart, who was even more pleased to have a girlfriend than I was to have a boyfriend, so pleased that he'd go out with a girl who didn't want to kiss him. He wrote me tender, heartrending love poems, but my heart was not rent, it was gladdened because I'd made a man fall in love with me. I took the poems to school and, if I was sorry to see the other girls passing them round in maths and giggling behind their hands, I hid it behind giggles of my own. I despised him, poor, sweet, thoughtful Stuart, for parting with something so precious to someone who didn't want it. Winning his love was like being handed the prize before the race had even been run.

They all leave you with something, your lovers, even those you don't love. I didn't love Stuart but I wanted to feel what he felt — the ache and the soul's sickness that was in his poems, the pain that showed in his eyes. This was passion, this was living. This was what books and films were all about.

Stuart had his revenge, although he never knew it. He made me believe that love and pain were inextricably linked.

Chapter 3

It's so hot in here. I open a window myself and pull down the blinds, but it doesn't help. The heating is still on; the nurses say the thermostat is broken. I can't breathe. I've been trying to read but I can't concentrate, and no one feels much like talking. But you can't help thinking about it. Every time I look up I see Jamila's empty bed. Millie is crying because she thinks it's an omen that she will lose her baby too.

Jamila was crying after lunch and I sat with her, holding her hand. I thought she was just depressed. She didn't tell anyone that the pains had started; perhaps she knew there was no hope. She lay back on her pillows, staring upwards and praying in a low murmur, tears streaming down her face. I should have called the nurse. But maybe she wanted this time of quiet. When they wheeled her away she clutched at my hand – 'I love him!' I told her that God would love her baby too, and knew what was best for him. But now I don't think it was her baby she meant, it was her husband. She thinks that if she loses the baby she will lose his respect and his love. I suspect that she is right. I am glad I misunderstood her.

Jamila has been moved to a private room and we have

been told not to visit her. But our shared grief doesn't bring us together, because Jamila's empty bed is like a grave. Which of us will be next?

I am fifteen. It is Annette's party. I sit on a sofa in Annette's mum's living room, with Janet and Linda, as though glued there. We are eager but afraid. The curtains are closed and the light comes only from a standard lamp in the corner, although it is only seven o'clock and still daylight outside. This is our first party with boys. Other parties were girl-only affairs, visits to the pictures and outings to the zoo. But Annette has a boyfriend at the local boys' school and he has invited his friends. In the middle of the floor stands Eddie, tall and good looking, whom we know as Annette's boyfriend's friend, with another boy, not so tall but even better looking, whom we have never seen before.

'He looks nice,' murmurs Janet, but I say he is not my type. It's my natural defence mechanism to say I don't want what I don't expect to get.

Both Eddie and his friend are smart in dark suits and ties with hair barely touching their collars. I tell Janet that I prefer Nick, the boyfriend of Susan, who wears beat-up jeans that cover spider-thin legs, and has straggly hair and glasses: an intellectual. Nick has never looked at me, but how could he when he is going out with Susan? I tell myself.

'He's coming over,' says Janet, meaning either Eddie or the new boy, I don't know which and dare not raise my eyes from the floor to find out.

'Would you like to dance?' He has a husky voice and I see his shoes, dark and shiny. I wonder why Janet doesn't answer him.

There is a short silence then Janet elbows me hard and hisses, 'Answer him, you idiot!'

I don't move because she is obviously mistaken, and then I see his feet shift slightly, so that they are pointing towards Janet, which must mean that previously they had been pointing to me, and he says, 'Would you . . . ?' And Janet leaps up but now I leap up and answer quickly, 'Yes, I'd love to.'

His hair is sleek and Chinese black but not so straight. His eyes are dark too, with the longest lashes I have seen outside an Eyelure packet. With his high cheekbones and fine full mouth he looks like a film star.

'Why didn't you answer me?' he says as we make our way to the middle of the carpet, the area designated for dancing.

'I didn't think you were asking me,' I say.

'Why not?'

I look at his beautiful face and think of my own visage when I look in a mirror – sallow complexion, too small eyes, too large mouth, hair in no discernible style. 'I can't think,' I say.

I went out with Neil for three months and he taught me two major lessons: one, that either I was more attractive than I knew or that you don't have to be good-looking to attract the best-looking man in the room; and two, that you can be sexy even if you don't know what sexy is.

Neil could make me feel sexy, but this was not, I discovered, the same as feeling randy. He made me feel that I *was* sexy. With him I felt wanted and desirable though devoid of any sexual feelings towards him. We used to meet at his house and I'd sit on his lap and we'd kiss and he'd fondle me and I'd think: This is boring, can't we find something more interesting to do? So we'd go for a walk, and then he'd want to stop somewhere to kiss and fondle some more, and so the day would go on.

Once, when his parents had visitors, we went up into his bedroom and lay down on the bed. I'd never lain next to a boy before. How strange to feel the length of his leg down the length of mine. He rested against the pillows while I leant over to kiss him, and when I drew back I saw that his face was different, his mouth hung open a little, while his lips had grown red and heavy. I was frightened.

'Touch me,' he said, and I thought, What does he mean? I am touching him. But he took my hand and placed it against his groin. I drew away in alarm. He had something tubular and hard in his pocket, metallic I thought, a torch perhaps? Why did he want me to touch a torch?

'Don't you like it?' he whispered. I realised what it was. I felt so stupid.

'We better go back downstairs,' I said.

That was the furthest I ever went with Neil. He'd been further with me, sitting in the cinema with his hand up my dress, and I didn't mind if that's what he wanted to do, it had no effect on me, and it was better than kissing because at least you could still watch the film.

He phoned me one Sunday evening. It hadn't occurred to me that I could ever be chucked. I went back into the sitting room where the family was watching television and said, 'We're not going out any more,' sounding as casual as I could considering that I felt totally humiliated.

'Oh?' said my mum, surprised. 'I didn't know you'd decided to do that.'

I think she genuinely thought that no one would give up the chance of going out with me.

At school the next day, announcing the news to my

friends, I heard Janet reply, 'well we wondered what had happened when we saw him with Eva on Saturday night. So you'd already broken up then?'

I don't remember what I said, whether I told them or not. You pig, Neil, I thought.

But after all, I had the last laugh. A year later he phoned again — he was sorry, he said, we should try again. I was going out with two other boys at the time — neither was serious, just the odd date. But they gave me a confidence I hadn't had before.

'Okay, Neil,' I said, 'pick me up Saturday.' He had a car.

Age makes such a difference. He was a man now, and I was independent, I had two boyfriends and a Saturday job.

And most important of all was the Saturday job because now I had money my hair was no longer without shape, but cut to fall in casual waves to my shoulders: stylish but without looking like I'd tried too hard. My eyes were ringed in black, lips flesh coloured, almost invisible. And I could afford clothes. For our date I was kitted out in the best Etam could offer: a short tight dress, open at the throat, around which was flung a long silky scarf. A suede fringed waistcoat and brown boots completed the image.

Pretending I was hunting for my bag, I dashed into the sitting room where Neil stood waiting and then dashed out again, calling 'oh, hi!' over my shoulder as though I had hardly noticed him. Then I collected my bag from the kitchen where I knew it to be. I'd just glimpsed him but it was enough to catch a look of astonished admiration: however he had remembered me, it wasn't like this. I looked exactly like Twiggy, only fatter.

We saw a film. I fondled him more boldly than before; I felt safe now in the cinema.

'Why not?' he asked, mystified, when I said I didn't want to see him again. 'You just wanted to get your own back, was that it?' But he was wrong. I had thought that now I was old enough to understand what all this sex thing was about I'd find him exciting. I liked him and he still looked like a film star. But kissing in the car afterwards I felt nothing. It reminded me of the time I went to see *Camelot* with my friends. They were all crazy for Richard Harris and, though I could see he was attractive and interesting and sexy, he just wasn't particularly attractive to me.

'I'm sorry,' I told Neil, 'but it's not like when you read about it, is it?'

'Hello, Mrs Cope. How are you?' It is Steven, flowers in hand and grinning, arrived to see Rita, but she has been a permanent fixture in the dayroom lately, puffing away. Since Rita introduced us, Steven makes a point of greeting me personally. He says ''Ello' and ''Ow are ya?' and I have to bite my tongue not to correct him as I would my own children. He is always smiling, always happy. He still wears the paint-covered jeans, but it must be a warmer day outside because he has no jacket and his shirt is open at the neck revealing a silver crucifix. He sports a ring on each hand, and if he were to pull his sleeves up I would expect to see tattoos on his forearms. He is still wearing the baseball cap and I wonder if he ever removes it.

'I wish you'd call me Ellie, you make me feel so old.'

'You're not old. Bet you're a lot younger than my mum.' I am and I wince at the comparison.

'And what about you, Steven, how are you?'

'Oh I'm always all right, me.' He smiles broadly, the

picture of youth and strength. 'Where's me mum then? Not in the dayroom with them fags again, is she?' His expression changes to concern and I feel a sudden pang which must be loyalty towards Rita.

'She's just popped out to the loo,' I lie. 'I'll tell her you're here.' I start up out of the low chair but he shakes his head.

'No, don't rush her. I'll talk to you till she gets back.'

I can't think of another excuse immediately, and now he sits on the edge of Rita's bed and tells me about his new job and how he likes working in the open air. He has a graze on his knuckles and his fingertips look hard and dry. I hope that my son never has to work as hard.

'Don't you mind the cold? It must be terrible in January.'

He shrugs. 'You get used to it. It's only a problem if it's icy, but that's not the cold so much as the fact you can slip. The hot weather's worse really. Makes it harder to get on. But I like all the seasons really, seeing them change. It makes you feel . . .' He casts about for how it makes him feel and doesn't find the words, but I can see in his face what it is. It makes him feel poetic and romantic, at peace with the world.

'And you don't mind heights, I suppose?'

'Oh no. Heights is all right. It's the drop I'm not so keen on.' I laugh at that, only realising later as I repeat it to myself that it will be an old joke in the building trade. My response encourages Steven to tell me about his brother Darren who is very bright and could probably get some GCSEs. But I am using up Steven's visiting time.

'I've got to slip to the bathroom myself,' I tell him at last. 'I'll just see what's keeping Rita.'

* * *

I wonder what they're doing at home now. Rebecca will be coming out of school, moaning about what they had for dinner and the fact that Miss Read made her do P.E. even though she wasn't feeling well. I always feel a flush of love to see her emerging from the school cloakroom, her hair all pulled out of its pony tail, her shoes scuffed and her socks falling down. I like this part of the day. It takes fifteen minutes to walk to the school from home, past the greengrocers and the hardware shop, and I usually meet one of the other mothers on the way. If I'm lucky it's Wendy. Her daughter is in Rebecca's class and we met on their first day at playschool. Wendy enjoys motherhood more than I do; she makes playdough for the children instead of buying it, and lets her three year old push a doll's pram all the way to the school, despite the fact that it makes the journey last three times as long. But beneath all that, Wendy shares the same fears as me: that we have somehow stepped off life's roundabout and can't get up enough speed to jump back on.

'Do you think you'll ever have a career?' she asked me once. We were drinking coffee in her kitchen, where one wall was festooned with her children's artwork. This was before I began writing for the *Guardian*.

'I don't know. It's so late to be starting. Everyone else our age is already established. What would you like to be?'

She shrugged. 'What can you do with zoology? I could teach I suppose.'

'You said you'd hate to teach.'

'It would fit in with the children.' Our discussions always reached the same conclusion. It isn't what you want to do, or who you want to be, but what will fit in with the school holidays.

'It's just not fair,' she went on. 'Men don't have to make those choices.' Our discussions always reached that conclusion too.

I try hard to warn Rebecca of the realities of motherhood. When she tells me she wants to get married and have babies I remind her that they will all grow up to be like her brother Simon, and she must make sure she gets a good job so she can afford childcare. I tell her that babies are synonymous with smelly nappies and are always sick on your best clothes. That children catch headlice and threadworms which they then give to you, and are always fighting and coming home crying with grazed knees. Once, when I was tucking her in bed after one of these lectures, she threw her arms round my neck and said how sorry she was that she was such hard work for me and she would try to be as little trouble as possible. I made a mental note to incorporate 'and children make you feel guilty' the next time the subject came up.

Once I told Theresa, editor of the woman's page, that I wanted to write a piece called 'The Myth of Motherhood'. It would ask: what happened to fulfilment and satisfaction? What happened to children playing round your knee while you make bread and stencil the kitchen cupboards? How is it that the cleaning and the cooking, the washing and the ironing never feature when you're planning a family? As I told Theresa, you read the books — the Hugh Jollys, the Penelope Leachs — and because you learn about tantrums and teething troubles you think you know the worst. But you recover from the nappies and the sleepless nights. The washing and the ironing, the bickering and the squabbling, those things go on forever.

Theresa said I was a cynic and that even if what I said were true, it did women no favours to remind them of it.

('But we could warn the next generation,' I argued. 'The next generation don't read our page,' she argued back.) She said we needed a simnel cake recipe for Easter week and would I research that instead?

I don't think I used to be so discontented. Once I assumed that the world was full of opportunities and I would have the pick. As it turned out it was and I did, but no one warned me that opportunities come with a use-by date. If there's one thing I've learned about opportunities it's that they lie to you. In some respects, they're like one-night stands — they tease and seduce with their promises and by the time you've realised they're never going to ring you back, it's too late. So I didn't worry about my career, there being plenty of time for that ('The world's our oyster,' Carol said the day we graduated. She should have said 'oil slick'), but started with the most seductive opportunity of all: the chance to investigate the phenomenon of true love. I followed Robert, who was slim and gorgeous with broad shoulders, and who knew exactly what he wanted to do, and moreover where he wanted to do it, and I was happy to do so because while for a man a career is everything, a woman may also have the satisfaction of children (I thought). And in the meantime, seeing as I could type, I could always work as a secretary if nothing else came up.

The trouble with having something you can do if nothing else turns up is that it pretty well ensures nothing else will turn up. If you're not actively looking for opportunities you don't recognise them even if they present themselves. And it was always easy to get secretarial work, especially as we moved so many times. I was even optimistic about my future. To me it seemed logical that, if a secretary was good enough, she would eventually move into the boss's job. (I don't know why I thought this, since I never saw it happen.)

IMMACULATE MISCONCEPTIONS

I saw inefficient clerks promoted to management, dishonest managers promoted to become directors, but however good the secretaries, they stayed secretaries. The greatest honour bestowed was to be asked to be a secretary to someone more important than the person you were secretary to already. If you were so good they thought you might actually leave and do something better, they would honour you with the title of 'Personal Assistant'. This, apparently, is a very important distinction to a secretary, even though Personal Assistants do the same work they did before and don't get any more money. But this was all fine too because this wasn't a career for heaven's sake, I was just earning a little money until something turned up. Just as my grandmother used to clean her flat before the home help arrived, so I was just flicking a duster round this area of employment until my glittering career showed up. And latterly it had had its compensations . . . I could work hours that fitted in with the children.

I know: pathetic, but if there's one thing more pathetic than travelling hopefully, it's finding out that the train you were travelling on has been going in entirely the wrong direction. Thus it was that I was filling out an application form for yet another part-time secretarial job ('It'll be okay for a couple of months') when I noticed something. They were asking for someone under thirty-five. Suddenly not only were my old choices no longer available, but the newer ones weren't either.

Which is why, when I applied for – and got – a job on the women's page of the local newspaper, I was so thrilled. I had a career. Not quite as glittering as I'd planned but still, at last, I was a *career* woman. The words 'just a' no longer formed part of my job title (as in 'just a secretary'). It was prestigious (relatively speaking), satisfying (ditto)

— and, can you believe it, I could still work hours that fitted in with the children. I thought I had died and gone to employment heaven.

'Why don't we have another baby?' Robert asked, when I'd been writing on the paper for about a year.

'Why don't you piss off?' I said. Oh, I know 'because I don't want one' would have been an adequate answer, but if Robert didn't understand how important my job was to me then he didn't understand anything. That was when things started happening between Robert and me. Or, more accurately, not happening.

I've put off thinking about Robert, wouldn't be thinking about him now were it not that I'm bored with my book and I've lent Jean my magazine. Robert doesn't seem to be the man I fell in love with any more. He used to be easygoing and funny. Now he has adopted the reactionary views and sartorial habits of men twice his age and waist size. He used to be stylish in a relaxed kind of way, but now that relaxation has turned into a mixture of conservatism and lack of concern over what he wears. His glasses are old fashioned too. I want him to get contact lenses but he says we can't afford them. Actually, this is what he says whenever I want him to buy something new (unless the something is related to the car, his hi-fi or his computer). He says, 'We can't afford everything. You just buy what you'd like for yourself and the kids.' I buy him clothes sometimes but he changes them for more white shirts, sensible ties for work, or the denim shirts he favoured a decade ago (except that then they were Wrangler or Levi and now he gets them in Marks & Spencer). He means to be generous I know, but can't he see that his lack of taste reflects on me? He has become unattractive to me. That lock of hair falling across his face is just an irritation now. I see him flick it back, and think, 'Why don't you get your hair cut more often?'

I've been mulling over a few ideas for the women's page with Rita. I thought she might enjoy it, but she's scathing.

'I can't see what you want to work for, a young girl like you.' Rita is only ten years older than me but she could be my mother. 'Two lovely kiddies, regular money coming in. Catch me working.'

'Yes but writing isn't like the sort of work you do. It's very satisfying. It's a branch of entertainment really, isn't it?'

She doesn't answer so I continue, 'I thought something on reflexology might be fun. Or aromatherapy.'

'Reflexology? What's that when it's at home with it's feet up? If that's your idea of fun then you want to come down the bingo with me, that'd knock some sense into you.'

I should let it drop but I'm sensitive about what I do. 'You may not like it, but there are plenty of readers—'

'Plenty of readers, yes — readers wanting to sell their furniture and buy second hand cars. If you think anyone bothers with the rest of it, you got another think coming.' It's not like Rita to be unkind. Maybe she's just not feeling so well today. 'And what's better than having a beautiful baby and seeing it grow up healthy? Aren't you proud of your two? I'm proud of mine, never no trouble with the police, not even Alan, though that could've been a matter of luck.' Her eyes look watery and I begin to feel sentimental too. I remember Simon on his third birthday. I'd made him a cake in the shape of a fort. Robert was up till 2 a.m., melting chocolate to be cut into squares for the battlements, and fashioning a drawbridge from chocolate fingers. In the morning when we came downstairs we found Simon standing on a chair to reach the cake we had hidden, as we thought, on the dresser. He was playing with the knights in armour which I had arranged so carefully, flying them in like aeroplanes and galloping the horses across the once glossy surface of chocolate icing. Now it looked like freshly farrowed earth. Robert shouted at him, and then I shouted at Robert. Simon cried.

'Have you any brothers or sisters, Rita?' She has just two get well cards on her bedside cabinet, one from her son in the army, the second from her other children. I've been wondering if she has more family around and now, in the break between breakfast and the arrival of the drugs trolley, is as good a time to ask as any.

'There's my sister, Enid. She lives in Dagenham. I never had much to do with Len's side, they're over Watford way.' She makes it sound as though living in Watford would preclude visitors. 'Anyway, what would I want with them? Bloodsuckers, the lot of them. You should have seen them when Len's mum died, fighting over who had what. I've got no time for them.' Her fingers are drumming on the side of the hard hospital chair. She does this when she gets irritated, usually prior to having a cigarette.

'Think I'll just pop down the dayroom for a fag. You coming?'

I wish I didn't find Rita such good company, because the dayroom is sunless and airless, heavy with twice-breathed air and cigarette smoke. This morning the air is clearer because Rita is its first incumbent, but the smell is still there, stale and sharp in the throat. The curtains are a mustard colour, the chairs with their hard wooden arms the same, but stained with spilled coffee or what I hope is coffee. On the floor are greenish carpet tiles, the colour of bile; from the state of the windows you would think (if it weren't for the fact that that we're three floors up) that a dog had peed against them.

'Len's mum was good to me. People carry on about their mother-in-laws but she was all right. If I was ill she'd come round and look after the kiddies, and she didn't agree with Len always going off, she always took my part.'

I nod and hope the conversation will take a more interesting turn. I don't get on with my mother-in-law and was looking forward to treating Rita to a short résumé of my resentments.

'People complain about their mother-in-laws, but I say, it takes two. You do right by them, they'll do right by you. And you got to remember, it's their baby you're taking away from them. My Bernie and Steven, they're still my kids, big as they are. Any girl starts messing them about, I'll soon sort her out.'

She doesn't sound as though she will be the sort of mother-in-law Len's mother was. I want to tell her about Robert but she's not receptive to my problems today. Her cigarette lighter falls to the floor as she draws it from her bag and she curses. She knocks my hand aside as I try to retrieve it for her, and lights up with unusual concentration. Her lips pucker into hard lines as she draws on the cigarette. Breathing out, she coughs.

I pray a lot in here: 'Please God, let me get well soon.' 'Please God, let the tumour be benign.' 'Please God, let Robert not ask about sex again.'

Actually, I feel quite well. Robert says I have to think positive, which I do, it's just that things always turn out for the worst. But the tumour has to be benign because I have so much to do. When I woke up today I thought, 'Please God, let me go home and get started on the rest of my life.'

It turns out Millie is quite religious. She took mass today. Before the priest came Rita called out to her, 'Say one for me.' I was sitting with Millie at the time and she hissed, 'She can forget that, I'm too busy praying for myself.' I thought this gave an interesting insight into the minds of the religious.

But she's sincere, for all that. She said to me, 'If you believe in God you should ask for what you need. God always answers.' I nodded my agreement and we clasped hands for a moment. Simultaneously, it seemed, our eyes filled with tears. For a moment we seemed united in God, but while Millie prayed I just went on worrying. Supposing God said no?

Last night I dreamt of him again. I was lying on the grass next to him. Robert was a few feet away playing with the children. They were younger than they are now. I felt Robert watching me although when I looked up he seemed fully absorbed with Rebecca and Simon. Max said, 'I'm sorry.' I said, 'It's too late to be sorry.' He said, 'It's never too late.'

Then Bertha woke me to take my pulse.

When the consultant comes with my test results I am just finishing the second chapter of my P.D. James. I think, 'Now he will tell me the worst and nothing will ever be the same again.' When I start chapter three the world will be a different place and I'll be a different person.

'Hello, Eleanor,' he says, and the words swim a little on the page but I don't take my eyes off them immediately. I

IMMACULATE MISCONCEPTIONS

want him to think that I have been deeply engrossed in my book, not that from the corner of my eye I have watched his progress from Jean to Millie, to Rita, to me. I don't want the consultant to think I'm panicking.

He stands at the end of my bed, glancing over my notes, as though they're only of casual interest. His suit is a dark grey and has a matching waistcoat, and his shirt is the white of new snow. His face looks scrubbed and clean as do his fingernails. Considering his profession, I feel glad about that. Then he looks up.

'We've got the results back.' He comes to sit on the edge of my bed, perching uncertainly, hospital beds being so high and he is not a tall man. I try to arrange my face into a suitable expression and suspect that what I actually look like is a Hallowe'en pumpkin with its ghastly carved grin. I try to relax but my face seems fixed in position. He refers to my notes, turns a page over, turns it back. Unusually the ward is silent; the air hangs heavy with anxiety and fear.

'It's good news. The growth is benign.'

Glad chooses that moment to come lumbering in with the tea trolley. The rumble of the wheels on linoleum and the flap flap of her down-heeled slippers have the sound of applause. The toot of a bus passing by is like a cheer. Suddenly life starts up again.

'So you mean it's—' I understand what benign means but I want him to keep on saying it, to explain it in different words, to let me savour the feeling of being retrieved from death.

'It wasn't doing you any harm, but it's best to get these things out and have a look at them.' I'm amazed at his understatement; we're talking miracles here. I feed him with another question, just to keep him fixed on the wonderfulness of it, but he goes on to the size and nature of the growth, which is sick-making and gross and not what I want to hear about.

Then, suddenly, with the immediate danger over, a thought hits me. 'So the hysterectomy . . . ?' Is he telling me that it wasn't necessary? That I could have gone on functioning perfectly well without this invasion? I suddenly feel possessive about my womb. A vision of the children I might have had, playing at my knee while I stencil the kitchen cupboards, is conjured from nowhere.

'In my opinion, a hysterectomy is always a good idea for someone with your history. Once it's gone it can't cause you any more trouble, can it?' He pats my leg twice through my dressing gown which signals that the interview is at an end, but I grasp his hand and hold it tightly between both of mine. I can feel myself growing sentimental. I want to hug him. Perhaps he guesses this because he tells me how pleased he is with the outcome and quickly moves away.

The screens that are kept at the side of the ward are fluttering slightly in the breeze from the window I opened earlier. The sunflowers on them are dancing now, their brilliant petals undulating. The brown centres are the colour of rich and fertile earth and shaded to suggest smiling faces.

Sunflowers are such a symbol of hope and optimism. I wonder why I used not to like them.

Chapter 4

I watch him on the ladder, reaching up with one arm to reach the topmost area of the eaves. His T-shirt pulls out at the waist revealing a strip of tanned flesh. A ripple of pleasure flutters through me.

Later, as I pass the landing window I see him standing in the front garden. Suddenly he drags his T-shirt over his head and, wiping a wrist across his forehead, swigs from a can of Coke. He leans back, shading his eyes, to survey the house and I bob back guiltily as though I'm doing something I shouldn't.

We talk and I wonder, What do I see in him? His eyes are too small for beauty, and his hair is neither fair nor dark, but his face is lean, high cheek-boned, like James Dean's. He drops his aitches when he talks, and his t's, though on those occasions he corrects himself for my benefit. When I speak he smiles, his eyes slide sideways, unable to meet mine, while a faint blush crosses his face. His eyelashes are like a butterfly's wings.

He has a natural delicacy, forbears to swear in my presence (and tells me how he hates it when his brothers do – it quite upsets his mum), and when he sees me putting out the rubbish for the bin, leaps forward to spare me from this arduous task. I'm touched by his thoughtfulness; my usual experience is for Robert to add another bag to the load, saying, 'Take that while you're going.'

My heart leaps to see him walking up the drive, head down, hands in pockets, whistling. I want to wear sexy clothes, tight pants and those wispy little tops that let your tits move about. And short skirts and black tights, and heels even if they're not in fashion. Except that I must be fashionable so that I look younger than he thinks I am. Or so I only look as old as I hope he thinks I am. And music. I need to hear it all the time now, loud and fast, someone singing with a deep husky voice, raunchy, provocative. I want to read books in which someone is saying 'fuck', and having sex in explicit positions I wouldn't have thought of.

He must give something off — pheromones, is it? Or maybe it's visual because he affects me the way pictures of naked women are supposed to affect men. Just a glimpse of him sauntering up the path, the denim of his jeans across his thighs.

I look him hard in the face, lick my lips and tell him, 'Drop your pants.' But it comes out, 'Would you like a cup of tea?'

And so I make him tea calling him into the kitchen to drink it, though I know he would prefer it outside so he can proceed uninterrupted. I ask him about his hobbies (music, and going to the cinema — he doesn't like reading), about what his friends are like, how he got on at school. Sometimes Rebecca joins us. I think she has a crush on him.

It happened like this. I was in town buying shoes for Simon and I saw Rita at the end of the market. I hardly recognised her out of her dressing gown, with her fuchsia lipstick and a perm like a pan scourer. But she recognised me.

'Ellie, darlin'! How are ya?' She took my two hands and stood back, looking at me. 'You look lovely. Everything all right?' I told her I was pretty well recovered, and she said she was too, but for the odd twinge here and there. I hadn't realised she was so much smaller than me. She wore ancient leather shoes much like the slippers she used on the ward, and though I wore only low heels I seemed to tower over her. Her coat was shapeless and she seemed older than her years. I was in the suit I wear for the office, and our clothes seemed to point up the class difference between us. I felt uncomfortable.

'Are you back at work yet?' I cast about for the common ground we had shared.

'I've been back but I'm off again just now. Not quite back to me old self.' She didn't ask me about my work and there was a pause before she turned to Simon. 'You all right then?'

He said he was very well thank you and she asked him if he liked school and he said yes thank you again. There was another pause when I could have said goodbye, but we'd been close, Rita and I, at a time when we needed each other. She'd jollied me out of a depression more than once. I kept her talking.

'And your kids, Rita?'

'Fine, doing well. Darren done all right in his GCSE mocks, still got his paper round, and he does Saturdays now down Sainsbury's. Gina's getting on all right at school.'

'And what about . . . ?' I couldn't think of his name.

'Bernie? He's home on leave soon.' No, not Bernie. 'But Steve's a bit down. Lost his job. Company shut up shop.' For the briefest moment a shadow swept across her face, but then it was gone. 'He'll get another one. He's a good boy.'

I nodded and took a step back, preparatory to taking my leave. We inhabited different worlds and it was fruitless to pursue it just because we'd had a temporary residence in the same one. I couldn't think what I'd been doing getting into a relationship with a woman who wore lipstick on the outside of her lips. But she caught my sleeve.

'Not got any gardening you want doing, have you? Or painting? He's very good, Steven.'

I said no, hurriedly, the way I do when gypsies try to press lavender on me, and then felt mean and tried to cover it up. 'I thought Steven was a labourer.'

'Well he is, but he's been doing painting and decorating with someone he knows for a couple of months — when they can get it. Does lovely paintwork now.'

I wasn't taken in by Rita's recommendation, But Robert had talked about getting the house painted and I wanted to do something for her. Giving her son a few weeks' work would cheer Rita and help assuage my middle-class guilt. Robert would complain, but where was the harm?

'We might need some painting outside. I'll see what Robert says. I'll phone you.'

Actually, Robert said rather more than I'd expected. 'I don't know what you were thinking of. He could be a juvenile delinquent for all you know; you can't expect a mother to give you an unbiased reference can you?'

I supposed not.

'And what sort of a job d'you think he'll do? There'll be paint all over the windows.' There was a lot more along those lines, and in the end it was Robert's opposition that decided me. Steven gave us a very low quote and I took him on.

Of course, Robert was right really. Steven doesn't have a car, so I had to buy the paint, carting it back from the hardware store in Robert's car, with the ladder he was borrowing from a friend strapped to the roof rack. And he does get paint on the windows. I have to check them each night before Robert comes home, wiping the paint off with a damp cloth before it dries. Steven says he'll do it, but he doesn't notice.

He makes me laugh. Simon said he wants to be like Steven when he grows up and my heart sank, but when I asked why, he said, 'Because he's always happy.' Steven has a quick temper, and I saw him rein it in today when I dragged my damp cloth across his freshly painted sill, but he's quick to smile too.

He reminds me of my first boyfriend Stuart. This is strange because I wasn't attracted to Stuart at all. Perhaps it's because I feel in control of the situation now, as I did then. Steven will do as I ask, not only because I'm paying him, but because my superior age and position (I'm the householder, he the artisan) gives me power. It's a long time since I had this feeling. I like it.

'I've got something to tell you,' says Steven, looking into the kitchen where I am pretending to be busy. His voice is full of excitement. 'You know Gina, my sister? Well, she was on the radio last night. I got it on tape here.' He hands it to me and I put it on the radio cassette player I use in the kitchen. The quality of the tape is poor but I can make out a girl's voice and a disc jockey saying, 'That's it! You've done it!' She won a compact disc and two tickets to see a band I've never heard of.

'Isn't she brilliant? I'm so proud of her. I've phoned up loads of times and never got anywhere.' His face is flushed with delight as he tells me of his own efforts to achieve ten seconds of fame. His immaturity is frightening.

But, after all, not frightening enough. I find myself wondering if he knows how attractive he is. I meet his eyes and he smiles, and says he had better get back to work. I guess he doesn't know. Then suddenly he pops his head back round the door. 'You can hang on to that tape for a bit if you want. Show the kids.' He stands at the door a fraction longer than he needs.

Everything seems changed since I came home from hospital. It's like coming up for air when you thought you'd been drowning. The world looks brighter, like through new glasses. This morning I looked at the daffodils coming up through the lawn and I thought, Next year I'll still be here, and the year after.

'I'm starting to look forward to our holiday,' says Robert, getting out the ironing board. My being away was good for him (or do I mean good for me?). He has learned to iron things other than his own shirts, and now has a working knowledge of the programmes on the washing machine. (I could never understand why he, who could plumb it in with such ease, should have so much difficulty operating it.) His mother, who remembers days when a hysterectomy was an operation requiring months of recuperation, instructed him to take on my tasks when I came home from hospital, so much of the washing, ironing and hoovering suddenly switched to his domain. I could do it perfectly well now, but it's easier just to go along with it. Well, I wouldn't want to disagree with my mother-in-law, obviously.

IMMACULATE MISCONCEPTIONS

And this isn't the only new development. After telling me that we couldn't afford a holiday this year, Robert has arranged to borrow his brother's caravan and has booked up for us to go to France in a few months' time. It's not exactly the five-star accommodation I could have wished for but it's an affordable way of going abroad, and it's sweet of Robert to have organised this surprise for me (so a mended wardrobe door wasn't the only thrill he had in store after all).

'It'll be good to get a bit of sun,' I say brightly.

Robert looks wistful, bringing home to me just how much strain he must have endured these past months. 'Maybe there'll be someone who can babysit on the site and we can get a bit of time to ourselves?'

I conjure up an image of the two of us sitting in a smart French restaurant and try to listen to our conversation, but we don't seem to be saying anything. 'Yes. That'll be nice.'

I'm grateful and touched by Robert's thoughtfulness and try to remember it when he says things which irritate me – which he does now by suggesting that he leave Rebecca's frilly dresses for me to iron, as I do them so much better than he can.

Today I make Steven a sandwich at lunchtime and we eat together in the kitchen. I think he expected me to take it outside for him, but whenever I wander outside to chat to him he gives me only half his attention, his eye constantly roaming to the area of windowframe he has yet to finish.

'Are you going out tonight?' I seem always to open with this question, but what else does one talk to the young about?

'Yes, well just a few pints down the pub. Me mate Rich'll be there and some of the lads we were at school with. On a Friday we go clubbing but not tonight. We go to that new place by the market. D'you ever go?'

I can't decide whether he genuinely believes I might or is just making the general assumption of the young that everyone enjoys what they enjoy.

'I haven't been recently,' I say, which is true after all.

'Music's brilliant. My friend knows the DJ.' I nod, but evidently a greater response is required.

'He's brilliant. Could've been on Radio One.'

'Wow, he must be good,' I say with heavy sarcasm, realising too late that now I'm the one making the assumptions, assuming that he will think Radio One is naff just because everyone I know does.

My tone has embarrassed him and his disappointment in my response gives me a pang. I add enthusiasm into my voice, as though the sarcasm hadn't been there at all. 'He must be really good,' I say, 'if radio is interested in him. He's bound to get a break soon.'

He nods in agreement. 'This is it.'

I don't know what's happening to me. I've always liked intelligent men. Look at Robert, look at Max: independent, thoughtful people who arrive at their own conclusions. Steven gets his opinions second-hand from his dad, his mum, his older brother, his friends. He is prejudiced against immigrants, foreigners, and black people; against the very rich, the very poor and the unemployed (his own redundancy notwithstanding); against people who get into fights and against those who back off. Perhaps, in time, he will also get his opinions from me. 'You're clever, aren't you?' he says, catching sight of our wall-to-wall bookcase in the lounge. 'My mum said you was one of them clever ones.'

If Steven thinks I'm clever I don't know how he would have described Max. (I do know. He'd say, 'Max is one of them *really* clever ones.' His powers of description are not wide.) Max had exceptional verbal skills. He could take a statement you'd make — an innocent remark such as, 'I'm not keen on raspberries' — and spin it like a web to catch you in. He'd peel away your arguments and layers of defence until, to your astonishment, the heart is revealed — and there, just as he'd predicted, you find you *do* like raspberries. No use to point out that his having won the argument doesn't make them taste any better; the point of the argument is the argument itself.

Sometimes they were irritating, but mostly those fierce verbal battles were wonderful. In the afternoons we would lie on opposite ends of my bed while the conversation rose and fell like bubbles floating and bursting. Then suddenly he would pounce on a topic, and we were off.

It always ended in bed. He wasn't the gentlest or most caring of lovers, didn't believe in foreplay (and could prove, in discussion, that I didn't either) but he exuded a powerful scent of sex. The argument was the foreplay; it raised the temperature, got the juices flowing.

I have a cat these days, called Trevor ('You can't call a cat Trevor,' Robert said, thereby confirming my choice), and sometimes when I come home he is so pleased to see me he reminds me of myself when I used to greet Max. My cat loves me, wants me to hold him, stroke him, fondle him. If I so much as kneel down to open a cupboard he tries to climb on to my lap. But I'm busy, I have the meal to prepare, the beds to make, my column to write. I have other interests — I can't devote my life to one damn cat. Besides, I have another cat.

Max could be very cruel. Once he said to me, 'I've made up an allegory, I want you to hear it.' I didn't want to, I guessed it would be some kind of trick or joke at my expense. He would sometimes tell me of something which had happened to him, a yarn so bizarre it couldn't possibly be true, but he would swear it was until I believed him — and then he'd laugh at me for being so gullible. I sensed something of the sort this time, but he was persuasive. The allegory was of a man and a mountain, and the meaning that evolved from it was that a man loved a woman and couldn't tell her, while she, unknowing, pined away thinking her love unrequited.

I flushed with pleasure. He loved me! I'd always known it. I explained the allegory in as cryptic a way as possible to keep the thing going.

He laughed, and there was the hint of a sneer. 'I shouldn't have bothered telling you. You can't possibly know what it's about, it's about someone you haven't even met.' And then he smiled, or at least I remember his bared teeth. 'It's not about you, you know. Did you think it was?'

Josie comes round in the afternoon. 'Mmmm, he's all right, isn't he? Wouldn't mind licking the Häagen-Dazs off that.' She looks backwards over her shoulder as I let her in the front door. Steven has his shirt off and is cleaning his brushes in the driveway.

'Josie!' How dare she treat my friend's son as a sex object. She raises an eyebrow, and with this innocent mannerism irritates me as she so often does. 'I thought you only had eyes for Greg.' I make coffee and open a packet of Hob-Nobs which Josie refuses initially. I've asked her round because I want her to mind the children for me tomorrow when their half term starts, while I go into the office. They usually go to a minder on the two days a week that I work, but Cathy is ill. I need to be pleasant to Josie and already the conversation is veering in a direction I don't want it to go.

'I do only want Greg, you're right. But when you're in love it sensitises you to the attractiveness of other men. You don't want them, but you do appreciate them. Whereas for you, married to Robert all this time, it's like someone walking around with their eyes on the pavement. You're dead to what's around you.'

I always think she's so shallow, so her occasional flashes of insight are all the more impressive. But she is wrong in one respect: now I'm as open to new possibilities as she is.

'You ought to have an affair,' she says. 'Make a new woman of you.'

Lying here, huddled on my side of the bed so that I don't touch Robert, I've been thinking about what Josie said. Perhaps an affair would do me good, but the trouble with having an affair is that you have to have sex. I still haven't had it with Robert since being in hospital, though it's nearly four months now. We did try, but I said it hurt. It did hurt actually, but then I was squirming around and wriggling so it was bound to. I can't lie to Robert, you see — I can't just say we can't have sex because it hurts, it has to hurt really. Not being able to lie would make having an affair difficult too, I suppose.

What I really want is an affair based on mutual devotion

and passionate need that can never be fulfilled. Perhaps Steven will come up behind me and kiss my neck, and fold his arms round me, and when I turn to him I'll see his face tortured with love, and I'll say, we can't do this, and he'll say please and I'll say no, and he'll say, 'You're right. I respect you too much,' and he'll turn away, brave but broken, and keep me in his heart all the days of his life. I've been flicking through a Mills & Boon book that Josie lent me in hospital, you can tell, can't you? But even in Mills & Boon they have sex these days.

Robert is being very understanding about my not making love, and the more understanding he becomes the less I want it and the more I'd like to hit him — anything to provoke a response out of his calm demeanour. Where's the dynamic rebel he used to be? Why can't he be angry or indignant with me? He must know that there's no physical reason not to be having sex, so why doesn't he do something about it? He still thinks that all my difficulties are hormonal, psychological or due to the operation, and he's prepared to be patient until things get back to normal — although why he thinks things were normal before I went into hospital I can't imagine, because I didn't want sex then either.

'Are you asleep?' Robert has raised himself on one elbow and is bending over me. I don't respond but he leans down and kisses my mouth. I stir, as though disturbed from half sleep.

'Your breath smells,' I say unkindly.

'Does it?' He sounds surprised; he has every reason to be. 'I'll clean my teeth again.' He gets up and pads to the bathroom while I turn into the foetal position and fall into what (I hope) looks like a deep sleep.

I too wish our sex life could return to normal, though in my case 'normal' would entail the sort of frenetic sexual activity enjoyed by, let's say, a nun.

Chapter 5

I was sitting in the university arts common room with my new friend Carol, between lectures, when he came in from the street and sat down with a newspaper. There was something in the slight pout of his full lips, a fineness about his nose. Was it the way he walked? 'Look at him,' I said to Carol, 'wouldn't you say he's bent?'

'Bent?' she said. 'How bent?' Bent was a new word for homosexuals and she couldn't quite catch my meaning.

'Queer, gay. Don't you think so?'

'Where? Who d'you mean?'

It took me so long to point him out that clearly she didn't think so. 'Him? The one who looks like Jim Morrison?'

He did look like Jim Morrison now she mentioned it: languid and overtly sexual, with the same firm jawline. Okay, so he wasn't bent – slightly curved maybe. Anyway, he had something about him which set him apart from the majority, even if I was wrong about what it was.

It was another three weeks before I spoke to him. Carol had persuaded me to go to an English department social with her. She was doing Music herself, but thought I could furnish her with a few introductions. Carol and I had been friends for less than a term, having met in the hall of residence where we lived. I suspected that the real reason she wanted me with her was so that she would have someone to walk home with if she didn't meet any men she fancied, but as the halls were nearly three miles away from the faculty buildings I didn't hold that against her. Actually I was glad to be asked out by anyone, even a roommate.

The English social was held in a newly built extension, the white-painted walls covered in posters advertising past triumphs at the local theatre. A few posters were for the RSC at Stratford, and there was a notice inviting students to sign up for a coach trip. In front of one of them stood a group of five or six male students, uniformly dressed in loon pants of varying colours so wide at the ankle they almost covered their shoes. The pants outlined the soft curves of their testicles, and it was possible to see quite clearly to which side they dressed and whether they were wearing underwear. One of them had a small bulge that extended several inches down his thigh.

'Get a load of him,' said Carol, jerking her head in the man's direction. As I watched he turned to speak to a girl wearing a full-length cotton skirt and an off-white cheesecloth smock. Like the rest of us, she wore no bra and her large nipples showed through clearly. She looked like she was offering him two strawberries in a dish of cream. On balance I thought she and he made a good match.

'Shall we go to the pub instead?' Carol was losing interest now the man with the bulge was spoken for.

'Let's have a look at the notices before we go,' I suggested, meaning, let's put ourselves in the vicinity of the other guys with their balls on show. Two of them wore tight T-shirts the same as mine, slightly short at the wrists, and the others were in skinny rib sweaters that emphasised their scrawny chests and above which their Adam's apples bobbed. Carol believed that a large Adam's apple was a sign of virility, but neither of us had yet had the chance to test the theory. We didn't get it now either: they were discussing something heatedly and ignoring us totally. Carol pointed out one of the posters of an RSC production she had seen, giving me a brief summary of its strengths just to pass the time, and then I pointed out the advertised trip we could go on, for the same reason. Then we looked at each other.

'Let's go to the Union first,' said Carol, 'see who's down there.' It wasn't just we who were bored, in fact the only ones who weren't were the man with the bulge and the girl, who was moving ever nearer it, and a bunch of students feigning enthusiasm as they talked to a couple of lecturers feigning a laid-back demeanour. The sombre atmosphere was reinforced by the drying cubes of cheddar and pineapple on sticks, displayed without flare or imagination on a trestle table draped in a white paper cloth.

'Come on, then, not much going on here,' I said, raising my voice and casting a last glance at the group next to us. They continued to ignore us as we turned to the door, and that might have been the end of it but at that moment another guy, with hair down his back and a moustache, walked in. I didn't know him, but I saw from her face that Carol either did or meant to. She made a beeline for the door and 'accidentally' bumped into him, dropping her canvas shoulder-bag. He picked it up for her as she turned back from the door, and she fell into conversation with him, tossing her hair back and smiling with her wide mouth. As they passed me *en route* to the table with the wine she winked at me, and I heard her telling him that she'd known, the minute he walked in, that he was an Aquarius.

I didn't know what to do then. I didn't want to cover the several yards to the table with the things on sticks (people might have looked at me), but I felt exposed standing there by myself. On the other hand, I didn't want to go to the Students' Union either. The corner by the door to the Union bar, where I would have to pass, was the haunt of the crowd I took to be pot-smokers, though I had never tried it myself and was embarrassed to ask anyone else if that's what they were doing. Admitting you hadn't tried pot was almost as embarrassing as admitting you were a virgin, and they could tell, these guys. They had held out their cigarettes when I passed them earlier and invited me to join them, laughing when I tried to pretend I hadn't heard and wishing me love and peace. They were older than the students I knew — mature, very mature students. I didn't want to be around them by myself.

But if I didn't want to go the Union, even less did I want to go home. I'd spent fifteen minutes on my eye make-up and almost as long deciding which cheesecloth skirt to wear. I hovered by a table of leaflets which informed me that the purpose of tonight was to advertise to an eager populace the mystery and excitement that was the English Society.

'So, you're an English stoodent, or are you just looking us over?'

I spun round to see a small, thin figure, dressed from collar to ankle in skin-hugging leather. He wore a large gold earring in one ear and his long hair was receding and grey at the temples. He must have been at least forty-five. I looked at him non-plussed.

'You doing English, or what?' He repeated the question

and I noticed a mid-atlantic drawl which didn't sound entirely authentic. He had spurs on his black leather Chelsea boots.

'Yes, I'm in my first year.' I tried to sound relaxed but he made me uneasy.

'I can see that.' He leaned towards me conspiratorially. 'It's only people in the first year who come.' He laughed at the joke and I joined in.

'I take it that you're in the first year too, then.'

He roared with laughter now, making the group standing at the notice-board look round. He extended his hand toward me. The fingers were bony and long, and there was a ring on each one. 'I'm Cliff Rose. I'll be lecturing you in Anglo-Saxon poetry next year.'

I knew nothing at all about Anglo-Saxon poetry, and I hadn't expected to find myself displaying my ignorance quite so early in my career. There were plenty of questions I could have asked — about Anglo-Saxon or about the other lecturers, or the way the faculty was organised, or the drop-out rate among students. This was an opportunity to put one over on Carol, to make her feel that in abandoning me she had missed an opportunity to develop a personal relationship with an important and influential member of staff. All I needed was a clever and original quip with which to burn myself into his memory and make me stand out as separate from the others. I fixed him with my gaze and drew a breath. He looked at me expectantly.

'I'll look forward to your lectures then,' I said.

Cliff Rose decided he had extended his patience quite long enough. 'Let me introduce a coupla people to you.' He beckoned someone over, and it was the man I had seen in the arts common room, the Jim Morrison lookalike. It's embarrassing to find yourself being introduced to people about whom you have already formed an opinion, and I could feel myself blushing. He had been in the act of refilling glasses, and he advanced upon us still carrying a bottle of red wine and two clean glasses. He didn't look like the other students or, if Cliff was anything to go by, other lecturers. He wore an open-necked shirt and green cords which gave him a slightly arty look, and his hair barely touched his collar. He had a slight hint of eccentricity about him.

Cliff relinquished his grip on my arm. 'I caught her. Just about to leave, can you believe that?' Jim Morrison gave a wry smile. To me, Cliff added, 'He'll look after you. I need a fresh beer.' He didn't linger; I hadn't entirely impressed my new lecturer with the calibre of this year's intake.

'Would you like some wine?' When he spoke he wasn't like Jim Morrison at all. He had a public school accent and an air of inner confidence. He pushed the glass into my hand and filled it carefully. He had long fine fingers, and when he looked up I saw his eyes were granite grey. I reviewed my earlier prejudice and found it in his favour.

'We're a little short of women tonight,' he said. 'We need to hang on to all the ones we can.'

I nodded. 'It looks like you're short of punters generally.'

'Yes. Not exactly standing room only is it?'

'No, but there's plenty of room to lie down.' It was just the nerves talking — before Cliff Rose had arrived I was wondering about the man with the bulge and the girl, and whether they'd end up in bed — but it sounded like I was giving Jim Morrison the come-on. He looked me in astonishment. 'I mean,' I added hurriedly, 'if there aren't enough chairs, we can all sit on the floor.'

He glanced around at the thirty or so chairs, all empty,

and I saw with relief that he had decided to ignore my ramblings. 'It isn't as well supported as it should be. Are you going to join?' Waves of dark hair framed his face.

'I don't know. Presumably you think it's worth while.'

'Good Lord, I'm not a member, not my kind of thing at all. I only called in for a free drink.' We laughed at that and some of my tension eased.

'Are you reading English?' he asked.

'It's the only language I can read.' He didn't smile and, feeling suddenly self-conscious I went on, 'but I'm like you, I'll go anywhere for a free glass of wine.'

'Maybe you will,' he said, and added cryptically, 'but I don't think that means we're alike. What do you plan to do with your life?'

'Get a degree. Fall in love. Live happily ever after.' It was meant to be flippant but it sounded naive and foolish. In fact I had planned no further than to get a degree — I thought three years would last forever.

'You're not very ambitious, are you?' His eyes narrowed as he weighed me up, and I felt I had failed my second test of the evening.

He was studying English and Drama (I thought the drama explained that slight theatrical affectation), and was in his second year. He was born in Cambridge but lived variously in London, Birmingham and Manchester, as well as in France and Italy. He asked whether, in saying that I only read English, I meant I had no German or French, and I said I hadn't meant that at all (even though it was true) and it was just a joke.

'A joke?' he said, as though it was a concept with which he was entirely unfamiliar, reminding me of those high court judges sometimes quoted in the papers who claim never to have heard of Mick Jagger or rock 'n' roll. 'So you're something of a wit, are you? Then I guess you must be a fan of Wodehouse. I never got on with him myself.'

I re-reviewed my prejudice and decided he was a cut below, not above, the rest. Pretentiousness, thy name is Jim Morrison. I looked around for Carol to rescue me but couldn't see her anywhere. 'I'd rather have Monty Python,' I said to puncture his conceit.

'Oh God, not another telly fan,' he said, puncturing mine instead. 'I'll tell you my main objection to television. The people who watch it never have any conversation beyond what they watched last night.'

The injustice of that stung. At school we had discussed many other things: pop stars, clothes, boys, music, homework, boys, pop stars. What we'd watched on TV was only part of a larger whole. But beneath my inner protestations a little voice whispered that indeed many of my ideas and views had been formed by what I had heard on television. It warned me that I might want to conceal that fact in future. For the first time in my life, I was among people whose background and culture was not identical to my own, and from now on it would be unsafe to make assumptions about the thoughts and experiences of others. I might need to do more than just 'be myself' in such company. But who, then, should I be?

He had been continuing to talk while I considered this new perspective, all the time making me more insecure and afraid of what I was doing here among the articulate and well-educated. 'So, tell me your first impressions of university life.'

It was bursting in me to tell him how I despised him and all the others like him, with their pretentiousness, their elitism and their Adam's apples, but when I raised my eyes, his gaze was disarming. He wasn't laughing at me as I'd thought and, furthermore, he wasn't flirting with me either. Unusual, that, and oddly flattering. Perhaps after all there was nothing personal in his remarks. I was the one at fault for being unused to hearing such opinions expressed. Here was a man who focused not merely on my body, but who was attentive, responsive, waiting on my reply. At last — a guy whose interest in me was based on the quality of my mind (this idea was less encouraging than I'd have liked it to be).

The conversation lulled, but he seemed disinclined to end it. 'Shall we try some of those awful cheese things?' he said, leading me towards the trestle table. 'If they're free we might as well.' He threw a smile in my direction. His voice was soft but deep with a trace of huskiness. I wondered why I had thought he was gay.

'By the way,' he said, 'my name's Max.'

Max. He was older than me; only by three years, but there seemed decades between us. Mature and confident, he knew exactly what he wanted to do with his life. He would lecture, possibly abroad, research, write. His life was mapped out.

Later he was to tell me that he rarely went to English socials, had only gone to this one because, passing, he had seen me go in and wanted to meet me. He must have meant it, it wasn't his way to bother with flattery. That was something I liked at first. If he said a thing you could be sure he was sincere. Of course, that has its down side.

It was over a month before we met again. When we did, it was as I was coming out of a tutorial. I was on the verge of tears because I had just been given a B— for my essay.

'Haven't seen you for ages, how are you?' He made it sound as though force of circumstance had kept us apart, though in fact I'd spotted him in the common room several times and guessed he must have seen me. We walked back to the common room where I was meeting Carol and he bought us coffee, chatting like an old friend. I was delighted to be included in his coterie. He seemed to know everyone, and always the most interesting people. Even on the way to the counter he was stopped by three or four of them — a tall young man with long black curls and a large gold earring in one ear (a cause for comment: only women, gypsies — and Cliff Rose — wore earrings), and a group of horsy girls whose laughs sounded like coins rattling. When he came back to us I noticed them watching, checking us over. Max included Carol in our conversation, but his attention was all mine. I felt bathed in the soft glow of his gaze.

'Are you going to the disco tonight?' He hadn't struck me as the partying type, and we'd already decided against going, but if he was . . .

'We could do. What do you think, Carol?'

'I don't mind, but you said—'

I cut her short. 'I'm in the mood; it could be fun.' I smiled, satisfied that some sort of date, however casual, had been set.

But then he went on, 'Not really my thing, discos. I'll find out who else is going, maybe I'll look in later.' He took his leave then and strode off, leaving me open-mouthed and affronted, but Carol was oblivious.

'Glad you changed your mind about the disco. And Max is nice, isn't he?'

'Do you think so?'

'Yes, really sweet. And he's quite sold on you.'

'Is he?' In spite of myself, I heard hope in my voice.

IMMACULATE MISCONCEPTIONS

He came to the disco, though I wish he hadn't. Things might have been different had we just gone on meeting once a month in the arts faculty common room. That's the way our romance should have progressed — slow and sure. Slow, anyway.

I was dancing with — who was it? I can't see his face, but my arms were around his neck, and as we turned I was aware of Max, standing at the edge of the floor. Other students wore jeans and denim jackets or coloured loon pants and T-shirts, with Afro hair or tangled locks cascading down their backs, but Max was in the same green cords with brogues, with a calf-length leather coat over the top, his hair cut the shortest of anyone's there. He must have been unbearably hot, but he obviously thought it was worth it for the distinctive figure he made as he leant against the wall, flicking cigarette ash on to the floor. When he slipped the coat off he was wearing a brown sweater with a checked shirt underneath — studiedly casual; he looked as though he would smell of pipesmoke and tobacco. I can't imagine why he appealed to me. I thought, 'Does he know what he looks like? He's twenty-one and he could pass for forty.' But I could feel myself growing hot; I knew he was waiting for me.

When the song finished, I saw him take a step towards me and I went to him. We danced together, two dances, slow because it was late and the disco was drawing to a close, and I felt for the first time the breadth of his chest and the softness of the tiny curls at the back of his neck. And for the first time, too, I felt strange dark stirrings, a pulse that beat in time to the brush of our thighs. They say you can tell, from dancing close with someone, how good the sex will be.

Chapter 6

It makes you philosophical, illness. It has occurred to me that it's something to be grateful for. I've heard people say this before and thought they were idiots, that they had arrived at this conclusion because it was easier to accept than acknowledging that God has singled you out to have an especially bad time. But now I can see that it gives you a second chance. It reminds you that you have to live for today, and if you want something, to go for it. I watched Josie going off to the hairdressers this morning, getting herself beautiful (even more beautiful) for a Greg-filled weekend (a Greg-filled Josie), and I thought, why not? If she's not happy, why shouldn't she look for something else?

I've phoned a few other local newspapers to see if they would be interested in the occasional article, and I might try freelancing for magazines. I told Robert and he said, 'Don't run before you can walk.' But I'm sick of walking. If you keep on walking you never catch the people who are travelling by train.

'Did you – you know – go to university and everything?' Steven asks the question shyly, not looking me in the eye, as though he's requesting details of an intimate and private nature.

'Yes, is that what Darren wants to do?'

He scuffs the toe of a paint-splashed boot against the garden wall. 'No.' It comes out 'naaa'. 'We don't like all that studying in our family.'

I haven't met Darren and could hardly care less what he does, but I'm stuck on ideas for my column and it's cooler out here in the shade than in the study with the sun streaming in through the picture window. (I call it 'the study' but it's really the dining room — as we never have anyone over to dinner it's not too big a problem.) Steven often works stripped to the waist, and I observe the daily deepening of his tan from behind my curtains, but when he stops for a coffee with me he usually dresses again. I'm touched by his delicacy. I told him he should start wearing shorts to get his legs tanned and he blushed, so I said if he wanted some sun cream rubbed in to let me know, just to make him blush again.

'Don't tell me he's joining the army as well.'

Steven has already told me he applied himself and only changed his mind when a friend's father offered him an apprenticeship. 'The army's a good life. Nothing wrong with that.'

'I thought your dad bought himself out because he couldn't stand it any longer.' Rita had told me that. She always blamed the army for her husband's inability to settle in one place.

'Alan liked it, and Bernie.'

'Alan didn't like it for long though, did he?'

There's a pause just long enough for me to regret causing the shadow of pain that passes Steven's eyes. But how can Darren want to follow in the footsteps of a brother who was blown up crossing a road in Northern Ireland?

Steven pushes his baseball cap away from his eyes and

squints up at the roof. He raises an arm to stop the glare of the sun and I see that the elastic from the cap has left an indentation in the hair that's pressed flat across his forehead.

'I could get killed falling off this ladder,' he says. 'You can't not do something because you might get hurt.'

He's beginning to sound like Josie. I finish my coffee quicker than I'd planned and go back indoors.

This half term is dragging on. I hate the short school breaks far more than the six weeks in the summer. You get organised for that, sense it coming, so that by the time it arrives you've made your childcare arrangements, booked your time off, planned some outings. But half terms creep up on you. You think, well, it's just a week, forgetting that a week is seven long days with twenty-four hours to fill in each one. In this instance, a week is actually eight days: I've discovered today that the school has tacked a training day on the end of it.

Robert says I should take the kids to Brighton for the day. There's a special offer whereby one or two adults pay their full train fare and everyone else travels at a bargain rate. He says I should get a group together and we could all go. But Rebecca's best friend is away in Scotland for the holiday, and Simon's friend's parents both work full time. So many of the mothers work now, and the children seem to be farmed out to friends or relatives for the entirety of the holidays. It makes me regret not working full time so that I too could be relieved of the task of having to make the school holidays fun. The kids unite to remind me what a poor mother I am.

'But why can't we go?'

'Jenny's gone to Spain, and we can't even go to

rotten old Brighton. *And* she gets five pounds a week pocket money.'

'You never want us to go anywhere.'

I am explaining why it won't be much fun if we go on our own, how it will seem a very long journey with no one to talk to, that it's certain to be cold, wet and too expensive, and am just getting around to 'because I say so' when Robert adopts the sort of expression that in cartoons is normally enhanced by a light bulb over the head. 'I bet I know who'd like to go.'

It turns out that Steven has been telling him how his family won't be having a holiday this year, with Rita not working and still not in very good health. Robert thinks this is the perfect solution, in the way that people do when they're not the ones who'll be affected by it.

'Yes, but Rita's other kids might be awful.'

'Steve's all right. They'll only be like him.' I've begun to notice that Steven has become 'Steve' to Robert. I wonder if the fact that he has twice helped Robert jumpstart his car has anything to do with it.

'I thought you didn't like Steven.'

'I never said that. I only said he was about as good a house painter as you are. Apart from that he seems a good bloke.'

The question of whether Steven is a good bloke isn't the problem, of course, and the image of him stretched out on the sand in swimming trunks browning his thighs has a definite appeal, but I can't hold that picture without also seeing Rita in it. If I so much as glance at Steven she'll be bound to notice. Anyway, Steven is too old to want to come on a family day out, and without him, what would I talk to Rita about? Two minutes chatting to her in the market had seemed an eternity.

Robert is unsympathetic. 'She was a good friend to you in hospital. If you run out of conversation then split up when you get there, but the least you can do is see if she'd like to go.'

She'll probably be too busy anyway, but he makes me feel so guilty that I ring Rita straight away. She accepts at once.

Few things are quite so satisfying as offering to do a favour and then being turned down. You get all the credit with none of the inconvenience. This is what I'm thinking as I sit opposite Steven studying his three-quarters profile, his head turned to look out of the window.

Rita telephoned this morning when I was cutting the sandwiches, and I felt my shoulders droop on hearing her voice. She has a heavy cold and I felt a surge of resentment that she should let herself be ill and ruin my day, leaving me to a day full of nothing but my own kids' conversation. Simon has developed, just this week, a penchant for saying 'Why?' after everything. It's driving me mad. But I'd forgotten what Rita was like.

'Gina's been looking forward to it that much; you don't mind if they still come, do you? I know it's a cheek asking.' I said no, of course I didn't mind, thinking all the time, *damn damn damn*: not just my own kids' conversation, but her kids' too. She went on, 'Darren doesn't really want to go, but I don't want him hanging round with those boys he's got in with, so Steven'll still come and he'll keep an eye on them both. You sure you don't mind?'

Once, when I was pregnant with Simon and in constant desperate need of a loo, we got stuck in a traffic jam on the motorway. When I finally arrived at the services, the unimaginable relief I felt on reaching the ladies has been equalled only by what floods through me now.

'It'll be my pleasure,' I said, trying to keep the delight out of my voice, trying not to sound as though I could kiss her with gratitude, not to mention her son. 'I'm just sorry you're not feeling well.' We chatted on about her ailment for a few minutes and then I heard myself say, 'Maybe we can do it again later in the summer?' I held my breath, lest she take me at my word, but she was just touched by my sympathy and helpfulness. I hung up, while my conscience whispered 'hypocrite' and 'liar'. I ignored it.

Actually this isn't the only thing I'm thinking as the train passes the back gardens of England. I'm also considering what fun it would be if we got stuck in a tunnel and everybody, but especially all the kids, had to get off, leaving Steven and me behind for some heroic reason involving great bravery on Steven's part, which I would later reward by pushing him backwards across this seat and kissing him passionately . . .

'Can I have money for a drink?' Simon has seen my contented smile and thinks it signals an optimum time for getting money out of me. I give Gina enough for drinks for everyone and make the inspired suggestion that they all go ('. . . then you can choose what you all want'). My plan works brilliantly, except that Steven, who wants a beer and insists upon paying for it himself, also goes.

Still, we have all day. It was raining when we left home but it's brightening up now and maybe the sun will be out by the time we arrive. For me, personally, it's out already.

As I watch the kids make their way back from the buffet car, grabbing on to the the sides of the seats for support as the train sways, it seems to me that Gina looks younger than when I saw her visiting Rita in hospital. (I hope I look younger than when Steven saw me in hospital.) She has exchanged the dangly earrings for neat gold sleepers and wears no make-up. She's dressed in jeans and a sweatshirt, and Rebecca, who is dressed the same way (under protest — she would go everywhere in a party frock with frills if I let her), is delighted and thinks they must look like sisters. When Gina speaks Rebecca looks up at her with shy admiration. Gina tells me she hopes to be a nursery nurse when she leaves school. She has already taken charge of the children and now, while they sip their drinks, she sits by them, pointing out sights of interest — that is, what can be glimpsed through the windows of the houses that back on to the railway track, and the items of washing hanging out on lines (every time they spot a pair of knickers they score a point). I think the Connect Four and Battleships I've packed may be redundant.

Diagonally opposite me sits Darren, staring out morosely. He is trying to look as though he isn't travelling with us. This is fine by me; I very much hope no one thinks we're travelling with him. He has only been persuaded to come by the promise of unlimited access to amusement arcades and the threat of having to hoover the house for Rita if he stays at home. His headphones give off a metallic buzz and I keep finding myself trying to identify what the music might be. It's going *tusha tusha boom boom* over and over again. I signal to him that I want to speak and he lifts up one earpiece, saying, 'uh,' or 'Yeah,' or something.

'That song you're listening to: it isn't 'Chitty Chitty Bang Bang', is it? That used to be Rebecca's favourite.' Darren scowls and resumes ferocious chewing of his gum. A man sitting next to him catches my eye and grins.

'It's a shame your mum couldn't come,' I say to Steven,

not meeting his eyes but trying to sound as though I mean it. He makes me feel nervous. The day must be hotter than I realised because my pants are feeling damp.

'She's better off at home. She gets tired easy, and she'll have a nice day with none of us getting under her feet. I'll take her back something nice.'

Our conversations seem always to be like this — closed off, not leading anywhere, so that it is constantly up to me to keep them on the boil.

'What do you think she'd like?' If I keep talking, then there's a reason to look at him. And I'm too far away from the window to make looking out a comfortable option. We're passing countryside now but you've seen one field with cows in it, you've seen them all.

'I'll just get a souvenir. She likes anything like that.'

'Get her an ashtray with 'Souvenir of Brighton' on it then,' I say, meaning it as a joke about Rita's smoking, but he doesn't laugh.

'Naaa, she's giving up. She's cut right down you know.' Rita will never give up. His naïvety increases my affection.

'You don't smoke then?' I hold my breath for the answer. His breath should smell of cherries not fag ash.

'It was different when my mum started, they didn't know then. But these days you got to be stupid to smoke.' He goes over to Darren's corner of the carriage and lifts the ear piece of his headphones. 'I say, you gotta be stupid to smoke!' Darren scowls and pushes him off and Steven comes back laughing.

'You're not gonna smoke are you, Gina?' he says, turning to her for support.

She looks up briefly from her conversation with Rebecca. 'No, too bloody expensive.'

'Gina!' Steven is trying to look angry at the swear word, as though I wouldn't have heard it before.

'Sorry, Mrs Cope.' She looks sheepish and I smile foolishly. I don't want Rebecca and Simon to start swearing, but neither do I want to appear an elderly authoritarian whose sensibilities must be protected. (I wish they wouldn't call me Mrs Cope.)

Steven's eyes are fixed on me, and I only realise it's because he's expecting a stronger response when he leans across to Gina and hisses, 'If I hear one more word like that I'll knock your flaming head off.' His eyes are large and soft like a stuffed spaniel of Rebecca's that she likes to take to bed with her. Thinking about taking the spaniel to bed makes me squeeze my thighs together.

After that we all sit cowed and frightened to speak, especially me. Simon looks at Steven with renewed interest. I follow the line of his gaze but Steven is looking hard at me and I look away. Trying to focus on what little I can see out of the window, I drift off. I think of Max.

Chapter 7

After the disco, Max walked me back to hall.
'Do you want to come in?'

It was easier for a man to pass through the women-only hall of residence than for a camel to pass through the eye of a needle but only just. The porter might stop you on any of a dozen ruses: 'Did you sign him in?' 'Make sure he signs out.' 'Not so much noise on them stairs.' At night there was no porter, but it was still a challenge to slip in, using your own key, and tiptoe past matron's room, avoiding the loose bit of rug and the stairs that creaked. Did that add to the frisson of excitement I felt, or would it have been as intense anyway? Was it the danger that made me want him to stay, or his lips on the nape of my neck? Or was it just my desperation to be rid of my virginity? Sometimes I could imagine that 'Virgin' was tattooed on my forehead. And I wanted to be free and sophisticated like the girls I read about in magazines or watched in films.

'How do you want it?' he said. I didn't know there would be questions. I thought you would be overcome by passion, tearing each other's clothes off, unable to stem the flow of need. I should have told him it was my first time. But I thought the idea of a virgin as something special was out of date, that virginity was simply evidence of naïvety and lack of experience.

I wanted to undress him, seductively and slowly, but once I'd undone his shirt he said, 'Oh come on,' and pulled it off himself.

I hadn't seen a penis before. Not a real one, extended. It was very red and thick. 'You're a big boy,' I said. I thought it was what you had to say.

'Don't be stupid,' Max said.

It wasn't what I was expecting. But I remember the supreme pleasure of his bare skin against mine down the length of our bodies, and the coarse dark hair of his chest that scratched my face as he came inside me, and his closed eyes, and that expression of intensity bordering on pain. I watched, strangely detached, wanting to see what having sex was like, wanting to watch myself fall in love. I had read that it is normal for a woman to fall in love with a man who has made love to her. Somehow it hadn't occurred to me that men wouldn't react the same way. I didn't know then that women use sex to get love, and men use love to get sex.

I tried hard to make that first time feel as special as it ought to be. I moaned, I moved my hips, I kissed passionately. But I was shocked by the wetness — so much — and the hot stickiness that glued my skin to his, and in the morning the smell of fetid fish, the sheets, crumpled and damp where they weren't stiff and crispy. I had read so much about sex yet I had read nothing about all this. And then, briefly, I was panicked by the thought that the cleaners, in their weekly changing of the sheets, would find out what I had been doing. Then I was panicked, not so briefly, by the idea that I could get pregnant. I'd expected that he'd produce a condom at the optimum moment.

'You are on the pill, aren't you?' Max asked afterwards as he swigged from a bottle of lemonade on my bedside table. It was warm and he pulled a face.

'Oh yes,' I said.

'Hell! Is that the time?' Next morning, Max was irritated at waking late, and I had a sinking feeling that it was also at finding himself with me. He was even more irritated when he realised he couldn't leave before ten-thirty without alerting the commissionaire to the fact that he had been in hall overnight. I tried to recapture the mood of the previous evening. And I felt genuinely loving, notwithstanding the unwelcome discoveries I had made.

'There's no hurry.' I stroked his face as he lay on his back drumming his fingers on the bedspread. 'You said you've no lectures till this afternoon.' I couldn't understand his sudden urgency. I had missed Twentieth Century Poetry this morning and was missing Chaucer even while we spoke, and I was happy to sacrifice them in the interests of True Love. 'I'll make some coffee and we can go out and get an early lunch.' It seemed to precipitate him to action. He leapt out of bed, throwing the covers on to the floor.

'This doesn't mean anything. Don't tell anyone,' he said cryptically, thrusting one leg into his trousers.

I thought he was implying that I was about to break the news to matron and the principal, and I laughed. Besides, he looked so appealing with his hair still flattened from sleep, pulling his trousers up.

'Of course I won't, silly. But if you're going now, when will I see you?' I was embarrassed, afterwards, that it took me so long to fall in.

'Around. In the common room.'
'I'll see you in the common room later then?'
'Yes. Probably.'

He finished dressing and began to pace the room irritably, looking at his watch. He didn't kiss me goodbye.

I arrived in the common room in time to meet him from his lecture. I wanted to watch him enter, observe him from my new vantage point of knowledge (Tree of Knowledge, that is, upper branches). I wanted to see the way he carried himself (virile and strong), the slope of his cheek, turn of his head, his expression (delighted and eager) when he saw me waiting for him. I wanted to feel the bond between us stretching the length of the room, of which everyone must surely be aware. In case they weren't, I also wanted a public acknowledgement of our union; what I was actually thinking, as I sat drumming my biro impatiently, was that it was a shame there wasn't some exterior change to the body, something that would be a signal to everyone that two separate individuals were now eternally united as one — maybe your private parts could light up like neon, or something.

He was the last to arrive, and when he walked in I caught his eye at once and smiled while butterflies swooped and soared. He smiled too, but not at me. He obviously hadn't seen me because he turned and, his face relaxing into a wider grin, walked over to a group on the far side of the room. He stood with his back to me and I could see his shoulders shaking as he laughed and gesticulated. He was describing something; his head was moving and the others were hooting with laughter. A few minutes later he left without looking round.

I hadn't realised he was short-sighted. I used to do that

myself at school before I had contact lenses: smile in the general direction of faces, hoping that this would encourage anyone I knew to come over, so that I wouldn't have to join a group of people who, on closer inspection, might turn out to be total strangers. Sometimes friends who claimed I had passed them in the street would say, 'But you did see me, you looked straight at me.'

So this is what must have happened. Max had lost his contacts, or dropped one, or maybe he wasn't even *aware* he was short-sighted and would be mortified to find out that he hadn't acknowledged me. He obviously just hadn't seen me.

Only, he had seen me. I'd caught a flicker of an expression on his face as our eyes met, before he looked away. Consternation, or irritation, or maybe even fear.

A small ice cube of acid and bile settled solidly in my stomach and stayed there. Sometimes I can still feel it. And the neon light in my knickers went out.

I barely saw Max except in passing, in the corridors of the faculty, or queuing for snacks in the common room. He was always in a crowd.

'What put you off Max?' Carol said once, observing the coolness between us, and I marvelled that she had assumed the choice was mine.

'He's a pretentious snob.'

'Yes, I know.' How dare she agree with me! 'But he's quite sexy. Don't you think he looks like Jim Morrison?'

'I bet Jim Morrison never wore baggy Y-fronts.'

'Oh God.'

It was a lie about the Y-fronts (Max had worn the bikini type with narrow sides, in black), but I was gratified to realise that Carol had given the rumour legs when it came back to me, in confidence, via a girl in my tutorial group.

It's true that you learn from your mistakes. But sometimes you learn the wrong things. One thing I thought I'd learned is that you can get pregnant even if you only have sex once. I went to the students' health centre in a blind panic looking for help and sympathy and, when I undressed for the medical examination, found that my period had started. I came out clutching a pack of pills and a box of condoms, with a wad of tissues in my pants.

But that wasn't the only unhelpful lesson. The reason Max had dropped me, I decided, was because I didn't understand sex. I needed more experience, more relationships, to know more men, and (to be on the safe side until the pill kicked in) I needed more condoms.

Now I think I was looking, not for experience, but for comfort, someone to give me back myself. Max had taken my own idea of my specialness and trampled on it. I wanted to find someone who would cherish me, as Stuart once had.

Instead I found Phil, who was trying to make his girlfriend jealous; and Geoff, who was on the rebound and left when his girlfriend took him back; there was Paul, who said he just didn't fancy me — afterwards, that is; and Jack . . . Carol asked me recently how many men I'd been to bed with. I counted up, and then, later, I remembered two more. And she said, how can you forget something like that, were there so many? Of course there weren't so many, but I was never any good with names and how could I remember their faces when we always had the lights off? But the truth was not that there were so many, but that they were so insignificant. I can't distinguish between them.

Carol was going out with a medical student called Dan

that term, and it was at a party at Dan's house that I saw Max again.

Dan lived in a large semi, which he shared with five other medical students. When I arrived at eleven the place was already heaving with bodies, several of them already the worse for drink. Carol had said she'd meet me there but I couldn't find her and I didn't know anyone else. What is more isolating than a party where you have no one to talk to? I got some wine and sat on the floor in the lounge where Pink Floyd was playing very loud and a group of four or five men were smoking dope. I tried to get interested in a poetry book that been abandoned on the rug, or at least I tried to look as though that's what I was doing. But it was too dark to read and when the bearded man sitting near me was suddenly sick I moved into the hall in the hope that Carol would eventually have to pass through.

It was a narrow hall, with the stairs going straight up from the front door. One wall was decorated by a huge collage of cartoons and news cuttings which stretched from the front door, up the stairs, to the lavatory door across the top. I stood reading cartoons and trying to give the impression I was enjoying myself.

Gradually I became aware of another presence by my side, some other guest taking refuge from the fray.

'That's a good one, isn't it?'

It was a Snoopy cartoon, and not good at all. I thought, Why do I think he is so clever, when this is the best line he can come up with? But I said, 'Have you seen that one? That's funnier.' Max threw his head back and laughed, though that cartoon wasn't brilliant either. I thought: he wants to make it up.

We read on, pointing out to each other the choicest morsels, or pretending to.

'So how are you then?' he said at length.

'I'm fine.' I meant to sound light and careless but I could hear an edge to my voice.

He didn't notice because he smiled conspiratorially and nudged my arm. 'Amazing how these things happen, isn't it? We just got totally carried away, didn't we?'

I turned away to the collage in disbelief. So this was how he justified it, was it? Two people swept up in the heat of the moment? And he thought he could dispose of three months of heartbreak just like that? I toyed with the idea of turning on him, the way movie actresses do, a ringing slap across his unsuspecting cheek. Then while he was recovering, I'd thrust my knee into his groin, and as his head went down bring my other knee up to smash him in the face. Carried away? He'd need carrying away in a wooden box when I'd finished with him. There was only one kind of language a man like Max understood.

And that was the language of polite and careful understatement. 'I thought you were extremely ill-mannered,' I said.

You see, what you have to understand about Max is he always thought of himself as a gentleman. The important thing to him was that in public you were seen to be conducting yourself respectably. No swearing, no violence, no histrionics. His uncle, he once told me, had a second family which he had set up in Ireland, where one of the branches of his business was centred. His wife knew about it, but because it was carried on discreetly and without giving embarrassment, he was allowed to continue.

With Max, bully-boy tactics would have been no use whatsoever. He would have thought they said more about me than they did about him. And so we discussed the major tragedy of my life as though it was on a par with, let's say, handing one's course work in a day late.

'It *was* ill-mannered,' he said, with an expression of mock regret. 'I felt dreadful about it. But it would have been humiliating if anyone had found out. And I've often wondered — what were you thinking of? Letting me sleep with you like that. Do you always do that?'

I hadn't been brought up with the same idea of respectability as Max. The only thing keeping my hands off his throat was the knowledge he'd have found it entertaining.

'*Letting* you? I thought it was something we were mutually agreed on. It takes two, you know.' I could have kicked myself; I knew he'd pounce on the cliché.

'Ah but it doesn't take two at all. It takes one to ask and one to agree — which you did. In fact I didn't even have to ask, as I remember, I just accepted that which was freely offered. It's in the nature of a man to have sex when he can get it, you can't blame him for doing that which has been bred into him.'

There was a pause while he continued looking at me with an expression of mock severity, and I was thinking, shall I, shan't I? I couldn't hit him, but maybe there was another way to hurt him.

'Thank you for letting me know,' I said coolly. 'But I wish you'd mentioned it before. I just didn't realise, what with it being my first time and everything.' I had the satisfaction of seeing his jaw drop and knowing that I had wrong-footed him. He wasn't slow in grasping the equation. Me: young innocent. Him: cunning bastard.

He sighed, scraping his fingers back through his hair. I had embarrassed him. 'I had no idea,' he said. He looked away from me and over the heads of the people jostling to get into the kitchen, but I don't think he was seeing them.

'Ellie . . .' He turned to take my hand and now he looked regretful and sad, but this time I could be the one to leave him. I drew back, ready to sweep away and out of his life forever. I had him just where I wanted him. And in that brief moment I didn't want him at all.

Three of Dan's drunken friends came stumbling and swaying down the stairs and Max edged me into the corner by the front door to avoid them. Until Dan's friends moved on, I had no escape. Max gazed down into my eyes. 'I had no idea, believe me. I thought . . .'

I watched Dan's friends pushing through the crush, heading for the front door. It opened and a cool blast wrapped itself round my ankles. There were more people outside waiting to come in, but I could see the blackness of the night behind them. I could be out there, on my way home; I'd said what had to be said, I could put all this behind me. The new people, gatecrashers it seemed, forced their way in. The door closed.

'We got off to a bad start, Ellie. Let's try again.'

Oh Max. Your eyes, when you looked into mine, were wide with sorrow. You could be so tender. And your tenderness would be so rare.

He took both my hands between his and we smiled at last. The doorbell began to ring again but we ignored it. I had a sensation of having come home. I thought we were going to live happily ever after.

Chapter 8

'Have you seen something you'd like for Rita?'

He shrugs. 'Not really.' We've stopped at the first gift shop we come to on the way to the beach. The shelves are crammed with ornaments of china or glass, and the owner of the emporium sits huddled over the counter in a fug of smoke watching us suspiciously. I love these shops: the irresistible opportunity to be smart and superior about the sort of people who buy these things. I pick up a grotesque egg-shaped china money box which has a face painted on either side. One face is smiling (more of a leer really) and the other is scowling, and around the brim of the yellow china hat it wears is printed what might loosely be called a rhyme, to the effect that if anyone swears they have to put some money in the box. I can't imagine anyone paying £7.99 for this, or what kind of house it might fit into. Maybe a home that already has the plastic doggy-doo which I notice on the shelf below, to display alongside it. A souvenir from the footpaths of Brighton, presumably. I point these choice items out to Steven, laughing conspiratorially.

'Good, isn't it?' he says. 'My mum's got one at home.' (I hope it's the swear box he's referring to.) I rearrange my expression from cynic to guileless appreciation, like his, and turn to leave. As I do so I knock a plastic notice on to the floor. Bending to pick it up I read: 'Lovely to look at, delightful to hold, But if you should break it, consider it sold.' In its fall, the notice has cracked across the front. We beat a hasty retreat before the owner can charge us for it.

The kids are waiting for us outside, and on seeing them Steven reaches into his pocket and draws out some notes and a handful of change. At first I think he is going back to buy something from the shop (he had looked very thoughtful about a china kitten whose face was almost entirely made up of its doleful eyes), but then he calls Gina over and pushes some money into her hand. 'Get the kids a bucket and spade each.' I argue, but he insists. 'It's not much fun for you having us lot along,' he says, 'this is to say thank you.' I have to turn away so he won't see me smiling.

The day is warm but, with the sea breeze to contend with, not as warm as I'd hoped, certainly not sufficiently mild for me to assume that Steven will get his kit off. We arrange ourselves by a breakwater to get some shelter from the wind, and I hope that the patch of damp on the wood next to me is from sea water and not where some infant has crouched down for a wee (as the one at the next breakwater down is doing). Once the food has been eaten, or at least complained about (Simon: 'Why can't we go to McDonald's like everyone else?' Rebecca: 'Why did you bring 7-Up? You know it makes me sick!'), Gina takes the kids to build a dam at the water's edge. Even arctic temperatures would not dissuade the kids from stripping off, and soon they're down to their swimming costumes and running off to the water's edge, pointing a toe, running back. It really isn't warm enough to go in the water but I raise only token opposition. It's their day out and the chilly breeze doesn't seem to be doing the two elderly men on the nudist beach any harm. (I think they are nude. Either that, or their suits need ironing.) Besides, Steven might be seduced into believing he should strip off too.

Darren came down to the beach with us to join in the picnic (if you can call taking one sandwich and sitting by himself on the next breakwater actually joining in) but now he has wandered off by himself to look round the town.

'Have you got a girlfriend?' It's a question I've been longing to ask Steven for weeks, and now, as he sprawls out with his cap over his eyes, and I relax against the breakwater with a book on my knees, I wonder why it has seemed so difficult to ask.

'Girlfriend? No, not at the moment.'

Even though I hadn't really thought he had a girlfriend, and even though it could make not the slightest difference to me if he had, still a frisson of pleasure thrills through me, as though I had just learned of a rival's emigration to Mars.

'I did have one. Nice girl, long hair. But we didn't, you know, have much to talk about.'

I don't remember, from my earliest boyfriends, that having much to talk about was the main concern. Sometimes I wanted to say to them, 'Look, there's more to me than what the inside of my bra feels like.' I'm delighted he has such a mature attitude.

'How old was she?'

'Seventeen, eighteen. About the same as me. I have a better time with my mates really. Don't want to get serious with anyone.'

'You're very wise. Once you're married everything changes. You want to make the most of being single.' I sound about ninety.

'You like being married though, don't you?' He raises himself on one elbow and pushes his cap back to look at me. His sudden interests takes me by surprise.

'Yes, I like it, but . . .' I don't want to give Steven my long list of buts, but he is waiting expectantly. 'When you're married everything goes on being the same, year after year. There's not the variety in your life, with things changing all the time, that you get when you're on your own. You get into a routine and you have to stick with it because that's what holds things together.'

'My dad didn't do that.' From the sounds of it, Steven's feckless dad didn't do most things that other dads do.

'Your dad's not typical.'

He shifts to get more comfortable on the pebbles, oblivious of the enormous reserves of tact I have used up in this short statement. Seeing him move, I also shuffle on the stones. Whichever way you move there seems to be another sharp flint ready to dig into your backside.

Steven picks up a pebble and rolls it in his hand. 'I don't think my dad should have ever got married.' That much is obvious, but I don't feel in a position to agree. 'He hardly ever came home and when he did he was always shouting and thumping everybody.'

'Did he hit you?' This is something Rita has left out of the scenario. He leans forward over a pile of stones he is assembling, and his hair hides his face from me. I want to kiss better all the hurts he ever suffered, especially any that fell between his nose and his knees.

'Not so much as we got bigger. But still, that's why Alan never came home on leave. He'd stay round at his girlfriend's or sometimes he'd go over to our Auntie Enid in Watford.'

Rita had painted a picture of a loving father who adored his family but, through an incurable wanderlust, was unable to be with them as much as he would have liked. You could get terrible eyestrain reading between the lines with Rita, and I had, but the impression I had gained was the right one.

'Don't think I didn't love him and everything—'

'It's just that you hated him.'

He laughs to himself without looking up. 'He made life hard for my mum. She's had to do everything, never got no help.'

'Is that the reason you didn't join the army?'

He shrugs as though he isn't going to answer and lies back down again. But he goes on, 'When Alan was home we all looked up to him, being the eldest. He was more of a dad than my dad was. Then it was Bernie. Janice had already gone, so if I left too it would've meant the others being on their own — and Darren needs watching. He's bright but he's stupid with it, you know what I mean? Gets in with the wrong sort. He wouldn't take no notice of my mum but as long as I'm here he knows I could lay one on him any time.'

'So you gave up the army to stay with your family?' Steven, my hero.

'The apprenticeship looked a good thing at the time; we didn't know he was going to go bust.' I've noticed how Steven likes to be with Robert, engage him in conversation, hear his point of view. He's looking for a father figure, someone to look up to. (It crosses my mind that that would make me a mother figure but I chase the thought away.)

The conversation drifts somehow on to comic books Steven likes to read, and then the toddler I had seen weeing earlier comes over. She is wearing canvas sandals and a shiny pink swimsuit and has a mop of curls to rival Shirley Temple. She looks me hard in the face without smiling. I have the uncomfortable feeling, which I sometimes get from babies and toddlers, that she can see behind my façade and is unimpressed by what she finds there. I was on a bus once and there was a child on the seat in front who knelt up so she was facing me. She stared me out for about five minutes. Then suddenly she said to her mother, 'Why is that lady so ugly?' I've never quite got over it.

Without warning, Shirley Temple holds out her ice lolly to me.

I try to pretend I haven't noticed, on the principle that if you ignore a dog that's worrying you it will lose interest and go away. Any maternal instincts I ever had have been expended on my own kids. I never developed the knack of relating to children I hadn't given birth to.

'She's offering you a lick of her lolly,' says Steven, helpfully, as though I haven't noticed the melting confection being thrust almost under my nose. Out of the corner of my eye I can see her parents, a skinny youth with a hairless white chest which he has bared to the elements and a fat girl in a sun dress the size of a small marquee. She has a band of sunburn across her shoulders from wearing another dress with differently placed straps. They're smiling proudly, so honoured am I to be the subject of their two year old's attention. If she drips her lolly on my new T-shirt she will be honoured with the attention of my extensive vocabulary. (Lucky we didn't buy the swear box; I don't have that much cash on me.)

Perhaps Steven senses my lack of warmth. 'Cute kid,' he says and, getting up, takes her hand and leads her back to her family. He lingers in conversation with them, leaving me excluded.

'Don't you like kids then?' he asks, settling down when he returns.

'I've nothing against kids, it's their orange Lyon's Maids I'm not so keen on.' I mean it to sound humorous, but I'm irritated with the child for highlighting this unflattering side of my personality, and I can see by Steven's surprised expression that it shows in my voice.

Even so, a little later, he says, 'Your kids are lucky, aren't they?' I hope he means having me for a mother but he goes on, 'Got everything, haven't they? Bikes, computer, nice house. When I get married that's how I want it to be.'

In the afternoon Darren comes back and they all play ball, making enormous allowances for the fact that Simon always drops it and Rebecca constantly cries 'That's not fair' when she thinks they should have thrown it to her. I sit and guard the bags and buckets as I remember my own mother doing. I feel like a hen watching her chicks. A very old hen.

Three girls are walking across the pebbles, and I see both Darren and Steven pause to stare. Steven says something which makes Darren smile and he shouts something out to them. Rebecca chooses that moment to throw the ball and it hits Steven in the groin. They all laugh. I think, 'Serve you right, you bastard.'

The three girls have long hair, in varying shades of brown, and it flows out behind them in the breeze. One is shorter and stockier than the others, and her chubby buttocks protrude slightly from the legs of her too-tight shorts, but she has the same vivacity and glow as the others. Heads turn as they pass. At school and college, we were constantly comparing the attractiveness of ourselves with everyone else. Belinda has long legs but her eyes are too small. Christine has a good bust but that nose . . . Janet has beautiful hair but thighs like Geoff Capes'. Now I see that youth is attractive in itself. Firm flesh and clear eyes make everyone desirable.

In eighteen months I'll be forty. Looking down at my legs stretched out before me I observe that while my flesh may no longer be firm, at least my eyes are still clear: I can see with perfect clarity the faint blue line, like a biro mark, of a varicose vein making its way up one calf.

'Can I have an ice cream, Mummy, can I?' This is the first time Simon has asked since we arrived, which must be a tribute to Gina's way with children. She'll make a wonderful nursery nurse. I ask Simon to go and ask what everyone wants, but he assumes that I'm going to say what I usually say and starts, 'Why can't I? You never let us. Everyone else—'

Steven comes over, feeling in his pocket. 'I'll get them.'

'No, I will.' I'm still feeling bad about the buckets and spades. 'And Rebecca and Simon can help me. It'll give you all a chance to have some time on your own.' I think a game of ball, uninterrupted by the squabbles of my two, would be welcome. But the tide is going out now and Darren, free of his earlier aloofness, wants to build a castle with the children. I say I'll go on my own, but Steven says I won't be able to manage them all and he'll come with me. I don't argue.

We walk along the seafront in the direction from which

we have seen people coming carrying dripping ice lollies and King Cones. Perhaps we are both enjoying the stroll, because we agree that the queue at the first kiosk we see is too long and walk on. The three girls we saw earlier pass us and I see them looking at Steven. The stocky one nudges her friend. For some reason this makes me feel skittish.

'Do you ever take that cap off?' I ask him, flicking the brim of his baseball cap with my forefinger.

'No,' he says.

'Well you will today!' I grab it from his head and run off with it. I hear him shout and laugh but I don't turn round, I go on, past two people in wheelchairs who threaten to block my route, jumping sideways to avoid an oncoming skateboarder, between the crowds of holidaymakers who suddenly all seem to be coming towards me, as though united against me. I'm seventeen. I could run forever but so can he; I've just pushed into another crowd of barely moving bodies when Steven catches my arm and I feel myself swung round. Someone shoves both of us with force, and Steven is pushed against the sea wall with me pressed against him. For a few moments the pressure of other bodies keeps me there. We're still laughing. I put his baseball cap on my head, wearing it backwards.

'You look ridiculous.' He tries to pull it off me but I cling on to it.

'It's the way you always look.' We're pressed against each other. I can feel his hips against mine and my breasts are hard up against his chest. The bulk of the crowd pass on, and I move backwards a few inches, but his thighs are still brushing mine.

'It'll ruin your hair,' he says, removing the cap at last, but he speaks so quietly I can hardly hear him.

Without his cap he looks different, seems strangely naked and vulnerable. We aren't laughing so much now.

'It's made your hair go flat,' I say, and I run my fingers through his fine dark hair, the way my hairdresser does to give it lift. Except that it's nothing like this when my hairdresser does it. I'm concentrating on his hair, fluffing it up, smoothing it out, studying the contours of his eyes, not meeting his eyes. When I do, they're dark and heavy and I realise just how close we're standing.

The crowds have dispersed now. There's no one here but us. The air is warm but the breeze blows my hair across my face. I brush it away, and my hand moves slowly, I have the sense of the world slowing down, holding the moment. His lips are parted and we're so close. I think, if you want something go for it. I think, you can't not do a thing just because you might get hurt. I think, what you need is to have an affair. And I can feel his breath. His tongue licks dry lips, something I could better do for him, and I wonder what the nape of his neck tastes like. I can feel a burning and gnawing inside that I haven't felt for a long long time.

Suddenly I'm aware of another crowd walking by us. We aren't alone at all. A large woman in her fifties, her face as pink as the candyfloss she's eating, is saying, 'I wouldn't mind but it wasn't her lawnmower.' The gulls overhead are screeching out a warning.

I lean towards him but it's only to put his cap back on his head. 'I think there's a kiosk over there,' I say.

In the train going home I remark, 'It's a shame Rita couldn't come.' Steven doesn't answer.

Chapter 9

It's strange how, at one and the same time, you can be both happy and unhappy. When I was alone with Max in my room, he was all I ever wanted. Even his unkindness and sarcasm could be excused and forgiven. But as he walked out of the door, anxiety always walked in. When would I see him again? How soon would he call? For the benefit of the public at large, we weren't going out together. And the public at large were kept unaware of the extent of our staying in together.

No, you couldn't say we ever dated. In some ways it was like already being married to an unreliable and unpredictable spouse. We never went out to the theatre, to dinner or to films, or at least, not together. Our life fell into a pattern: we both had lectures in the morning, and he would call round to my room, it being so conveniently situated, straight after lunch. I ate in hall, but he would get a sandwich in the faculty building before calling on me. We would lounge around then, drinking coffee and eating fruit and arguing — God knows, we argued — not about any of the things that mattered to me: why he didn't introduce me to his friends, why we were such a well-kept secret, but endlessly on subjects we could do nothing about.

We had opposite views on everything – politics, education, Vietnam, music, art, drugs – they were all good for a row. Until, that is, about three o'clock, maybe three-thirty, and then the anger would wane, he'd settle next to me, or pull me on to the bed next to him, and we'd make love all afternoon.

And he was adoring then, delicious and loving and thoughtful. He would stroke my face and kiss me. Sometimes he frightened me a little. There was something dark in his love-making, some current seething beneath the surface which I couldn't identify and lacked the knowledge to satisfy. But we were each other's for all that; we belonged together.

'Hell, is that the time?' It always ended like that, the afterglow abruptly extinguished in the race to be dressed and in the Students' Union at the front of the queue for the evening meal.

'It's so discourteous,' I complained. I was good at this sort of understatement now.

'Oh, I'm sorry,' and he would pull a stupid cartoon-like face of aped sorrow, and then, wheedling, 'but you don't know what it's like to be at the back of the queue.' I did, though – every afternoon, around this time.

Once I played a trick on him. He had a habit, when he arrived each day, of going straight to my desk to see what I was working on. For no particular reason this enraged me. On this occasion I wrote a poem and left it on top of my work where he would see it at once.

> Maxwell is a friend of mine
> And often comes to visit me.
> We talk and then make ardent love
> Until it's time for Maxwell's tea.

I thought he'd laugh. It was quite apt after all. He was incensed. 'If that's what you think, I'll go now!' he stormed, stamping around the room, throwing his coat down then grabbing it up again. I hadn't realised he could be hurt.

To be with Max was always an education. On one occasion he wanted to visit an antiquarian bookseller at a town forty miles away, and said I could go too. I wasn't interested in antique books but I knew that to be asked was a privilege. He had never taken me along before.

Until then I had never heard of antiquarian booksellers. I thought either books were new and you bought them in paperback unless you were extremely rich or a public library, or they were old and you bought them from jumble sales because you couldn't afford the paperback. It was a revelation that there were people for whom the age of the book, the way it was bound and the paper it was printed on, were the most important things about it. Max could be snobbish about his enthusiasms, of which this was but one.

I took a perverse delight in deflating him. 'Look at the state of that,' I remarked of a yellowing volume that he was admiring. 'Wouldn't you rather have a new one?'

'Don't be stupid,' he said.

He often said that, and even if it was appropriate in the antiquarian bookseller's, it wasn't always. Sometimes he said it when I came up behind him to hug him. Or if I tried to hold his hand in public.

Another time, we drove out for a picnic. I was extraordinarily excited. Now, I thought, we'll be together like a proper couple. The pre-Raphaelite influence was fashionable then, and I had dressed in a flowing skirt and a fine cotton blouse with a dozen tiny pearly buttons from the neck to the waist. Unfortunately I was also wearing platform-soled sandals, not realising that the picnic would be, not in a country park, but by the sea. Fashion was another of the topics we argued about; he hated anything new and had a particular antipathy for platform soles. It was to assert my independence that I had bought a pair. They were both expensive and uncomfortable but I was wearing them to make a point. Unfortunately, as so often happened, it was Max who ended up making the point. It was never Max's way to make allowances; he wanted to walk down the cliff path to the beach, so I had to find my own way over the rough and uneven pebbles. My shoes wouldn't grip so I had to remove them and limp painfully and awkwardly over the jagged stones to the sand. My skirt caught in the brambles at the side of the cliff path.

'Stupid, coming out dressed like that,' Max said, but with good humour. He'd won, after all. I climbed on to a rock and sat looking out to sea while he wandered off by himself. It was a fine clear day with a bright sun. There was no point in putting too much weight on his behaviour, it was just the way he was. I tossed my head back and felt the breeze ruffling my hair. I wore it permed and long now, like Elizabeth Siddal, the woman who appeared in so many of the pre-Raphaelites' paintings, whom I thought I resembled as I perched against the sky, the warm air caressing my face.

'Who the hell do you think you look like?' It was Max, of course, laughing. I ignored him, but when he had passed I took out a pen and a till receipt from Woolworth, there being nothing else in my bag to write on, and wrote a poem, a short pithy bitter poem, about how I hated Max.

Later, lying in bed, he was sorry.

'You looked so pretty sat up on that rock,' he said. 'You were writing something. Was it about me?' He sounded loving and hopeful, wanting to hear my tender thoughts. I felt mean and sorry for what I'd written. I threw the poem away.

But such outings were rare. Most of the time we followed a routine: sex in the afternoons, Monday to Thursday, possibly Friday, but never at the weekends because Max was busy with other friends then — I never knew whom — or else he was studying. I didn't see him in the evenings for the same reason. At the time it didn't seem strange.

In between times I was lonely, but love carries you through all that. I spent my evenings at the Students' Union, hanging out with whoever was there. Often it was Robert. He was part of the rugby crowd and they were always to be found in the same corner, making a noise and throwing food about. If they'd had a particularly good match, one of them would usually get up on a table and drop his trousers. ('The rugby rowdies are at it again,' Carol would say, 'letting it all hang out.') Strange to think that Robert was ever like that. He was very good-looking and it was a boost, arriving miserable and alone, to catch sight of him across the bar and see him coming over. He was patient too, he let me talk about Max. And I loved to talk about Max.

'Don't you mind him seeing other girls?'

Max didn't 'see' other girls in the way Robert was suggesting, but there were one or two with whom he was friendly. 'They're just people on the same course as him.' This is what Max told me whenever I asked to see him in the evenings. 'And it's only the same as me seeing you, Robert.'

'But it's not the same, is it?' Robert could be infuriatingly persistent on occasions. 'I'm not screwing you.'

'Max isn't screwing them either!'

He let it pass and there was a pause. 'You know he's queer, don't you?'

'He isn't!' I answered too quickly and felt my face go hot. Robert had said this before, and it made me mad, perhaps because at first I'd made the same assumption.

'He's friends with Cliff Rose, isn't he?' Cliff Rose was the lecturer in Anglo-Saxon poetry who wore the skin-tight leather. Max claimed the stories about Cliff's bizarre lifestyle were rumours and I believed him.

'Oh I see,' I said, sensing a weakness, as I thought, in his argument. 'He's queer *and* he's screwing other women. Neat trick if you can do it.' I was so naïve then.

Robert looked at me oddly. 'Well, Cliff Rose does,' he said.

We fell into silence then. I needed time to consider this new concept. Of course, I had heard of bisexuality, but real people didn't do that, did they?

'Just ask yourself this,' Robert said, getting up to refill our glasses at the bar, 'does he make you happy?'

'Of course he does,' I said. As he took the glass from my hand I found I couldn't meet his eyes.

The college holidays yawned long that first year. Max sent two postcards, one from Italy, one from Edinburgh. But he didn't invite me to visit or arrange to see me. And I didn't ask to see him in case he said no. I always felt the threat of losing him hanging over me.

When we returned to college things were worse. Max came back with even more power than he'd had before. It was as though he was flexing his muscles.

I lived in different accommodation that year. Carol and I found a self-contained upstairs flat that was reasonably clean and gave us more independence than we had enjoyed living in hall. But it was further from the faculty buildings and as a result, not so convenient for Max to call. I should have thought of that. Because now I only saw him perhaps two afternoons a week, and even then he didn't always turn up, or he would arrive very late, *en route* to somewhere else. I always tried to be studying when he arrived so that it didn't look as though I had been waiting for him; but he wasn't fooled. I knew that by how sweet and attentive he would be – his level of kindness in inverse proportion to the amount of time we had together. The less time he intended to stay, the kinder he would be. I hated myself for being so glad to see him.

It's cumulative, this sort of need. There was a constant ache – to touch him, to be with him – an ache that was never satisfied, because he always gave short measure. Even when we were together he held something in reserve. Sex was unsatisfying, because with the first kiss came the dread that it would soon be over, and the need to scheme to see if I could make him stay an extra ten minutes, maybe even half an hour. My love made him secure. The more I wanted him, the more careless he became of me.

It wasn't just someone on my course now, it was one other woman, Angelique. I hated that name.

'It's not serious or anything. Justin just asked if I'd take her out; she's been ill and she's lonely.'

'I'm lonely,' I said.

'Oh, you can cope. And it's only the one date.' Invariably when I complained that was his reply: you can cope. I think about it now I'm married, now I'm Mrs Cope.

And then, just when I didn't think I could take it any longer, he did something so beautiful and caring I could have curled up and slept in the warmth of him, like a kitten in a blanket.

He wanted to take me out for the day. But not like those other days, when I'd been taken along like some troublesome niece he was obliged to babysit; today was to please me, to make it up to me for his negligence. He said so, he actually said all that.

We were to go to the Natural History Museum. And my first response was, how typical that a treat for me should comprise what he'd like to do himself. But it wasn't like that. He was astonished to hear that I had never been, thought that he had an obligation to ensure I went before I grew any older. 'It's an essential part of a person's education. We must go as a matter of urgency.' He could be such an idiot.

Max called early for me and was attentive and sweet. He'd bought me a box of liquorice allsorts to eat on the journey. 'You like those, don't you? And they're not as bad for you as chocolate.'

When we arrived he didn't wander round on his own, leaving me to occupy myself till he was ready to come away, as on our picnic and the visit to the booksellers. He walked me round the exhibits, held my hand, pointed out items, filling in the background detail, bringing each object alive for me. He took me into the teashop and bought cakes, too many to eat, so that I had to wrap them in a serviette and hide them in my handbag to bring them home. And in the gift shop he chose for me a scarf printed with a motif from one of the exhibits we had looked at, and a scarf ring to wear with it, and a biro with 'Natural History Museum' printed on it, and oh-so-many things –

'You'll like this'; 'this is pretty, would you like it?', 'this is to remind you of today.'

When we were ready to leave Max realised he had left his jacket in the teashop. He ran back upstairs to get it while I wandered round the model of the dinosaur in the main hall. I looked up to see him leaning over the balustrade watching me. He was smiling, dark and handsome and lovely. And I saw that at last he was seeing in me what I had always seen in him. He ran down the stairs.

As we waited on the platform for our train he turned to me. It was a precious moment. His eyes were liquid and the rugged lines of his face had taken on a softness I hardly recognised. 'I do love you,' he said, scarcely audible. He pulled me to him and kissed my hair. 'You've waited a long time to hear that, haven't you?' I didn't answer, but I laughed; for all the times I'd doubted my sanity in clinging to him, for Robert and Carol who had been so wrong, but most of all for myself and all the good things he would bring to me.

We settled ourselves in a carriage and he took my hand between his, resting his head against mine.

'What shall we do tonight?' I said, glowing. It was the first time, in eighteen months, I had dared presume he would spend the evening with me. There was a pause, long enough for the scenery to have changed from urban to suburban. I assumed he was considering the options. In a way he was.

'Look, I'm sorry,' he said. 'It'll be the last time, but I have to see Angelique tonight. It's too late to get out of it.'

The ice cube of acid and bile was back now, and I wondered why I'd ever thought it would go away.

Somewhere in the back of my mind was a box into which I had filed all the various hurts, insults and injustices that had been Max's true gifts to me. It was marked 'Pain – Do Not Open', but now I did open it, just enough to squeeze in this one last item.

'You understand, don't you?' said Max, and he was sad and sorry. 'But I just can't let her down this late.'

We collected his car from the station car park and he drove me home. 'Ellie,' he called, as I walked towards the front door, 'you've left all your presents.' But I'd only left the bits of junk he'd bought me. I wish I could have disposed of his real gifts as easily.

Chapter 10

To tell you the truth, I'm a bit sorry to have to give up the moral high ground with regard to Josie. I've enjoyed feeling I'm a better person than she is; it's made up for the fact her hair is sleeker than mine, her waist slimmer and her legs longer. But who else can I talk to? And I have to talk to someone.

'Go on then, what have you got to tell me?' I'm hardly in the door and this is how she greets me. How can she tell? 'Well it's obvious something has happened, you look like all the lights have been switched on. Have you got a new job?'

I'm partly relieved she is so wrong, and partly disappointed. I'd have liked to think I was exuding love and passion.

'It's nothing like that.'

'Robert's got a promotion? You're moving – somewhere exotic – somewhere like – California!' This used to be Josie's own dearest wish. I tell her that she's wrong again, and no, we're not buying a new house either, or a new car, we haven't just come into money, and I haven't just met Tom Cruise in Sainsbury's. She's stumped, and I realise telling her isn't going to be as easy as I was expecting. The truth is going to sound disappointing.

'It's nothing really,' I tell her.

'Come on, out with it.'

'You'll think I'm stupid.'

'I won't, I won't.' She will, she will.

'Okay – I've got a thing about someone.'

'A *thing* about someone?' She doesn't know what I mean.

'You know Steven— ?'

'Steven? Mary's husband?'

I have a sudden impulse to throttle Josie. 'Steven-the-boy-who's-painting-the-house! Look, forget it—'

She draws up her knees and hugs them, giggling. 'You fancy him! And you told me you didn't think he was sexy.' She pauses and looks up at me coquettishly from under carefully made-up eyelids with sweeping lashes. I can see why men find her attractive. 'Have you been to bed with him?' She's gleeful at having her own immorality condoned, can't wait to compare notes on our wrong-doing. She talks as though it was all so easy. She's going to laugh if she knows I haven't even kissed him.

I stand up to go. 'It isn't like that, Josie. I just can't tell you.' Her eyes open wider and she looks hungry. She thinks we have done something unrepeatable, like in readers' letters to men's magazines. A fleeting image of doing such things with Steven comes into my mind and isn't entirely displeasing. I file it away for later consideration.

'You can tell me, there's almost nothing Greg and I haven't done.'

'We didn't do anything.'

'Look, I'll just say something and you say yes if that's what you did. Was it, say, oral?'

I think I will throttle her. That way I could go to prison for life and never have to think about any of this again.

'Okay . . . was it bondage then?'

'For goodness' sake, we haven't done anything! I just fancy him, that's all!'

The smile disappears and her brows knit together. The concept of fancying someone and not acting on it is a new one to her.

'Then what's all the fuss about?'

Josie makes coffee and we sit in her recently installed kitchen considering my new and unexpected situation. Her kitchen looks very hi-tech with its dark grey work surfaces, pale grey floor and white units. Her last kitchen was all pine. She has a new kitchen every five years. Her old one is now my new one. Perhaps in five years time this one will be in my house too.

'You seemed so lit up I just assumed something had happened. Something physical, I mean. He's very sweet, I can see why you're hooked.'

I tell her I'm not hooked, but I say it too insistently so she raises one of her lightly plucked eyebrows to show that she sees through me. But really I'm not hooked. Right now I have a choice. He finishes the painting this week and that could be the end of it; he could go, we'd say goodbye, and I'd be left with a clear conscience and a newly painted house. But Robert is already suggesting that we pay him to dig over the vegetable patch (or what would be one if we ever got round to planting anything) and weed the flower beds. And he certainly wants Steven to help him when he builds the new patio. He could be here for weeks. And if he is here for weeks, something will happen. It's inevitable.

Josie has a way of interpreting events in the way which

suits her best, just one more of her characteristics that irritates the hell out of me. But it's different now she is doing it on my behalf. 'Look at it like this. Robert can't be giving you what you need or you wouldn't have to look somewhere else. It's not your fault he doesn't satisfy you, is it?' Robert would take issue with that but we're discussing my needs, not his. 'And look at it from Robert's side. He does his best; maybe it's not his fault either. So are you going to punish him for that? Break up your home because you can't get things right in bed? Because that's what will happen, you know. Problems always start in bed. Could you really bear to do that to Robert?'

I might be more convinced if it wasn't Josie urging me to be so selfless; Josie who never does anything that isn't good for Josie. This is all that her concern for me — and Robert — comes down to: she wants a partner in crime.

'And think of the children.' I knew she'd get round to them eventually.

'I am thinking of the children. That's why I haven't done anything.'

'Children need stability. And how stable will your marriage be if you're unhappy and tired of it?'

'Well I'm not exactly unhappy—'

'If you were happy, you wouldn't be looking around. You've got a choice. Throw in the towel and accept that you're on the road to splitting up—' She sees I want to disagree but steamrollers over me: 'You are! Boredom is where it all starts. Or you can take some preventive medicine. And once you've got some fun back in your life it'll probably rekindle your feelings for Robert.'

'It didn't rekindle anything for you.'

'I'm still here, aren't I? And nothing I do affects David.' She sees my expression. 'Not really,' she adds.

'Well, I don't know . . .' Talking about the long-term consequences is having a curiously dampening effect.

'As long as you go into these things with your eyes open, there's no threat to your marriage — just the opposite. And who knows better than me?' She goes on in this vein for some time and the more she says, the more shallow and silly she makes me feel.

There's a knock at the door. Josie answers it and comes back with a brilliant shine to her eyes, and a curious jerking of the head towards the front door. 'Someone for you.'

Steven is standing there holding a parcel. 'Someone just delivered this. Thought it might be urgent.' It's only a dress I ordered for Rebecca from a catalogue, but I'm touched by this small attention. I ask him to leave it in the kitchen for me, not listening to what I say, aware only of his nearness and the splash of paint on his eyebrow. For a moment I visualise licking it off. He goes, and I linger at the door to enjoy his retreating back.

I wonder sometimes where this lusting came from. When he first came all I felt was a sense of protectiveness towards a friend's child; my developing fondness seemed only natural. I even told Robert how taken I was with Steven. 'You'll be needing a chaperon next,' he said lightly, 'or he will.' He's right. Suddenly I don't know whether to date him or adopt him.

I think it started the day I called Steven indoors to take a phone call from Rita. After he finished the call, while he wiped the black fingermarks he'd made on the handset on to his shirt front, we got talking. It was about nothing in particular, but that must have been the first time I noticed him, looked at him properly. I was still talking to him, but all the time I was transfixed: by the strength in his square rough hands; by the hollow of his throat where it met the rise of his chest; the way his shirt fell open at the neck and was pulled out at one spot from the waistband of his jeans. I remember thinking that I could just reach out and tuck it in. He must have noticed I was distracted because suddenly he said, 'Are you all right?' Steven, I thought, you are eighteen and I am thirty-eight. I am not all right.

'I think I left the bath tap running,' I said, and ran upstairs.

Josie resumes her attack with renewed vigour but I could match her if I wanted to. What I can't counter, though, are the soft-winged butterflies that are swooping from my stomach to my throat and brushing my nipples with their wings.

She tells me about falling in love with Greg and how her life is transformed. I nod and adopt a stance of concentration, but she can talk on this topic unaided for ages which gives me space to retreat behind my eyes to my own thoughts. I'm still dwelling on tucking Steven's shirt in when she starts up again.

'Anyone could see something special has happened to you, and it's what you need in your life, especially after your illness. You looked dreadful in that hospital, all grey and puffy round the eyes. But look at you now, it's taken years off you.' Several people have made the same morale-boosting observation, so I know she must be right. As I ponder this thought I catch sight of myself reflected in the switched-off television screen. The image is too far away to detail my features, but there's an unmistakeable jauntiness about my head and shoulders which I don't remember seeing before. For just a moment I resemble Josie.

'And remember, you can't get pregnant now.' This, of course, is what is making the whole thing possible. I'd never have considered it if the outcome were likely to be life-threatening — and the very thought of another baby would threaten my life. Prior to my operation I was using the coil, as the precaution of least evil, but I know of two women who had babies while using it. One story, hopefully apocryphal, had the baby being born holding the device. Now that monthly anxiety is a thing of the past. And I am hardly likely to catch anything more serious than a cold off Steven.

'If he's doing you this much good just by being there, then just think what . . . He's good for you, Ellie.'

Still watching my reflection, I toss my hair to make it swing the way Josie does. Maybe I could lose a little weight, but I look healthy — and alive.

'He's just what you need. You can't afford not to.' She raises her mug in a toast. 'Go for it!'

So in the end I decide to have an affair on grounds of my health.

That night we make love for the first time. His voice is husky with tenderness.

'Doesn't this feel good?' It does feel good, the warmth of him, Steven's legs entwined around mine, his mouth pressed against my neck. My back arches and I am Kim Basinger, I am Sharon Stone, I am Michelle Pfeiffer. I kiss Steven's face, nuzzle his chest and bite his shoulder with helpless passion as he cries out. Afterwards he collapses on his back, exhausted but jubilant. 'Well it was certainly worth the wait,' says Robert.

As we settle to sleep, with me cradled in his lap, the sleeping posture we always used to favour, I wonder if it matters. After all, fantasy is encouraged these days isn't it? When I was first married, I read a survey which said that most women thought of a different man while they were having sex. It upset me at the time; wasn't thinking about it with someone else as bad as doing it? But when you've been having sex with the same person for a long time, maybe fantasy is the nearest thing to excitement you can get. And where's the harm? I mean, while you're doing the washing up you listen to the radio, while you're ironing you watch TV, so why shouldn't you have something to occupy the mind while you're doing that other chore that has to be dealt with every couple of days?

Anything that improves a marriage must be a good thing; so what if it happens to be the memory of Steven's tanned bicep?

I drift off to sleep rehearsing these and similar arguments, but fail to convince myself.

Chapter 11

'So. What have you got in mind for next week?' It's the weekly editorial meeting. Which is to say that Theresa, the woman's page editor, and I are drinking coffee, having exhausted our discussion of our children, last night's TV and sale bargains currently available in Marks & Spencer, and have now resorted to the subject of the newspaper that employs us.

Theresa is in her forties, with mousy shoulder-length hair which she tucks behind her ears. She has thick ankles accentuated by calf-length skirts and the neat court shoes from which her plump feet spill. In the past I've rather despised her for a tendency to squash my most brilliant and innovative ideas with a doubtful shake of the head and a 'best be on the safe side,' but she was solicitous while I was ill, phoning weekly with her quiet enquiries and the words I most wanted to hear: 'Your job's here whenever you want it.'

The office is open plan, providing an unrestricted view of desks floating in a sea of typed copy (A4, double-spaced), black and white photos (we have colour on the front page only), and an assemblage of dirty coffee cups and abandoned McDonald's boxes. 'Organised chaos,'

Theresa likes to say, though which bit is organised she doesn't say.

In fact, Theresa is rather more talented than any of us give her credit for. The other staff constantly tease her about her contribution, but she has an unerring talent for sensing what the readership wants. We often get letters praising us for our economical recipes and thought-provoking articles on wholefoods and homeopathy; our readers seem delighted with the happy coincidence that the very item we are addressing is being advertised in adjacent columns. But I'm tired of conjuring up pieces with titles like 'Fifteen Places to Visit for Under a Fiver', and I haven't the time to read the book which sits by her coffee cup and which I know she will ask me to review. It's time to kick our gentle readers out of their complacency.

'Why don't we run a series on relationship problems?' I say.

Theresa sucks at a morsel of bourbon biscuit stuck in her teeth while the considers. 'Family relationships?' she asks.

I hadn't thought of it quite like that, but husbands are family, I suppose. 'I thought I'd start with what makes women want to have affairs.' She blinks but I push on. 'Not so much the having of them as the thinking about it. What it feels like, who does it, why they do it. We could call it "Contemplating Infidelity . . ."'

Theresa reaches across her desk for the packet of biscuits and offers me one. She has a faint moustache which I haven't noticed before. Perhaps we should do a spread on dealing with unwanted hair; I could investigate what it's like to have your eyebrows plucked and your bikini line waxed. Not that I've got a bikini line, more a bikini spread, extending from impenetrable forest at its densest point out to hedges and shrubs with a creeping undergrowth, like ivy, that nothing will hold back. It would be good to wear swimwear without worrying about what might be poking out of it. I've tried hair-removing creams but I'm allergic and I hate shaving – you get black stubbly regrowth before you've even washed the soap off. It'd need industrial-strength wax to cope with that lot.

When I drift back from my reverie Theresa is nodding her head and smiling, still on my infidelity piece, and for just a moment . . .

'It'd be brilliant, wouldn't it? I'd love to do something like that,' she says.

'Then why don't we?'

'Can you imagine Phoebe?' Phoebe is a reader who once won a cake-icing competition Theresa organised, and she has been corresponding regularly ever since. I hate her cosy all-girls-together letters.

'So do we have to set our standards according to what Phoebe likes?'

Theresa dips her biscuit in her coffee and sucks on it. 'I used to be like you, wanting to set the world on fire. But we're as important to our readers as any of the *Daily Telegraph*'s. Or *Woman's Own*'s. Our readers are all Phoebes. We're their friend.' She pushes her glasses up her nose and leans forward purposefully. 'And don't forget, we're the most successful provincial paper in the group. The editor hates the woman's page, but advertisers like it, and if I want to keep my job –' she waves a pencil at me – our jobs – I have to keep it that way.'

It's embarrassing to be lectured on principles, and especially when the one doing the lecturing is someone to whom you've always thought you were superior in some undefined way, and had assumed she thought so too. Plus, she has such terrible dress sense.

'In-depth analysis of social issues? That's not for the likes of us.' I feel my face redden at the thought of being bracketed together with Theresa and her thick ankles. 'So what other ideas have you got? Must've come up with a few while you were lying in that hospital bed.' In view of her moustache, it would be undiplomatic to mention the hair removal idea and, on consideration, I'd want a general anaesthetic before anyone poured hot wax on my pubic area. We settle on aromatherapy, and something on acupressure facelifts for the week after.

She picks up the book next to her and flicks through it before handing it over. 'You'll enjoy this.'

I've just arranged an interview with a local aromatherapist when the phone rings again. Theresa answers it and hands it to me with a look of concern.

'It's your childminder.' This is only the second time Cathy has ever telephoned. The last occasion was when Simon fell off the swing and had to be rushed to hospital with a hairline fracture of the skull.

'Cathy? What's the problem?' She hesitates, and I think: hospitals/doctors, next week's headline and a spokesman moralising about working mothers.

'Is it Simon? Is he injured?'

'It's Rebecca. She isn't hurt or anything, but the school's sent her home.'

'What's she done?' Stabbed another child with a dinner knife? Thrown paint at the teacher? Told the teacher her mother says 'bugger' when other drivers cut her up at the lights?

'Nothing to worry about.' Cathy's attempts to break

the bad news gently are agonizing. 'I just thought you might be embarrassed. She's got nits.'

Relief makes me bad-tempered. 'Why didn't you just say so? I thought it was something terrible.'

'I'm sorry, I just thought . . . I've put a headscarf on her, I don't want the others to catch it.' She's sullen now; I've offended her, which I can't afford to do. I'll have to get her some Black Magic for her trouble.

'Thanks for dealing with it, Cath. I'll come straight home.'

I put the phone down. Theresa is still wearing the same expression of concern.

'Nits,' I say, scratching my head.

She laughs. 'Suleo-C, here you come.' Suleo-C is the preparation the health visitor brings you to cure what they are pleased to call 'an infestation'. It's a foul-smelling liquid with which you have to wet the entire head, and then it has to dry naturally without benefit of hairdryer. You have to do the whole family at once and the house reeks for days afterwards. My chemist told me, when Simon got them, that there's a shampoo which does the trick just as well but it's Suleo-C which the health visitor prefers, and she will bring a pack and hand it over on the doorstep, declining to come in because she is in a hurry but really because she doesn't want to catch them herself. It's the twentieth-century equivalent of making you shave your head: shameful and embarrassing. It is also, it occurs to me, the precise opposite of aromatherapy: the mere smell can make you feel bad. I scratch my head again.

'Do you think you've got them?' Theresa asks. 'I got them each time my kids did.'

'I'd have noticed,' I say, and a tickle, just like a tiny insect scuttling, goes from my neck across the top of my head. I raise my hand to my head but Theresa is watching me and I rub my nose instead.

'Well, use the stuff anyway,' she says, helpfully. 'Best be on the safe side.' I gather up my bag and notes and stop off at the loos on the way to the car. Leaning over the sink I sink my fingers deep into my hair and scratch my scalp all over with both hands.

'Oh God, not again.' Thus Robert, on opening the front door.

It's not only the smell he recognises but the sight of me bending over Simon with the metal nitcomb, wiping off the brown eggs that collect on it with every stroke. I've finished Rebecca, fortunately. Her long hair combs into tangles and she has only just stopped crying. Simon's hair is shorter and in any case he's making a great show of being braver than she was. 'You've got to wash your hair too,' he says to Robert, brightly.

'You must be joking.'

'My teacher says you've got to or we'll catch it back off you,' says Rebecca. Robert flicks back the lock of hair on his forehead and I watch to see if anything falls out of it. My friend's mother had an itching scalp for ages and only found out she had nits when she went to her doctor. She went home and shook her head over a sheet of newspaper, and so many tiny bodies fell out that the paper was covered. 'You could see them running,' my friend said. I tell this story to Robert.

'Look,' he says, 'I haven't got them, so stop going on about it.'

But after he has changed out of his suit, he comes back downstairs with wet hair and smelling like the rest of us.

Simon leaps at him to be hugged. 'I thought you said you weren't going to, Daddy.'

'I didn't want to be left out,' Robert says, swinging him round.

Once the kids are in bed I get out my Basildon Bond and the pen I had for Christmas to write to Carol, my friend from university. She's still my closest confidante, even though she lives in Manchester while we're in London, so most of our confiding gets done over the phone. But I'm not phoning tonight; if I write it down then it might help me get it clear in my mind.

I want to tell her about Steven. I want to see if she thinks it would be such a terrible thing to do. In theory it is, of course; marriage vows are not to be taken lightly. But I'm not taking them lightly and life isn't as straightforward as moralists would have us believe. These days we understand about self-fulfilment, and the need to be true to oneself. We live in liberated times, no longer hidebound by outmoded systems of behaviour, constricted by outmoded family values. We no longer concern ourselves with what our parents or parents-in-law would think. Which is fortunate: my mother would have a fit.

These days we recognise that few things in life are entirely good or wholly bad. Already Robert has reaped the benefit of a wife who suddenly wants sex once more (and who may even be willing to have it again tonight; and consecutive nights of sex haven't happened since pre-Rebecca days). Josie is firmly convinced it would help me and that it is only her affairs which keep her marriage going (I brush away the several 'buts' that come to mind as I think of this). But then there's Steven. Am I treating him like a pawn in all this? What would his opinion be? If, when he arrives tomorrow, and I hold his gaze, reach out and touch his cheek and say the things I burn to say, will he melt with helpless desire? Or will his face just turn red?

Steven is an unknown quantity as regards his sexual experience. I've read that most boys in his social class (but Steven is himself, not a statistic in a social class) have had sex by now, probably with a fifteen year old in a doorway at the back of the Odeon. But Steven isn't like that. I think he's probably still a virgin. He smells of innocence; of innocence and testosterone, a heady combination from my point of view and maybe from his too. He wants it, but he doesn't know where to get it. I could form his first introduction to loving, caring sex. To experienced sex. He would not have to start with a fumbled quickie on his parents' carpet while they were out at a church social, as Carol did, or ignominiously in the back seat of a mini, as did Josie. Or with someone who didn't care about him and didn't even know it *was* his first time and who wouldn't speak to him again for three months.

Your first time should be so special, but is it ever? What I remember is wetness, sweat and a smell I hadn't smelled before. What Carol remembers is 1001 carpet cleaner. We discussed our earliest experiences once, sitting in her kitchen while we breastfed our new babies. 'At school we learned how tiny a sperm was,' she said, 'and I thought there'd be just the odd drop or two, like water, barely visible to the naked eye. But I'd no sooner got my pants off than this guy started coming by the bucketful — and he hadn't even got inside me. Most of it went over my mum's Axminster.'

'How awful.'

'It was, we had to stop and get the stain removal kit out.'

'And what happened?'

'Nothing. It all blended in with the carpet.'

Josie had been equally disillusioned (though if you start off on the back seat of a mini your romantic expectations can't ever have been very high). 'I was only sixteen; I thought your vagina would sort of seal up afterwards. I hadn't realised his stuff would all run out the moment you stood up. It ruined my suede shoes.'

It wouldn't be like this for Steven. He would never have to tell of his first time with a wry smile, a funny story told against himself and his ignorance. He would be nurtured and cherished, his innocence a quality to be prized. I wouldn't let the mess we made be the main thing he would remember afterwards; I wouldn't rush off, or drive off, or clear off before he'd even got dressed just to get to some lecture on seventeenth-century drama. I could fill the entire experience with unbridled passion coupled with sweetness, delicacy, caring and tenderness. And I might, if I was in the mood (and I would be in the mood) toss in the randy raunchiness of the confirmed seductress, debauched and devoid of shame, hot enough to make the sternest stud go weak at the knees. I would be the woman men read of in the pages of *Penthouse*; the older woman younger men wet dream about.

'Dear Carol,' I write. 'I hope you are well.'

Later, as I watch the news with Robert, trying not to inhale the eye-watering blend of Suleo-C and the alpine air freshener I've tried to mask it with, Robert says, 'He's a bit of a lad, old Steve.'

'Oh?' I keep my eyes fixed on Trevor McDonald's countenance.

'Saw him when I was on my way to work this

morning. I was waiting at the traffic lights and there he was, snogging some girl in a shop doorway.'

I begin a doodle in the margin of Carol's letter, which still hasn't proceeded beyond paragraph one. 'Doesn't sound like Steven.'

'Oh, I don't know.' He sounds almost admiring as he folds the newspaper to get better access to the crossword.

'I've noticed kids these days are much more inclined to touch and hug each other than we were.' I'm trying not to sound hopeful.

Robert picks up his pen and begins again the enterprise which he has never yet entirely completed. 'Then it was a pretty good friend, from the look of her. And she had the most enormous bust – what I could see of it. I don't know when I've seen anyone being so throughly groped.'

I screw up the letter to Carol and throw it in the bin.

Chapter 12

I'm having a lazy afternoon. It must be in the eighties. I've dragged the sun bed out here and now I'm lying in the shade of the umbrella. Steven said he'd carry it for me but I can manage perfectly well on my own. He's digging the garden behind me but I'm ignoring him.

When I came out here in my bikini (black with white polka dots, underwired bra; my operation scar is well below the line of the pants) I felt his eyes on me, all the way from the house up to the greenhouse at the end of the garden, where the sun bed is stored. I thought, Dream on, loser.

I saw my aromatherapist this morning. Originally I was just to do an interview, but unusually the paper ran to paying for me to try it out. It wasn't what I was expecting: no glamorous treatment room replete with rubber plants and pale carpeting, just a poky corner in the basement of a hairdressing salon, with the plaster peeling from the door frame and dents in the woodchip-papered partition wall. Perhaps this made the effect of the oils with which I was massaged all the more startling (except that I wasn't startled, I was soothed and calmed and led to the very borders of sleep). Without the façade of magic and promise I hadn't expected it to work.

Sandra, slim with small neat hands, and wearing a white overall to suggest a medical connection (though she is a hair stylist by profession and is still learning aromatherapy via a correspondence course), anointed my legs in a slow caress, while keeping up a running monologue about her career prospects. Fortunately I left the tape recorder running because the soporific mood she induced in me was not the stuff of which a probing interview is made. In fact, I barely listened to her at all, but her dull south London monotone was soothing and I drifted off, dreaming of other hands, attached to male bodies.

She hadn't warned me that she would oil my feet too. My feet were so slippery in my shoes I could barely walk to the car.

The tape recorder and my note pad are on the table next to me awaiting my attention but I already know what I will write, and Sandra too knows I mean to give aromatherapy the thumbs up. I've booked another session for next week.

The sun is scorching my toes, but when I move the sun bed wobbles on our uneven lawn. I could get up and move it, but then I'd have to move the umbrella too and even thinking about it makes me drowsy. Besides, a colony of ants are running amok over the umbrella base and one of my sandals, and it would be a shame to disturb them.

'D'you mind if I get a drink?' Perhaps I've been dozing because I didn't hear Steven approach. He is outlined against the sun, seeming monstrously tall now that I am lying down. His silhouette shades my feet, bringing temporary relief.

'Help yourself.'

'Shall I get you one?'

'Yes. Coke.' And then, as he lumbers off, 'Thanks.' Falling out of love with him has made me lose my manners.

I feel hypnotised by the heat, and it seems only seconds before he is returning with our drinks which he has put on a tray. Outside the back door he bends down to pick something up, and when he arrives with my drink, the glass half full of clinking ice, I see that he has set a sprig of mint on the top, plucked from the bush that grows by the back door. I am conscious that he is looking at me, waiting for my comment.

'Thanks,' I say.

It's strange what puts you off people, but the image of Steven snogging in the street has taken him out of the realms of romance and fantasy and brought me back to earth with the force of a meteorite. If Robert had just said 'kissing' I could have coped with it. 'Kissing' is to making love as a rosebud is to a full bloom, and Steven is entitled to be attracted to girls. But 'snogging' and 'groping' is backstreet stuff, animal and coarse. How could I have got so carried away by someone who could be so vulgar? And at a bus stop? On the way to work? It's just my hormones making me vulnerable; I still haven't recovered from the operation, not in that sense. Steven's just a boy, and not a particularly desirable one at that. When he's hot and takes his shirt off, as he does now, he wipes his face on it. I've only ever seen him in his working clothes, except for the day we went to Brighton (and it was just my reprieve from death carrying me away then). His favourite reading is science fiction comics. His idea of sartorial elegance is probably to wear his cap the right way round. If he wants to look even sharper he probably tucks his T-shirt in.

In the distance I can hear Josie's phone ringing. She must be out; she always answers by the third ring, she loves a phone call. I've been thinking about our conversation. I think she's wrong that I need an affair but she's right that I need some more fun in my life. I need to make a few changes. Maybe I should look for another job. Or join a club, make some new friends. The magazines to which I offered freelance articles all turned them down, but two said they'd be interested in any other ideas I had. I should contact them again. I haven't the energy for an affair, even if I had the inclination. And I'd be a fool to do anything that might jeopardise what I have . . . including the chance to doze in the sun on this lounger.

I reach out for my drink but the ice has melted and a wasp has drowned in it. I must have been lying here longer than I thought.

Turning, I see that Steven has finished digging over the flowerbed and is leaning with one arm on his shovel looking up at the house. Maybe he's admiring his handiwork. Now the house painting is finished, Robert has arranged for him to start on the garden, and then when that's straight, he can start digging out for the patio. I suggested he should come on the days I don't go into the office. ('Won't he be in your way?' Robert asked. 'I'll manage,' I said, 'and I really ought to keep an eye on what he's doing.') But that was before the information about the snogging. Now the sight of that lop-sided grin is just a reminder of what a fool I've been.

I passed Josie as I drove the kids to school this morning and she gave me a knowing smile.

It's time to start thinking about dinner, so I drag my body, which seems to weigh twice as much as it did earlier, off the sun bed and let down the umbrella. I don't know whether it's the aromatherapy or the heat of the sun but I feel warm and content. Life is good. I will be here next summer and for summers *ad infinitum* and, barring accidents, will live to be old and cantankerous and make my children's lives a misery.

The umbrella is awkward and won't clip shut, so I drag rather than carry it up to the greenhouse at the top of the garden. Soon, since we now have a gardener, we'll recommission the greenhouse for its proper purpose, but for now it houses the garden furniture, the lawnmower, the kids' bikes, and all the other things which would go in the shed if the shed wasn't already full.

The umbrella keeps trying to reopen itself, and perhaps this is why I only realise Steven is in the greenhouse when I back into him. He has placed the shovel against the bikes and is arranging a garden trowel and spade neatly on the wooden shelf.

He turns, half smiling, and leans in for me to pass. He has put his shirt back on but it's undone and I glimpse beads of sweat shining on his chest. As I pass, my back to his, a tiny cord, seemingly inside my stomach but stretching from my thighs to my navel, pings and reverberates. A shower of tiny sparks light up my insides. Must be some kind of after effect from the operation.

I lean the umbrella carefully against the adjacent shelf and close my eyes, enjoying the small sensation of pleasure. Ripples continue to echo from its source; my thighs begin an old familiar ache, but I can't immediately think why it's familiar or why I should be feeling it now. I feel heady as though from too much wine, and when I open my eyes, the air is throbbing and pulsating. I turn slowly and carefully — I could almost fall, my eyes are hazy as though I'm just awakening — and then I see Steven. He is still turned away from me, lining up the garden tools the way Simon straightens his set of felt pens. His hair brushes the collar of his shirt, a brushed cotton check; it hangs loose, covering the seat of his jeans which are creased at the backs of the knees; one leg is frayed at the ankle where it has rubbed against a trainer. His ignorance of the danger he is in, the passions beating their loud wings behind him, adds to his sudden appeal. I take a small step forward and for a moment I stand poised, uncertain. He's only inches away and still he doesn't know. My heart begins to beat. I take a breath and lean forward so that my face is resting against the soft brushed cotton of his shirt, and place my hands on his shoulder blades, inhaling the damp warmth of him. He stiffens and straightens up, his shoulder blades emerging further from under softer flesh, and I run my hands round and up under his shirt and on to his chest. His sweat against my fingers makes our intimacy almost unbearable. He draws in his breath; his heart too is thumping. He places his hands, rough with dried-on soil, on mine, but I slide them from him and slowly trace the wiry hair that protrudes from the waistband of his jeans. He grasps my hands now and turns, and for one heart-stopping moment I think I have misunderstood the signs and he is going to push me away; in response a blush begins in my neck. But the face turned to mine is heavy and flushed with longing, a long naked look, his lips unusually red and full. Placing both hands on my waist, he lifts me on to the slatted wooden shelf behind me. He cups my face in his mud-caked hands and kisses me. I wind my legs around his waist, drawing him nearer.

'Someone might see,' he says huskily, looking round us at the clear view the glass walls of the greenhouse provide. I follow his gaze and then close my eyes.

'I know,' I say.

'You look like you've caught the sun,' Robert remarks.

'Whose son?' I ask, a flash of Rita looming before my

eyes. For once I'm grateful that Robert doesn't listen to a word I say.

For the first time ever, Theresa asks me to rewrite my piece. 'It's a wonderful piece of creative writing, very sensuous,' she says, handing it back without looking at me, the way I've seen the editor do to her. 'Unfortunately, we've no room for creative writing here, have we?' She begins to scribble busily and I stand by her desk like a child being set lines. 'And we don't want people getting the wrong idea. You make it sound like a French massage parlour.' I take the sheet of paper from her hand and the words 'swoon' and 'caress' seem to jump out at me, the memory of something else sending a small tremor down my spine. 'Put a few quotes in,' suggests Theresa, softening a little.

'In the *greenhouse*?' Josie's laugh is like silver coins rattling in a glass. She is in blue today, the blue of June skies over a summer meadow: blue shorts, blue espadrilles, blue earrings, blue beads. Only a white T-shirt gives relief, and emphasises her careful tan. My own legs are the shade of pork crackling at the front, still white at the back, with a faint bristly regrowth of hair just beginning to make itself apparent, tiny black shoots peeping through the pores, like blackheads. Josie has regular waxings and her legs gleam like the ceramic earthenware mug from which she now sips. 'Go on then, dig the dirt.'

'There's nothing to tell really.' But her words remind me of Steven's fingernails, black with fresh soil; the sharp edge of cuticle that scratched my nipple. His kiss was gentle and his tongue darted in and out like a silver fish, at once both startling and teasing.

Josie tucks one leg underneath her and stirs her coffee

with the faintest suggestion of irritation. 'You can't say, 'I put my arms round him', and then say there's nothing to tell. What did you do?'

He's so sweet, you know. I looked in his eyes, and he was so shy and uncertain. He was doing what they all do, his hands as quick and dexterous as a magician's (later I was to say to him, 'You have magic hands.'), but his eyes asked, 'Am I doing it right? Will you forgive me if I make a mistake?' I remembered Stuart and Neil and how I never forgave them anything.

He pulled down the strap of my bikini top and licked my nipple with his tongue, eager yet somehow uncertain, and when he drew back I tightened my legs round his waist and rested my arms on his shoulders. I was sixteen again but free of the teenager's prissiness. Reckless and beautiful I would be, a fuck to remember all his life — and mine.

I tightened my grip still further and lifted myself on to him.

But he wasn't ready. I caught him off balance and he fell forward, landing me back on the greenhouse shelf with a bump, a splinter of wood scratching my buttock and tearing into my bikini pants, and then the umbrella flopped sideways, opening out and catching the shovel which fell with a clatter against the spokes of Simon's bike's front wheel. The handle hit Steven smartly across the toes.

'It never happens like this in the movies,' I said as Steven bent to pick up the umbrella. He didn't answer but he was blushing a deep red.

'We just kissed,' I tell Josie. 'It was a bit of fun, but I don't think I want it to go any further.'

* * *

I told Josie about it the day after it happened, and I believed what I said at the time, about not wanting it to go any further. Even yesterday I believed it. But this morning, stripping our bed while the morning sun streams on to my back, I realise I am singing and there is a sense of excitement in the room which I am at a loss to explain. We aren't going on holiday; I'm not going anywhere, I haven't received good news. At first I think it's a resurgence of the sense of pleasure I get periodically since my reprieve from death, but then I start to trace my thought processes back, and I don't have to trace them far. Today is the day Steven comes again.

The garden is deplorable, seen at its worst from our bedroom window. There has been little rain this summer and dry yellow patches are spreading rapidly. The flowerbeds are nothing of the sort, just strips of bare soil either side of the lawn boasting the odd overgrown bush. Last year I planted a few bedding plants, and the remains of some alyssum have made a brave attempt to survive in the far corner, but new growth is being choked by old dried-up dead material that I never got round to pulling up. There's enough work here to keep Steven going for a week or two. And when he's finished, he'll still need to come back periodically to mow the lawn.

It could be very pleasant, this. A man around the house periodically, employed almost solely to boost my morale. And it's all very innocent; we haven't done anything, nothing has really changed. Not really. In a global sense.

There's still no sign of him, so I get out the clean sheets and set about putting on fresh pillowcases. Placing one of them back on the bed I imagine Steven's head on it as he wakes up in the morning, but I'm ashamed of my own day dreams; fortunately the effort required to get the duvet back into its clean cover takes my mind off them. When I've finished, Steven still hasn't arrived, so I straighten the curtains and check the garden to see that's nothing's changed there either.

I've got butterflies but I'm not sure why. I don't know what I want to happen when he gets here. His kiss was nice but I don't think I want another one. Sex is too messy and complicated, and in any case I feel now that perhaps the important thing was to know that he was interested in me. I didn't think I'd given much thought to not having a womb, but maybe I needed reassuring that I was still feminine and attractive. My scar is neat and fairly small, though it still has a look of raw meat about it. I'm glad that Steven hasn't seen it. The main thing, now that we've responded to each other and acknowledged we're attracted, is to discuss how we feel. Too many relationships fail from a simple lack of communication. What I want to do today is actually very simple: to sit across the table from him, sip wine and stroke his fingers. I just want to look into his dark innocent eyes and talk to him.

The phone rings. 'Steven can't come,' says Rita abruptly. 'He's hurt his foot.'

'Haven't you rung to see how he is?' Robert asks me when Steven still hasn't returned a week later.

'I've been so busy,' I lie. In fact, the impulse to ring him arrives hourly; were he anyone else of my acquaintance I would certainly have telephoned. But I'm embarrassed by my own eagerness to hear his voice. So I don't phone; it's my punishment for wanting to.

It's the end of the following week when Steven returns. He always knocks at the door when he arrives, but today when I look out of the kitchen window he is already hard at work. He's obviously shy of meeting me, and to an extent I feel the same. But age gives you power. And it's my house.

Earlier it seemed like another scorching day, but clouds have moved in and I decide to change my shorts and cropped top for something less revealing. I don't want to look too obvious so I plump for jeans and a sweatshirt, just as though I wasn't trying to impress him at all.

Checking my reflection before I come downstairs I decide after all that a little light lipstick wouldn't do any harm. And some mascara. Blusher.

'Hi, Steve. Is your foot better?' Why do I call him Steve? I never have before and it sounds so false in my mouth.

He straightens up and turns to face me but his eyes don't quite meet mine. 'It's fine, thanks.' He doesn't look at me. 'I been down with flu as well, that's what really kept me off.'

'You must've caught it from that girl you were kissing.' I could kick myself for being so stupid; then I feel even worse when I realise from his embarrassed expression that he probably thinks I mean me. 'Robert saw you kissing a girl, when he was going to work,' I add hurriedly. I feel as though I'm driving a car on which the steering is locked and the brakes have failed.

'No, I don't know no girl.'

I want to let it go but the car just hurtles on. 'At the bus stop,' I persist. 'In the high street. Very passionate, from the sound of it.' I adopt a smile and try to give my words a light touch but it still sounds like he's being cross-examined.

'I don't go down the high street. And I don't know no girl.'

'Oh well, it's not important.' The car judders to a halt.

He looks sullen and there's a stubborn jut to his jaw. I stand there foolishly.

'D'you want me to stop coming?' He still isn't looking at me.

'Of course I don't.'

He casts a swift glance at me as though he isn't sure I mean it.

'I want you to keep coming,' I say, hoping he will take that to imply, 'We need to talk about what happened last week', and, 'Steven, I like you; please don't act like this.' What I actually say is: 'Those weeds are shooting up.' I mean to reach out to his hand where it rests on the shovel but he is already turning away to resume his work.

'Better crack on,' he says.

I've been back in the house no more than a few minutes when he taps at the door, looking like someone who is trying not to look awkward and ill at ease, which is how I must look myself.

'Did you say you was making coffee?' he says.

He stands in the kitchen, leaning idly with one elbow on the work surface. His face is tanned and healthy, and he looks taller indoors, seems to inhabit more space. I flutter around, filling the kettle, looking in the wrong cupboard for the biscuits. He has to direct me: 'Don't you usually keep them in that one there?' I spill the sugar while refilling the bowl. (Yesterday I returned a blouse I had changed my mind about to a local boutique. The manageress was awkward about it, but I was determined and stood my ground. Eventually she capitulated. It's scarcely credible that I'm that same assertive person.) Steven takes his milky coffee from my grasp and slowly stirs in two heaped spoonfuls of sugar. I pick up my own mug and wonder what to say now that I have him here. Our kitchen isn't large, but six feet of cushionfloor separates us – an impossible distance. I see now why, in films, lovers always run towards each other across a field: it's not their eagerness, it's just too embarrassing to walk. The unspoken questions hanging in the air between us are almost audible.

We discuss the progress of Steven's digging, and he asks for details regarding the patio. I know only one thing about the patio: that when it's finished it'll be a perfect sun trap for me to lie in. But I don't mention the one thing I know. Instead I ask after Rita's health, Darren's progress, Gina's latest boyfriend.

Steven drains the last of his coffee. It's almost too late. If I don't say something now, I'll never be able to. I can't casually mention in six months' time, 'Oh, by the way, that day in the greenhouse . . .' How can I introduce the subject now? What else can we talk about while I think of a way? Think. Concentrate. He rinses his mug under the cold tap and stands it in the sink. He's going to walk to the back door, and out of it, and he'll be gone and it'll be too late. And still I say nothing.

'Can I wash my hands?' he asks. His question is so unexpected (why didn't he wash them before he ate three digestives?) that I hesitate for a moment. But then I hand him the soap and he turns on the hot tap.

'That day in the greenhouse,' he says, rubbing up a lather between his hands, 'did you – I mean . . .' He pauses, seeming thoroughly absorbed in his task. I watch the lather forming, surging up between his clasped fingers. 'Was it an accident?' He turns on the tap again and rinses his fingers. I reach for the towel from the rail by the sink. I smile.

'It was an accident that the shovel fell over.'

I offer him the towel but as he reaches out I take his

hands and dry them for him. Neither of us speaks, and then I drop the towel and rest my hands on his waist, looping my fingers in his belt hooks. He rests his hands on my shoulders and we regard each other. It's so easy. Why did I think it wouldn't be?

'I like you,' I say, 'you're very attractive.'

'I like you,' he says. 'But I think you must be crazy.'

'I am,' I say, 'but crazy people have the most fun.' The clouds outside part and for a moment a shaft of sunlight catches us like a spotlight. It feels like a cue.

I turn my face up to be kissed and pull his head down to reach me.

Lying in bed, I watch the scratch marks on his buttocks disappear as he hoists up his jeans and buckles his leather belt. He suddenly pauses, his back to me. 'When can I see you again?'

'You're working here Tuesday and Thursday next week, aren't you?'

'You know what I mean.' Yes, I know what he means, and I smile to myself that he has been the one to ask. I've been wondering if I might have disappointed him, with my tits that flop sideways under my arms when I lie down, and my scar, and my thighs like orange peel. It's a long time since I've been examined so closely by someone I wasn't married to or who doesn't have a medical qualification.

I dab at the wet spot on the sheet with a tissue. The taut muscles of his back relax and he bends to pick up his shirt. When he gets up he too is smiling.

'I hope my mum don't find out.'

He's joking, I know, but a sickly feeling of guilt accompanies his mention of Rita. I screw up the tissue and toss it across the room along with all thoughts of her. For just a moment I feel like doing the same with Steven. The only way a relationship like this can work is by pretending that nothing exists for us outside it. If he doesn't know that then he knows nothing. How have I got into this?

I swing my legs out of bed and start pulling the sheets off the bed, angry that the afternoon has so easily been spoiled.

He stands motionless, watching me, wondering what he's done wrong. 'It was all right, wasn't it?' He knows it was; we've already discussed all this, the wonder of it, the unexpectedness. I have made him doubt me and now he is doubting himself. for some reason I see a brief vision of Max.

'I don't know about next Tuesday,' I say, 'I may have to go out.' It's a total lie, but I can't resist seeing him caught and knowing it's up to me when to reel him in. I gather the sheet into a bundle and throw it into a corner of the room, and still he stands there, forlorn and lost. Momentarily I see another brief vision, but this time it isn't of Max, it's of me.

I put my arms around him and hold him tight and he pulls me down on to the crumpled sheet at our feet.

That's how I thought about it after he'd gone, sitting on the floor in my bedroom making cryptic notes in my diary, wanting to capture it forever so I could go on enjoying it just the way it was. But that isn't quite how it was, doesn't capture the essence. It doesn't mention the musky smell of him, the warmth of his breath, the unbearable appeal of his uncertainty. Or my own: that sudden terrible doubt as he lay there, so eager, trusting me. Naked he was so vulnerable. How could I take the clean slate of his inexperience and scribble over it, like a juvenile delinquent with a can of spray paint? I wanted to draw back, to say I'm sorry, find someone your own age to hurt you, the way it ought to be. But by then it was too late: the tide was already surging in, beating its great waves through our bodies, until nothing mattered but this – now, *now*, harder – and even if he'd known he would still have cried out 'do it, do it, do it' just the same.

And it's only the innocent ones, the guiltless and the guileless, that you can do it to. The others are the ones who do it to you.

I am part of his history now. Whoever he meets, whoever he makes love to, I will always be there, he will never be rid of me. I am in his memory, part of his knowledge. I will be his first dysfunctional relationship.

A voice is whispering in my ear, an echo of something long past. It's Max.

'Welcome to the club,' he says.

Chapter 13

I decided not to go home for the Easter vacation following my break-up with Max. I hoped Carol would stay too, but she had to get back for a christening, ironically, so I was left by myself.

During the day I did a little study on the nineteenth-century novel, but it was a month until the exams started and I couldn't work up any enthusiasm. On the first evening of the vacation, I went down to the Union bar to see if anyone else was around. It was too early really, only eight o'clock, but when you've had nothing but the nineteenth-century novel for company all day eight o'clock feels quite late enough. I bought myself a shandy and opened *Silas Marner*. I hated George Eliot, so this was by way of a penance. As it happened, Providence had a different punishment planned. I'd read less than a page when Cliff Rose came over.

He plonked his pint down on the table and, instead of moving the chair to one side, cocked his long thin leg over the back before easing into it. He wasn't a tall man and he achieved this feat without quite maintaining the degree of cool he had hoped for. He was dressed in denim so tight it looked like a tourniquet. He had lost a little more hair since we last spoke.

'Hi. Long time no see.'

I dredged my memory for a suitable line from the movies to answer with. 'Hi,' I said, failing miserably.

'Putting in a little extra study?' He nodded towards *Silas Marner* and I smiled wanly. Cliff was the sort of man who assumes any lone woman must be glad of his company; in that respect he was like most men I'd ever met.

'How are you enjoying the Anglo-Saxon?' This was the course Cliff ran and which I had started this term. I found it turgid and incomprehensible and I was out of sympathy with the Anglo-Saxon poets who, according to the work we had studied so far, seemed to do nothing but moan about how cold it was and wouldn't it be nice to get near the lord's fire in the great hall and warm up. Carol said I had no soul.

'It's fine.'

'Great, glad you like it. Students' — he pronounced it 'stoodents' — 'often find it difficult. But it has a kind of byoody . . .' (beauty) 'when you get into it. And it's a foundation for all your other course work.'

I nodded, wondering in what way it was helping me with *Silas Marner* except to demonstrate that, by comparison, *George Eliot* was about as demanding as the Mr Men books. If I was looking for a punishment, I'd been too easy on myself.

He took out a pack of cigarettes and offered me one. I reached for it, then waved it away. I ought to give up, I supposed. 'What do you think of *The Dream of the Rood*?'

I reached for my glass and sipped slowly. *The Dream of the Rood* was a poem around which Cliff had centred an unusually dramatic and, some said, inspired lecture. That was as much as I remembered about it, being in the throes of an out-of-body experience at the time — that is, my body was present but my mind was heavily engaged elsewhere.

'It was very dramatic,' I said, remembering Cliff striding about the stage of the lecture theatre and nearly stepping backwards off it, 'and inspiring.' At least that's what our friend Nigel had said, and he was widely reckoned to be in line for a First, which was good enough for me.

Cliff leapt eagerly on what he took to be my enthusiasm and for thirty minutes subjected me to his. In between surreptitious glances at my watch I tried to make mental notes, because such one-to-one tuition was invaluable as well as unheard of, but I could feel another out-of-body experience coming on. Finally he subsided into silence. We'd long since finished our drinks and when he stood up I breathed a mental sigh of relief. Prematurely.

'What are you drinking?' He picked up my glass and studied it as though the former contents might be named on the side.

'I should be going.' I shut *Silas Marner* with a snap and shoved him into my bag in such haste that the corner of the cover bent back.

Cliff stilled me with a finger. 'Not yet. I haven't finished.'

When he returned he placed the drinks down then turned the chair round and sat astride it, resting his forearms across the back. If he'd said 'Howdy, pardner' I wouldn't have been a bit surprised. I racked my memory for intelligent questions to ask on whatever poem he was going to discuss now.

He raised his glass and considered the head of beer

before taking a swallow. 'So, you're no longer seeing Max.' He spoke as though he was continuing a subject we'd started earlier. I wasn't sure whether this subject was an improvement or not. Probably not.

'Er, no.'

'Shame. He thinks a lot about you.'

'Does he?' And why would he tell Cliff? 'I didn't know you knew Max that well.' At least, not well enough for Max to have spoken of me, especially when I'd always been such a well-kept secret.

Cliff laughed, revealing a gold tooth. 'I'm his landlord, I thought he mighta mentioned that.'

I thought so too. 'Yes, I know that,' I lied, not wanting it to sound like I was less in Max's confidence than Cliff was, 'but my relationship with my landlord ends at negotiations over how much rent I pay. I don't discuss my love interest with him.'

He smiled a smile that on a woman might have been coquettish. I didn't know what it meant.

'We've been friends a long time. And I do discuss love interest. I have it written into the small print.' He took a long drag on his cigarette and blew smoke out of his nostrils. How ironic that I should be presented with someone who could tell me something of Max's history just at the moment I'd stopped caring about it. I wished Cliff would go away but he was only a third of the way through his drink and I'd barely started mine.

'You know what I think?'

I smiled my keen interest at the man who would be marking my Anglo-Saxon paper in six weeks' time.

'You should get back together. So, he made a few mistakes. You can take it.'

I wondered what he was getting at. Max didn't admit

making mistakes to himself let alone to anyone else. 'He knows where I am.' Hell, now *I* was talking like a B-movie too.

'He's a decent guy, you could do worse.'

And then the door opened and a guy I could do worse with walked in, right on cue. It seemed prophetic.

'Excuse me, Cliff, but I'm meeting someone. I'll see you later.'

He called, 'Bring him over,' to my retreating back, but I had no intention of dragging my rescuer down with me. I caught Robert at the bar. I could have kissed him, I was so pleased to see him.

'Ellie! I thought you'd have left for the holidays.'

'I thought *you* had! I decided to stay on and get some revision done.'

'Likewise.'

I gave him the smile you share with someone who has made the same bad decision you have yourself. He paid for our drinks and I led the way into the corner, carefully avoiding Cliff's gaze. We sat down and smiled at each other, a little awkwardly. Our relationship had never been defined, which made things difficult when we were alone together. I leaned back from the table to maintain a proper distance between us.

'Quiet tonight,' Robert said at last to fill the silence. I was sorry he'd drawn attention to it because it was worse than quiet: it was dull and empty with all the leading lights now home for the holidays and only those with nowhere to go left behind. Three whole weeks of this; how could I bear it? Though it wouldn't be quite so bad if Robert was going to be here too. Time to think was what I'd wanted, but what I really needed was to have no time to think at all. Thinking was depressing.

'How's the revision going?' I asked after another pause. Someone hit the jackpot on the games machine and the thump-thump-thump as it coughed up its fortune drowned out speech for a few moments. A small cheer sounded from three lads in the corner.

'Okay. Yours?'

'Brilliant,' I said, hoping my bright smile didn't look as forced as it felt. 'I've just been getting some extra tuition from one of the lecturers. I think it pays to be here without the majority. It makes you stand out.'

Robert nodded and sipped his drink. I sipped mine.

'Has Carol gone home?'

'Yes.' We talked then about Carol and conversation flowed more easily, but I didn't feel any better. I knew I should have told Carol. If this had happened during term time I'd have had more support, but how could I break the news when she was all packed up to leave? She had to get home because she was to be a godmother at her niece's christening. At the thought of christenings I felt a pricking behind my eyes and took a sip of my shandy.

'Ellie, what is it?'

'Nothing. Grit in my contact lens.' I dabbed at my eye with a tissue, and when I took the next breath it came in staggered gasps that seemed to go on and on. For a moment it felt like I'd never breathe out again.

'Ellie, sweetheart!' Robert moved round the table and slid his arms round me, resting his chin against my hair. 'It's okay, it's okay,' he said soothingly, and momentarily it was okay – if I could just stay like this, in this quiet corner, with this sweet, kind man's arms round me, everything would be all right.

'What's the problem? Is it Max?' We'd had long talks about him and his wickedness, and there was nothing I hadn't told Robert. Well, perhaps one thing. But this time it wasn't about Max, it was about me.

I started to say no, but the sobs came again and I tore at my handbag to find a dry tissue to muffle the sound. Through bleary eyes, I became aware of emaciated denim-clad legs standing in front of us.

'Is she okay?' It was Cliff Rose, sounding concerned.

'She'll be fine. I think she feels a bit lonely without all the usual crowd here.'

Cliff seemed to be nodding though I couldn't see his face. He lowered his voice a little to indicate, I supposed, that he was about to say something confidential.

'I was just talking to her. About a boy she just broke up with. Think I mighta upset her.'

'Thanks for telling me. I'll see to her, she'll be okay.'

The legs stayed still for a few moments and then walked off and out of the door.

'Just tell me about it,' said Robert again. But I didn't tell him until later when we walked home and the cool air dried the tears on my cheeks, making my face sting. I'd been so stupid. I was crying for the way I had thought, as you always think, that it can't happen to you. As long as you go on doing what you did the day before and the day before that, then nothing worse can happen to you than has happened already. And that was all I'd been guilty of, doing the same as I'd been doing. That's the only drawback to a form of contraception that's so simple you forget you're taking it: you can also forget when you're not taking it. By the time I'd remembered I should have put a cap in I was past caring. And I thought, well, it's just the once.

I'd asked to come off the pill because I was putting on weight. Well, now I was really going to pile it on.

Robert was quiet for a long time after I told him, and in

the silence something changed between us. Something delicate and finely balanced was lost, but something infinitely precious grew in its place. It wasn't the aching, burning I always felt with Max, but by comparison those feelings seemed shallow and empty. What I sensed beginning was a deeper bond, a foundation from which to move forward. With Max I'd been trying to build on sand; no wonder I could never sustain a proper relationship. Robert, by contrast, was granite: strong and reliable. And he was like a brother, someone you can tell absolutely anything and he will never think any the worse of you. Though by the time Carol returned for the start of term, when I was already spending most nights in Robert's bed, he would seem not like a brother at all. But at this moment, with his firm assurance and steady command, that was how I thought of him.

'Are you sure?'

'Of course I'm sure!'

'I mean, have you had a test done?' I hadn't had the result yet but I just knew. My periods had always been irregular so the non-arrival of one wasn't cause for alarm, and feeling queasy in the mornings was so usual for those among my friends who spent their evenings at the Union bar that I didn't remark on that either. It was only this week — when I still couldn't face Carol's scrambled eggs by lunch time, and she made an old joke about morning sickness — that I realised why my breasts were getting bigger. I'd had a test the day before, but that was for the doctor's benefit not mine.

'You'll have to inform Max,' Robert said at last, very matter of fact, as though it was like contacting the Inland Revenue.

But I didn't inform Max. I went to the college health

centre for counselling and Robert came too, saying he was the father. In those agonizing discussions over what to do – to have or not to have, that was the question – when each day the opposite answer presented itself as the right one, we developed a kind of understanding. An abortion would have been such an easy solution, but somehow I couldn't go through with it. I'd always thought of myself as unmaternal, but that decision brought all my instincts to the fore; maybe that's what used them up, leaving me fewer than required for the children I would have later.

When term started I told my closest friends I was pregnant, though not who the father was, and Carol took to referring to the baby as my 'immaculate conception'. As Robert and I seemed so close by this time it was generally assumed to be his, and we didn't trouble to deny it. I liked to think of it as a case of immaculate misconception. We were just coming round to the idea that I should not only *have* the baby but actually *keep* it – Robert's finals would soon be over and he could support us over the early months – when I miscarried.

'You should cry if you want to,' Carol said, sitting by my bed when I came home from hospital. But I didn't want to. It was like discovering you have an incurable disease and then, before you've even fully come to terms with it, finding that you've been cured. The baby hadn't yet taken on a personality for me; it was just a burden which I had accepted I must carry but which was suddenly and miraculously taken away. Strangely, losing Max's baby didn't seem to have any repercussions for me at all. In some ways I even felt exonerated, as though God had tested me and, like Abraham and Isaac, the fact I was prepared to make the (to me) ultimate sacrifice was enough. In other ways I felt that making such atypical religious comparisons was a sign that getting pregnant damages the brain cells, and so it was an even bigger mercy than I'd thought that it had lasted such a short time.

Of course, there was one repercussion. It was the cause of bringing me closer, much closer, to Robert. We fell in love, and in that respect it changed my life entirely.

Chapter 14

It's a little short, this dress — the sort of thing Josie wears that I thought I was too old for. But I needed something new, and the dim lights of the store and the boom of the music that vibrated through the polished floorboards made me think — why not? Age is relative, and I'm actually twenty years younger than the managing director of the company for whom Robert works, who will be sitting with us at tonight's dinner. The sight of my knees might even boost Robert's promotion prospects.

The dress sits off the shoulder and is scattered with black sequins. I had a lot of trouble finding it; it's only July so the shops won't have their winter evening wear in for *days* yet. Twisting round to see my reflection from the back I'm pleased at what I see, save for the varicose vein snaking up my calf which makes me look like I'm wearing one seamed stocking. Tonight I'll be in shiny black tights and patent high heels, but for this last minute try-on before I finish packing my feet and legs are still bare. For a moment as I gaze in the mirror I see Steven next to me, hair brushed back, standing straight and tall in a black evening jacket and bow tie. But I can't hold that picture; his fingernails still have dirt under them.

Robert's mother is babysitting for us and is staying for a few days. She only lives ten miles away, but she's seventy-three and in poor health, and regards coming to us as a holiday. She's only five feet tall, with short stumpy legs inside thick support stockings. She is thick all the way up, in fact, there's barely a change in width from her knees up to her shoulders. But her wavy grey hair and glasses give her the look a granny ought to have. She looks as though she will have boiled sweets in her apron pocket to produce for the children, and endless patience to play Snakes and Ladders and Monopoly. And she has. My mother wears track suits and trainers and has her grey hair rinsed blonde.

'What time are you leaving, dear?' Robert's mother is obsessed with timekeeping, even other people's. We don't need to leave for half an hour and I wonder why she's so keen for us to be on the move.

But then Simon appears at the bedroom door 'When are you going? We want to play a game with Nanny.' At first I can't see why they can't start until we've gone, but of course it's not a game he's after, but watching the video she will have rented and brought with her. We strictly forbid the watching of videos during the day, but grandparents exist to flout house rules.

'The more you ask me the longer we'll take,' I say, as the expected scowl forms on Simon's face.

Robert emerges from the shower looking ghostly pale after all the tanned bodies I noticed on the high street today. His hair is usually bleached white-blond by the sun at this time of year but that's because we have usually taken our holiday by now. I've always admired his body, slim but tough — the legs of a tennis champion, the shoulders of a rugby player. Both are things he used to be, actually. (Okay, he wasn't a tennis *champion* but he was jolly good.) But now he stoops over his sock drawer with the girth of middle management. From the nipples up he's still the same, has retained the boyish grin, and if the face is fatter than it used to be, with just the suggestion of a double chin, well, on him it still looks good. But from his mid chest to thighs he is thickening and filling out. He has stopped resembling sports stars and started looking like their managers. It occurs to me that his mother may not always have been the shape she is now.

By contrast, Robert's white torso reminds me of Steven's hardened frame. I lick my lips at the mirror and pout at the sweep of my mascara-darkened lashes.

'You look fabulous.' Robert comes to stand behind me and looks in the mirror over my shoulder. Naked and still damp from the shower, he nibbles my ear and cups my right breast with his hand. 'What do you say? We don't need to go yet.' I can feel his flaccid penis springing into life, pressed against my bottom.

'For goodness' sake,' I snap, 'is that all you think about?'

In the car I try to make it up to Robert. 'Tell me who's going to be there and everything I need to know about them.' There is scant chance of my remembering, assuming I actually listen to what he says, but it will please him that I'm asking. It's a big night for Robert. His company is being presented with an award, which the managing director and Robert are to accept. In addition to this, it's a rare opportunity for him to impress the MD with his genius and wit. Something of that responsibility also falls to me, but I know how to act the company wife well enough: keep your mouth shut and look interested.

Of course, all the company wives do the same thing, that's what can make these occasions so tedious. As we turn off the M25 I remember the last one we went to. Robert had said, 'Be sure to look after Mrs Hepworth, she's very shy. Her husband is director of Astley's and I need to keep on the right side of him. Don't worry about the other two couples. Bill Jackson is only coming because the people we really wanted have dropped out. And Jed Tyrrell's a wanker, don't bother with him.' When we arrived, the husbands introduced everyone by their christian names, and I instantly forgot who was who. I did remember that the shy one was to have my attentions, and Sheila, who answered all questions in monosyllables, certainly fitted that description. In fact, of course, I'd attached myself to the new girlfriend of Jed the wanker, and those present who knew that he had only recently left his wife for her looked askance at my attentions. The woman I should have been chaperoning turned out to have known the other couple from dozens of other dinners and spent the evening in avid conversation. When eventually I realised my mistake I felt I'd already made as much effort as could be reasonably expected in return for my meal. Consequently I didn't feel inclined to explain my mistake to Robert and he thought I'd done it on purpose. He was furious with me.

By the time our car draws up at the nineteenth-century hotel I'm feeling excited. With Robert's mother staying over, we've been able to book a room for the night. It's years since we had a night away without the children, unless you count my Bertha-ridden nights in hospital.

The hotel stands in its own grounds; signposts to stables and tennis courts abound. 'Should've brought our rackets,' Robert remarks. It's odd that he has forgotten, he used to carry it around with him just in case. He hasn't played at all this year. For my part, I'm glad he forgot – I haven't played since Simon was born.

Ivy winds its way round the entrance and hangs over the heavy bays that lie to either side. One room must be the lounge: chintz sofas are arranged either side of an inglenook fireplace, and occasional tables are scattered around the room with armchairs pulled up, creating little oases of cosy intimacy. A wave of affection for Robert mingled with regret surges over me and for a terrible moment I think I'm going to cry. But it could all come right; it's not too late.

'Let's take coffee in the lounge,' I say, in an effort to enter into the spirit of the thing. We could sink back into that sofa and flick through *Country Life* while servants minister to our needs in hushed reverence. Perhaps marriage counsellors are right and a break can revitalise a flagging relationship. Experimentally, I flash Robert a smile of love and affection.

'You go,' says Robert. 'I need to go over my acceptance speech.'

In the way of hotels, our bedroom doesn't quite live up to the splendour of the downstairs rooms. The desk and wardrobe are teak and streamlined, the emphasis being on the practical with just a nod at style. But the window is of leaded lights, festooned, as they say, with an Austrian blind. If you stand with your back to the desk and wardrobe, the effect is cottagey and almost quaint. You might think that the helicopter pad, situated directly below, would mar the impression, but the idea that people who own helicopters also stay here gives my morale an extra fillip.

While Robert hangs up his suit, I arrange my make-up on the dressing table and then lie on the bed, from which

I can see the woods and a clear expanse of brilliant blue sky. Robert kicks his shoes off and lies next to me, with his arm round my shoulders.

'What do you think of it?'

'Blissful.'

It's strange to be free of the burden of having things to do. I can't think how to spend my sudden spare time, the afternoon spreading itself before me; it's like being let loose in a cake shop with a full purse and no dietary restraints. Robert squeezes my arm and shatters the illusion.

'While I go over my speech, why don't you make a few notes on what we need to say to Simon's teachers next week?' Parents' evening at the school is looming but in this place it feels like light years away. I'm astonished that he has brought his concerns about it with him. 'Then we could have a walk round the grounds before we start getting ready.' He has my entire afternoon planned, it seems. He lies back, regarding the ceiling, satisfied that he has resolved the dilemma of how to occupy the wife. He is apparently relaxed, but I can sense he's itching to get up and start work.

As I take in the room, I notice that he has hung up the rest of my clothes for me. He's such a good person – he's caring, he's thoughtful, you'd have to be very ungrateful to find fault with him as a partner. You could even call him romantic, yet his constant wanting for sex no longer feels like an indicator that love is alive and well, any more than the kids' perpetual demand for sweets when we're shopping is a sign that they love me. They ask me because who else would they ask?

Robert squeezes me again and gets up. 'We could have a good time tonight, couldn't we?' He isn't referring to the dinner.

IMMACULATE MISCONCEPTIONS

The banqueting room is hung with old masters. Literally: the old masters who used to own the place, white haired and stately every one, posing in his best suit and best expression. Every son who inherited followed the tradition, right up till the last one, in 1952, after which they must have sold out to the corporation that owns the hotel now. Their poses of authority and regality should imbue our proceedings with their sense of history and tradition, but the unnaturalness of their postures only serves to remind me of how we're all here playing out a pretence of one kind or another. The tinkling laugh and 'Oh darling' of a woman behind me seems to emphasise the point. On the face of one of the old masters, I think I see an arched brow and an unexpected twinkling eye as though he too can see the hypocrisy underlying these gatherings.

But there's no denying the beauty of the surroundings. In each corner of the oak-panelled room stands an enormous flower arrangement supported on a slim stand. The curtains that frame the leaded light windows are crimson velvet, drawn back with heavy gold braided ties, and the atmosphere is one of opulence and grandeur. I'm aware of a flutter of pleasure despite myself, and try to rise to the occasion. I stand taller, square my shoulders and tuck my bottom in, but this only has the effect of making my dress ride up.

'Wine, madam?' A waiter, nineteen years old or so, inclines his head a little and proffers a tray of white wine and Bucks Fizz. I catch his eye for a moment, searching his youthful expression for traces of Steven, but this boy is weasel faced and narrow lipped, and inexplicably I'm pleased at the contrast. He smiles at me a little awkwardly, disconcerted by the stare of this strange woman who is taking so long to select a drink.

Arranged periodically along the length of the trestle tables are delicate flower arrangements of pinks and purples, set in pale wicker baskets. At the end of the evening the managing director will present them to some of us to take home; it won't be me — Robert and I are family, so to speak. Along with the MD, we're the hosts, but I hanker after one all the same. Josie buys these flower arrangements for herself. Once I went into the florists to get one, to see if the presence of flowers was what gave her house its atmosphere of serenity and style. When I saw the cost, I bought some oasis and tried to make one at home, with flowers from the garden, not knowing that oasis crumbles if you keep altering the position of the stems, or how quickly blooms wilt if you keep sticking them in oasis and then taking them out again. In the end I threw the oasis away and stuck the flowers in a jam jar, and Robert complained that they looked better outside and I should have left them alone.

'Beautiful, aren't they?' I say to Robert, hoping I don't look as I once saw Simon look, arriving at a birthday party and catching sight of the party bags, already assembled to be taken home. I'd felt ashamed of his acquisitive gleam.

'Too fussy for my taste.' Robert leads me to our table and we join another couple who are looking for their name cards. I watch them with the sort of detached objectivity you're free to direct towards people to whom you have not yet been introduced; I can see from the studied way in which they keep their eyes on the table without looking up that they're intending to make us speak to them first. If it were left to me I'd play the same game they are, but they're Robert's guests and he leaps to their aid, dragging me with him by the arm. He and Derek shake hands with such enthusiasm you would never guess they've only met once before. Derek's wife, Christine, is in her early thirties with hair of pale orange and a freckle-scattered complexion to match. She looks faded and wan, like a T-shirt washed too often, which isn't too bad a description of her light gold dress either. She smiles as she greets me, but I sense a hint of alarm as I step from behind the table and she notes the expanse of leg I have on show.

Immediately our other guests arrive, or to be more precise, Hugo's charisma appears followed by its owner. He's a big, jovial chap, with a chest that pushes out the frill of his dress shirt in a sweeping curve over the waist of his evening trousers. He exudes charm and good will and I'm delighted to find myself sitting next to him. Robert has told me he is only forty-five, but he is probably one of those people who looked the same at twenty-eight as they do now, and will still do so at sixty-eight. I'm less enamoured of his wife, Eileen, a spare and mean-looking woman with blondish hair that hangs in the loose waves of what could once have been a cheap perm. (Women who favour expensive perms have them redone before they decline into this condition.) Her roots are growing out too — there's a good half inch of brown hair at the scalp — and I feel a twinge of antagonism that she should come as our guest without making a hair appointment first. Her too-bright lipstick saps the colour from her face but matches, more or less, her dress of red polyester. It is trimmed at the neck with gold braid that looks like she sewed it on herself, inspired by one of those 'How to Revamp Your Wardrobe' items that I used to read in my mother's magazines when I was a child. (The sort of magazine I despise and yet am still not good enough to write for. This unexpected reflection floods me with despair just as Robert is introducing me. I take a generous sip of Buck's Fizz before shaking Hugo's hand.) Eileen moves round to stand next to me.

'If my bra straps show, you will say won't you?' she says.

Having established Hugo and Derek in conversation, Robert is playing host, talking to Derek's wife Christine, making her laugh. He's a head taller than Derek, which adds to the impression he gives of being in charge. He's good at socializing. It's always Robert who notices if someone's glass is empty, or if they need rescuing from the person they've got stuck with. If I can fix his good points in my mind firmly enough, perhaps they'll begin to mean something to me.

Gerald, Robert's managing director, who is good at none of these things, arrives fifteen minutes later, escorted by a girl of dazzling vivacity. Tall, with waist-length fair hair with highlights, she wears a short turquoise dress which shimmers as she moves. Her heels must be a good four inches and make her taller than Gerald. He doesn't look as though he minds; in fact, he has the look of a man who will never mind anything again. Expressions of wonder appear on several of the men's faces, though they're working hard to conceal it. Suddenly I feel silly in my short black dress.

An arm snakes round my waist and I turn in alarm — I thought Robert was still talking to Christine but now he is behind me, his mouth by my ear. 'That girl doesn't look a patch on you,' he murmurs. Oh Robert, oh Robert. His tenderness, and my inability to respond to it, make me want to cry. I do what I'd do if I *was* responding to it, and squeeze his hand briefly before he moves away to be introduced. Part of a line from *Macbeth* steals into my consciousness: 'Be like the innocent flower but be the something under it.' I don't remember the rest of it or even what it means. Something about a snake. It makes me feel uncomfortable.

'So,' says Hugo as we chase round our plates the three melon balls of varying shades in a pink gravy which constitute Medley of Melons in Raspberry Sauce, 'you're a journalist.' I guess that Robert has told him this. When he tells people about me he manages to give it a gloss I don't deserve, but 'journalist' is a description guaranteed to win my love and affection, and I warm to Hugo for not having questioned it.

'In a small way,' I say modestly.

'I'm sure you're just being modest,' he says. He quizzes me about my job, how I get the ideas for my features ('Pinch them from the Sunday papers,' I say, making the truth sound like a joke), the management structure of the company, how disciplined I must be, how talented. The Medley of Melons slides down like oysters.

'So what does Eileen do?' I ask, a little wickedly perhaps.

'Novelist,' he says, wiping his mouth with a flourish. 'Very successful. She won a prize last year. You've probably heard of her.'

After I've heard all about Hugo's prolific and successful wife, and his own career history (which includes a detailed report on the fluctuating fortunes of the construction industry over the last decade and his apparently not inconsiderable role in its resurgence), conversation flags. Hugo uses his bellowing voice to strike up a conversation with Gerald but my voice carries less effectively so that I have no choice but to settle back and arrange my features into what I hope resembles satisfied contemplation. Eileen catches my eye and smiles. I try not to grit my teeth.

It'll be five days before I see Steven again.

As we are finishing coffee, the presentations start. There are five awards, for architectural designs of various sorts, and Robert's comes second to last. Gerald and Robert go to collect it together: Robert's design and Gerald's company. I see tension around Robert's lips as his name is called but he looks confident and cheerful as he accepts the certificate, and his speech is flawless — he even manages an impromptu joke which is all the more effective for being funny. Robert seems to tower over the portly and greying Gerald, who looks like a man nearing retirement who has not yet come to terms with the fact. It's time to make way for a younger man; I will him to notice the candidate standing next to him. If Robert got a promotion that might take some of the pressure off me.

Robert is holding his audience, a fact which momentarily surprises me, but then for a moment I'm back at college, listening while he argues with a colleague in defence of innovation over conservation. He flicks his hair out of his eyes as he reaches his closing words. The applause is enthusiastic and Gerald slaps him on the back as they return to their seats. Gerald's girlfriend kisses him on the cheek and squeezes his arm. It prompts me to do the same to Robert.

After the speeches we're free to wander around. My first impulse is to wander up to bed, but it's only ten-thirty. Gerald's girlfriend is standing with the men. She isn't speaking but there's something in the demeanour of the men that suggests her presence isn't going unnoticed.

Christine comes over and settles herself next to me with a shy smile.

'Enjoying yourself?' I say, wishing I could find a more original opening.

'Oh yes, lovely. Lovely meal.' I didn't enjoy the meal, actually. It was roast beef with Yorkshire puddings that had been kept warm just long enough to breed bacteria. I could taste them multiplying as I chewed, but that wasn't the only reason I hadn't enjoyed them. They reminded me of hospital dinners and Rita. I'd promised myself then that my life would change, but had it? Seducing a young boy certainly wasn't what I'd had in mind. The memory of Rita slicing a ribbon of fat from her beef and popping it into her mouth brings with it a sickly feeling of guilt, which now extends to include my guests whom I'm failing to entertain. I drag myself back to reality and beckon to Eileen who is standing gazing upwards, pretending to admire the paintings.

'Eileen, come and join us.' She comes over, looking irritable. 'What did you think of the meal?'

She shrugs. 'Oh, fine. I've had better though. I mean, roast beef in this weather . . .' Something in her tone irritates me so that, instead of agreeing, I spring to the defence of the top rib as though it were a personal friend.

'I thought it was an inspired choice,' I lie, smiling to take the edge off the fact I'm disagreeing with her. 'Refreshing to have something a bit unseasonal, after a summer full of salads. Don't you think so, Christine?'

'Oh well, yes.' She's floundering, not wanting to take sides. 'But I don't mind what they feed us, I'm just glad to be asked.'

Eileen shrugs again and takes out a pack of cigarettes, offering them with the sort of movement which suggests she expects them to be refused. She pauses, cigarette in mouth, lighter poised. 'You don't mind, do you?' I say of course not, as you do, but I push a dish of petit fours away from the proximity of her smoke to hint at my real feelings.

'Hardly anyone smokes any more,' she says regretfully. 'People make you feel an outcast. Can't smoke on trains, can't smoke on buses, can't smoke in shops. I don't hold with it.'

I search for a middle course between what I feel and what I can say. 'It must be very difficult if you can't give up.'

'Why should I give up? It's my right; it's a free country, isn't it?' I fix my face into an expression of sympathetic understanding and wonder why the phrase 'it's a free country' is making anger rise in my throat. And then I'm in hospital again, in the day room. I'm remarking on the parlous state of the carpet, the chairs, the coffee table, pockmarked with cigarette burns and grey with spilled ash, the windows opaque with smoky grime. I wasn't intending to criticise Rita personally, but she took it that way, never asked me to sit with her in there again.

'But it's a free country for non-smokers as well,' I say, hoping Rita can hear me. Why am I always so scared to say what I think? 'Why should the rest of us have to get cancer from cigarettes we never even smoked?' I can't hold back the resentment in my voice.

Eileen is a lot calmer than me, in fact she isn't fazed at all. She appears well practised in defence. 'That's just a fallacy. They fix the figures. Massage the statistics. If what they said was true, we'd all have been dead long since.'

'I used to smoke,' Christine says quietly, 'and I found it

very hard to give up. But once I become pregnant I really felt there was no choice.'

'Oh I felt the same,' I said, weighting the evidence against Eileen. 'The minute I knew I was pregnant I gave up, just like that.'

'I've got three kids,' says Eileen, and she inhales deeply and speaks on the outbreath of smoke, 'and they're right as rain, the lot of them. It's all a load of rubbish.'

Christine doesn't respond but produces a polite smile. And so do I.

A glass and a half of claret later, during which Eileen and I have papered over the cracks sufficiently to discover TV sitcoms that we mutually love, politicians we mutually hate and, and film stars we consider over- (or under) rated, Eileen suddenly says, 'And that's another thing I can't stand.' She is pointing her cigarette at the earnestly talking group which now consists of Derek, Robert, Gerald and Gerald's girlfriend.

'What don't you agree with?' Now that I've acclimatised to her and the wine, I'm warming to Eileen. She calls a spade a spade and that can be diverting, especially once you're moving into the warmth and tolerance of early inebriation.

'That young girl and that old bloke.'

'That old bloke happens to be your host,' I point out, in mock reproof. 'As such, and as our managing director, he's allowed to do what the hell he likes.' Because Eileen's earlier frostiness has thawed, I assume we're joking.

She ignores me. 'She's twenty-five, I asked her. And he's — what? Late fifties?'

'But if they're happy. Good luck to him.'

'I asked him what kids he's got. He's got a girl two

years older than she is. It's almost incest.' I still haven't realised that Eileen's mood has changed.

'Well, hardly.'

'Incest by proxy. He can't have his daughter so he gets a girlfriend who looks like her.'

'I wouldn't mind,' Christine chips in, 'but the men all think he's done something rather wonderful. It wouldn't be like that if it was the other way round.'

I throw in a generalization to take the focus off poor Gerald, who chooses that moment for a particularly voluble guffaw so that several people nearby turn to look. 'Well, I don't know,' I say, 'if it's wonderful one way, why not the other? If people care about each other, age doesn't come into it.'

'It'd come into it if she was sixty and he was twenty-five.' Christine is unexpectedly tenacious. 'People would be disgusted. And did you see those heels?'

They have a damn nerve criticizing the man whose company is paying for their dinner, and so what if the girl is a few years younger than him? He can date who he likes. In the back of my mind Rita points out that it's a free country as Eileen goes on: 'A friend of mine had an affair with a younger man. She said she used to lie in bed and think of those old "Love is . . ." cartoons. In her case it was: "Love is . . . never having to explain your operation scars."' They both laugh.

It must be because I still feel embarrassed at getting so overheated about the cigarettes that my voice comes out almost shaky. 'People can be very narrow minded, but in the end does it matter what other people think, if you're happy yourself?' They're both looking at me but neither answers, so I go on, 'If two people are attracted to each other, and it's what they want, then is how old they are really relevant?' They still don't answer, which somehow makes me feel they're disagreeing. 'I don't see it's anyone's business but theirs,' I say, lifting my glass which I had forgotten is still empty.

I see Eileen nudge Christine. 'Not thinking of picking up some young lad yourself are you?' Christine smiles but looks down at her lap. I toy with my glass, and I can feel my colour rising.

'I'm off to the ladies,' says Eileen drily, stubbing out her cigarette. 'I could never have an affair, I'd be sure to blush every time the subject came up.'

Back in our room I make coffee while Robert kicks off his shoes and bounces on to the bed. He's jubilant. 'Gerald was very impressed. Did you see his face when they made those comments about my design? There ought to be some money coming from this.' It's Robert's oft-expressed hope that a pay rise is about to materialise, whereas it's clear to me that Gerald's strategy is to pay his loyal and hardworking employees the minimum in the certain knowledge they won't leave, while giving bonuses to the less committed as a bribe to stop them going elsewhere. It still amazes me that Robert hasn't yet learned that simple fact. Carrying his coffee to him I see his face lit with hope and feel a pang.

'If he doesn't give you a rise now, he never will,' I say, knowing Robert will put a positive interpretation on my words, and intending that he should. 'What did you think of Gerald's girlfriend?'

He pats my leg and repeats his earlier phrase. 'Not a patch on you.' It isn't only his company that Robert has loyalty for.

As I undress for bed, unpeeling my expensive shiny tights

and trying not to snag them on my toenails, painted red for the occasion, I consider what a relief it is not having to feel self-conscious about your body. Eileen's story about the 'Love is . . .' cartoon struck a chord, and I remember how I held my stomach in when I got out of bed to speak to Steven. Leaning forward like this, naked but for my pants and the tights which are, after all, caught on my big toenail, it's possible to see the full effects of gravity on my breasts; and I know from the unexpected view I got of my backside when I was trying on my new dress in the changing room that that isn't the perky specimen it once was either.

'She was sexy all right, but a bit, I don't know, obvious. And too young for Gerald. What did you think?' Robert, bless him, is hedging until he gets my opinion.

'I thought she was gorgeous,' I say. I'm not normally so fulsome in praise of other women but the man I most desire to impress isn't here so competition isn't a problem. Besides, Robert no longer judges me by the criteria he brings to other women. He remembers me as I was when we first met, or to be more precise, as he imagines I was. Occasionally he refers to how sexy I looked when we met. The picture he paints bears scant resemblance to the tale told by photos of the time. His bias is comforting and soothing, and I feel a sudden surge of frustration that I can't be happy with that.

'What's the matter?' Robert is ever sensitive to my shifts of mood; out of long experience he knows how a sudden change of temperature can bode ill for his sex life.

'Nothing,' I say brightly, and search in the bottom of the suitcase for the satin teddy I brought with me. Perhaps if I look sexy I will feel sexy, and Robert deserves some reward for his clever speech and efforts with the guests.

I want to compensate him for the pay rise Gerald won't be giving him.

Suddenly he springs out of bed and flings his arms round me. 'I do love you.' His voice is muffled and thick. I squeeze him tighter in response. 'I couldn't manage if it wasn't for you. You make my life possible.' It's so unlike Robert to be emotional. He leads me to the bed and we sit, hand in hand.

'I was so scared when you were ill. But now – tonight – everything is wonderful again. I can't believe how lucky we are. We've got everything we want, haven't we?' The light from the bedside table makes his face shine. I don't know what to say.

The teddy does all that could reasonably be expected and afterwards we fall asleep.

Chapter 15

Steven knocks on the back door and hands me a note from Rita which he has forgotten to deliver. She wants us to go to tea on Friday — the kids and me. My heart sinks at the prospect of finding conversation to fill up two hours with her, and we can hardly stay for less time than that. I look regretful.

'Oh I don't know, Steven. It's very kind, but Friday's a busy day, not sure I can make it. Maybe next month.'

'Just take a few hours,' he tips his cap back and his smile speaks helpfulness. 'I told her you finish early Fridays. That's why she chose it. Come when you pick the kids up.'

Josie has taken to calling me Lady Chatterley and I don't like it. I've started slipping Steven's wages inside his bag when he's not around; I feel embarrassed at giving him money.

Steven maintains his pose of polite deference in front of the family and sometimes I think he forgets he can do without it when we're alone. He continues to knock at the door before entering the house, even when he knows everyone is out. This, from the man who last week whipped my knickers off and said he was taking them home as a souvenir. This morning he knocks and asks if he can have a word. His uncertainty is embarrassing. 'Don't ask if you can ask me a question, just ask it, okay?' I don't mean to sound sharp, but honestly . . . He looks a bit taken aback, and spends a moment screwing up his courage.

'I want to do some GCSEs. I want you to help me find out what to do.' Of all things I thought he might be going to ask ('Can I kiss you?' 'Can we go upstairs?' 'Do you love me?'), it wasn't that.

Briskness conceals my disappointment. 'Yes, I'll help you. What subjects do you want to do?'

'I don't know. I was good at maths at school. And woodwork.'

I ignore woodwork. 'What about English?'

'Nah, I weren't no good at English.'

'All the more reason to do it,' I say. 'Get a few prospectuses from local colleges and I'll give you a hand filling the forms in.' He smiles his gratitude and goes back outside.

I think he's a little frightened of me. It tends to be I who take the initiative, or if it's him it still follows some fairly clear signal from me. When he's working in the garden and I walk up to him, he just stands there looking shy. I think he's worried that I might just be arriving to offer him coffee and he'll get the wrong idea and look foolish. I could be imagining it. I'm enjoying the novelty of my superior status in this relationship but at the same time I'm uncomfortable at how unequal we are, in all senses. Other men I've loved haven't been so reserved. Not that I love Steven.

I should be pleased he's asking me to help him with

his qualifications, and in one respect I suppose I am. He's trying to improve his prospects and I want that for him. But it reminds me that I used to like men I could look up to and I no longer know any. I was in command of my relationships with both Stuart and Neil, but even so I was aware that Stuart was wiser, Neil more experienced. Robert, of course, was both of those and with a clear vision that saw straight to the heart of a problem. Max was all of that and then some.

Robert used to have the casting vote on all our major decisions (when to get married, where to live, which house to buy), but now he looks to me for advice and support. I have to guide him on how to confront the MD about a promotion, on how to talk a prospective client into taking him on, on which tie to wear with which suit, just as I have to tell the children how to approach their teachers if they don't want to do P.E. or if they can't keep up with their work. And now I have to take charge of my lover's life as well. Why won't they leave me alone? I don't want to be the one with the greater intelligence, experience and wisdom. Or the age.

Steven is telling me about a trailer he has seen for the latest Harrison Ford film. I've heard about it and half suggested to Robert that we go, but right now I'm more interested in the turn of Steven's head as he describes the film clip with his usual gusto and delight. His eyes have a light in them today, but his enthusiasm is for my benefit, part of his effort to entertain me. I am contributing to his mood of exhilaration at least as much as the film.

'You ought to go,' he says, 'if you like Harrison Ford.'

'We probably will. At least . . . the thing with Robert

is, he wants to do these things but when it comes to it he has to travel away for the night, or it's the evening he goes to his photography class, or he's just too tired. We always intend to but we hardly ever go anywhere.'

'You should.'

It's so easy for people who have no responsibilities to give advice. 'Perhaps I will,' I say without conviction.

'You could go with me,' he says suddenly. 'I was going on my own anyway.'

It's a good idea, in the way that it's a good idea when people you meet on holiday say we must keep in touch. For that fleeting moment you see the chance to recapture the magic of the drinks you shared at the mountainside restaurant overlooking the bay, the food and the ambience, the air of geniality that goes with the sun and wine.

'We ought to do that,' I say. It doesn't occur to me he might take me at my word, any more than I'd expect any of those holiday friends to turn up on my doorstep just because I'd said any time you're passing, drop in.

Suddenly, Steven is dropping in. 'What about Tuesday?' he says. 'In the afternoon. Get your childminder to pick the kids up from school. You'd be back for their tea.'

I smile at his childish eagerness. He hasn't considered how it will look if someone I know should see me, arm-in-arming it with a lad young enough to be my (friend's) son. Or what if Robert were to be unexpectedly driving by and see us coming out, eagerly discussing the sex scenes. A public date with Steven is the stuff of which fantasies are made, but fantasies are dangerous if you let them intrude on real life. Steven hasn't yet learned this, because he adds, unaware of his own recklessness, 'I'm fed up of only seeing you indoors with the doors locked. I want to go out and show you off.'

It's such a ridiculous suggestion that I almost want to laugh.

'Okay,' I say. 'Tuesday it is.' My answer takes me by surprise.

'It's made a real difference to him, working for you.' Rita pours from a large white teapot, holding in place with one finger the cracked lid which is too loose a fit. 'He's told me all you done for him.' I laugh, wondering what terrifying path the conversation is about to take. But after all she is only referring to his return to education, which she thinks is my doing, and the many cups of tea and the odd sandwich with which I try to keep his strength up. 'Well it's done him no end of good, whatever it is.'

Through the window of what would once have been the scullery, I can see Rebecca and Simon playing cricket in the small garden. So far the ball hasn't gone over the hedge but it can only be a matter of time. Gina and Steven are fielding and it looks as though Rebecca is sulking until it's her turn to bat again. Steven steps forward and adjusts Simon's hand position on the bat.

Rita's dining room leads directly off the scullery kitchen through French doors. Both rooms are dark, this being the rear aspect of the basement flat, but this room is the darker, the only daylight being that which comes through the scullery window. The table is spread with a white damask cloth under which the fringed edges of a velvet-type table cover are evident. A well worn sofa of green velvet is pushed against one wall, and two armchairs, one matching the sofa, one of an older vintage, rest either side of the gas fire. Rita has shown me the front room which she keeps 'for best'. Presumably we don't qualify. Steven has already told me that family are only allowed in there on special occasions but, as the television is in here, they tend not to go in then either.

'I saw a piece of yours in the paper.' Rita draws me back from my fascination with the garden. 'I cut it out to show my neighbour. I told her, I know her!' She laughs wheezily.

'I'm glad you enjoyed it.' I take another sip of the eye-wateringly strong tea to which she has automatically added sugar. As in our meeting at the market, our conversations lead up blind alleys, I wonder what we found to say to each other in hospital. Hospital! 'Do you ever see anything of Jamila, or . . .' Already I've forgotten what the other woman's name was.

'Millie? Well it's funny, I did, down Sainsbury's. She's split up with that bloke. We said she would.'

I don't recall that we ever discussed it, but perhaps it was in one of the several conversations we had in which Rita talked and I just nodded and thought about whether I was going to die. It all seems so long ago.

'Do you remember that time my kids came down the hospital? The look on your hubby's face! I don't think he knew what hit him.' Outside, Steven is just stepping up to bat. No, I think, and he still doesn't.

When I've drunk as much of the tea as I can manage, concealing how little this is by spilling some in the saucer, I say I'll help Rita clear away. She bought sausage rolls for the children, and chocolate marshmallows and mini swiss rolls in coloured foil (to which Rebecca and Simon are particularly partial), but out of politeness they ate only one each. I saw Simon's look of frustration as Steven ate his fourth. Watching Steven throwing the ball so gently that Rebecca can't possibly miss it, I wonder if I'm dreaming my relationship with him. How could I be drinking tea with his mother if there were anything between us? How could my kids possibly be playing ball in the house of my lover?

While Rita goes to get a swiss roll each for Rebecca and Simon to eat in the car, Steven helps me on with my jacket. 'Everything all right?' he whispers close to my ear.

'Fine.'

'I mean, did you say anything?'

'Only that you're good in bed and hung like in a donkey.'

He grins and digs me in the ribs. 'You never.'

When I arrive at the Odeon on Tuesday Steven is waiting in the foyer with the tickets and a box of popcorn. Some of the local schools have already broken up and a group of youths lounge by the ticket office waiting for their girlfriends. Steven could almost be part of them, which makes me feel conspicuous as I climb the steps to join him. People over thirty don't go to matinees. Well, only if they're pensioners.

His face lights as he catches sight of me and he holds out his free arm to embrace me.

'Steven! Someone could be watching.'

'Good. Hope they are.' He's in high spirits as he leads the way through the corridor to the auditorium. He opens the door for me and stands back with exaggerated rather than natural politeness. He wants me to notice how well he's behaving. We settle down (back stalls, naturally), and Steven takes his jacket off and puts it on the seat next to him with the popcorn. We're early; even the advertisements for local curry houses haven't started yet. The group of youths enter noisily, also heading for the back row, but choose the opposite end from us. Apart from two other groups of kids and a couple, the cinema is empty.

Suddenly Steven slides his arm round my shoulder and in a single movement pushes my head back and kisses me. His other hand slides inside my jumper.

I fight my way out of the clinch. 'What the hell are you doing?'

He backs off, astonished and mystified. 'There's no one else around. What's wrong?'

'I don't want it like this. Take it easy. And the lights are still on; I don't want everyone watching us.'

'No one's watching us.'

He's right actually: one of the youths sitting adjacent is already exploring his partner's epiglottis, and another seems to be trying to get something out of the front of his girlfriend's blouse. But that's not the point.

'Can't we just enjoy being together without a lot of groping?' I don't wish to be confused with anyone he's ever met in a shop doorway.

Steven withdraws his arm from round me and goes into a huff. His bottom lip is pushing out; he looks like Simon.

When the advertisements are finished and the usherette has appeared forlornly with her ice cream tray, Steven takes my hand again. I can see why he waits for me to take the initiative. It's so easy for me to crush him, even when I don't intend it. We have such different assumptions about what is normal in a new relationship that I don't see how we can ever make it work, even short term. I squeeze his fingers gently.

He slides his arm along the back of my chair, not quite touching me. I remember Neil doing the same thing — the first move, feeling the way, so that if you don't want his arm round you, he can say he was just resting it there. I accept the cue and lie my head against his shoulder. His arm comes round me a little more tightly. As the British Board of Film Censors inform us that this is a PG, I turn my face up to be kissed. Goosebumps cascade down my skin, from the roots of my hair to my toes. There must be a draught in here.

Josie thinks it's a hoot that I've had tea with the mother of my lover. I haven't seen her for over a week – she's been away with David for a short holiday – and today I've found her catching up on the weeding round her bedding plants in the front garden. Josie is the only person I know who looks as elegant dressed for gardening as for an assignation. Even the yellow washing-up gloves she's wearing to protect her manicure co-ordinate with her T-shirt.

'And she didn't guess?'
'Why would she?'
'Greg's mother'd guess if she saw us together. We can't keep our hands off each other.' She pulls up a tiny nettle and shakes the earth off it.
'We obviously have better self control than you do. Anyway the kids were there, and they're about the best appetite suppressant you can get.'
'I always forget about them. What will you do when they break up from school? It must be quite soon.'
'They've broken up already. Last Thursday.'
'Gosh. How will you manage?'
I've been wondering about this myself. I haven't even kissed Steven in over a week, since we went to the cinema. He has a perfect cover for continuing to come, even though the digging is all finished, because I found out what books are coming up for the English GCSE. It turns out that a friend of Theresa's will be taking the English classes

Steven will start in September, so he bought the books and I've suggested we make a start straight away. But I haven't yet worked out what to do with the kids. All their usual friends seem to be away. Perhaps it's because Josie has no children of her own that I hadn't thought of her.

'You must be desperate!' Josie is horrified at the idea of going without sex with one's lover for a whole week. 'You must have some time together,' she says. 'I'll take the kids swimming or to the pictures. Just tell me when.'

I always accuse Josie of thinking only of herself, so it's surprising to find she can be altruistic. The uncharitable thought that she wants to see me get in as deep as she is flickers into my consciousness and out again. These days I like Josie, perhaps because I identify with her in a way I couldn't before. But Josie and David have drinks with us at Christmas; she and Robert like each other, she always has a special word or joke for him. I don't like to think of her being in collusion against Robert.

I say all this, supporting my argument by letting her know how uncomfortable I've felt in the past at keeping her secret from David. Josie listens while smoothing the earth around a clump of pansies. When she looks up she is sympathetic.

'I know, it's awful what we have to do, isn't it? All this lying. Do you think you'll finish with Steven then?'

I like to think I can see through people but I forget that sometimes they can also see through me. We air our consciences in the sunshine and then I accept Josie's offer to take the kids swimming on Friday afternoon.

I finally got around to writing to Carol and her reply comes almost by return of post. Knowing that Robert will assume he's as free to read what she has to say as he always has been, she's careful and cryptic — to the point of incomprehensibility.

Glad you're feeling better but re some of these changes you're thinking about, you must be off your head. Just think what you could be losing — baby and bathwater refers. It's just the operation that's unsettling you, give it six months and you'll be back to normal. Maybe you should talk to your doc. about your hormones — get put on HRT or something. I think you should come and stay for a few days — you need to get away from IT all. Fancying a new 'job' isn't a good enough reason to risk losing the Old One.

'She's losing it, isn't she?' comments Robert, reading over my shoulder. 'I mean, what's she put "job" in inverted commas for? She'll be putting an apostrophe in "tomatoes" next. She's missed her vocation; she should have been a greengrocer.'

You and your Job were made for each other — taking on extra 'work' isn't the answer. Don't do anything you might regret.

'I didn't know you were thinking of leaving your job.' Robert is puzzled and I explain that Carol must be referring to the freelance writing I've been thinking about.

'I just mentioned it in passing but she's taken it seriously and evidently thinks I couldn't cope with it.'

Robert shrugs and puts his arm round me. 'You can do anything you put your mind to.' He gives me a squeeze. 'Got to be going. I'll read the rest later.'

I'm glad to hear this, because later he will have forgotten the letter even exists and, scanning ahead, I see, *I tried to ring you but then Dan came home early and you know how he hates me using the phone*. She's telling me that she couldn't phone because Dan was in earshot. Even if Robert hadn't worked that much out, he'd have known something was awry. Carol's phone calls are legendary and Dan has about as much power to curb them as our cat. If Carol didn't want to talk on the phone Robert would know she had a very good reason.

Robert wanders back into the kitchen looking for his car keys and eventually finds them underneath Carol's letter. 'I wonder why she didn't just ring,' he says.

'Mummy! Mummy!' The back door opens and Steven comes into the kitchen carrying Rebecca. She has cut her knee on the steps in the garden where Steven was chasing her and Simon. She has her arms round his neck and her face is buried in his shoulder.

'Darling, let's have a look.' I dampen some kitchen towel under the tap while Steven lifts her on to the draining board. The knee is hardly grazed but she's in urgent need of soothing and sympathy, and I hug and coo gently while Steven takes the kitchen towel and dabs at her knee. Rebecca begins to calm down and takes a tissue from me to wipe her eyes with.

Despite the drama, I'm aware of how close Steven is standing to me. He's bending down, pressing the kitchen towel against the wound so gently. 'Is that okay, Becky? You're doing fine, nearly over.' He throws the finished tissue in the bin and reaches for another. It doesn't seem quite right that he should be attending to my daughter quite so intimately.

'Here, let me.' I take a fresh piece of kitchen towel but Rebecca fends me off.

'No, mummy. I want Steven to.' He moistens the paper under the tap and leans closely over her knee once again. He doesn't look up but I can see he's smiling. So now he has us both.

He arrived ten minutes ago and has been occupying the kids by playing catch while I clear up from lunch. He looks fresh and scrubbed, strangely unfamiliar in jeans that aren't dusty or paint-covered and a Persil-white T-shirt over which he wears a tartan shirt, left open. I'm sure I can smell talc and aftershave.

Today is the day for starting on his GCSE set novel: *Cider with Rosie*. He has begun reading it already and I want to talk about it with him just to see how he's getting on. He's not much of a reader, he says. I'm looking forward to it, it's a book I've always been fond of. Later Josie is taking the kids swimming.

When Rebecca seems fully recovered she settles on the sofa with a comic and I take Steven into the kitchen.

'So, what do you think of the book?' Steven sits at the kitchen table, where we can keep an eye on Simon but not be overheard by Rebecca. It feels so formal to sit across a desk from him, and I don't want to remind him of school. I get him a can of lager and take a long time straightening and tidying the remaining kitchen detritus – a cup Rebecca has used, a glass Simon has finished with – before I sit down.

Steven picks up the book in his hands and turns it through 360 degrees. 'Dunno really.'

'Are you enjoying it?'

He shrugs. He's wearing a self conscious half-smile, but he looks unhappy.

'Okay, well tell me what you think of the narrator. Do you like him?'

'Narrator?'

'The one telling the story.'

'Thought that was the author.'

'Well, yes. In this case it is. What do you think of him? Do you like him? Do you want to know more about him? Does he make the story interesting?'

Simon appears at the window and presses his nose flat against it to make a face at Steven. Steven jumps up and, with his nose almost up to the glass, pulls his bottom lip over his top one, crosses his eyes, and sticks his tongue out. Simon does the same and then runs off.

'Steven, does he make the story interesting?'

Sitting down again, he flips the book up in the air and catches it. 'Dunno really.'

Glancing into the garden to check that Simon isn't looking, I take a swig of Steven's lager. Steven's head is bowed, avoiding my eyes.

'Come on, Steven. It isn't difficult.'

Mrs Jessop, French teacher, fourth year at grammar school: 'Come on Eleanor, it isn't difficult. *Pourquoi est-ce que M. Corot a passé la nuit a l'hôpital?*' I don't know the answer, and as hands began to shoot up around me, the chance of my ever knowing it retreats. Eyes are drilling into my back, my sides, my face. 'Eleanor, *pourquoi est-ce que M. Corot a passé la nuit a l'hôpital?*' My face is reddening. Mrs Jessop signals for the raised hands to be lowered. A hush of expectancy. Jane Driscoll, sitting next to me, hisses the answer, but I can't say it. Won't say it. 'Eleanor, *pourquoi est-ce que M. Corot . . . ?*' Now it's a battle of wills. Keep staring at the floor and there's nothing she can do. 'Eleanor, if you don't know the answer, say so.' Stare at the floor. 'Jane is telling you the answer; why won't you say it?'

I reach across the table and stroke my finger down Steven's cheek but he leans back in his chair so I can't reach him.

'It's no bloody good. I said I was no good at English.'

'I'm just no good at French,' I told Mrs Jessop when she kept me behind afterwards. She set me extra homework and warned me there'd be more every time I refused to answer in class. She kept her word too, but it didn't help with my French O Level. It was being unable to ask where the loos were on a day trip to Calais with Neil and Eddie that altered that.

Leaning back in my chair to mimic Steven's posture, I hold his gaze. 'I want you, now. Here, across this table.' His jaw drops so fast it's in danger of hitting the table. 'But I want to hear a few observations on this book first. So get talking.' He blinks at me, and I keep going to maintain the momentum. 'First, do you like it?' He doesn't answer. 'Come on, quicksticks! Do you like it?'

'No.'

'Okay, why?' He hesitates. 'Come on, first thing you can think of.'

'It's boring.'

'Apart from that.'

'I – I don't like the – what d'you call him? Narrator. He's wet. The story's too slow.'

'Go on.'

'Nothing's happening – no one's dead, no one's stolen anything. If it was TV I'd switch over.'

Every time he pauses I jump in with another question, making him answer it as quick as he can. It's like running a relay, and after five minutes we're both beginning to sweat. He stops and we look at each other. He's relaxed now, having fun. He may not have learned much about *Cider with Rosie*, but I have. I had no idea it was so erotic.

'Have you read the chapter on the two grannies?' I asked him to read this far but guessed he wouldn't. He shakes his head.

'Okay, read it now.'

'Oh come on, we've done enough.'

'I said now.' I slip off my sandal and feel for his chair with my foot. When I can feel the flat plane of the seat I work my toes along until they're resting against the top of his leg. He begins to stroke my foot but that isn't the idea. 'Read your book.'

'No.' He's laughing. I draw my foot away and see his expression change; then, slowly, I begin to stroke his thighs with my toes and nestle them into the tiny space between the chair and his crotch.

'I said, read.'

He reads.

By the time Josie arrives, my skin is prickling with sweat and I'm tingling. She's ten minutes later than agreed but Steven is still on the first page of his chapter. Rebecca collects up their swimming things, her injury forgotten, and runs out to the car with Simon. She pauses at the kitchen door to toss Steven a coquettish smile.

'Bye Stevie. See you next week.'

Josie nudges me. 'You've got competition,' she says as I follow the children down the path to see them off. 'Have fun,' she whispers.

As she leaves, I take Steven's hand to lead him upstairs but he pulls me back and pins me against the fridge.

'You promised me the kitchen table,' he says.

'You *didn't* finish your chapter,' I say.

* * *

In the lounge we close the curtains and I light the gas fire (one of those which burns just like a real one only at a much greater cost), and Steven closes the doors against the light. Now it's a snowy winter's night and we're alone in the mountains with the wind howling outside.

Kneeling on the rug, I push his shirt from his shoulders and pull his T-shirt over his head. His eyes are lit by the flames, and his tan is even deeper in the half light. The blue flames are licking up the chimney, casting shadows across his chest. I have never seen anyone more beautiful.

Later he whispers something urgent, something desperate and tender against my neck. I don't quite hear it, but I know what it is.

'I love you too,' I murmur into his hair. Perhaps it's true.

By the time Josie gets back (and she's been wonderful, taking them to McDonald's after the swimming baths and then on the swings at the local park) I'm exhausted. Not only are my knees like jelly, but my arms ache from scrubbing the kitchen table and washing the cushionfloor. (I have a dread of a pubic hair turning up in the butter.) Steven got his wish in the end (getting it in the dining room as well as the kitchen, in fact), and now I just want to curl up and relive it all.

In fact, I get my wish too – well, half of it anyway.

'I want all the mucky details,' says Josie.

Chapter 16

'I want all the mucky details,' said Carol. It was the period when Max and I had begun sleeping together regularly, and she had just started to get serious about Dan. It was obvious from the dreamy look in her eyes that their sex life had moved on to a higher plane — a plane upon which people listen to ballads and violins and buy each other cards of soft-focus lovers walking hand in hand along a sunset shore. My sex life had never achieved such dizzy heights and I didn't fancy being quizzed on it by someone whose had.

'Is he good at it?'

'Brilliant.'

'What does he do?' Max didn't do anything much. He kissed a lot, felt me all over, then he just did it. What else would he do?

'I love the way Dan does it.'

'Oh, yes.' Of course I loved the way Max did it too, would have done even if it had entailed him standing on his head and singing a chorus of Ye Banks and Braes' while his penis swung upside-down in time to the tune. That's what being in love means.

But actually ... Well, I had the suspicion that his

technique only worked for me because it was *his* technique. I could imagine there would be better ways. For one thing, once he got going in earnest it was over so fast; in fact, once he got going in earnest you could say it was over already. But it was uphill when, as you might say, he wasn't in earnest. That was when he liked to vary his rhythm – very fast, then very slow, almost stopping. Then, just as you thought you'd got the knack of it, he'd start up again, like a piston engine. Sometimes he made me feel like I was being unblocked with a sink plunger. Sometimes it sounded like it.

'Does he – you know . . .'

'What?'

'Do oral stuff?'

'No.' Until I'd had other lovers, those one-night stands, I hadn't realised real people did this. I had thought it was just in books, like bondage. Now I thought of it as something a man might do to impress a new partner with his expertise. And Max wasn't the type to go in for that sort of shallow posturing. 'Does Dan?'

'No.' But she looked away, making me think that maybe she just wasn't going to admit to it if I wasn't.

It would have been good really to open up with Carol, to find out if there was something I ought to have been doing. Because how do you know? Maybe my technique was strange too, because the first time I did it with Max, after we got back together that is, he said, 'Do you always do that?' and I said, 'Doesn't everyone?' and he said, 'I don't know, I haven't slept with everyone.'

What I would really have liked to ask Carol was if Dan ever made her feel inadequate, or insecure, or just plain stupid. But catching a glimpse of that dreamy look of hers, I was glad I hadn't.

* * *

Steven hasn't slept with everyone either; in fact I guess he's slept with hardly anyone. I haven't asked him yet, it seems somehow vulgar. Actually, the real reason I haven't asked is because I know I couldn't keep the eagerness to know out of my voice, and I don't want to lose the image of control and sophistication I try so hard to maintain.

I've been dreading facing Robert since Steven left (he'll sense Steven's presence on me, sniff strange pheromones in the bathroom, notice the sex smell that pervades the house, even rooms we haven't been in) but when he finally arrives home an hour late I'm the one on the attack.

'Your dinner was ready ages ago. Why didn't you ring?'

'I'm sorry.' He looks harassed, too weary to flick back the forelock that hangs over his forehead so listlessly. 'I've had the worst day of my life.' For a terrible moment I think he knows. But then he says, 'We're losing that contract from the looks of it. We've got to go through all our figures and see if we can get them any lower. And there's a new job coming up that we need to tender for. Gerald's in Bangkok sorting out that other fiasco so I'll have to do it.'

I don't feel as involved as I should, but I go through the motions. 'Sit down, I'll get you a drink.'

'No, I want to see if I can cancel our ferry crossing.'

'What?'

'Well we can't go away, can we? I've got to handle this job. There's no one else. We'll have to forget the holiday.'

I haven't been looking forward to our holiday, to be honest. Caravanning is hard work: so little space, the kids running up and down the gangway while I'm trying to cook dinner. But now it's being snatched away I want it more than anything else in the world.

'This is our holiday! You can't just cancel it!'

'You don't seem to realise — the company is going right down the tubes.'

'Of course it isn't. Everything is fine. Gerald told me.'

Gerald had certainly put an optimistic gloss on things at the awards dinner. But then he would, wouldn't he?

'This is serious. If I lose my job there'll be no holidays at all — not this one, not ever. I don't see us having many on what you earn.'

I know he didn't mean it. He was just het up and worried and disappointed and he would never say anything like that to hurt me normally. But he'd hit me on raw spot — he'd reminded me of something I always feel and hope no one else will comment upon: that I have a pathetic little job that brings in hardly any money at all.

'How dare you? I've given up everything for you and your kids. What sacrifices have you ever made? Whatever you've wanted you've had, wherever you wanted to live, that's where we lived. If you saw a better job, you've taken it. I always said we should've stayed in Birmingham, then this would never have happened.'

'Just drop it! Can't you see what sort of a day I'm having?'

'And can't you see what kind of a life I'm having?'

He pushes me aside and goes into our bedroom. I can hear him hunting through old brochures searching for the travel documents that will have the ferry company's phone number on them. I've kept all our travel details separate, and I take them down from the kitchen notice-board and carry them upstairs to him, taking my time. He's in a fury by now.

I hand them to him regally. 'If you cancel this holiday,' I say, 'I'll never forgive you.' He looks up at me helplessly and I wonder why I'm saying all this. I know it's not his fault. He's trying to salvage what he can, at least if we can get a refund we can go some other time.

I draw a breath, surprised to find I'm shaking, with the intention of retracting. Okay, I'm sorry, I understand, we'll make the best of it. But then he says, nastily, 'Why don't you go on your own with the kids? Or get Josie to go, or your mother?' He wears a snide, sneering expression as he makes his helpful suggestion. I'm scared of driving on the wrong side of the road; I couldn't do it even when Robert was taken ill with food poisoning once in France when the children were small. We had to park at the roadside with Robert slumped over the wheel until he was well enough to continue, with Rebecca crying, 'Please don't die, Daddy.' We had to keep stopping for him to vomit at the kerbside.

'We should never have left Birmingham,' I say again as Robert begins to dial.

In the lounge, Rebecca and Simon are sitting in front of the television, not watching but wide eyed and fearful. 'Why are you shouting at Daddy?' Simon asks, climbing on to my lap.

'He made me cross, just like you do sometimes,' I say, smoothing his sweatshirt out against his back. The action reminds me of Steven. I no longer feel guilty.

Chapter 17

I've always loved the journey to Manchester from London. Not by road — mile upon mile of motorway from which the most interesting thing you see is a service station — but by train it's bliss: plenty of time to sit and stare and do nothing and, more to the point, with nothing you ought to be doing. (Just like being in hospital really, but with better food — assuming you've brought your own, that is.) Today, admittedly, the bliss is more elusive than usual; a toddler is crying at the other end of the carriage, which wouldn't be such a problem if the mother didn't keep shouting at it to shut up, and Simon and Rebecca have been bickering since we boarded. (In fact they've been bickering since Simon was born, but getting on a train has made it worse. Simon: 'There's a scarecrow in that field!' Rebecca: 'So what?') Now, though, I have sat Simon and Rebecca by the window either side of the table with paper and pencils, and set them a competition to see who can produce the better picture. It'll be Rebecca, naturally — she's the artistic one in addition to being two years older — but Simon isn't daunted by the challenge and is giving it his best effort, tongue between his teeth, felt pen gripped like a dagger. They chose the subject for the competition themselves: a picture of Steven.

I have a new novel open on my lap. I bought it in W.H. Smith's while we waited for the train to be ready, seduced by the heaving bosom of the heroine on the cover and the raven-haired Adonis who stands behind her kissing her shoulder. It's not the sort of thing I'd read normally (or ever; the hero is called Storm) but the way she leans her body heavily against his brings the smell, the feel of Steven to me with exquisite clarity. (I try to imagine what Steven would be like if he'd been christened Storm, but the image defeats me.) The picture is like a snapshot of our relationship, frozen in time. Steven stands behind me, protective and strong, and yet in truth I am the greater force (symbolised in the defiant gaze of the heroine's black-lashed eyes and thrusting cleavage. If my cleavage thrusts at all it's only metaphorically, but still I'm glad to see such generous mammaries. They're already beginning to have an invigorating effect on my fantasies). I gaze out at the fields rushing past, remembering Steven's equally dark eyes, though the memory is tempered by the realization that every passing mile puts me further away from him.

'Is anyone sitting here?' The train has stopped at Milton Keynes but so busy have I been with Steven that I barely register the stocky woman struggling down the carriage until she speaks to me. She is in her fifties, with glasses and orange hair that is grey at the roots, and her lipstick is painted outside her narrow lips to make them look fuller. (It doesn't.) She probably shops exclusively from catalogues; she would never have bought a polyester dress like that unless she'd seen it being modelled by someone younger, slimmer, taller. Our coats are piled on the empty seat by which she hovers and now I have to feign willingness to

IMMACULATE MISCONCEPTIONS

move them. I take my time because there's an empty seat in the adjacent section where she could easily sit, but that would place her opposite the teenage lovers (heavily into grunge; I count seven earrings between them) who have just got on but are already carrying out a thorough investigation of each other's dental cavities. (As I'm watching, the boy comes up for air and then makes a dive for the girl's ear. His hair is matted and grey. I hope she's had her tetanus jab.) I heave our jackets on to the already over-full overhead racks with difficulty and the woman sits down with a smile of satisfaction, a mission well accomplished. She rests a shopping holdall on her knees. I smile back in a way that isn't meant to be encouraging and return at once to my book. If she thinks I'm reading perhaps she will let me daydream in peace. I close my eyes briefly and Steven's lovely face appears.

'That's a nice picture,' I hear the woman saying to Simon. He responds briefly, then she says to Rebecca, 'And yours.' I open my eyes and hold my breath, waiting for her to turn her attention to me — and she does. 'They look the same age as my grandchildren. They live in Manchester. I'm going to stay with them.'

I say, 'Oh, really,' and nod, bending down to retrieve a pencil Simon has dropped. The woman's calves are knotted with varicose veins and she is wearing an ankle bracelet under her support tights. I blink, but when I look again the bracelet is still there, poised above the battered slingbacks.

'People never believe I've got grandchildren,' she says proudly. I can't see why anyone would think that. She certainly looks old enough, although if what they mean is that they can't believe she found someone to marry her, they may have a point. I know this is an unjust thought even as I think it, and she takes out a bag of Maltesers and offers them round just to make me feel worse. She begins to tell me about her son and how successful he is, and I listen with great interest and what I hope is not a glazed expression.

I should never have come; I only did it to spite Robert. He hates to be alone in the house without us, so coming away was an appropriate punishment for putting his job before his family. But also we needed a break. The kids had been promised their holiday and I couldn't expect them to be cooped up in the house for the entire vacation. I had to do something. I realise now there were lots of things I could have done: taken them on a series of day trips ('I'm going to take the children to Blackpool on the coach,' the woman is saying), perhaps involving an overnight stay; or rented one of the numerous holiday cottages advertised in our local post office ('This is Debbie, she's seven,' she says, handing me the photo, 'the image of her mother.'). Steven would probably have turned up unexpectedly to surprise the children . . . At the very least, Josie could have come. We could have sat up all night drinking wine and comparing our lovers' techniques. Steven is coming on in leaps and bounds. ('Debbie is a good little ballet dancer. Coming on in leaps and bounds.')

But no, I opened my mouth in rage and what came out was, 'Well, sod you. I'll go to Carol's.' It was her fault. If I hadn't just got her letter I wouldn't have thought of it. When I telephoned she could hear I was in a state and said we should come straight away. It was only as I put the phone down that I realised it meant leaving Steven. I could have kicked myself. ('This is Oliver. You should see him kick a ball!')

Theresa isn't as reliable as I'd thought, either. She

should have made me keep to the holiday dates I'd asked for, but no, she said it was no problem at all if I went away a few weeks early. She would use the piece she was reserving and I could write the next one, which we'd already discussed, at Carol's and fax it in. You just can't depend on people.

'Whose is better, Mummy?' Simon holds up his picture for adjudication. Rebecca's is infinitely superior. There's something in the defiant stance of her man which speaks adolescence. She's drawn him wearing his tartan shirt over a white T-shirt, the clothes he wore on Friday. Simon has given him an enormous head and he's pulling a face (when I say this it turns out he isn't supposed to be pulling a face). It looks nothing like him and yet there's something in that lop-sided grin that tugs at my heart.

'I think they're both smashing,' says the woman. 'I couldn't possibly pick between them.' Her diplomacy does her credit and I'd be more than happy to leave the adjudication to her, but the children turn to me for a decision. I announce a draw, which satisfies Simon but leaves Rebecca insulted. I hand them some coins to choose a prize from the buffet. As Rebecca squeezes past me in a sulk, the woman beckons her over and whispers that Mummy had to make it a draw or her little brother would be upset, but as Rebecca is so much more grown up Mummy knew she would understand: of course she's the winner really. She brightens at this all-girls-together approach, and the woman says she will go with them to the buffet car as she has to go the lav anyway.

I feel a pang of sadness, watching the lumpy legs on their slingbacks making their way up the carriage. Simon stumbles and she grabs his wrist before he falls. Her ankle bracelet — a nod at the sensual being she wishes she still was – is caught on the back of her support tights. She's just like me underneath it all (underneath the lack of taste and dress sense, that is); she still wants what I want: to be young and vibrant with a (even younger and more vibrant) virile lover. In twenty years' time, will I be like her, still looking for love, my life comprised of old photos, my hair dyed the colour of a Jaffa orange?

I settle back to look at my book cover again, but it's just a cheap picture of an idealised couple, all in the worst taste, and I can't retrieve my earlier saucy feelings. The toddler at the end of the carriage starts to cry again.

Carol is to meet us at the station in the village where she lives. The children drag their cases along the platform and for a moment I miss Robert, who always does the carrying, as I heave mine off the train. A guard stands by, ready to blow his whistle, and observes our struggle patiently. I remember, as I stumble into Rebecca who is moving at a snail's pace, that since my operation I'm not supposed to lift anything.

As we emerge into daylight, we see Carol and her kids waiting by her Volvo. Carol's chestnut hair is longer than when we last met, its natural curls falling in waves to her shoulders. Whenever I think of her I remember her hair as a short neat cap, the way she had it at college. She looks lovely, but in a year or two she'll need to have it short again; there comes an age beyond which long hair becomes unacceptable unless you're a witch or a hippy, or want to look like Nanette Newman. It could be a shade lighter than it used to be, but perhaps that's the effect of the sunshine. She has a fresh, dewy look to her skin, the result, as she will no doubt tell me once again, of a low-fat diet and long country walks. At college I watched

Carol pass from what used to be called bonny through all stages en route to 'fat'. But she has actually lost weight since having children, and the woman who holds out her arms to greet me is as slim and athletic as I used to be.

'Don't look at me,' she says as we hug in greeting, 'I've grown huge. I'd slimmed right down then it all went back on again.'

There isn't an ounce of fat on her, but she has the obsession with her size of the once-overweight. She used to be permanently on a diet that was equally permanently doomed to failure. In her heart she could never accept that a pat of butter contained more calories than half a loaf of bread, or that a bag of crisps could be more fattening than an entire sandwich. She never came to terms with the idea that big things don't necessarily contain more calories than small. That was one thing I really liked about Carol: she was always fatter than I was. But now she won't have butter in the house and lives on wholemeal bread; if you offered her a crisp she'd think you were trying to poison her. She sees the open packet of chocolate cream eggs in my bag and pulls a face.

'Well the train was late. We had to have something, didn't we?' I sound like I'm on the defensive, and I am. The waistband of my jeans pinches me as I breathe in.

The twins, Mark and Jamie, who are the same age as Simon, stand by the car eyeing Simon shyly. They get on famously but it takes time for them all to break down their reserve. They've changed too since I last saw them, but then that must be over a year ago. Annalise and Rebecca are already renewing their acquaintance, admiring each other's outfits. Rebecca is entranced by Annalise's newly bobbed hair and is struggling to conceal her jealousy.

Carol takes the kids' cases and puts them in the boot,

lifting them with ease, and I lug mine in next to them. The Volvo is only a few years old — I only realise this when I check the number plate later — but it is heavy with dust (in which someone has written 'Don't wash this car, plant something'). Inside the seats are stained and the floor littered with chewing gum wrappers and tissues. The back seat is cloaked in a rug covered with dog hairs. They have three dogs; one had puppies and they couldn't bear to part with all of them.

Carol drives erratically through the narrow streets of the village and then we turn into a small wooded private road and into her drive. Her house is large, rambling and welcoming. It is also untidy beyond belief, but perhaps because of its size the debris just adds to the homely feel.

Dan must have been looking out for us because he comes out, accompanied by one of their Labradors, as we're unloading the suitcases. Dan is over six feet tall, and towers over Carol. He's heavily built, and getting heavier from the look of the beer gut pushing out the front of his T-shirt, but with his height the effect isn't unattractive. Dan has always had charisma and the gift of exuding bonhomie. He gives me an enormous hug, squeezing me tight as well as kissing my cheek.

'Are you better now? You're looking fine.'

I don't want to talk about my operation, so I smile and pull at his beard which always seems in need of a trim. 'You want to ring David Bellamy,' I say, 'you've got something nesting in there.'

'Piss off and carry your own cases,' he laughs, taking them from Carol.

Dan didn't qualify in medicine after all. He failed his first-year resits and switched to biology. I don't remember what brought him into computers, but now he runs his own company from home. Carol says they have money worries, but she has always said that. To judge from the house and land, the Range Rover Dan drives, and the gardener they employ regularly (but then so do we, I suppose) their worries are of the sort most people only dream about.

We gather in the kitchen where there are still the remains of lunch, or it could be breakfast, or maybe both.

Carol opens the dishwasher and is dismayed to see it hasn't been emptied yet.

'First things first,' she says, gathering the dirty dishes from the table and piling them by the sink, 'what do you all want to eat?'

I can think of nothing but Steven. Carol's window cleaner came today. I just caught sight of his ankles disappearing up the ladder and my stomach lurched. I went outside and looked up at his disappearing bucket just to be sure it wasn't Steven, somehow transported here — and he was a man of fifty, white haired, with the neck of a chicken. He saw me looking at him and I had to say I'd come to see if he wanted a cup of tea. Carol complained I was setting a precedent and he'd expect one every time now.

We're supposed to be here for a week and a half, but how can I manage for that long? I can't even phone him. Every man I see reminds me; the tilt of a head, shape of the brow, shade of the hair.

Robert phoned last night, sounding penitent and lonely. He says he needs me, evidently unaware that it's his incipient need that I most want to get away from; it's not my responsibility to see that he doesn't crumble. He wanted us to make up and be friends again but I hardened my heart against him. I don't want to hear his endearments down the telephone (though better that than in the flesh). And it's his own fault. If he hadn't sprung it on me about the holiday I wouldn't have minded not going; I'd have had time to realise it meant I needn't be apart from Steven after all.

Maybe what I'm going through really is hormonal. Gradually I'll get back to normal and fall out of love with Steven. (And he'll fall out of love with me at precisely the same time, of course. I don't want to hurt him.) Then I'll start wanting Robert again. He'll develop inner strength and a firmer bottom, and I'll be swept up on a tide of passion. I hope so. Otherwise I don't know what I'm going to do.

'Can I see your scar?' Carol likes to think she has a medical bent. We are sunbathing on her patio which sweeps across the back of the house in a semi circle. Hanging baskets and tubs give the house what we used to call a chocolate-box look, although boxes of chocolates don't seem to look like that any more. The kids are chasing each other with the hose pipe. They've been threatened not to spray us on pain of death, but that hasn't been sufficient deterrent for Mark. Carol finds his disobedience cute, but I'd like to hit him.

'You don't want to see my scar. You'll only say "Ugh!"'

'I won't. Go on. I only want to see.'

I pull my bikini trunks down and Carol peers over to look. 'Ugh!'

I aim a punch at her head and we both laugh.

'Are you self-conscious about it?'

'Only with you.' It's a neat scar, beginning to lose its

raw look now. About four inches wide, it sits along the line of my pubic hair. When I lean forward my stomach hangs over it. I'm more self-conscious of that than the scar.

'I mean with him, that boy.'

That boy. She can't bear to refer to him by name; she feels how I used to about Greg. As long as they have no name they have no identity. Her antagonism can't prevent a wave of heat passing over me, like warm water. At last I can talk about him. All day I find myself looking for opportunities to bring his name up, ways to keep his image alive alongside me.

'I told him about it. But he knew about the operation — I was in hospital when I met him.'

'It doesn't put him off?'

'Since when did you meet a man who could be put off having sex?'

We both laugh and are instantly friends again. But then she says, 'Go on then, tell me about him. I can see you're bursting to.'

'No, you don't really want to hear.' It's embarrassing to be so transparent.

I wait for her to push me on it but she says, 'Okay, please yourself,' and settles back with her face lifted to the sun. Damn.

Later, as I finish off Simon's half-eaten cornet, she says, 'You're making a terrible mistake, you do know that, don't you?' I don't answer. She may as well get it off her chest, she's been very restrained so far. 'Robert's a wonderful father. He works hard, he's loving, there's nothing he wouldn't do for you.'

'I don't want him to do anything for me.'

'It's your age. Some kind of mid-life crisis brought on by your illness. It's understandable — and God knows young boys can be attractive.' Carol gives piano lessons. She's commented before on the deliciousness of one or two of her Grade VII pupils. 'But you don't want to go risking everything. Where would you live? How would you manage? Dan's sister is a single parent and it's no picnic.'

'I don't love Robert any more.'

There's a silence after I've spoken. I'm frightened of what I've said.

'Yes you do.' Carol gets up, very matter of fact, and gathers our glasses up from the table. 'I'll get us a top-up.'

I have the impression that the subject is closed, but after the kids have gone to bed and Dan has volunteered to clear up from dinner in the absence of Carol's or my offering to, she picks up the conversation again. By now we're on our third bottle of wine and mellowing.

'Have you actually slept with him?' We've been talking about the Margaret Atwood she's reading, and the question seems to have come out of nowhere. All the same, I'm surprised she has to ask. I'd thought it was obvious. I lean forward to pick up my wineglass so that I don't have to meet her eyes. I don't answer. 'Frigging hell, you have, haven't you?'

I smile lightly and look down into my glass. I've drunk plenty, but not enough apparently to prevent me from feeling embarrassed at scandalising my friend.

'Jesus, you better not let Dan find out.'

'You haven't told him anything, have you?'

'No, of course I haven't. He'd think you were some terrible corrupting influence.'

In spite of the doubts and insecurities I'm feeling, I'm

enjoying the impression of living on the edge and dancing with danger. Carol doesn't seem to appreciate that my life has taken on the force and momentum of a widescreen movie in glorious technicolour and that I am the star.

'Talking of corrupting influences,' she goes on, 'do you see anything of that nympho neighbour of yours? What's her name? Jackie? Jocelyn?'

'Josie?' I look surprised. 'Occasionally.'

'There must be something in the water in your street.' I don't respond and there's silence for a few moments. 'So what's he like?'

'I thought you didn't want to know.'

'I don't want to know. But I have to, don't I? You are my friend; I can't pretend it isn't happening. If I'm going to help you, I have to know all the details.'

'You can't help me.'

'I am already, aren't I? Letting you put some distance between you and this boy.' It's astonishing how people can misread a situation.

'It's distance from Robert that I needed.'

'You only think that.' Carol also has an interest in psychology. 'Subconsciously you needed to get away to see the situation objectively. I'm very touched, actually, that you felt you could come to me.'

I'm tempted to let her know she has misread this situation too, but instead I say how tired she's looking (which she will know translates as 'haggard and ageing') and that I'll give Dan a hand in the kitchen.

Next morning I wake to a tapping at the door and the smell of school dinners. The door opens and Dan enters with a cup of coffee.

'Sorry, were you asleep? Thought you'd be awake

already — the kids have been running riot for hours.'
I've heard squeals and the thump thump thump of feet along the landing, but they'd been incorporated into a dream in which Robert was running along the corridor of a train and couldn't find me even though he kept passing the compartment I was in.

'What's that smell?' A sickly aroma of meat and herbs is rising from the kitchen.

'Chicken. I'm doing you a picnic to take to Alton Towers while Carol gets ready.'

For a moment I wonder if the saintly Dan is also part of my dream. I sip my coffee and am reminded that Carol indeed mentioned visiting Alton Towers. I hadn't realised she meant today.

'We won't all get in one car.'

'Oh, I'm not going. I'm working. Carol's got some free tickets but you have to go today. She didn't realise till she checked them last night — that's why it's a bit of a rush. She'd intended going Thursday, then I could've come too.'

Alton Towers is thus explained, though not why Dan should be preparing the food for a jolly he isn't even coming to. But then the wonderful Dan is just another of life's mysteries.

Perhaps he interprets my look of admiration as doubt, because he goes on, 'That's all right, is it? You do want to go?'

I'm still tired from yesterday's journey and feel queasy from the red wine and the smell of chicken. A day on the patio in the sun would have been more to my taste, but I arrange my face into a mask of unmistakeable enthusiasm.

'Can't think of anything I'd rather do.'

'Oh really? I'd no idea you had such a boring life.' He laughs and I manage not to blush.

By the time we arrive at Alton Towers the sunny morning has given way to a grey sky that threatens rain. Carol carries the rucksack containing the day's provisions — a whole roast chicken ('I thought we could just pull bits off as we fancied it'), plus ham rolls, crisps and cocktail sausages. Dan assembled the feast single-handed. He even remembered a wad of tissues and babywipes for our sticky fingers. I begin to sing his praises but for some reason this irritates Carol. 'He only does what I tell him,' she says, as though this wasn't wonderful in itself.

I carry the kagouls, sweatshirts (despite a cooling breeze the kids insist T-shirts are all they need), a large flask of coffee and the kids' purses, which they insist on bringing with them despite the fact we all know if there's anything to buy it'll be Carol or I who will end up paying for it.

'I'm worn out already,' I say as we heave the bags on to our shoulders.

'Can't wait to go on the slide,' Carol answers, stepping up the pace. She goes with the kids up the helter skelter and comes down screaming and careering from side to side. Annalise and Rebecca, who are behind her, progress far more sedately; in fact Rebecca, with her arms folded, her hair tucked behind her ears, and her face arranged into the expression of one who has done all this before, has the appearance of an old-fashioned school-marm. As they come to a halt at the bottom I see in Carol something of the girl I met in the faculty common room twenty years ago. Inside every middle-aged woman is a young one trying to get out.

'Mum! Everyone's looking at you,' hisses Annalise, wishing the young one would stay in.

Carol minds the bags while the kids and I go on the pirate ship, but I come off feeling green and wobbly. We both balk at the Corkscrew. 'You still haven't told me', she says, as we watch Rebecca and Annalise climb into the car and have the heavy harnesses fastened, 'what this boy is like.'

A ray of sun peeps through the clouds on to us like a blessing. 'He's beautiful. He's tall and dark and sexy. He's funny, he's thoughtful.' My rhapsody continues like this for some minutes before I realise she isn't listening.

'Frigging kids. I told Mark and Jamie not to run off. This place'll be mad busy before we get to the Log Flume.'

By the time the girls have finished, stepping off the ride looking pale but claiming they loved it, the boys have come back. They charge ahead while we struggle behind with the bags. Carol tries to tempt them with a ham roll in the interests of lightening her load, and for the same reason I tell them they'll be cold on the Log Flume and will need sweatshirts, but they're out of earshot before we've even finished speaking.

Waiting in the queue for the Log Flume, that is snaking past the thirty-minutes marker, she resumes her questioning while we pick at the chicken. 'What did you say he does?'

I search my brain for a definition that will make odd-job person sound more prestigious. 'He isn't academic. But he's gifted with his hands.'

'I bet he is.' She gives me a wry smile and then goes on, 'Like a sculptor?'

'He hasn't had that sort of education—'

'What sort of education has he had?'

I'm sure I put something of this in my letter. She just wants to make me say it so she can pour scorn from a greater height. 'His family aren't educated. He left school at sixteen and he probably truanted half the time before that. He's not like us, Carol; I won't pretend he is. But that doesn't mean he hasn't got qualities worth valuing.'

'Just don't go thinking he loves you.'

This is cruel and I wonder why she has to say it. I tell her how wrong she is.

'You're fooling yourself. He's using you. Oh I know you like him, I'm not arguing with that. But listen to yourself. He's a loser, isn't he? You're risking your home, your family – your whole life – for a complete no-hoper.'

I turn away to watch a log-boat poised at the top of the final drop. The dad sits in the front, the hood of his kagoul pulled up; behind him sit three children already screaming. The log drops and a tremendous arc of spray rises as it hits the bottom. The dad gets out, shaking the water off his hands and laughing. I concentrate hard on the view and blink my eyes but I can't stop them filling up.

'You okay?' asks Carol, seeing me dabbing at my face with a tissue.

'Grit under my contact lens.'

'Shall I look?'

'It's out now.' I can feel her looking at me.

'You think I can't understand the true situation because I'm not involved in it, whereas I think that you can't because you are. There's no future for it, is there, you don't deny that much?' I don't answer which she takes as assent, and perhaps it is. 'In six months it'll be over and you could have lost Robert, your home, maybe your kids – and he'll just walk away scot free.'

Without apparent warning, the queue moves ahead

several feet and there's a commotion while we gather up our bags to move with it. Carol calls the boys to get back in line and I think about what she has said, frustrated by my inability to prove how wrong she is.

The queue seems to move faster as we near the front, and suddenly it's our turn to be handled in to the log canoe. I sit at the front with Carol, the girls in single file behind me. The boys get into the next canoe. The logs are pushed off; at the highest point our canoe pauses while the automatic camera takes our photos. Carol leans forward and hisses in my ear. 'You do realise that the one at the front gets the wettest?'

The log drops through the air, snatching my breath away so that I can't even scream. The spray rises roof high above us and a shock of cold rushes over me. When I start to breathe again I realise I'm sitting in some kind of hip bath. My jeans, shoes and hair are soaked. As the log draws to a halt and I get out my jeans stick to my thighs and bottom. I look like I've wet myself. I'm surprised to see that Carol has her kagoul on and is completely dry. The boys think it's wonderful to see me in such a state. 'Look at Mummy,' yells Simon with glee, while Rebecca and Annalise rein in their laughter until they're certain I'll see the funny side.

'You cow,' I laugh to Carol, wringing a stream of water from my hair.

'Serves you bloody right,' she says.

I love the Log Flume usually, but today all I could think of as the log balanced precariously at the highest point and everyone screamed in fear of the drop, was that I wanted it to be over, done with, finished. Because as our log canoe had begun its swaying and bumping journey through the narrow channels Carol mentioned something: 'Remind me to tell you,' she said, 'last week Dan saw Max.'

I don't know what's the more shocking: the idea that Dan has seen Max, or that we've passed twenty-four hours together without Carol telling me.

I contain my curiosity until we're seated in the picnic area. The kids are at a separate table and once they're settled with everything — food, drink and money for an ice cream — I introduce the subject as casually as I can. Which is not very.

'So Dan saw Max?'

'Yes, in Sainsbury's. He was coming out with his trolley — Dan, that is — and Max was paying for a newspaper at the front desk.' Max in Sainsbury's sounds like an anomaly; supermarket shopping would be far too common. He probably only eats Italian bread made with sun-dried tomatoes, dipped in extra *extra* virgin olive oil. His milk would come from a rare breed of goat fed on organic vegetables.

But then Max *was* only buying a paper.

'How did he look?' I'm astonished to realise that I feel nervous.

'Exactly the same, from the sounds of it. Well, he always looked old before his time and now his time has come. He's actually as old as he always looked.'

'Did he say anything?'

'He was just passing through. He owns a bookshop, did you know that? He has written a book on early theatre.'

Well, that followed. I couldn't have imagined him selling computer software like Dan, or managing staff like Robert. As I remember he couldn't even manage his own cheque book; in view of that, I wonder how he runs a bookshop. Maybe his part in the venture is just to read the books. I want to ask if he's still in the area but don't know how to put it.

'Dan told him you were coming over,' Carol says, taking a bite from a chicken leg. 'But he said he was only here for a few days. Just as well, because Dan would've ended up inviting him for dinner. You know what men are like.' She laughs at the insensitivity of the male gender and I try to join in.

'Fancy him turning up after all this time.' I pick up a cocktail sausage and turn it slowly in my fingers, looking at the brown wrinkled skin. Food doesn't always survive such scrutiny and I suddenly find I'm repulsed by it.

'He isn't married. I asked Dan if he was still carrying a torch for you. Know what he said?'

'No, what?' I want to give the impression of sharing the joke.

'He said he thought he'd lost the torch but he's still got the batteries. I thought that was quite funny. For Dan.'

I think so too. I pick up the sausage and pop it in my mouth.

Chapter 18

From my bedroom I can see into the house opposite. The people who live there often leave their curtains open at night and sometimes, as I go to close ours, I can see them undressing. The husband wears a singlet and boxer shorts.

From my room at Carol's house the view is rather different. A field stretches to the left, flanked by a wood, and to the right a hill rises in close proximity. I'm not used to seeing hills except from a train, and then they're usually in the distance. I was born in East Anglia, and the nearest thing you get to a hill there is a steep camber in the road, so hills have always held a fascination for me.

On these hills cows are grazing; those at the peak have the appearance of being balanced against the horizon, as though they're tightrope walking across the top of the world. (When Rebecca was tiny I told her that was what the cows were doing, and she believed me.) Carol thinks I've got a headache and am lying down, but I just want to be on my own.

Robert rang again when we got back from Alton Towers and the day was suddenly spoiled. I felt a well of rage surging up inside. Strange that I feel more antagonistic now I'm away from him than I did when I was there.

His call was a mix of good and bad news: he told me the plug on the freezer had fused but he'd mended it, and just as I was getting up a head of steam to ask why he was phoning long distance to tell me that, he mentioned that Steven had phoned. Steven wants to know when I'll be back. 'He's very conscientious,' Robert said. 'He wants to get on with this GCSE stuff but he needs you to help him over the next bit.' The idea of Steven being conscientious about his GCSE made me smile, but I was touched to hear he'd phoned. Perhaps he has the same need to talk about me that I do to talk of him. I'd rather he didn't do it with Robert, though.

'He says he's doing maths as well. I said I'd help him if he liked.' I told Robert that was a kind thought, determining to nip the idea in the bud as soon as I got back. The idea of my husband and lover becoming closer friends isn't to be contemplated.

I lie down on the bed and think about Steven, who I will be with again in a very few days. But when I try to imagine him, it's Max's face I see.

'What an extraordinarily dull room. Why don't you put some pictures up?' I didn't know then that Max's usual form of greeting was in the form of a criticism albeit with a smile attached. He had been in my room before, of course, but obviously he hadn't been looking at the decor on that occasion. He was right: the walls were painted a pale green that had dulled with the passage of time, but it was against hall rules to put sellotape on the walls, and if you used drawing pins the plaster came away (which you could see from where braver souls than me had tried it). 'Well, use Blu-tack then,' he suggested when I told him the problem. But I was dubious about that too. Dad would never let me use it at home, saying it left greasy marks on the wallpaper, though as we'd never used it I did wonder how he knew.

'What a strange girl you are,' said Max, sitting down and kicking off his shoes. 'You don't mind breaking the rules about not having men in overnight, but you won't stick up a few pictures.'

I spent the afternoon in Athena choosing posters, and came away with a Dante Gabriel Rossetti, a Millais, and a very classical looking representation of a well-formed youth being pursued by a beseeching female. I thought Max might appreciate the irony of that. The latter was a sombre choice, with its dull browns and deep shadows and the rather anxious face of the young man, but I thought it had all the feel of an old master and that Max would certainly be impressed.

When he called later in the week he laughed out loud. 'You've made your room even duller, you dunce. You really do have the most extraordinary taste.' It was difficult to find strengths in the old master, particularly as I'd rather expected Max to tell me what was good about it, but I had less trouble defending Millais' *Ophelia*, as she floated pale and ethereal down the river, surrounded by leaves and flowers. She was beautiful and likely to prove comforting to other young women with boyfriend troubles. I pointed all this out, with feeling.

'You do know how he painted that?' Max asked lightly.

I hesitated. What did that 'how' imply? 'With a paintbrush' probably wasn't the answer.

'He got Elizabeth Siddal to lie down in the bath,' he said, 'and it looks like it, don't you think?'

He didn't comment on the Rossetti directly but, glancing up at it, mused, 'The pre-Raphaelites are much overrated. They were story-tellers, not true artists; they missed their vocation, you know, they should have been book illustrators.' I argued in defence of the pre-Raphaelites' 'jewel-like colours', a phrase I'd read once, but they weren't evident from the pictures I'd chosen and, besides, I was out of love with them now. I kept them until I moved out of that room but that was only so Max didn't think he'd been able to bully me into taking them down. I hated them after that, and even now a Christmas card printed with a Millais or a Burne-Jones can cause a sinking feeling in my stomach.

It's the twins' birthday on Wednesday, which I only remember when Carol starts talking about the arrangements she's making for their party. We're on a country walk at the time, making our way up the same hill I can see from the bedroom window. At home having 'a long walk' means covering the distance from Tesco's to where the car is parked. At Carol's it means hiking boots, mud, and steep hills with cows on them. We don't own hiking boots, but fortunately the mud is dry and hard at this time of year. Carol understands that namby pamby townies suffer panic attacks if not in sight of a pub. I haven't seen one for the last half-hour, in fact, but she assures me that The Fox is waiting for us over the next bridge.

'So what have you got in mind for the twins?' I ask, as I unhook my sweatshirt from a splinter sticking out of a stile, made too narrow for people of normal girth.

'Larry's coming, he's a magician friend of Dan's. He's Magic Circle but he loves to entertain the kids. The twins saw him at a friend's house and they were desperate for him.'

This sounds like an excellent idea. The kids will be occupied for the afternoon and we can lie in the sun and read.

Carol looks surprised. 'He'll only be on for half an hour. We'll be peeling the spuds for their chips then. Then Dan's going to run a few races for them and referee some football while we cook the burgers.'

Chips? What can she be thinking of?

'Sunflower oil,' she says airily. 'Just use it once and chips are actually quite good for them.'

I have to admire Carol. When I give a kids' party (which is a rare occurrence but it has happened), the criterion is what will be easiest for me. That usually means taking them bowling or to the cinema, but whatever we do it has to include tea at McDonald's. Carol has already made the birthday cake, she tells me (pale lemon sponge cut into the shape of a tennis racket which lies upon a lawn of green desiccated coconut — tennis is the twins' latest enthusiasm), and bite-sized meringues. I haven't made a birthday cake since the fort-shaped one for Simon. It put me off — all that work, and then all he wanted to do was gallop the soldiers through the icing and eat the turrets.

All she has to do now, Carol tells me, is buy a few marshmallows and some ice cream, and get the mince for the beefburgers. ('They're so easy to make, I can't be bothered with the frozen ones.') I try to introduce the idea of oven chips (the prospect of peeling all these potatoes is lowering my spirits) but she tells me the freezer is too full with soft fruits from their garden. Briefly I think of Josie's immaculate house and wonder at my friends' ability to make me feel guilty in so many different ways.

The twins have invited about ten boys, which is the sum of the boys in their class. They go to the village school, which is approached via the narrow lane down which we now walk. Carol often brings us in this direction. I don't know whether it's because the track which leads to the school is more user-friendly to people wearing imitation-designer trainers, or because she wishes to remind us of the inherent superiority of village life which the school so ably demonstrates. The nineteenth-century building of old grey stone is faced on two sides by rolling fields in which horses graze. The third side is flanked by the village church, and next to that the rectory. It's a picture of the kind of Englishness that is often supposed to exist no more. The heavy scent of flowers from the cottage garden makes me want to retch.

'Isn't it beautiful?' says Carol, leaning on the dry stone wall that runs along the side of the lane and taking in the view.

'You've seen one blade of grass, you've seen them all,' I say.

It's not that I'm above sentimentalising over a sunset or rhapsodising at a poppyfield, but for my money nothing beats the rush of adrenalin you get walking over Tower Bridge or wandering round Harrods Food Hall and wondering at the price of caviare. And an undoubted advantage of both is that you're not a million miles from a cup of coffee.

My kids surely have a duty to stand up for the suburbia that is their home, but as Carol points out the small size of the classes, the homely mateyness of the staff, the various activities that take place in the schoolroom (all of which sound stimulating, challenging and fun and yet still, mysteriously, result in a sound grounding in the three

IMMACULATE MISCONCEPTIONS

R's and virtually automatic acceptance into the fought-after local private schools), I see both Rebecca and Simon look pathetically wistful.

'Why can't we live in the country?' It was only a matter of time before Rebecca asked that, but she could have held out just a little longer, say until Carol wasn't around to hear her. I explain the 'grass is greener' syndrome ('But I like green grass,' she says) and point out how deprived Mark, Jamie and Annalise must feel upon visiting us when they discover our easy access to national museums and West End theatres. (Annalise, who is within earshot, looks astonished.) Rebecca remains unconvinced, which perhaps isn't surprising considering that her only experience of West End theatres was a pantomime at the London Palladium throughout which Simon howled whenever the villain appeared. Annalise is quick to point out that they have an excellent museum in Manchester which her school has just taken them to visit. ('See?' complains Rebecca. 'Our school doesn't take us anywhere.' I make a mental note to ask why not when term starts back. And another mental note to hit her with a stick as soon as we get back.)

We turn in the direction of one of the rolling hills, the one behind which, Carol assures me, the pub nestles. And then, as she leans on yet another damn stile to admire the view while I shake a stone out of my shoe, she says, 'Do you ever think about Max?' People are strange, aren't they? It's like asking me if I ever think of eating.

'Not really,' I answer.

Larry is slightly built, with narrow shoulders and the pink complexion that often goes with red hair. In fact Larry's hair is a mousy grey, but perhaps it was more brilliant in his younger days. He is in his fifties, and strangely diffident for a performer, though this retiring manner changes the moment he steps out before the children, just as though a switch has been pulled. One end of the patio has been arranged as a makeshift stage, with a cloth-covered table on which are arranged a few pieces of equipment and to one side of which stands a cardboard box. Mark runs up and looks into the box, and has to be hissed at by Carol. He goes back to sit on the ground with the other boys but not without a swagger that says 'My birthday, my party, my entertainer'. Simon watches him thoughtfully.

I was press-ganged into peeling the potatoes during the morning, so Carol and I are free to watch Larry's performance after all. He begins by twisting coloured sausage-shaped balloons into various animals, all of which resemble a dachshund whatever he may call them. I drift off, imagining Steven standing behind me so that I rest against his chest, just like the picture on the cheap book I bought. I wonder what he's doing right now and if he's thinking about me . . . The sudden bang of a burst balloon drags me back to the present. The kids, and Carol, are laughing; I have been too dense to realise that the similarity of the dog-shaped balloons is part of the joke. Carol nudges me. 'Good, isn't he?'

Dan is laying the table for tea, I can see him through the dining room window, so I go in to help him. I've been waiting for days to speak to him but he has been out constantly since Carol told me the news about Max. We've met at mealtimes but I haven't felt able to ask him then. The kids are unanimously agreed that we adults lead boring and monotonous lives, and thus ignore anything we say in their presence, but they have an unfailing knack of picking up anything you would have preferred them not to hear. Rebecca can spot intrigue at fifty paces (she has only missed what's going on with Steven because she is in love with him herself).

I place a serviette decorated with Bart Simpson on each plate and make small talk about Larry. There's a slight pause and I seize the opportunity to fill it.

'Carol says you saw Max last week.' My voice sounds a little high-pitched but Dan doesn't seem to notice.

'Yes, recognised him but couldn't think who he was. He remembered me, though.'

I hope that Max hadn't remembered referring to Dan as 'that tedious young man'. Dan's warmth and openness were anathema to Max. 'If it's faithfulness and devotion she wants,' he said of Carol's choice, 'she should get a Labrador.' Of course, now she has both.

'How did he look?' I've asked Carol already but I want to hear it from Dan.

'Oh, the same, you know.' I should have known better than to expect anything more from Dan.

'Is he — you know . . .'

What I want to say is; 'Is he happy, contented; has life been good to him?' Another woman would have understood without my having to spell it out, would understand why such things can't be spelled out. But Dan just says, 'Is he what?'

'Is he — married?' It's a waste of a question since I've already asked Carol, but it's a way of prolonging the subject while I form a better one.

'Dunno. Don't remember.' It's strange how you can ask a man a question and end up knowing less than you did before. Carol said he *hadn't* married. Been quite definite about it. Then Dan says, suddenly confidential, 'Not thinking of getting back with him, are you?' He laughs and I add him to my mental list of people who need hitting with a stick.

The conversation seems to be over, chopped off before it's really started, as my chats with Dan so often are. I always feel we would like to be friends, to be as easy with each other as we both are with Carol, yet somehow in conversation we seem to miss each other so that we retire mystified and confused.

But as he sets by each place an enormous cup, souvenirs from Disney and Seaworld (where, despite their money troubles, Dan and Carol have spent several holidays), he picks up the subject again. 'Strange bloke, I always thought.'

'Oh?'

'Wasn't well liked, was he?'

It hurts me to hear this and I retort a little too quickly: 'Being liked isn't everything. Neville Chamberlain was well liked and look where that got us.'

Dan looks at me oddly, no doubt wondering what Neville Chamberlain has to do with it. I'm angry that I couldn't come up with a slightly more contemporary comparison. 'He wasn't a bad bloke, I don't mean that — but I never really took to him. I was glad when you started going out with Robert. Max had too much side for my liking. Bit of a poser. Whatever he said, you always felt he was trying to create an effect.'

Well of course he was, that was the point. But you can't expect a puppy to have that kind of perception. 'He was just very conscious of the English language,' I explain patiently. 'He planned his words before he said them. He *was* trying to create an effect — the effect of someone who is meticulous in everything he thinks and does.'

Dan stops in the act of placing down the next cup and

looks at me under his brows. 'Happen you're right,' he says, adopting a Lancashire accent and straightening a fork that the cup has misaligned. 'You knew him better than I did, obviously. But all in all you made the right choice with Robert, didn't you?'

This isn't a question but one of those uncontroversial and unifying statements designed to create accord between parties who have had some slight disagreement. As such I assume it requires no more than a nod, but as I stand back to admire the table I realise Dan is still looking at me, waiting for an answer. 'Oh, absolutely,' I say, and put the remaining serviettes back into the sideboard.

Larry stays on after his performance (generally well received except by Rebecca and Annalise who are very superior about it, claiming to have seen most of the tricks already on TV, and able to explain some of them) and sits on the patio with us, drinking wine. The kids have finished tea, and in this last hour until the parents arrive, they're free to run riot in the garden.

'Have you got children, Larry?' I ask. Carol is breaking up a tiff among some of the boys, and Dan is opening another bottle. I have to keep the conversation going in their absence.

'A boy and a girl. But they're grown up now — one's at university. I don't see a lot of them.'

'Your wife doesn't mind you being out every Saturday afternoon?' Carol has told me that his act is very popular.

'I'm divorced.'

'I'm sorry to hear that.' I'm not sure if this is the right thing to say to divorced people. Perhaps he's glad.

'Oh I don't mind it now. I've got a nice little flat,

plenty of friends. I do quite a lot with Rotary.' As he tells me how happy he is he seems to shrink. 'And I love kids. I'm always busy.'

He doesn't go on and we both let our gazes wander over to Carol who has now been joined by Dan. The dispute has just been settled and as the two boys involved run off, Dan bends to Carol and whispers something to her. She laughs and puts her arm round his waist while he puts his round her shoulder and pulls her still closer to him. Annalise and Mark come running up, poking at each other, and looking for adjudication. Astonishingly, Dan says something to make them smile. Standing there, united, they are the perfect family group. The kids turn and wander off and Dan and Carol kiss briefly. I feel isolated and lonely, suddenly overcome by an overwhelming sense of loss.

'Good to see a couple so happy, isn't it?' says Larry. But there's nothing to be gained by watching happy people. It's not like studying a magic trick, there's no secret someone can teach you.

'How long have you been on your own?' Maybe it doesn't take so long to adjust as people say. You read all kinds of things about the trauma of divorce which probably aren't true at all.

'Ten years,' he says with an attempt at brightness. 'I like it on my own.'

'Marriage — who'd have it?' I say with an effort at humour.

'Not me!' he says, without conviction.

Carol arrives before our forced jollity can sink any lower.

'Show Ellie that trick you do, the one with the stick.' He demurs, but Dan joins in and demands a free show in return for the wine Larry has drunk. Larry, I soon realise, is happy to agree. He's one of those people who think they're only ever asked to do things out of politeness, not because people truly value they're skills. Carol has told me that Larry would like to get more work in night clubs but that he lacks push.

We gather closely round Larry and he produces a stick from his pocket. It's like a lolly stick, but is black with a white line drawn across it. He turns it over to show us there are three lines on the other side. Then he turns it back and astonishingly the line on the first side has disappeared completely. When he turns it over again the original line is on *that* side. We're too close to him for him to be palming it, replacing it with a different stick or hiding it up his sleeve. The lines keep changing and disappearing, and none of us can see how it's done.

'Larry, you're brilliant,' I have to say when he's finished. His pink face blushes a little pinker.

Talking to Carol about it afterwards I comment that the magic trick reminded me of the way relationships operate. You start with one thing, think you understand it, but then it changes and when you try to change it back you find what you thought you had was never there in the first place. You puzzle over it, try to work it out, but you never really understand what's going on.

'You don't half talk some crap sometimes,' says Carol.

The next morning Theresa rings about the piece I'm to write next, on facial massage. A book has just come out and I'm supposed to have tried out the techniques and be reporting on them. Actually I did try the techniques. It took twenty minutes to run through the sequence and I couldn't tell from the instructions whether I was doing the tiny tapping movements too hard, not hard enough, or just right but in all the wrong places. I didn't think it had worked at all. Mind you, I only did it the once.

Theresa tells me she has heard of two other books on the same subject and wants me to look over all three. 'Do a comparison,' she says, 'and find something positive to say.' She means: 'If necessary, lie about your conclusions.'

I hate doing research. As soon as you have to travel to a bookshop or library you double the amount of time you'll have to spend on the piece — and that's assuming that you actually find the books you're after. Either they've just parted with the last copy, it's out of print (sometimes they say it's not yet in print) or they have it on order but don't know when it might arrive. Foolishly, I tell all this to Carol.

'Don't worry, you won't be doing it for much longer, will you?' she says, weighing out wholemeal flour for pastry. 'If you leave Robert you'll need something that pays a bit better.'

Thus it is with a bad humour that I set off for Manchester in search of *Facelifts Without Surgery* and *Look Better in 28 Days*. I've already tried to talk Carol into making a day of it — that way I could at least have got a lift — but she wants to do some baking and ensure the kids stay out of Dan's way. He has a client calling this afternoon.

Once I'm actually aboard the train and on my way I'm grateful to be alone. Much of the twenty-minute journey is through open countryside and the effect is calming and soporific and conducive to sweet thoughts about Steven. I'm going to phone him later, and just the thought of hearing his voice sends a flutter through my stomach. When I get back I'm going to take this relationship in hand — spend some more time with him (preferably time which isn't overshadowed by the possibility of kids arriving home early, friends calling, Robert telephoning). The first time I went to bed with Steven someone from the bank phoned. I had to answer with no knickers on and Steven stroking my bottom.

As the green fields outside the window give way to the unlovely backs of houses, so my contemplative mood is overtaken by a ripple of excitement. I always get a surge of adrenalin arriving at a mainline station.

When I'm through the ticket barrier I stop for a moment and look around: all those people, all those destinations. A group of Japanese tourists gather next to me and I'm caught up by thoughts of where they've come from, what their own homes are like. One of them, a small slightly-built man with glasses, asks me where nearest McDonald's. I direct him and he thanks me, saying Manchester very nice place.

A flush of pleasure washes over me, as though Manchester's niceness were all my own doing. Somehow this meeting combines to increase the inexplicable excitement I'm feeling already. It's as though my consciousness is moving on to another, higher plane. As I watch them walk away I see my life in a new perspective. I'm here, I'm alive and I'm in love. Life is good.

I've noticed before how, if you're in a positive mood, good things seem to happen. The cynic would say, of course, that it's simply that your positive mood affects the way you perceive what might otherwise be unremarkable events. Or if the events *are* remarkable, that it's just coincidence. This is what I think too, being a cynic myself, but sometimes things happen to make you sit up and think. I once needed two hundred pounds in an emergency. I prayed and prayed for it and the next day a cheque for that precise amount arrived in the post.

I'm reminded of all this when the first bookshop I go into has both the books I need. It isn't quite as satisfying as a cheque in my name, but still it's a rare enough happening and the sort of thing that makes you think either everything is going to go your way or something nasty and unforeseen is waiting round the corner. (In the case of the cheque, it was: I got a bill for tax arrears only days later.) But today I can only think of good things. I reflect now that the train arrived on time, another unusual occurrence, and that the gang of noisy teenagers I had noticed on the platform and whose enormous tape deck would have ruined my journey, had got into a carriage further down. Even the assistant who wraps my books is smiling; she tells me she may get *Look Better in 28 Days* herself. (She's not a day over twenty, with the complexion of a two year old.) Clearly this is a day on which nothing can go wrong.

A book sale is in progress and, on this wave of feel-good emotion, I decide to choose books for everyone. Carol is a great reader; Dan isn't but ought to be; the kids would prefer comics but have to be set a good example.

I choose the Whitbread winner for Dan, another Margaret Atwood for Carol, a book on birdwatching for each of the girls, and books on fossils for the boys. I'm on way to the cash desk, weighed down by improving literature but buoyed up by good intentions, when something else catches my eye. *Is There Sex After Forty?* It's a slim volume of cartoons and wacky advice, seemingly leading to the conclusion: 'Yes there is, if you don't mind having it with people who are as fat, old and ugly as you are.' I snap it up for Dan, and immediately feel that if he's entitled to fun then the kids should be also. I dump the nature books along with the Whitbread winner, and gather a random selection of comics that includes the *Beano*, *Smash Hits* and *Mad*. And then I have another idea. Maybe the shop has Max's book on early theatre.

The history section is tucked away around a corner — and I see what I'm looking for almost immediately: M. P. Lawson, *Medieval Mysteries: A New Perspective*. It sounds deadly dull — that's bound to be it. I can't quite reach it, loaded up as I am with magazines that threaten to slide from my grasp, besides which a man is standing directly in front, blocking my way. As my eyes drill into his back, willing him to move, he reminds me, just for a moment, of Max. It must be the combination of the bookish setting, us having been students together, and his being on my mind right now. But it hits me that I have been expecting to see him all along. It used to happen constantly — I was always seeing his figure disappearing through a doorway, round a corner, driving off at speed — mostly when he was on the other side of the country. I had a fantasy in those days, that it would really be him not wanting me to see him, just to be near where I was. Pathetic, I know. Sometimes, in my clearer moments, I could have cried for myself. But self delusion makes all things bearable.

The book the man has taken from the shelf is the very one I want. As I gasp in irritation, Dan's book of cartoons slides off the top of the pile of magazines I'm holding. As I lunge to stop it, the parcel of books also slips, taking the Margaret Atwood with it. I cling on to *Smash Hits*, but succeed only in retaining the cover, the innards scattering around my feet. A loud thud is followed by a gentle rustling.

Suddenly the day seems full not of good things but

only of bad — I shouted at Rebecca this morning for getting chocolate on her new sweater, caught my heel in a flagstone as I walked to the station, scuffing the leather; the kids had eaten all the Raisin Bran, leaving me with corn flakes which I hate.

As I bend to gather my things, the day has taken on a different hue. Absently, I notice the shoes of the man who has been blocking my way. Shiny brown shoes, unusually broad and heavily creased at the point where the toes join the foot. A slow queasy feeling of butterflies — of butterflies vomiting — develops in my stomach. I don't know whether it's excitement or dread, but it's a long time before I find the strength to stand up. As I do so, he turns towards me.

I wish I could say I am delighted, that my heart has missed a beat and it is love at second sight. In fact, it is like my tombstone being lifted, to reveal dozens of scuttling insects underneath. A blank, deathlike expression passes fleetingly across his face, but then he starts to laugh.

'Good Lord,' says Max, 'it's Ellie.'

Chapter 19

Max folds his arms across his chest and looks me up and down, smiling. 'Are you well?'

'Yes, thanks. You?'

'Oh, tolerably. Carol's husband — forget his name — said you were visiting. But I never thought to see you.' I smile wryly at the conclusion he has drawn which was so different from my own. 'Is she with you?' He looks around as though Carol might appear round the corner.

'I'm on my own — not even got the kids with me.' Damn, why did I mention them? I change tack fast. 'I'm doing some research for a piece I'm writing.'

'You're a writer too? I'm impressed. What line are you in?' I'm disappointed that he hadn't found this information out from Dan. I'm also embarrassed when I notice his own book still in his hand as he turns it round and round. He thinks I mean I write books.

'I'm a journalist,' I say, moving on swiftly before he can ask for details. 'I hear you write on theatre history.'

'Yes.' He holds the book up for me to see. 'Not exactly bestseller stuff.' He manages to sound modest while implying that his book is superior to that category.

'And you're a journalist? I didn't know you wanted to do that. Is this on a newspaper or a periodical?'

'Newspaper.'

'I knew you'd get on. Well done.' For a moment an expression of tenderness crosses his face and then it is gone. Perhaps I didn't see it, just wanted to. Whichever, it calms my racing pulse and any lingering fear that he might belittle my achievements. Hell, I can always do that by myself.

'I'm just on a local paper,' I tell him (who cares what he thinks anyway?), 'nothing very grand, but it's the area I always wanted to be in and it's flexible. It's unfashionable to say it, but mothers still have to fit their lives round their children.' Why shouldn't I say what I feel?

He nods sagely and indicates the comics I'm still holding. 'I take it that's who those are for.' He goes on to ask about my children, their names and ages, while I hide Dan's cartoon book under *Smash Hits*, wishing I'd stuck with the Whitbread winner and the books on fossils. Even though I don't care what he thinks, I don't want him to think the wrong thing.

He tells me about the book he is currently working on, and that he is staying in Manchester only temporarily while he does some research, and we discuss the relative merits of Manchester and London, where he lives. I'm interested in the minutiae of his life, not the broad spectrum, but there's only so much you can ask in the way of small talk with someone you haven't met for fifteen years. The boundaries over which we may not cross without appearing to pry are soon reached. When I hear myself comment on the dryness of the summer we're having I acknowledge, with something akin to relief, that it's time to draw the meeting to a close.

'Better get these paid for,' I say, foolishly, of the books and magazines on which I still have only a precarious grip. But I don't move, giving him a chance to make me linger if he wants to.

'It's been lovely to see you,' he says, with the sort of fond smile you would give a child. I feel I've been dismissed.

As I stand in the queue at the cash desk, I wonder whether I've missed an opportunity or had a narrow escape. Perhaps I should have got his number. Maybe it's a good thing I didn't get his number. I glance back over my shoulder and at that moment he appears round the corner of the literary criticism section. He sees me looking and smiles, embarrassing me; he could think I was looking out for him. *Smash Hits* starts to slide from my grip and as he approaches he catches it before it hits the floor.

'Please, let me help you with those.' He takes the comics from me and looks bemused when he catches sight of *Is There Sex After Forty*? 'I was just thinking, if you're in no hurry, perhaps we could have coffee? It seems a shame to bump into each other like this and not take advantage of it.'

I'm so astonished at this twist of fate that I hesitate in answering, which Max takes as prevarication.

'Come on,' he says, in those old wheedling tones that time hasn't altered, 'just ten minutes. I'll take you to the Royal Exchange. The coffee is absolutely divine, you'll love it.' His voice, so richly familiar, warms me down to my feet. 'And the company will make it even better,' he adds, turning on me the full force of his charm. Suddenly I'm glad I didn't get his number; I don't need it. It's the pleasure of the sentimental and memories savoured that I'm experiencing, not reality; he is nothing but an old photograph discovered in an attic. It's strange to be able to stand back and view objectively someone you have loved so deeply. Why has his memory had so much power over me?

The shops of the Royal Exchange are dark and atmospheric. As Max holds open the glass door for me, a heavy aroma of spices and men's aftershave wafts towards us. I carry my purchases to a table in the corner while Max buys the coffee. Odd that the only table vacant should be the same one I sat at with Carol when we visited two years ago. If I'd known then that I would one day sit here with my old love, what would I have thought?

He leans forward a little on the counter, chatting to the horsy-looking assistant, who is charmed. I used to think he was so distinguished and distinctive, but is Dan right in believing that that was just a pose? He takes his change and checks it briefly in his palm; is there a small affectation in the turn of his head?

He slides the cappuccinos on to a tray along with two Danish pastries and, as he carries them carefully, beaming so broad and warm, I think, How can I be so unkind? This is a man with whom I loved and who loved me (loosely speaking). I spent countless too-short hours squeezed into a single bed with him. Why am I being so uncharitable?

But this isn't lack of charity, it's just that I'm seeing him as other people do. I'm Titania, with the spell lifted and new glasses.

'So do tell — are you happily married?'

'Oh, very.' I laugh gaily and hear Dan whisper in my ear, 'You made the right choice with Robert.'

'I made the right choice in Robert,' I say, and feel a blush surge up from my neck. Why the hell did I say that?

IMMACULATE MISCONCEPTIONS

'Absolutely. Solid as a rock, old Robert.' He means that Robert is reliable if dull and uninteresting. 'I remember him telling me he wanted to be a director by the time he was thirty. Did he make it?'

'Oh, that ambition changed once he got out in the market place. The trouble is, once you're promoted above a certain level, it's all admin and management skills, and you lose touch with the subject that brought you into the business.' (Or: 'No he didn't', as you might say.)

'That's where the academic life is so blessed. The more successful you become, the more you can afford to write – which is to say, the more time you can spend on the subject you enjoy. In a sense that's even been true with the bookshop. I employ someone to manage it now, which means that I can enjoy the books without any of the tediousness of having to serve people.'

'Did you ever serve people?' I can't keep astonishment entirely out of my voice.

He laughs. 'No, not really. I wasn't very good at it. The general public can be very quarrelsome and argumentative.'

I attack my Danish pastry with my fork so he won't see me smiling.

'Are you married?' I'm glad the conversation has moved into the area where I can ask this without feeling self conscious, but as I do so I realise that the answer no longer matters as once it did; his voice isn't so provocative nor his presence so irresistible as they were. Meeting him again has exorcised my fascination.

'I was, just briefly. Sweet girl but it didn't work out. She was French and we lived there for a while. But when I had to come back to England she couldn't settle. Terrible cook too.'

'Poor you.' I'm being sarcastic — let him do his own cooking.

But he goes on, 'You know what every man is supposed to want — an angel in the kitchen and a whore in the bedroom? Well, she was a whore in the kitchen.' He laughs, so I laugh too, pretending I haven't heard it before.

'I'm a whore in the kitchen too, but it's got nothing to do with how I cook.' I'm thinking of Steven and my kitchen table as I say this, but it sounds like I'm flirting. Which is ridiculous. He tries to hold my gaze but I go back to sawing through the Danish pastry. 'What men actually want', I say, 'is some sort of sex machine that can also clean up — half whore, half hoover.'

I expect him to laugh; if there's one thing I can't stand it's a man without a sense of humour. But he just jabs the air with his dessert fork. 'So you're a feminist these days. Good for you.'

He hasn't quite lost the knack of needling me, but I let it wash over me. Being with him is like watching old home movies: They remind you of past felt emotions without quite enabling you to recapture them.

His eyes are as dark and long lashed as they ever were, but his complexion is ruddier and his jawline has thickened; he has lost that gaunt high-cheekboned look that was so alluring. He looks less like Jim Morrison than Alan Morrison. (You won't know him; he used to teach geography at my grammar school. He had just the sort of jowls that Max is surely working towards.) The comparison makes me smile again, just as though I've put one over on Max. And in a way I have, because he's trying to hold my gaze again, thinking I'm still under his thumb — whereas I have crept out from under and am holding two fingers up.

'What's so funny?'

'Nothing.'

He's as irritated at having this said to him as I used to be when he said it to me, and it's encouraging to know that I can needle him too. But actually I want him to know what's making me smile. 'You suddenly reminded me of someone.'

'Someone charming, clever and dazzlingly good looking I hope?'

'No.' I keep a straight face so he'll see I mean it but he laughs uproariously. I should have produced my insult immediately, not worked up to it, because it's given him time to get one in first.

'You reminded me of someone too, when we first met.' Here it comes. 'Virginia Woolf.' Gosh, I've impressed him as someone who is both intellectual and literary — and, more importantly, wasn't she also thin? I can feel myself glowing. 'Only you're fatter, of course,' he adds, with what could be a twinkle in his eye but is really a steely glint. He's teasing me, mocking my literary achievements, drawing attention to my (slightly) increased girth. (He needn't look so smug, he has thickened in all the wrong places too, though, as so often on a man, this seems only to add to his presence and air of maturity.) So, he's still adept at spotting Achilles' heels from fifty paces — and I still haven't learnt how not to reveal them. I laugh for all the world as though I think it's funny.

'No, but seriously,' he goes on, 'you're looking wonderful.' (Perhaps my laughter wasn't as convincing as I thought.) 'Radiant. Far more . . .' He waves his fork in the air then stabs the right word with it. '. . . assured. You used to be such a nervous little thing.' I fix my face into an expression that doesn't register my offence at the way he remembers me. Of course I was always nervous; I never knew where the next psychological injury was coming from.

'Whereas you haven't changed a bit,' I say casually. 'Still the arrogant bastard you always were.' My resentment shows through only in my words; from the way I say them you would think I was joking. Which he does, because he laughs again.

'Marriage must suit you. You've developed an edge, do you know that? It's rather attractive.' I sip my cappuccino without answering. If I acknowledge his compliment he'll only add something else that will transform it into another insult.

When I've finished my Danish I'm ready to leave. Somehow the early lead I had in our conversation has slipped away from me. I invent urgent research I must do and hedge when he tries to question me on it.

'I'll give you my card.'

I'm rising to go, collecting up my books, but I haven't been quick enough.

'And give me your number, I'll give you a ring.'

I don't want to know his whereabouts, or for him to know mine, but he pushes the card into my hand.

'This is the shop address, but I'll put my home number on the back too. It's a shame when old friends lose touch. I should like to see old Robert again.'

I gather up my bags, pretending that I haven't noticed he is waiting, pen poised, to write down my phone number.

The Easter vacation. 'I'll give you a ring,' he had said. We had been dating (*dating!*) for six months, but 'I'll give you a ring' was the closest to a formal arrangement I had got out of him. Once home I hardly went out, jumped when the phone rang, made excuses to myself in my diary (entered nightly) for why I hadn't yet heard from him — lost my number, too shy, couldn't bear being apart, terrible accident . . .

'I thought you might have brought Max home for a few days,' my mother said. 'Poor Max.'

It's only when I get into a taxi at the station that I remember I didn't phone Steven.

Chapter 20

'I'm going to Oxford on Sunday. Taking our old television to the aunts.' Max could be unbearably cryptic, but I asked questions at my peril. I made some kind of non-committal sound while I tried to calculate why he was telling me this.

'Do you see much of them? Your aunts?' A question that was slightly off the point might give me a few clues.

'Good Lord, no. They keep themselves very much to themselves. A bit eccentric. But dear old ducks really, and Mum is very fond.'

'Why are you giving them your television?'

'Not my television — my mother's. The aunts' has gone on the blink and Mum thinks they can't live without it. Which they can't, actually. Mum's just bought a colour portable and she never uses the big one, so they might as well have it.'

'That's very generous.'

'Really? Wouldn't you give your aunts an old telly if they needed it?'

However carefully I covered my tracks I always landed in the wrong somehow. And I still wasn't sure why he was telling me. I mean, Max didn't just offer up this sort of personal information about his activities without a reason.

'So, will you be coming?'

I stopped myself just in time from falling to my knees with gratitude at being asked. After all, it was quite possible that his question. was entirely unrelated to the trip to Oxford, and could turn out to mean, 'Will you be coming to the Students' Union later?' Or even, 'Will you be coming to the front door with me?' He was quite capable of arranging this sort of confusion as entertainment.

'Are you inviting me?'

'No, of course I'm not inviting you.' There was a pause while he waited for my next question but I refused to come up with one. 'I'm not inviting you, but the aunts are. Mother must have mentioned that I was knocking about with some little townie and they obviously think a trip to the country would do you good.'

I went to open the window so he wouldn't see the expression on my face. It was no good his trying to bluff it out; the fact was that he must have talked to his mother about me, and said sufficient for her to consider that we formed some kind of couple. I couldn't keep the smile from my face. A student I knew vaguely looked up as she passed and assumed I was greeting her. She waved and I waved back. My shoulders were shaking with laughter and I had to put my fist in my mouth to keep quiet.

'Ellie, are you crying?' He sounded incredulous rather than sympathetic but, nevertheless, he came and put his arms round me.

'Of course I'm not crying,' I said. 'You fool.'

He rubbed his nose against mine, Eskimo fashion. 'Ten o'clock Sunday,' he said. 'And don't be late, I'm not waiting for you.'

* * *

It was difficult choosing what to wear that would favourably impress two eccentric aunts and yet not strike Max as frumpish or old fashioned. When I consulted my wardrobe, however, the choice was made for me. I wore suede boots under my best cheesecloth skirt, and a neat little top (it clung to my breasts, which I hoped would appeal to Max) with a long cardigan over it. Demure but elegant.

'I don't know where you think you're going,' Max said, looking me up and down, when he arrived.

I offered to change into something else but he wouldn't hear of it, saying there wasn't time, although I'm certain the real reason was that he liked knowing that he had made me uncomfortable. When we pulled up outside the aunts' double-fronted Edwardian house he said, 'I hope they like you.'

'Why shouldn't they?' I exclaimed with a confidence I didn't feel.

In fact the aunts were charming. Elsie was small and thin with her hair cut into a silver cap, while Marjorie was younger, perhaps early sixties, and still upright and stately. They came to the door together and Elsie at once came forward and took my hand to lead me in. 'Maxwell, she's delightful,' she called over her shoulder. 'Where have you been hiding her, you naughty boy?' I turned to look at Max but he was in conversation with Marjorie and had missed hearing my compliment.

The house had once been a vicarage, and Elsie and Marjorie had lived in it all their lives. Occasional tables of oak or mahogany filled the few gaps between the large chairs and heavy sofas. A portrait of their father gazed down contentedly from above the fireplace.

'Thank goodness you've brought the tellybox,' said

Marjorie appreciatively as Max carried it in. It looked incongruous set next to an ormolu clock on top of the carved and polished card table, but the ladies were delighted. Max plugged it in and adjusted the aerial.

'Ssshh, it's Harry Secombe.' We sat in silence while he finished his song and then the aunts applauded. Elsie switched it off just a trifle sorrowfully.

Marjorie made tea and we sat round the large ugly fireplace while she poured Earl Grey into china cups. I was surprised, when their possessions seemed so beautiful, to find that the cup she handed me had a brown crack running down it. In fact, when the level of tea went down as I drank, I saw that the cup had broken and been stuck back together. The seam of white glue was clearly visible in places. They were strange cups too; very round, with too small handles, the saucers wide and flat with unnaturally high rims. The edge of each piece was a brilliant but gaudy green.

'I see Eleanor is admiring our cups,' Elsie said to Marjorie, embarrassing me for having noticed the state of them.

But Marjorie smiled proudly. 'Only four of them left, I'm afraid. There were six, but Charlie broke two walking on the draining board.'

A friend of theirs was to join us for lunch. Was that Charlie? They were too old for it to be a child, though perhaps one might visit. I could see why Max thought them eccentric.

'Charlie is . . . ?' I ventured.

'He's sitting under Max's chair. Such a rascal.' A large Burmese stretched itself out from under the chair, kneading the rug with its paws as it did so.

'They were made in the mid eighteenth century,' said

Elsie, holding her cup up and perusing it happily. 'They are beautiful, aren't they? I love to imagine all the changes they've seen. But we only get them out for visitors.'

My hand was trembling as I replaced the cup on the saucer. I refused a second cup of tea.

After lunch the aunts' friend took Max round the garden to show him the progress of some shrubs he had planted for them, and I sat with the women in the conservatory. They were serene and gentle, and they made me feel comfortable and welcome among them.

At last Elsie placed her hand on my knee. 'We're so pleased to meet you, my dear. You know Max is a dear sweet boy, but his mother has been very worried about him. He has mixed with some rather unfortunate types in the past. A good steady girl like you is just what we've been praying for for him.'

I hadn't realised I was being vetted, but what did it matter, seeing as I had evidently passed. They asked about my family and seemed surprised that my father had been only a railway booking clerk. But I'm proud of how my parents helped me get on, despite their own lowly (as Max would say) origins.

'It was so kind of you to ask me here,' I said, when conversation lapsed a little. 'Max is so secretive about his life, I really know very little about him.'

The aunts nodded and I saw a look pass between them. I thought Marjorie was about to speak, and that perhaps at last I would discover a little more of his history, but at that moment Max and the aunts' friend started back in our direction.

'Ah, here they come,' said Marjorie. 'I'll make us some fresh tea.'

* * *

Travelling home that evening, I was filled with lightness and gaiety. Things were working out my way. So much of Max's behaviour was just a bluff, then — some kind of façade to conceal his true feelings. Well, now I knew, I could deal with that.

'Your aunts were wonderful,' I said. 'And I think they liked me.'

'Yes, they did rather. And I thought you handled the whole thing rather well.'

'Wasn't anything to handle, was there?'

He laughed, the cold harsh laugh that always acted as a warning, and I felt a sense of dread flow over me like cold water dripping down from my hair. 'They were a bit astonished to find out your father was a booking clerk — so was I, come to that. They thought he was a foreign diplomat.'

'Why ever would they think that?'

'They obviously got confused when Mum was telling them about some of my friends.' He paused, just briefly, ready for the strike. 'You did realise they had you confused with another girl?'

I rehearsed saying lightly that of course I realised, and it was of no significance as they liked me anyway. But suddenly my tongue felt swollen and fat and, besides, I couldn't find the words that would prove I believed it.

Max laid his hand on my thigh briefly. 'Anyway, who cares what two batty old women think?'

I wasn't fooled by his pretence at offering comfort. What he was really doing was making the fact of their liking me worthless. My face was turned to the side window, but I could feel his eyes looking at me, trying to see how upset I was. He always liked to measure the effect of his unkindnesses; with Max every silver lining had a cloud. For every pleasure there was pain not far behind.

Chapter 21

As we hug farewell at the station, Carol assures me that now I've had a short break from routine I'll be able to see everything in a whole new light. I do, too, but the light I see things in is that of a dim and guttering candle in which Steven provides the only ray of warmth. (Max whispers in my head that Steven isn't the *only* ray, but he's wrong.) But I protect Carol from this insight, seeing that she has made such a great PR effort on behalf of Robert.

Robert. I feel an inexplicable irritation at the thought of him, which is somehow made worse for not having seen him for over a week. In the flesh, his presence has a moderating effect on my antagonism; left to itself, it seems to be running riot.

'Come up again at half term,' Carol is saying, 'and make Robert come with you. We haven't seen him for ages and Dan really misses him.' I say of course we'll come, and try to look as though I mean it.

On the train the kids settle down with comics and I read a magazine article on self-hypnosis. It explains how to lull yourself into a trance-like state while envisaging attitudes or behaviour you would like to have. I focus on being a better wife, on feeling more contented and less hostile to Robert. I'm dragged out of the trance rather more quickly than recommended by Rebecca's urgent need for the toilet, but as I come to I feel surprisingly buoyant. Perhaps my problem is just that I get too intense about things, what I need is meditation, more thoughtful reflection, to learn to relax. Of course, one session of self-hypnosis on a crowded InterCity, with a toddler being sick in the seat behind isn't likely to achieve much, but it's a start, and it'll be interesting to see if it makes any difference to my feelings when I actually see Robert.

I get off the train feeling warm and receptive towards him. It'll be nice to see him, after all. We'll be a family again; and I always think it's romantic to be met at the station. I hurry the kids along with the cases, excited at my own revised behaviour.

The surge of rage I experience when he isn't outside waiting comes over me with the speed and force of an express train passing through a station it isn't stopping at. I toss the magazine into the rubbish bin (self-hypnosis? Self bloody delusion more like), but then have to despatch Simon to get it back because I need the editorial address for future reference.

By the time Simon returns with the magazine we've moved to the head the taxi queue, and I open the door and slide the luggage in.

'Why aren't we waiting for Daddy?' asks Rebecca, who knows that Robert is always late and will arrive in a minute or two. We set off and, as the taxi pulls up to the traffic lights, I see his car go past. The kids are looking out of the other window. I don't say anything.

Rebecca and Simon are delighted to be home. Simon races into the garden to check the well-being of the guinea pigs, while Rebecca tries to caress our disdainful cats, Trevor and Ginge, who have taken umbrage at our absence. For me, though, the house has no welcome. Although the sun is shining, the lounge seems smaller and darker than I remembered, the hall narrower. It seems as though I have been away for a decade and the accommodation has shrunk and shrivelled in the interim, a disappointing replica of its old self, enclosed and devoid of the essential spark. It's like a dead thing, with the spirit gone.

Suddenly the get well card Simon made for me catches my eye. It has been on display for almost six months now, waiting for me to find the heart to put it away. I remember how I felt then, coming home from hospital, as though a new life was waiting, with opportunities to be sought, fresh hope ahead. Well, where is it? Why should I have to live here just because Robert works in this town? Maybe the kids really would be better off in the countryside with Carol, living on wholesome home-grown food and attending a little village school with no crime, even if it would make them sound like characters out of the Famous Five books. Something has to happen; something has to change.

Right on cue the phone rings. To have your prayers answered so swiftly shakes you a bit, and my heart is beating when I pick up the receiver. I almost expect to hear God on the line telling me what he has in store. But it isn't God, it's Theresa.

'Oh, hello, I thought you might not be back yet.'

I wonder why she's ringing me if she thought that, but as she's my boss I don't say anything. She sounds somehow different from usual and I'm eager to know what she wants. I have a feeling it isn't just about my next piece, 'Short Cuts to Perfect Pastry'.

'Yes, we've just walked in. What can I do for you?'

'Oh . . . well, you'll find out anyway but I thought it was my place to tell you . . .' So that's it. The deputy editor's left and she's getting his job. She's talked of this in the past – and now they're going to offer me hers. Working on the women's page of the local paper could sound quite impressive if you had charge of it. ('What do you do?' 'I'm a journalist. Editor of the Woman's Page.') And I'd have an assistant. Plus I'd be on a career ladder; I could move up, the way she's doing. And now at last I can have a go at some of the interesting pieces Theresa always squashes. I make a quick deal with God: okay, I'll stay with Robert and try to be happy in exchange for Theresa's job.

'It's bad news, I'm afraid,' she's saying. I'm still smiling, thinking I've misunderstood. 'They're cutting back. Reducing the women's page to half . . .'

I am a long time understanding the significance of her words. Perhaps it's always like that for those who suddenly find their services redundant. How can the paper survive without me? My half-page of perfect prose is the only bit worth reading. Yet someone thinks it can, because they're giving me a fortnight's notice. From now on they just want one item a week which Theresa will do.

'I'm so sorry,' Theresa says with a shake in her voice, and I realise that she has enjoyed our editorial coffee mornings as much as I have. 'I didn't want you finding out from a letter.'

I tell her I understand, surprised to hear how calm I sound, but it's just that the time for tears is not yet, I'm too shocked to take it in. I assumed that my job was a forever present, like finding water in the tap when you turn it on. Clichés such as 'having the rug pulled out from under your feet' clamour round inside my head.

I catch sight of myself in the mirror over the telephone table and notice the bags under my eyes, and the way my cardigan makes my shoulders seem to droop. When I put down the phone, the walls of the already shrunken hall come squeezing in on me, elongating until I'm standing in a long thin tunnel down which I must walk, with no suggestion of interest or colour on the journey and no light at the end of it. Even the guttering candle has gone out.

I'm still standing there when Robert arrives.

'Ellie? Are you all right? Not going to faint, are you?' He looks tired and drawn, but most of all he looks puzzled. 'Why didn't you wait for me? I saw you in the taxi. Did you forget I was coming?' I start to say yes, unable to explain why I waited less than five minutes, but knowing that I've been punished for it — and then the kids come in to kiss and hug him and I sit down so that the dizzy feeling starts to fade, while the kids clamber over him and make him forget his disappointment.

When they finally let him go I tell him about Theresa's phone call. He shrugs resignedly. 'Cutbacks are everywhere. No one's safe. You've been lucky to have your job as long as you have.' I should have preferred some show of the outright indignation I feel myself, along with a declaration that the entire newspaper group would be bankrupt within a month and the MD would burn in hell but his words are comforting, and I'm chastened to realise that I still need his moral support. (His financial support, of course, I'll need more than ever.)

Later, when I have told him all about our stay with Carol (the endless walks, the day at Alton Towers and the party, but have somehow forgotten to make any mention of Max), he says, 'Oh by the way, Steve said he'll drop round this afternoon. He sounds very excited about this new course.'

My mood shifts as swiftly as if I've just changed a TV channel with the remote control, and I give him an enormous hug in gratitude for the good news. The imminent arrival of Steven is as good as an Elastoplast over the wound of my lost job.

'I've missed you,' Robert murmurs into my hair, caressing my back.

'And I've missed you,' I say, trying to mean it, trying not to think of Steven, trying to forget about Max.

I don't have to try not to think of Steven for very long, because he arrives within the hour. The sensation of seeing him, the sunlight making a halo around him as he stands in the doorway, is almost like a religious experience. I draw him in quickly, accidentally cutting off Robert in mid-sentence as he shouts something from where he lies on his back under the car in the drive. Steven turns and waves to him but I pull him indoors before he can get into conversation.

He has grown taller in a week, and his lashes are even darker, his eyes yet more heavy-lidded, come-to-bedded. But the dimples in his cheeks are turning to gaunt lines, and he's a little thinner in the face. The feelings he inspires are the opposite to those the house gave me: he's all light and air, hope and the promise of pleasure. But there is nowhere we can be alone together, what with the kids playing upstairs and Robert liable to glance through the lounge window at any time or appear in the kitchen looking for Swarfega. The safest place is right here, behind the front door. My arms go round him and he clings to me tightly, urgent and desperate. His chest is warm through his shirt and he smells of aftershave, but also of his own smell which is both soothing and exciting.

'I've missed you,' he says into my hair.

'And I've missed you,' I say. I don't think of Robert at all.

We go through to the kitchen — where at least we'll have Robert's footsteps and the unoiled latch on the back gate to warn of his approach; a face at the lounge window would be a silent intrusion we might miss — and sit at the kitchen table. (Our table: the table where we made love. Other people have a special tune to remind them of romantic moments. I have a piece of furniture.) I open *Cider with Rosie* and arrange his A4 pad so that it looks like we're working. Then I slip my feet from my sandals and rest them on his shoes. He squeezes my fingers and we gaze at each other. The agony of longing is unbearable and delicious.

'You didn't ring me,' he says.

'You didn't ring me,' I said to Max. The Easter vacation from college had come and gone without the looked-for call. The only time he had promised such a thing. When I first saw him again he didn't mention it so I didn't either, unwilling to give myself away. Several days passed before I asked him.

'Did I say I'd phone?' he said. 'I must have been busy. I was in Germany all Easter and there were people around all the time . . . We had a wonderful time — this girl I was staying with . . .'

'I'm sorry. I wanted to,' I tell Steven, 'but there were people around all the time — the kids, or Carol — I didn't get a moment to myself. Besides, I was a bit worried what

Rita might think — what reason could I have given for needing to talk to you?'

'I'd given her a reason.' Is there a suggestion of sullenness in his face? 'I told her I was stuck on my studying and Robert was going to ask you to ring. Robert's supposed to have told you all that.'

He had told me, I'd forgotten. 'He must have forgotten. I'm sorry. I've been desperate to talk to you. It's been the longest week of my life.'

The pout leaves his lips and he smiles. His mouth is wide and sweet and it becomes impossible to sit here so close without touching it. I begin to trace the outline of his lips with my forefinger and he opens his mouth to suck it. I wriggle my feet inside the legs of his jeans until I can feel flesh, and scratch one leg with my toe nail. He gasps faintly with surprise. 'Bitch,' he whispers, and takes a second finger into his mouth. Our eyes are locked together. I think I may come just sitting here.

'Make us a coffee would you?' Robert must have left the back gate open and, of course, he's wearing trainers, that's why we haven't heard him come in. I begin to stand up but my feet are caught in the ankles of Steven's jeans and I have to grasp the table to stop myself toppling backwards. Fortunately Robert is studying the oil on his hands and goes straight to the tap without looking at us. All the same I can feel myself blushing.

'You okay?' he says, as I stand next to him to fill the kettle. 'You're looking very flushed. Not going down with something, are you? I thought you looked rough when you got home.'

I make the coffee and Robert brings his to the table and sits down with us. He begins relating some tale about the carburettor, which Steven seems to know something about — remarkable considering he doesn't even have a car and cannot, as far as I know, even drive. I feel the same swelling of pride in the breast I get when Simon or Rebecca displays some unexpected gift.

'Shall I have a look at it?' Steven drains his cup and starts to get up. I've noticed how Steven loves to do things with Robert, listens to what he says, follows his lead. When Robert tells him something — about the car, the garden, the house painting — he listens with a sharpness and intensity he doesn't give me, no matter how fascinating I'm being about *Cider with Rosie*.

'It's okay, Steve, you're in the middle of your work.' Robert hasn't forgotten why Steven is supposed to be here even if Steven has.

Steven catches my eye and has the grace to look embarrassed. 'Ellie, would you mind . . . ?'

What can I say? so I answer, 'Of course not,' but do it with bad grace and then see them exchange 'We're in the doghouse' type glances. Bloody men.

Seeing Steven preparing to get under the car in the shirt I thought he'd chosen specially to please me, I fetch him an old one of Robert's to change into (watching with apparent casualness as he undresses), and then go next door to see Josie.

She is in her back garden reclining on one of those sofas that swing and are covered by canopies. It's brand new, and still has the plastic cover on the seat. A glass of white wine is on a table next to her, and she's wearing headphones and reading a magazine, idly drumming out a rhythm on the table with one manicured hand. I remember Max catching me with my arms full of washing and wonder why I don't seem to project this sort of glamour and grace when my visitors arrive unexpectedly.

She looks up as I approach and smiles with perfect teeth as she removes the headphones.

'Ellie! You look wonderful.' Even though this is her standard form of greeting lately, my travel-weary face is glad of it. She brings a glass out for me and immediately I start telling her about Steven going off with Robert and wasting our precious time and after he'd made such a thing of missing me too.

Josie thinks I'm being too hard on him. 'He's looking for a father figure, that's all. He's got no dad and he lost his brother; he just needs an older man to look up to. It won't be that he doesn't want you. It's that, seeing as he can't have you, he thinks he might as well be doing something with Robert. He kissed you didn't he?'

I nod.

'Well there you are, then. He got what he came for, and he can see he can't get any more.'

'But I just wanted to talk to him.' I know I sound pathetic, but I feel pathetic.

'If you'd just wanted to talk to him, you'd have phoned when you said you would.' As a ploy for sympathy I told Josie that not only have I been deprived of a few hours of Steven's company, but we haven't even spoken by phone for over a week. 'Anyway, *you* might want to talk, but if that's all *he* wants, then he's not like any man *I* know. And naturally he'd rather be stripping down some engine than doing his GCSE work. Bloody hell, *I'd* rather strip down an engine than do a GCSE. He's a red-blooded bloke, Ellie, it's what they're like.'

'Max isn't.'

'Who's Max?'

'And what about Greg?' I didn't mean to mention Max, and I'm glad to be able to convert my comment into a dig at Greg. I still haven't met him, but that doesn't stop me not liking him.

'Oh, Greg, well, he's different. Anyway, I've got something to tell you. About Greg and me . . .' I don't want to hear about Greg and his wonderful good-in-bedness. I want to keep talking about me.

'What's happened?' Let's get it over with.

'He's leaving his wife for me.'

'*What?*' I feel as shocked as if Sweep were leaving Sooty. Josie and Greg are just having an affair, for goodness' sake — it can't become permanent.

'Isn't it incredible? He's leaving in a week or so and we're going to move in together.'

I don't know how to respond to this. I can see that the seeds of disaster are being sown, but how to convey the knowledge to Josie? There's as much chance of her taking my advice as there is of it not raining on a bank holiday.

'Josie, don't do anything hasty.'

'Hasty? How many years have I been waiting? And now it's going to pay off. Say you wish me well.'

'Of course I do,' I say, and I mean it, only not with Greg. I still believe she will fall back in love with David given time.

There seems nowhere else for the conversation to lead and Josie has retreated into blissful dreaminess, so we sit in silence for some minutes nursing our wine. Eventually she rouses herself to ask about my holiday with Carol but I've lost the energy to tell her, and now I have to cover up my slip about Max. She has tunnel vision when it comes to relationships and she'll never believe that old flames can go out, especially one I've kept burning for so long. She goes indoors to top up our glasses, giving me an opportunity to get my story straight. She might just have forgotten my reference to Max, but if she hasn't then all I need to do is convert Max into Larry — say that he was a friend of Carol's who came to entertain the children. And that he was a bookish, child-like man which is why he wouldn't spend time on stripping down an engine.

'So,' she says, handing me a fresh glass of wine. 'This Max, where did you meet him?'

'We were at college together,' I say.

Well, I suppose I wanted to tell her really. I had told Carol of course, but only the facts of it: meeting him in the bookshop; having coffee. It was only gradually that the implications of it were bearing down upon me. It was such a strange experience — bizarre, that something you've secretly hoped for should so astonish you when it comes true. But then it was the sort of dream, like becoming rich and famous, that you don't expect can ever happen. Now it has, I feel somehow empty; a cherished longing has evaporated and left nothing in its place. I ought to feel relieved that I can work out the answers now to the old 'What if' questions, proud that I'm no longer taken in by Max's pose of superiority. But instead I want to go back to before that time, when I still thought the love of my life was someone unfathomable and exquisite.

I tell Josie all this, and see the look of the scavenger in her eyes. She can't wait to start picking over the bones.

'Have you got his number?' she says.

I tell her I haven't.

When I get back home again Steven is sitting on the front

step. He stands when he sees me and leans against the door frame with his hands in his pockets, wearing the expression of someone who is proud of himself and expects to be congratulated.

'Where's Robert?' The car's gone, but Robert could just have put it away in the garage, and I don't want to say something incriminating and then have him appearing round the corner.

'It's okay. He's gone to fetch a spare part. Taken the kids with him.' He grins broadly.

'How long will he be?' To think I've been killing time round at Josie's.

'He's only just set off. It won't take less than an hour. He's got to go to the main dealer.' His grin grows even wider and he strokes a finger down my cheek.

Suddenly wild fire is tearing through my veins. I push Steven back into the house, slamming the door behind us and, taking hold of Robert's shirt with both hands, tear it open, laughing at the sound of ripping cloth and flying buttons; laughing less as Steven's glistening chest is exposed and that terrible ache takes hold of my body. Hot needles are pricking at my nipples and in my pants. I take his hand to lead him upstairs but we can't wait that long. He pulls my pants down and slips his hand inside in a single movement.

We make love where we are, with my legs wrapped round his waist and my arms clinging tight round his neck.

By the time Robert gets back from the garage, I've finished mopping the stains from the hall carpet and Steven and I are in the kitchen having a post-coital coffee, deeply engrossed in *Cider with Rosie*. 'I didn't need the part in

271

the end,' he tells Steven, going to the sink to wash his hands. 'Jeff, the guy who usually services the car, took a quick look for me – he reckons it just needed a bit of adjustment.'

Steven says he's glad to hear it, but the look he gives me says he isn't exactly surprised.

After Steven has gone home, the phone rings. For one stomach-churning moment I expect it to be Max, somehow conjured up by my conversation with Josie – but it's Eileen. At first I can't think who Eileen is, but then I remember it's the novelist from the banquet, wife of Hugo – the one who made me green with envy and red with embarrassment. Remembering her comment about people who have affairs, I blush again.

'I'm organising the charity second-hand clothes sale this year,' she says, 'and I just saw your name on the rota. I had no idea you lived near us.' In fact we don't live all that near, but the charity clothes sale attracts women from a wide area. She seems delighted to renew our acquaintance; far more pleased than she seemed at meeting me first time round. 'I didn't know you were interested in this sort of thing.' I didn't know I was either. It's one of those things where you do it once and are forever committed. When we first moved here it seemed a good idea to sell the children's clothes through this annual sale, and to pick up usable stuff for them too. But no one has wanted the things I have to sell, and the clothes we've bought have languished in the wardrobe or turned out to have hidden tears or stains I didn't notice in the poor lighting of the church hall. After last year's fiasco, when someone nearly bought Simon's new school coat which he had only taken off to try on an old sweatshirt, I swore I'd never go again. ('This one hasn't got a price on it.' 'Oh, call it three pounds;

it's got a mark on the sleeve.' Three pounds? I'd paid over twenty quid for it in BHS only a fortnight before.)

I tell Eileen I have to check I'm available on that date, but I know that the calendar will be yawning empty and that without a bona fide excuse I lack the resistance to turn her down.

'Some of them said you wouldn't do it again, but I knew I could rely on you,' she says with satisfaction, ringing off.

I've hardly seen Steven this week. Not only are the kids constantly around, but he has got a job house-painting for Freda, one of our neighbours, who has got him doing work inside as well as out. For all Robert's initial reservations, Steven's decorating skills have turned out to be surprisingly good. In the winter, when he is no longer needed to work on our garden, perhaps we could call him in to do our spare bedroom. For now, however, I am having to make do with stolen moments when he tells Freda he is popping out for turpentine. Since I no longer have to call in to the newspaper office (my two weeks' notice turned out to be 'pay in lieu of . . .') the highlight of my week looks like being the second-hand clothes sale. I spend Friday morning going through the kids' cupboards, discarding any items that no longer fit (which turns out to be seventy-five per cent of their belongings), and Friday afternoon making labels with our name and a price on then. Deciding the price takes an astonishingly long time: is an anorak with a torn pocket and a zip that does up only if you do it fast to skip over the bit with the teeth missing worth more than a child's dress which is in perfect condition but only cost £5.50 new?

By the time I get to the sale in the evening I'm in

the depths of depression, and being greeted at the door by Eileen doesn't help. She has come outside to snatch a quick cigarette.

'Fire hazard, with all those clothes about. But I can't face three hundred marauding women without one.'

'Three hundred? Is that what we're expecting?'

'Was last year. And you have to keep your strength up for breaking up the fights. Weren't you here last year when a woman tried to buy some kid's new coat?'

Funny, I must have missed that.

I take my clothes in and join the other mothers involved in sorting the clothes. There's a special rail for anything of particularly high quality, and as we sort I note that no one suggests anything of mine belongs there. Not even the child's dress in perfect condition (even if it was only £5.50 new).

Before the doors open for selling we take up our positions on our stalls. I'm doing baby clothes, nought to six months, along with Selina, a burly woman with glasses who looks to be in her early fifties but on acquaintance turns out to be only twenty-nine. She has two children of four and five and twins under a year old. I'm surprised she looks as young as she does.

'They're a handful, my lot,' says Selina as we watch two women eyeing each other over who has first refusal of a hand knitted matinée jacket, 'but I think I'm lucky to be able to stay home with them. My sister, she works all hours, off abroad here there, all over, and I say, Settle down, start a family before it's too late. I mean, what's the point of going all through pregnancy and everything and then not being there to enjoy them?' I nod, and take two pounds in exchange for a baby's shawl the colour of vomit. 'Do you work?' asks Selina as an afterthought.

I straighten up the matinée jackets which neither woman wanted after all. 'I never seem to stop,' I say.

After the first hour Eileen brings us a cup of tea and pauses to ask how we're doing. Actually, we're having an easy time of it, most women being interested in clothes for older children. It's unfortunate when there's so much time to chat that the only person I have to talk to is Selina. She's the type of woman who, if you gave her a computer, would try to get *EastEnders* on it.

'What brings you here, Eileen?' I ask, hoping to detain her, if only briefly. 'Your kids are older, aren't they? And I didn't take you for the committee type.'

She puts her tray down and looks around with satisfaction. 'No men here, that's what I like. No one battling their way up the career ladder, no one racing each other away from the lights and putting two fingers up. Look at us — everyone's happy. We've all got families; we're all trying to do our best for them one way or another. No bullying, no backbiting, everyone getting along.'

'It's camaraderie,' says Selina, surprising me with her long word, and then, looking at me with the attitude of one who offers advice which will prove invaluable, 'you want to come to NHR.'

'National Housewives Register,' explains Eileen helpfully. 'National Women's Register as they call it now. You'd like it.' She picks up her tray, calling over her shoulder as she moves off, 'It's full of women just like you.'

While we sort the unsold clothes into piles for collection at the end of the sale I have time to wonder. Is it the way I'm dressed? Is it my demeanour? Is it just the very fact that I'm here instead of going off abroad here, there and everywhere or engaging in activities involving ambition, backbiting and racing people away from the lights? Why does Eileen think I'm like Selina? Or could it be that, under that respectable exterior, they all — even round-faced, bespectacled Selina — have secret lovers and unutterable dreams just like mine? I'm still pondering this as I carry back to the car my pile of clothes, which is almost as big as when I arrived. However I've done better than last year. I got one pound fifty for the anorak with the faulty zip, so at least I've covered my petrol.

I've never minded Mondays: a chance to straighten the house after the weekend; the comfortable routine of having the kids back at school and Robert at work, the house to myself; and then time to plan what ideas to offer Theresa, or finish off the current piece. But not today. Today I strip the beds and know that when I have done that I have nothing else to do. Last week's Sits Vac columns offered no part-time job vacancies, and I lack the energy to tackle the job centre just yet. Besides, with the kids still home from school I'd have to take them with me, and I can't face that.

Suddenly I remember Josie. Suppose she should really leave David? Calling on her will be something to do once I've finished the beds, so with renewed vigour I gather up the sheets and carry them to the top of the stairs. The kids are playing at a house along the road but it sounds as though one of them has come back into the hall. I glance over the banister and the sheets drop from my grasp.

At the bottom of the stairs, leaning against the telephone table, stands Max.

Chapter 22

From our very first meeting at university I saw that Max was inconsistent and unreliable, but the upside of that was his ability to surprise constantly, and maybe that's what kept me hooked. Uncertainty had its own appeal, making me more grateful for the times when everything worked out right.

The other thing about him that kept me guessing was that I never knew, of the various tales he told, which ones were likely to be true — if any. There was the matter of his parentage, for example: was his mother really descended from a love child of Francis Drake, and with the documentary evidence to prove it? Had his father really spied along with Kim Philby, only deciding against defection at the eleventh hour, and doing a deal with the government that kept his activities a secret? And what about his elder brother who, he maintained, was an early lover of David Bowie and had broken his heart; or the rock group, then storming the charts, Max claimed to have smoked dope with at boarding school? Each story was more unlikely than the last, and the more I heard, the more sceptical I became, especially since my family had had no dealings with the rich and famous whatsoever (unless you count the fact that my dad once shared a urinal with Ken Dodd).

But when I had tea with the aunts it somehow emerged that the Francis Drake connection was true.

And then there was the day I turned up unexpectedly at the Students' Union. It was after I'd finished with Max — hadn't seen him for a month or more — and I was supposed to be going to the cinema with Robert. But when I called at his flat I found him ill with flu, so I beat a hasty retreat and wandered into the Union to see if Carol was about.

She saw me at the bar and came over. 'Quick, come and see this band. They're terrific.'

I'd heard music emanating from the adjoining room where groups performed, but as it was only seven o'clock it seemed too early for a band to be playing in earnest. I paid for my lager and followed her through, surprised that no one was at the door taking money although the audience was standing shoulder to shoulder. Evidently, the group had originally been setting up for a rehearsal but relaxed into a jam session which so far had lasted nearly an hour. They were a new group, Ghost. I didn't recognise the name, but three of them had got together, Carol explained, when their previous band split up after a huge and sudden chart success.

'Have you seen who's on sax?' Carol asked, nudging me. I didn't have a clear view because the room was packed and I was standing behind a man the size of the Incredible Hulk, but I could still make him out. Max was just completing a solo, red in the face, eyes closed, his face tortured with feeling. As the band rejoined him the audience broke into a round of applause.

'Did you know he could play like that?' asked Carol.

'I didn't know he could play at all.'

The sight of Max's face, bursting with all the emotions he fought so hard to conceal in daily life, exonerated all the things I had ever felt about him. It was still over between us but I was right to believe there was another, better man, hidden beneath the one he'd mostly shown to me.

It's this memory of him that springs to life now as I watch him, arms folded, waiting in the hall below. His resting face is free of that supercilious grin, the superior lift of the jaw. Maybe this time we can have a different relationship. I'm talking friendship, of course — there's no going back over old ground. But it could be rich and rewarding, a comradeship which got below the patina of the surface.

Unfortunately I can't reach below the patina of my own surface for the moment, because my next thought is that Max is standing only yards from me and I haven't got my make-up on.

Hearing my movement, he looks up. One of the children must have let him in as they went out. I say nothing and neither does he, so I have to say, 'Oh. Max,' trying to sound surprised and delighted, to break the silence. I come down the stairs, wishing there weren't so many of them (or maybe that there were many more so that I need never reach the bottom), holding on to the banister and trying not to look like I'm shaking. I'm dreaming this, I'm dreaming, I tell myself, but I never dreamt of stripping the beds before.

It's awkward being alone in the narrow hall with him and I can't think why he's here. I lean against the newel post at the bottom of the stairs, trying a casual pose, but my body has forgotten what casual means and my elbows and hands can't find what they should be doing. Somehow I want to be near him but I don't dare look him in the face.

I'll make coffee, that's what I'll do. But a magnetic pull is holding me fixed to the spot. Even at this distance the air around us is sizzling and crackling like static electricity.

At last I find something to say: 'What brings you here?' The cliché makes me blush but he answers in kind.

'I was just passing.' He swallows and indicates outside. 'A boy let me in. Your son, I think.' He feels as awkward as I do. Sensation returns to my legs now that I've rediscovered my use of speech, and the nervousness in his voice gives me confidence.

'Excuse all the mess. Come into the kitchen and I'll make us—' I'm moving past him, still avoiding his eyes in this enclosed space, but it's no good, I can't resist the pull. I turn round to face him and it's like a bolt searing through my flesh — a destructive, reckless force — but he doesn't take me in his arms in the best tradition. My God, I am thinking, surely he's old enough *now* to see how it's done. Hasn't he seen the films? No; he grips my arms to hold me off.

And it all comes back. He was always like that, even in bed; distancing me at the point of greatest intimacy, pulling away in the afterglow; withdrawal was something he understood in all its guises. God, I think, you bastard — all this time and you're still the same. My face is reddening with anger and he's still gripping my arms — the bastard. But then I look in his face and, as I do so, his hold slackens and his arms come round me, not drawing me to him but leaning towards me, so that his face rests against my neck. We stand still while I wonder what the hell this is all about — not friendship, not sex — but then I feel the muscles of his back trembling and he draws a long shuddering breath. Max is crying.

His tears are a momentary lapse. I've no sooner realised

what's happening than he has recovered himself and is turning away, brushing his fingers across his eyes. 'You must have changed your perfume,' he says. 'It never used to have that effect on me.'

I laugh at this, relieved that the awful moment has passed and we can return to being who we always pretend to be. When someone cries, what are you supposed to do? Jolly them out of it? Be sympathetic? Join in? In this instance what I've actually done is to let him lean on me while I absorb the slow discovery that Max has vulnerabilities too. In fact he has pre-empted what would surely have been my next reaction: to feel that if anyone had the right to cry it's me.

'Have you had breakfast?' I know I'm falling back into the role of housewife and provider, but you have to find some kind of activity to fill the gap between awkward silences.

'Yes, I've been up since six. Haven't you?'

'I get up with the kids when they're on holiday.' Actually this morning I got up rather a long time after them.

'So you don't have to go into work today?'

'No, I don't work Mondays.' Or Tuesdays, or Wednesdays . . .

'I didn't really expect to find you at home, but I was virtually passing your door so I thought I might as well call.'

Where we live isn't really on the way to anywhere — certainly nowhere that Max is likely to be going. But I decide not to embarrass him by following this line of questioning, even though that's what he'd do if our positions were reversed. I start to lead him into the kitchen, remembering too late that it resembled the Mad

Hatter's Tea Party when I looked in earlier. As I push the door open I catch sight of the corner of the table which is free of debris, and for one shining moment I think that the children have cleared up for me, but as the rest of the kitchen springs into view I'm soon set right. Four cereal boxes are still on the table (Simon likes a cocktail of the varieties), two cartons of orange juice (one finished and one new, to judge by the pool of spilled juice by its lip; opening the cartons always results in some minor catastrophe), the cereal bowls and glasses have been abandoned where they were set, and a piece of toast is lying on the floor. In the corner by the washing machine a festering heap of laundry is awaiting attention. If Max's tears were caused by any suggestion of regret he'll think again now. I decide to brazen it out and march over to the kettle, kicking a stray pair of my dirty pants into the pile as I pass, without mentioning the war zone we've entered.

'I'm having toast and coffee, if you'd like some.'

'No toast, thanks, but I wouldn't mind a little tea with lemon.'

I rarely buy lemons except for Pancake Day, but a few weeks ago Rebecca found a recipe for 'real' lemonade in her *Bunty* annual and begged me to buy a couple. I fish in the depths of the salad box and find half of one, mouldy down one side, in the sticky pool of water at the bottom. I carry it to the sink surreptitiously and carve at it to retrieve a bit that's free from bacteria. It looks a strange shape, but he'll never notice.

'So where was it you're off to?' I've forgotten that I didn't mean to ask this. Max pushes the breakfast detritus to one end of the table and hitches a thigh on to the corner, the other leg still on the floor. He always preferred sitting on a table to any available chairs. (Not that our chairs are available. Spilled milk has spread on to two of them and Ginge has charge of the other, batting at cornflakes with his paw.)

'I was just out driving around; I do that sometimes when I'm working on an idea. It's very relaxing, you should try it.' The idea that battling with our local one-way systems can be relaxing is a novel one, but I don't say so. 'I'm staying back at my London flat for a few days. A few fringe plays have opened that I'd like to see. I expect you go quite a lot, don't you? I remember how you loved Gilbert and Sullivan.' His sudden laugh registers astonishment at my taste along with fondness at the memory. But I've only ever seen *The Mikado*, and that was only because the college newspaper offered me free tickets if I'd write a review. It's irritating to find you've been wrongly filed away in someone's memory.

'We don't manage it very often,' I say, 'but we have seen some brilliant productions. *Aladdin*, Zippy and Bungle, the Sooty Show . . .' For the first time in my life I really don't care if he knows the truth about me. Already he can see that we're less upwardly mobile than I might once have hoped – okay, that we live in semi-squalor; plus I'm in my old leggings with the baggy seat, a sweatshirt with gravy on the front, and sans lipstick. Yet for all that, the sight of me has made him cry. (It's only afterwards that I realise maybe this is why.)

But right now he's smiling at the highlights of my theatre-going. 'Yes, it must be tricky if you've got kids. But I'm sure you could get away sometimes if you got organised.' I don't rise to this. His brief pause makes me suspect he knows how aggravating is this advice to the child-ridden. 'Did you know I had a play on last year?'

'You?' I hope my note of surprise sounds mildly offensive,

though I should have remembered you have to be more than 'mildly' anything to get through Max's façade of self-confidence.

'Yes. It was on the radio first, then I adapted it for theatre. Only fringe of course, but it was well-reviewed.'

I make congratulatory noises to cover my irritation about his success and to conceal the fact that, for some reason, I feel hurt for Robert. It's as though any achievement of Max's detracts from his. None of Robert's architectural designs are likely to receive media attention, unless they fall down or are of the 'carbuncle on the face of . . .' variety.

I hand Max his tea and he pokes at the lemon suspiciously with his spoon. He's wearing jeans with a waistcoat over a white cotton shirt, and a burnt orange cotton sports jacket. With his slightly too long slightly unkempt hair (which is nonetheless not unflattering), he looks like the sort of man who gets interviewed on arts programmes.

'I've got another play on early next year. You should come along.' He starts to tell me what it's about as well as his next book, and I listen, not listening, while I pile the washing into the machine and start to clear the breakfast table. As I bang about with the cups and plates I realise how he's irritating me with his tales of his rise to mediocrity. How could I ever have loved him? I don't even like him. Arrogant bastard. It must have been some sort of carnal attraction that kept me blinded to the truth. I want him to shut up about his stupid play and the stupid people who have told him how good it is/how talented he is/what a loss to humanity it would be if he doesn't write more of the same. I'm not even making affirmatory noises now, but he isn't deterred.

And yet when he stands to go I suddenly panic. We've unfinished business here; he can't just walk in, bawl, walk out again. In fact he has only got up to help himself to more tea, but it's a warning to me to say what I have to say, even if I'm not sure what it is.

The tea-pouring causes a short break in his monologue and I take the opportunity to fill it.

'Max,' I say, but I can't look at him. 'What was it that upset you earlier?' He's been stirring his lemon around; now he stops, then he starts again.

'Why don't you show me your garden?' he says.

Max carries his tea and my coffee into the garden, and places them down on the path while he moves the chairs and table back on to the lawn. Robert cut the grass yesterday and the garden furniture is still stacked at the side, but Max can see where they belong by the yellow balding patches of grass. Robert says I should move the furniture around, but we get a little shade from next door's apple tree in this spot.

'How long have you lived here?' I know Max isn't interested really, any more than I am to tell him, but I relate our recent history, and the few improvements we've made to the house, making them sound more. He drains the last of his tea and I wonder what happens now. I could make some more, but that would just lead to more pussyfooting around, getting us nowhere. The short silence that has begun grows longer and I refuse to fill it. And so does he.

'Mummy, can Steven come to lunch?' Simon comes flying in through the back gate and skids to a halt on grass still damp from last night's rain.

'Not now, darling.' I smile my piss-off smile but Simon reads only 'Mummy smiling', not subtext.

'Yes, but can he?'

'We'll discuss it later.'

'It'll be too late later. He's going home after lunch today because Freda's going out.' Now this is a quandary. I weigh up the necessity of seeing Steven against the problems of getting showered, changed and made up while not knowing how much longer Max is going to hang around.

'Who's Steven? Your friend?' says Max to Simon, leaning back in his chair languidly.

'No-o-o-o. Steven's Mummy's friend.' Max raises one eyebrow quizzically and Simon rolls his eyes which he does whenever he's about to say something *risqué*. His giggling strangles his words, but not as efficiently as I'd like to strangle him. 'Mummy loves Steven.'

Max laughs and slaps his thigh, and Simon's knees give way with the hilarity of it all and he rolls from side to side on the damp grass. It's his latest thing. 'Rebecca's in love with Scott at the library.' 'Mummy's in love with the milkman.' 'Daddy's in love with the girl in the Flake advert.' But knowing that doesn't help.

'I do believe you're blushing,' Max says to me.

After I've persuaded myself into having Steven here for lunch, and Simon has gone to tell him, Max gets up to go. I was wrong about our unfinished business. We're just two people who used to know each other. We make small talk about the garden as we walk through the back gate and towards his car. He feels for his car keys in his pocket but then, with his hand still on the door handle, he suddenly turns back to me. 'I made a mistake, didn't I?'

Is he about to tell me that he has made all the wrong life choices? That he shouldn't have come? Or just that he should have had coffee instead of tea? 'Oh?' I say, feeling my way, hoping this is sufficient response.

Perhaps it isn't, because there's another silence so long

I wonder if I've missed something. Unusually for him, he looks embarrassed.

'Last week, when we met—'

Trevor comes trotting down the drive and takes a run at me, settling precariously against my shoulder.

'My other cat,' I say unnecessarily, but glad to lighten the mood that threatens to descend.

Max laughs and reaches out to stroke Trevor's neck. He opens the car door but then hesitates again, not looking at me. 'It was seeing you with your own house and a family and everything . . .' He falls silent and begins scraping at an area of rust by the wing mirror. I wish he'd leave it alone. 'Strange, I'm not the emotional type.'

'Probably it was realising the passage of time,' I say gently. 'Seeing how my life has changed made you realise how yours has too. And I'm glad you came anyway; it's good to see you.' I want to shift the conversation from the personal to the general. Now we've got down to the nitty-gritty I find after all that I preferred the pussyfooting.

'You're not glad to see me at all. I'm embarrassing you.' He smiles his superior smile. Superior, even though I'm at my own house and in the ascendant, since he's the one making the confessions. Even when he's at a disadvantage, he doesn't seem to feel at a disadvantage. I wish Simon would come back again. This is too much for a Monday morning when the most taxing thing I'd expected to think about was whether or not to use fabric conditioner. 'You were always easy to embarrass. Oh, I could be a bit mean, — but it was your fault, you know.' How did he make that out? Maybe I've spoken aloud because he goes on, 'You encouraged me. Whatever I did, you came back for more. I always thought you must have a strong masochistic streak.

Then suddenly you were walking away, without a word of warning. It wouldn't be allowed these days, on-the-spot dismissal.'

Somehow he's keeping a lightness in his tone; anyone overhearing him and listening to his intonation but not his words could think he's commenting on the state of our marigolds.

'Why didn't you say something at the time?' I can't believe he let us break up and never tried to stop it. And he hadn't. The day trip to the museum, when I'd got out of his car and left my presents behind, was the last time we had been together. He phoned once after that, but I said I was busy and he accepted it. Although I finished with him, it always felt like he'd finished with me. A few flowers, just his presence at my front door, was all it would have taken if he'd wanted me back. But he hadn't seemed to.

He shrugs. 'I thought we were playing games, and had reached a stand-off.'

'And you were always good at games.'

'Still am.' There's the superior smile again and I wonder for a moment whether he's serious even now. 'Not so good with reality, though.' He grins at Trevor ruefully.

If I'd married you, Max, how would it have been? I'm relieved to realise I haven't spoken aloud.

He opens the door wider and is about to get in when Steven arrives with Simon. He wants to check that he's really invited for lunch. I introduce them, and Max extends his hand which Steven shakes rather awkwardly. Steven is taller than Max; broader at the shoulder but narrower at the hips. He makes Max look older, more tired, but also even more arty and intellectual. It's arousing to have your conquests meet in ignorance of each other, when you're the only one knowing how much they have in common.

'So you're Steven,' says Max, weighing him up. 'I've been hearing all about you.' Steven glances towards me, smiling uncertainly, and a deep blush begins at his throat. Seeing it, Max laughs loudly; so I'm not the only one who knows what they have in common.

'Steven is a painter and decorator, he's done an excellent job for us.'

'Oh, really?'

'Absolutely. He has quite an artistic flair.' For all I know he might have, though I'm hardly likely to have discerned it from having my gutters repainted. But I want to boost my darling, who can hardly compete on grounds of academic brilliance.

'As it happens I might need some work done myself.' Max reaches in his pocket for a business card and hands it to Steven. 'Give me a call.'

'Steven doesn't have a car,' I chip in helpfully, 'so you'd have to get the paint in yourself, Max.' I don't want him raising Steven's hope of employment unnecessarily. 'And anyway you're right on the other side of London, so it probably wouldn't be worth his while.' Not that I'm possessive of my protégé or anything, but Steven wouldn't want to traipse across London, would he? And we might want our spare room doing soon.

Simon *is* possessive, however. He stands close to Steven, trying to get his attention and embarrassing me with his presence in this sexual heat. I send him indoors to tidy his bedroom while Max and Steven discuss the relative merits of rag-rolling, and when I return to the conversation I'm irritated to find Max arranging for Steven to give him a quote.

Chapter 23

Steven arrives for lunch just as I'm coming downstairs, showered and changed, and it takes me aback a little to look over the banisters and see him standing where Max stood only hours before. But this time there are no awkwardnesses, and Simon is shooting him with a make-believe revolver from behind the dining room door, which punctures any tendency to passion. Steven falls dead as I reach the bottom of the stairs but his eyes are still on me.

I come over to him and tend his wounds.

'You've shot him in the heart,' I tell Simon, lying my face against Steven's chest. 'Shall I see if mouth to mouth resuscitation will bring him back to life?'

'I don't want him brought back. Anyway, you don't use mouth to mouth for if you've got shot,' scoffs Simon. That puts paid to that idea then. Steven is laughing and my back is screening us from view so I rest my hand on the zip of his fly instead. He twitches slightly in surprise.

'He's moving!' yells Simon. 'You said he was dead.'

'Dying, I meant,' I say, as Steven's legs go into spasm in his death throes. Simon comes out from behind the door and shoots him again. Steven's legs flop loosely, his head lolls sideways, and his eyes close. I stand up and push his lifeless body with my foot. 'One less for lunch then,' I tell Simon.

Simon charges off upstairs to get his new racing car to show Steven, and abruptly the corpse returns to life. He grabs my ankle and bites it.

Watching Steven taking the wheels off Simon's car, I wonder why I was in such a frenzy to get changed for him. He's dust-covered, even his hair from rubbing down Freda's paintwork, and is wearing his old paint-splattered jeans and workboots. I knew this is how he would be dressed and yet irrationally I'm irritated by it.

I'm also irritated by something else.

'I liked your mate,' says Steven of Max. He has no right to go liking Max; can't he see that Max, effectively, is his rival? 'Knows all about decorating. Seems like a good bloke.' Max doesn't know all about decorating either; he told me once that you need only two facts on any topic to convince your listener that you're familiar with their subject. I know it works because I've seen him do it before.

I punish Steven with *Cider with Rosie*. 'Have you finished that book yet?'

'What book?'

'You know what book.'

He sighs and rakes paint-stained fingers through his hair. 'I don't like it. I told you I couldn't get on with it.'

I give the scrambled eggs the beating of their life. 'Don't be so defeatist. Just do it. I want you to have read the whole thing by Friday.'

'All of it?'

'If you don't, you can forget about any help from me.'

He looks at me helplessly, making me realise what an effective aphrodisiac power is.

Simon draws Steven's attention back to the car and he turns it over in his hands miserably.

If Steven hadn't arrived so soon after Max it wouldn't have been so noticeable. But seeing him where Max has stood and pontificated, I can't avoid acknowledging the contrast. If there were any justice in the world, Steven should shine; he's the more genuine, honest and likeable. Viewed strictly objectively, he's the better looking too, with the undoubted bonus of youth and virility (okay, so currently Max is an unknown quantity in the virility stakes). But there isn't any justice in the world, and Steven's lack of ambition and achievement, his readiness to be content with so little, the way he never questions what happens to him — all this counts against him.

'By Friday,' I say. 'I mean it.'

After lunch Edward, a neighbouring child, calls for Simon to play. It takes some persuasion to convince him that Edward will be as much fun as Steven, but when Steven says he has to be leaving shortly Simon finally accepts the invitation.

When he's taken his bike from the shed and gone, Steven comes to put his arms round me where I stand washing up. From his general demeanour I can tell that he's still upset.

'I'm sorry about the book. I'll get it done, I promise.' For just a moment I wonder if perhaps I can push Steven around the way Max did me. I could be harsh and unkind and he'll take it and apologise as though it's his fault. But I wouldn't do that to him; I'm not that sort of person.

I undo his shirt and rub my soapy hands over his chest.

'I want to have you in every room in the house,' he says (and to think I've called him unambitious). He locks the door and I lead him upstairs to the spare room, feeling that familiar burning growing and spreading while I watch him close the curtains. He starts to unbuckle his belt, pushing my hands away and teasing me as I try to help him, and I tear a fingernail fighting with the button at the waistband of his jeans. I slide them down over his legs, stroking the coarse dark hair and the smooth skin of his inner thighs, damp with sweat and desire. We move on to the narrow bed and I lie on top of him, feeling him pressed hard against my stomach. Held here, between my thighs with my two hands that stroke him slowly back and forth, he is trapped on the edge, ready to fall, scared to let go. Such teasing is almost unbearable to him but still I caress him with whispered words and fingertips, making it last, making him wait. He tries to stroke my back but I grasp his wrist, controlling his pleasure.

Around five o'clock there's a hammering at the back door. I throw on my dressing gown and hurry down; it was a mistake to let Steven lock the back door, because Simon will naturally assume something is wrong when he can't get in. In fact it isn't Simon, it's Rebecca. She has been at a friend's house all day and I wasn't expecting her back so early; I thought they were giving her dinner.

She looks horrified to see me in my dressing gown.

'Mummy! Were you just getting up?'

I blink at her, for a moment thinking she said 'getting it up'. 'Er, yes. I had a headache.'

'You're not ill again, are you?' This is her biggest fear, and I feel angry with myself at being so careless as to let her draw that conclusion. At my age I shouldn't be getting myself caught in this position. ('No, not that position, this one,' I said to Steven.) I know my hair must be dishevelled too and my make-up must have been largely sweated, if not eaten, off.

'I'm fine, darling, just a bit tired, we've had so many late nights lately.'

'You went up at nine-thirty last night; I heard you.' I had an early night to write up my diary with sweet reflections of Steven. I'd forgotten that.

'Yes, but I started reading and that tired me out. Why don't you get some milk and watch the TV?'

She slumps in front of the screen with bad grace. 'I hate milk.' I begin to recognise the symptoms.

'Did you have a nice day at Sian's house?'

'She had another friend there and they kept leaving me out of everything.' The thrusting bottom lip is a warning that tears are on the way. I haven't got time for this. If I'm not back upstairs in thirty seconds Steven will be dressed and climbing out of the window. Rebecca's fear that I'll be ill is equalled only by Steven's fear that we'll get caught (and mine that he will fall out of the window, and that's when we'll get caught).

'Tell me what you want and I'll get it for you.' ('Tell me what you want and I'll do it to you.')

'I want you to sit down and watch this with me.' She holds her arms out for a cuddle but I can't sit anywhere until I've had a wash and cleared this creeping innuendo out of my head. And the tissue I'm gripping in place between the cheeks of my bottom feels very precarious.

'I'll just get dressed,' I promise, giving her a hug, 'I'll be down in five minutes.'

I creep upstairs to the spare room and find Steven hiding

behind the door struggling into his jeans and looking watchful and hunted. I'm telling him what a coward he is and that he's over-reacting, feigning a cool control, when there's a shout from downstairs. Simon.

'Mummy, I'm home. Can Edward stay for tea?'

'No.'

'Why not?' He's standing at the bottom of the stairs, then he sees me leaning at the top of the stairs and starts to come up.

'It's all right, Simon, I'm coming down.'

'Why have you got your dressing gown on?'

'She isn't well and you're not to bother her.' Rebecca has come out of the lounge now to join Simon (if there's any bothering to be done, she wants to do it.) 'Hurry up, Mummy, it's starting.'

'Why can't Edward stay?' It would be simpler to have the entire road here for tea than to find a reason that won't produce another question.

'Okay, he can stay.'

'He says he wants fish fingers.'

'Okay.' Just clear off.

'And to eat it in the garden.'

Yes, anything.

'Mummy?'

Now what? 'Yes?'

'Is Steven still here?'

I sense Steven holding his breath. I answer carefully. 'Why do you ask?'

'Well, Edward and me we wanted to ambush him and we waited by the gate but he never came out.' He smiles at me with the innocence of youth, brown curls framing his face. I could kill him.

'You must have missed him.'

'We never,' chips in Edward, the swine. But I have the final word in this house.

'I'll be down in a minute,' I say.

Simon takes Edward into the lounge where a small argument strikes up, probably because the boys want to watch something different from Rebecca. I hurry back to Steven.

'Mum!' Now Rebecca is back at the bottom of the stairs. 'The boys won't let—'

'Go away and let me get washed!'

She goes into the lounge and starts shouting at the boys, soundingly worryingly like me, and ending with; 'Because I say so.'

'I'll never get out without them seeing me,' Steven whispers miserably. He is sitting on the end of the bed, head bowed, like a condemned man. 'If my mum finds out she'll go mad.' The only thing worse than the kids finding out (and thereby Robert) is Rita finding out. I like having my own teeth and would prefer to keep them.

'Don't be so melodramatic. I'll keep the children in the lounge and you can creep down the stairs.'

'They'll see me.'

'Make sure they don't, then.' I pad back to the bathroom and scrub at myself with a flannel, then try to mask any remaining odours with talc. Instead of smelling of sweaty sex I now smell of sweaty sex and lily of the valley. I put on my discarded knickers with distaste.

When I'm dressed, Steven is still waiting behind the bedroom door. He's as anxious as ever but I'm beginning to find the risk factor exciting. Not quite as good as when your parents might walk in, but in that general area. His uneasiness makes me want to show off my calm. I slide one arm round his neck and start undoing his fly with the other.

'We could still have it,' I whisper, 'we didn't try it on the landing, and they can watch TV for hours on end.' It'd be a challenge to seduce him in these circumstances, but he's impervious to my advances and his zip jams which weakens my resolve. 'What are you, man or mouse?' I hiss, but from the feel of the flaccid member inside his jeans, curled up hamster is nearer the mark. He pushes past to peer over the stairwell.

'I'll make a bolt for it now.'

'Okay.' I don't want to draw attention to my failure to excite. 'But let me go down first and make sure they don't come out.'

In the lounge I agree a compromise over the television. Rebecca and I will watch *Blue Peter* and then Simon and Edward can choose the next programme. I occupy the kids by engaging Edward in conversation concerning his holidays, how he's doing at school, what subject he likes best. But this occupies me more than it does the children so that I fail to notice Simon going to the window.

'There he is!' Closing the curtains to stop the sun reflecting on the TV screen, Simon has caught sight of Steven on his way down the path. He bangs on the window excitedly.

'I said he was still here! I said he was.'

Rebecca also comes to look. 'Where was he then? I didn't see him.'

Steven is hovering on the path, uncertain of what to do. The sunlight glints seductively off his earring.

I open the window and call out: 'So, you came back for your wallet, then. I thought you'd realise you'd left it here.' He looks at me blankly. I speak slowly and with precision. 'You must have let yourself into the kitchen and found it. Your wallet.'

At last he falls in. 'Oh yes. I found it in the kitchen. I let myself in.' From his expression I see that inspiration and originality have hit him. 'But I didn't call because I thought it might disturb you.'

'That's all right. See you soon.'

'Bye.'

I close the window and collapse on to the sofa next to Rebecca.

'I don't think he should have just wandered in without saying anything,' says Rebecca prissily. 'You might've thought he was a burglar.'

Edward and Simon begin throwing cushions at each other while Rebecca and I watch *Blue Peter*. I dream of being sneaked up upon by Steven the Burglar, while we learn to make Sindy furniture of such skilful design that, when finished, it's almost identical to the matchboxes, washing-up bottles and sticky-back plastic it started out as.

Chapter 24

'What's the smell in here?' Robert is walking through the house opening windows. 'Musty, damp smell. You ought to open more windows, let the air blow through.'

I was changing into clean underwear when he arrived home from work, and had to hurry so he wouldn't catch me only just getting dressed at six o'clock in the evening. Now I'm following him guiltily from room to room, on the look-out for tell-tale signs, while he tells me about the conference he's been to, how he wiped the floor with the speaker. Unfortunately he spots a tell-tale sign before I do.

'What's this doing up here?' It's Steven's baseball cap, nestling behind the washbasin pedestal in the bathroom. 'It looks just like Steve's. How's it got up here?'

'Simon probably hid it to tease him. Simon brought him home for lunch today.' Gosh, the way the lies trip off the tongue.

He picks the cap up, opens Simon's bedroom door, and sends the cap spinning on to the bed as though he's skimming pebbles. He watches with satisfaction as it lands neatly on the corner of Simon's bedhead. Suddenly he turns to me.

'Oh yes — Simon said you had someone else here this morning. What was that all about?' I've been standing behind him, idly waiting for him to stop scouring the rooms, but now I find urgent tidying to be done back in the bathroom. I smooth the screwed up flannels and mentally line up the jobs to be done: put caps back on the bottles of bubble bath, shampoo and shower gel; fold and straighten the dry towels and lay them over the rail; collect damp and grubby towels into a heap on the floor. A conscience-free woman would have told her husband about the college friend she hasn't seen for nearly twenty years the minute he arrived home. 'Darling!' she would say. 'You'll never guess who called today! Yes, Max! Couldn't believe it! I absolutely insisted he come back and have dinner tonight so we can have a good long talk!' The bathroom mirror is speckled with soap, like snowflakes, and I rub at them with a J-Cloth, creating broad smears.

'Did you hear me?'

'What?'

'I said, who was it called today?' Robert is standing in the doorway and I'm cornered. The most intense cleaning can not save me.

'Oh. It was strange really.' I spit on the mirror and rub harder. 'It was Max.'

'Max who?'

'Max-from-college Max.'

Robert has been undoing his shirt and loosening his tie, but now he stops in mid movement.

I register his astonishment at the appearance of his old adversary but run on, diminishing its significance as best I can. 'He bumped into Dan a week or so ago, evidently. Carol did tell me when I was there but I didn't realise Dan had given him our address. Max has a flat in London and he just decided to call when he was passing.'

'Passing? Why would he be passing here?'

I give up on the spit and get out the Mr Sheen. 'Probably just nosy,' I say. 'It was a bit embarrassing really. There were all these awkward silences. I mean, what do you say to someone you haven't seen for half your lifetime?'

'In his case, bugger off,' says Robert.

After dinner, apropos of nothing, Robert says, 'So Max just turned up out of the blue? You didn't see him when you stayed with Carol?'

'No, of course, not.' Robert looks at me for a moment. 'Besides,' I add, feeling a need to support my denial, 'if I were going to have a romantic tryst with someone, I'd arrange it to be somewhere more romantic than our kitchen – and I wouldn't choose a day when both the kids are home from school.'

Robert's features relax, but even so he says, 'Who said anything about a romantic tryst? I only asked if you'd seen him.' I really should keep my petard under better control, it's all too easy to get hoisted with it. But Robert seems satisfied and picks up a biro to start the crossword.

'Glad I wasn't here,' he says.

It's another two weeks until the kids go back to school and I wish it were sooner. I need some time to myself to get things straight in my mind. Steven, for example. I have fun with him and he has beautiful eyes and a strong hard body – but now I'm wondering, 'Am I risking everything just for that?' I thought there was something special between us, something rather fine and poetic – but getting caught by your kids is just silly, as well as being dangerous for all concerned. Whenever I'm with with Steven I feel I am stepping outside my workaday existence, but now my workaday existence is pushing its hand in mine and coming along with us.

Wednesday morning Josie calls to see if I fancy going shopping. She's rather pleased that I'll be home more, now that my job is finished, and she's anxious to get me involved with all the activities she enjoys herself. She wants me to join her badminton class, but I can't see the fun in batting a shuttlecock about; quite frankly, if I'm going to hit anything it'll be the bottle.

But shopping I can cope with, and the kids are thrilled at the prospect of a ride in Josie's BMW, not only for its obvious sleek style and dark, rich (and clean) interior, but because it has electric windows and four doors so they don't have to clamber over the front seat to get in. As we glide along the road we pass Edward; Simon and Rebecca wave like royalty.

We abandon the kids in a toyshop the size of a small factory (but which probably still won't stop them complaining that they're bored) and promise a visit to Pizza Hut if they're still there when we get back. I disagree with bribing kids by buying them sweets but Josie gives them some money, thereby relieving me of any guilt I'd have felt if I'd had to do it myself.

'He's not the type I thought you'd go for,' says Josie, as we wander round Next. She picks up the sleeve of a white silk blouse and then lets it fall. She saw me sitting in the garden with Max, and it occurs to me that this shopping trip is just a means of setting aside an entire afternoon for talking about him.

'I don't *go* for him. He's someone from the past – in the

past I used to like watching Popeye and eating Marmite soldiers. I don't like them now either.'

She gives the collar of a navy blazer a knowing smile. 'But you will be seeing him again?'

'I can't think why we should.'

'A guy doesn't walk into your life after all this time without a reason. He's obviously interested.'

'Yes, but I'm not.'

'Oh of course: Steven. That's all still going on then, is it?'

I say yes, but I hesitate momentarily. We did make love in every room in the house, as Steven had predicted, though this was fewer than it sounds — what with Rebecca's and Simon's rooms being out of bounds by agreement and Steven wasn't including those rooms we'd christened already. Even so, it still left the spare room, conservatory, bathroom, and the walk-in cupboard which houses the tumble dryer and which I'm pleased to call the utility room. After the first coupling of the afternoon, somehow I found the novelty wearing off. He kissed my temples as we finished our session in the spare room and I found myself calculating how long we could allow in each venue in order to fit them all in.

In the utility room, things were fine. I sat on the tumble dryer with Steven leaning up against it and we switched it on, which added a certain frisson — not least, as far as I was concerned, because it meant the sheets were getting dried at the same time. But in the bathroom I couldn't keep the mood at all. As I knelt on all fours with my chin on the floor, I got a clear view of the accumulated dust and fluff under the bath through which peered a Lego man, a blue plastic boat with the sail missing and the comb I've been looking for for months.

'Steven,' I said, 'this isn't working for me.' He helped me sit up, all tender concern, and then rolled me over on to my back.

'Okay. Try this. I read it in a magazine.'

'I thought you didn't like reading.'

He grinned and began running his hand over my thighs and stomach, so lightly he was hardly touching me. 'Is that better?' It was very erotic and I began to feel the urge rising again. His face grew heavy with tenderness. He was very lovely.

And yet, when my back arched and I raked my fingers down his buttocks it wasn't my poor sweet lover whose name was in my mouth.

Josie notices my hesitation.

'Cooling off, are we?'

'No, he's a sweetie.' 'Sweetie' isn't a word I ever use. I can't think why I've said it.

'He's a hunk and you were tempted — that's nothing to be ashamed of. But you shouldn't blame yourself if it turns out not to be the real thing. He's just a boy, after all. Intellectually he's not exactly your equal is he?'

I never think of Josie as my intellectual equal either, so it seems odd to hear her say this.

'I'm not cooling off exactly. But I don't think I feel quite as I did.'

'Hmmm.' Josie considers my plight while she holds up a beige calf-length skirt to test the length against the one she's wearing. 'Oh well,' she says over her shoulder, as she carries the skirt to the changing room, 'off with the old, on with the new.'

When I hear his voice I know I've been expecting him to call all along. I'd just given up on scraping the new potatoes and resorted to the potato peeler when the phone rang. Simon answered it, and when he come skipping into the kitchen saying, 'There's a man on the phone,' I just knew.

'Hello, Ellie. Are you well?' He doesn't announce himself. He sounds different than in the flesh and I realise I've never actually spoken to him on the phone before; in itself that probably says all anyone needs to know about the nature of our relationship, though it doesn't strike me at the time. I'd like to puncture his self assurance by not recognising his voice but don't think quickly enough to do it.

'Hello, Max. I was just thinking of you,' I say, hoping he'll take this to imply there'd be times I wasn't. 'I'm fine. What can I do for you?' Keep it businesslike, ignore the suddenly beating pulse at the throat.

'I want to see you.' And there it is, no prettying-up or skirting round, just a bald statement of his needs. He's changed. In the past he didn't even know what his needs were.

'Why?' I want to make him say it, but also I'm playing for time while I think what excuse I can make to Robert.

'You know why. Just yes or no. If it's no then I won't bother you again.' I know we're still in some kind of game, but I also know, as does Max, that you can't always tell where the game ends and real life begins.

'Okay, when?' If I'd thought it through, I would realise that I have the upper hand here; it is for me to specify the date, make a few conditions. But you learn the pattern of a relationship and you go on repeating it. If I'd understood that at this moment I might not have gone at all.

'Six o'clock,' he says. 'Tomorrow. You can get to Waterloo can't you?'

'Yes.'

'Then I'll meet you outside the Royal Festival Hall. At six.'

'Yes. Okay.' And then he rings off and it's done. I wonder why he's settled on meeting at Waterloo (which isn't exactly convenient for me; it'll mean changing trains and won't be a very congenial journey during the rush hour). Perhaps he wants to take me to a concert, or to have an early supper sitting in the evening sun at one of the little tables overlooking the river.

I think of how, according to Josie, Greg makes her feel when he rings unexpectedly (warm and loved), and of how Steven has made me feel (hot and excited), compared to how I'm feeling now (cold and vulnerable). And yet I do want to go.

I tell Robert that I'm meeting Theresa for a meal.

'But why have you got to go right into London? Aren't there perfectly good restaurants around here?'

'She thought it would be fun to go further afield. And it's a bit special, a kind of farewell meal.'

'And it's a bit early isn't it, to go out to dinner?'

'She's going shopping first,' I say, thinking on my feet and impressed with my own resourcefulness. 'Actually she wanted me to go with her, but I can't ask Josie to have the kids for the entire afternoon.'

Robert resigns himself to coming home from work a little early and declines my suggestion of what he should feed the kids, offering them another visit to Pizza Hut instead.

When I get off the train I'm early, which is annoying because I wanted to find him waiting for me, in the best romantic tradition. At any other time I would use the odd half-hour at a station to flick through paperbacks on the station bookstall, or window shopping for fancy pants in Knickerbox, but this is the rush hour. Being pushed and jostled I can cope with but when my foot is stepped on for the second time I swallow my pride and set off to meet Max. So what if I'm early? Seeing the bust of Nelson Mandela, I become engrossed in the strength of purpose behind those eyes, the texture of the skin, absorbed in the inscription — so that when he arrives he'll see how interested I am in the arts these days. But when I've done all this and finally look to either side of me there's still no sign of him. I decide to walk towards the river where I can find a seat and try to look like someone engrossed in the architectural beauty of the area, but as I give up and walk on — there he is. He's on the footbridge, leaning on the railings and gazing up towards St Paul's. His white shirt has its sleeves rolled back to reveal tanned wrists, and his jacket is flung over one shoulder. Relaxed and contented, he has struck the pose I'd have liked to; of someone entranced by everything around him, who isn't waiting for anyone at all. Alone there, with commuters and tourists brushing past, he even looks vulnerable. I'd like to hold this moment, the prospect of him forever excitingly before me, but held safely at a distance.

He turns towards me as I approach, adopting a languid smile, but there are other emotions shifting beneath that calm surface, an eagerness or sense of anticipation he's trying to conceal. I walk towards him steadily, bravely, and we face each other. His cheek is rough and dark, he needs to shave again, — and he smells of books and cigarette smoke. He doesn't speak but his arms reach out and as he pulls me to him I'm swept back in time. His mouth is warm and familiar, and when we kiss he holds me tight, while ferries pass along the river unaware of the trembling of the earth above them.

The river has been wide and deep and the crossing hazardous, but surely, this time, I've come home.

Love, I discover, gives you unbridled energy which is why I've given in to Josie's urging to join her aerobics class. (Where did that stupid name come from? It sounds like a biscuit covered in Aero. *Aerobix! The lighter chocolate snack!*) Unfortunately, love has only given me enough energy to get here and there isn't much left for the class itself. But the music, loud and insistent, is what I want to hear, and the contrast between being here and doing what I would normally be doing — washing up after the kids' tea — is enlivening. It's novel too to be in the company of women. Without the presence of men, I sense an immediate kinship between us. I don't feel one of them exactly, but they're friendly to me and in some subtle way we're all in sympathy. They include me in their hellos, their how are yous, careful not to let their eyes dwell on the outfit I'm wearing. They're all in leotards that shimmer like jewels while their tanned legs glisten above gleaming white trainers. These women must be the ones Josie dresses for; even the largest and lumpiest of them exudes style and elegance. Pert bottoms, like Josie's, are encased in brilliant cycling shorts or cropped-off leggings; hair is pulled back by toning headbands or, also like Josie's, into jaunty ponytails; their stomachs are so flat that if they laid down you could serve drinks off them. They wear full make up to come here, and I hear two of them discussing a nose job and liposuction that a mutual friend has just had done. Personally, I would never trust

IMMACULATE MISCONCEPTIONS

liposuction: it might suck up all kinds of things you still wanted, like my hoover does; but I can see that the loss of the odd internal organ wouldn't be a serious worry for these women. We're in a total line- and wrinkle-free zone here; they wouldn't know a crow's foot if it were still attached to the crow.

I, on the other hand, present a slightly different image. My hair is flopping over my face, my usual styling mousse being quite unused to the new demands placed upon it, and my (once) white trainers are the ones I throw on for nipping down to the shops. One of them is tied with a black lace because Rebecca, judging her own fashion needs to be greater than mine, took a lace out when her own broke and I've had to use one from Robert's old shoes. My leotard dates from bygone days when I had a brief dalliance with yoga, and when Lycra was a mere twinkle in the eye down at Du Pont. It's too tight for me now, and also too short. When I raise my arms it disappears up the middle and there's never a convenient moment to hook it out again. No one else's leotard — not even the large lumpy women's or the woman's whose gusset is only a thong — seems to do this. While I bend over with a straight back keeping my head up, and feeling my leotard cutting me in half again, I think about the thing I have to ask Josie. I need plenty of time to do it, and after the class, when we go for a drink, seems the optimum moment. I want to savour it, see the look on her face, take time working out the options, the variables, the logistics.

'Enjoying it?' whispers Josie as we straighten up and jog in place, knees and arms raised high. I smile, lacking the breath to answer. I'm going to get some grey pedal pushers, like the woman Josie introduced as Gerry, and a cerise cropped top that shows the midriff. Why shouldn't

I be the sort of girl who has nose jobs and goes everywhere in full make-up? I wanted changes in my life and here they are, happening all around me. After ten minutes I have to sit down with my head between my knees, but I am not disheartened. This is just the beginning.

I haven't reckoned on Gerry, the woman in the grey pedal pushers, and Veronica and Deirdre et al coming to the pub. My news is already beginning to feel like an anticlimax because Gerry has, just this week, left her husband for a man five years her junior and this is her first night away from him. There's much excitement and innuendo from which I feel excluded, being not quite on smutty-comment terms with the others, and I feel slightly offended too that they all know at least as much about Greg as I do. I'd thought that Josie's extramarital relationship was our special secret. I like them less now than I did at the class ('I bet you feel better after that,' said one. 'Yes, I do,' I said, 'because then I was dying of exhaustion and now I'm not.') Their interests tend too much to the trivial for my taste; no doubt this is why they have the time to grow perfect nails which are painted the same shade on hands and feet, and time for fortnightly trips to the hairdresser for the touching up of roots. Gerry is getting out a gold bangle which her new boyfriend has bought her, and everyone oohs in admiration and several of them try it on. I don't bother because I had one similar once. Okay, mine was in stainless steel and had a green plastic bead set in it, a present from Stuart when I was fourteen, but a bangle is a bangle.

When the women start to leave Josie says it's time to go too, but I still haven't told her the very thing I came out for, so I persuade her to stay by a simple expedient.

'I've got something I absolutely have to tell you.'
'Oh, okay then.'

I get her an orange juice and a packet of peanuts which she tut-tuts over but eats anyway.

'Go on then.'
'It's a brilliant idea, you're going to love it.'
'Good, let's hear it.'
'It'll need working out but I think we can do it.'
'Just tell me.'
'Okay, well, what would you most like to do in all the world?'
'Right now, wring your neck. I told David I'd be in by ten. Will you get on with it?' She shakes out a few peanuts into her palm.
'How would you like a weekend in Paris with Greg?'
'I'd love one, but who's paying?'

I hadn't thought of that side of it, but Josie's got plenty of money. 'Just listen. Think of it. The Champs-Elysées, the Louvre, candlelit dinners in tiny bistros.'

'I am listening. But why are you so keen for Greg and I to have a good time all of a sudden? I thought you wanted me to stay with David.'

'Oh no, we all owe it to ourselves to be happy.'

Josie raises one eyebrow, letting me know that, shallow though she may be, she's not as shallow as I am. This conversation isn't going as I'd hoped, but I can't control the smile on my face which is so wide I can hardly get the words out.

'You'll be my alibi and I'll be yours. We'll say we're going to Paris together — and we will, only you'll be there with Greg and I'll be there with Max.'

She looks puzzled for a moment. 'Max?' Then she remembers. 'Max — the one you're not interested in?' She does the thing with the eyebrow again. If I hadn't had two gins I might have blushed.

'I know, I know. I met him again since then and everything's changed. He wants me to go away for a long weekend with him, and if you were my alibi I could. You said Greg's already left his wife, so he won't need an excuse, and I could be your alibi for David. Max is suggesting a fortnight's time. What do you think?'

Josie looks down at her orange juice and swishes it round in her glass. After our exercise her make-up has taken on an unattractive sheen which a glass of white wine and two orange juices has done nothing to temper; I can feel the start of a prickle of antagonism towards her. She isn't reacting as she should; her eyes should be lighting up with excitement now, and we should be clinking glasses, drinking to love, life and debauchery. She drains her glass and places it back on the table with care.

Don't you want to do it then?' I can't believe she's turning me down, Josie the risk-taker. Perhaps she thinks the whole idea is seedy, or that she doesn't need any help with alibis — but surely an entire weekend is a little different from the odd overnighter (which is the best she usually manages).

Then she looks up and her eyes are sparkling. 'I always thought you needed watching,' she says, laughing. 'Yes, we'll do it. I'll ring Greg tomorrow.'

The bell is ringing for last orders as we walk to the car park, and the night is warm with the promise of things to come.

'So come on then,' says Josie as she unlocks her door, 'spill the beans on this man you're not at all interested in.'

I get in and tell her of the magic of our first kiss, the

sense of returning to the beginning, but a better beginning with all the problems ironed out. She turns the engine on, puts in a cassette of Elton John, and by the time we reach the main road she's already telling me how wonderful the sex was with Greg that first time.

I am hanging out some washing when he comes up behind me. His chin feels bristly as he kisses my neck and he catches my ear with the brim of his baseball cap. I can feel the hard rough skin of his hands through my T-shirt. He smells of paint and turpentine. I shrug him off, but my arms are full of washing and he doesn't respond immediately.

'You do realise that the neighbours might see what you're doing?'

'You didn't used to worry.'

I 'didn't used to' do a lot of things, I think. I didn't used to get myself romantically involved with my friends' children, for one thing. His youthful exuberance is beginning to grate.

'I love you,' he says, and his voice is almost inaudible. I wish it was inaudible. His face looks fixed and tense, as though he might cry at any moment.

'You don't love me,' I say, with a stupid brittle smile which I can't seem to help, 'you only think you do.'

I keep up the smile, conveying, I hope, sympathy and my superior understanding of the situation. And I suddenly remember Max and me, one sunny afternoon. We were lying on my bed in that period which in other circumstances, with other lovers, would be the afterglow. With Max it was a time always fraught with uncertainty and doubt, but that day there was something I wanted to get out in the open. I leant over and kissed his cheek.

'I love you,' I whispered. There was a pause. A long pause.

'No you don't,' he said. 'You only think you do.'

I lay back down again, still with his arm round me, and hatred welled up like lust. I wanted to stab him and bite and kick. But most of all I wanted to prove him wrong.

And he was wrong. After all, if you think you're hungry, you're hungry. If you think you're cold, you're cold. It's not for someone else to tell you you're not cold or hungry. Or in love.

Lying next to him, very still and composed, I told Max all this. And he said, 'A sixteen year old gets in a car and he thinks because he knows where the accelerator is and the clutch, and he can make it go backwards or forwards, that he can drive. So he drives it at seventy miles an hour the wrong way down a one-way street and wraps it round a lamp post. He thinks he can drive, but he can't.' And then he leant over and kissed my cheek, the way I just had his. And for a moment I thought he was going to say it ... Then he began to nuzzle my breasts. 'I can't believe it,' he said, 'I want you again already.'

I look at Steven, and his eyes are wide in hope and confusion. I want to put my arms round him and comfort him but he's taller than I am, so I take his hand and press my lips against the knuckles. There's a graze across them; he must have done it today. I intend saying: Steven, this can't go on; Steven, it's over; Steven, it was a mistake and I'm sorry. But all the options sound so blunt and unkind and I can't find the right words. 'Oh Steven,' I say, and hope that my voice will convey all the things I can't find words for. But he hears what he wants to hear, what he has grown used to hearing. He puts his arm round me and pulls me to him.

So strange to be the one not making a commitment.

Chapter 25

Waiting for the plane to take off from Gatwick, I feel like a bride going on her honeymoon. The groom is next to me, delicious in a cream silk shirt, open at the neck, clasping my hand between both of his and resting it in his lap. Periodically I stroke his crotch with my forefinger.

I too am dressed in my wedding finery: a floral sun dress from Laura Ashley, an extravagance purchased with the last of my wages. I probably don't look any better in it than in my old one from M & S which this actually resembles, but its cost is a tribute to the significance of the occasion. I feel I have waited all my life for this moment.

'So Robert was entirely taken in?' There's a hint of exuberance in Max's voice at the notion of fooling Robert, which would sadden me if I wasn't so entirely immune to sadness just now.

'He doesn't realise there's any reason not to trust me. He was a bit surprised I wanted to come away with Josie, but then he knows we've been getting friendlier these past months. And he also knows how upset I was when we had to cancel our family holiday to France — he even told me to find someone else to go with.'

Max squeezes my hand. 'Hoist with his own petard. Good old Robert.'

'Yes, good old Robert.' Inexplicably, saying Robert's name makes me want to cry. I hate to be taking my happiness at the expense of his, even if he doesn't know how unhappy he ought to be. He's taking Simon and Rebecca to Thorpe Park today, Saturday, along with two of their friends, and tomorrow is driving them down to another theme park — this one being on the theme of the seaside. It's called Brighton. Cathy will have them on Tuesday until I get back, but on Monday Robert has arranged to work at home so they can both have friends over to play and Steven is coming over to start digging out for the patio. Robert has been so sweet and attentive, anxious that I should enjoy my break and not be worrying about them. He even ironed my T-shirts ready for packing. He wanted to drive us to the airport too, but I persuaded him that Josie and I could manage perfectly on the train so he, the children and David, saw us off from the station instead. It was imperative they didn't take us to Gatwick. Josie isn't coming to Paris at all. Greg is strapped for cash and Josie thinks it's unbecoming to contribute to the costs, so they're staying at a small hotel in Dorset. He picked her up at the next station. I caught sight of a tall wiry man with a dark beard embracing her on the platform as my train pulled out. He wasn't how I'd imagined. Not nearly as good looking as David. (In fact, not nearly as good-looking as Mr David, the manager of the shop where I had my first Saturday job — and he was bald with eyes that looked in different directions and a hare-lip. Okay, so I exaggerate — he didn't have a hare-lip.)

'Happy?'

I nod, assuming that Max has mistaken the cause of my

brimming eyes, but then he adds, 'And you don't have to feel guilty. You were mine before you were his.' This thought temporarily assuages my conscience and, when Max orders champagne, we drink to us and our future.

The Hotel Florence is situated near the Place de la Clichy which the brochure describes as 'less exclusive, but with a great deal to offer' without saying exactly what but Max says this is the hotel he always stays in and we only got in on such a late booking because August is so quiet.

'It always entertains me to come to Paris and stay in a hotel that models itself on something from another city,' he says as we climb narrow stairs to our second-floor room. The decor is faithfully Italianate, with a gold-painted balustrade above which a frieze of cherubs cavorts. When we reach the first-floor landing the balustrade gives way to a more modest handrail, but it's still painted gold and the wall paper which replaces the frieze is a red and gold flock.

'I always get this room if I can. I like the wardrobe being at the end of the bed.' The bed is covered in an ornate quilt of pink and coral flowers, edged with gold braid, and the headboard is quilted in the same fabric but edged in gold-painted wood in the style of Louis Quinze. The wardrobe, which takes up half the length of the wall, has mirrors on the front panels of each of its three doors. I smile but make a mental note to keep the light off or the sheets over me. I don't want Max seeing my fat bottom from multifarious angles.

He sits on the bed and points at the mirror. 'I'll be able to see you from all angles,' he says, patting the bed for me to sit next to him. 'It's tacky but it's rather fun, isn't it?'

I don't think it's tacky at all, I think he has whisked

me away to another time filled with the spellbindingly magical. The en suite bathroom is a late addition to this building that probably dates from the last century, and consists of three walls which jut out like a box into what was originally a simple rectangular room. When I open the door to the bathroom the walls shake alarmingly, but what is lacking in substance is made up for in the artistry. Each of the walls of the en suite section forms part of a painting of Venice, a frieze which extends across the door so that when closed the picture flows on uninterrupted. Gondolas pass in stately progress along the centre wall, the grand buildings forming a back drop, and the scene is continued round the sides, with more buildings and clusters of people alighting or waiting to board. The painting is not, as I think at first, a print or some kind of wallpaper, because when I look more closely tiny splashes of paint prove its originality. I feel like I'm staying in a stately home.

'I think it's beautiful.'

He laughs. 'I come here for the location and the service, not the decor. You do realise which painting that's supposed to be, don't you?' he asks. I don't at all. 'And the cherubs in the entrance hall, did you recognise that?' I try to look as though the name is on the tip of my tongue. 'Well wait until you see the lounge. They've got Michelangelo's *David* in there and someone has had a go at doing the Sistine Chapel on the ceiling.' I join in with his laughter, but I wish he wouldn't spoil it for me. I want to believe he chose our hotel for its charm and majesty, not its proximity to the Metro. I would also prefer not to be reminded that he's been here before. I hope he won't be comparing my performance in the mirrors with others with younger, trimmer backsides.

'You always did have terrible taste; I suppose I'll just

have to get used to it.' He takes my hand and pulls me down next to him and I rein in the ache I've been feeling. He can still come out with something unexpected and hurtful when I'm at my most vulnerable. He releases the strap of my sun dress and brushes my shoulder with his lips, undoing his shirt buttons with the other hand. 'I'll show you something beautiful,' he says.

I tried so hard to be restrained but I couldn't overcome the urgency, having him here to myself, wanting me. The smell and feel of him came back to me, though he had changed – thickened in the waist and thighs, but his stomach was still as flat as a boy's. His chest was broader, but I liked that, and the T-shaped curl of hair that ran down to his navel and to the length of him beyond (which I would have known anywhere; he's been the measure of the rest). I could have stayed indefinitely lying next to him, stroking, caressing, enjoying the new but entirely familiar texture of his skin, the taste of him, but he pushed me down on to my back and began the long slow progress that was his love-making and which was so sweet, so selfless and so changed from how it used to be. I had loved what he did because it was him doing it, but now the sensations were their own thing and all for me, infinitely sweeter and geared to my needs, not his. I felt taut and tuned, responsive to his every breath, his whisperings, his subtle movements and intrusive caresses, and when I opened my eyes he was watching me, his face devoted and heavy with longing, watchful of each attention upon me. I felt weak with yearning and waiting, teased to a frenzy with his intimate kisses and the tiny explosions like space dust on the tongue where his fingers stroked. And then slowly, pinpoint bubbles of heat, like water starting to boil, began to rise through me, growing more and bigger, breaking with tiny explosions, themselves growing bigger, joining with others becoming bigger still until suddenly this was it — I was, I was coming, I was coming now, *now* — but no, not yet, not yet, and then — yes, it was now now *now* and he was ready and strong, fast and urgent, moving faster, harder, faster, harder, faster and stronger and harder.

Afterwards we lay for a long time in silence. I had felt his tears as he had mine. He was mine now; this face upon the pillow was the one I would wake with forever, and all that had gone before was mere incident and interruption to this passionate and intense reality.

When I had lain in hospital hungering for the life I hadn't known, the love I hadn't shared, I still hadn't guessed that I had missed so much.

Later, as we sit in Max's favourite brasserie waiting for our soup to arrive he tells me about the itinerary he has mapped out for tomorrow. I wonder why he wants to waste tonight talking about tomorrow; I want to take the moment and hold it between our hands, making a pressed-flower memory out of it, so I can take it away with me and still have it when I get home.

Max is telling me about Montmartre, and I make listening noises, although what I'm really doing is simply basking in the warmth of his undivided attention. But not even the clatter and buzz of conversation from the bar and the passage of diners past our table can hold me in the present. I want to be here, relishing the moment, but the aroma of filter coffee and something in the stance of the waiter and the joke he and Max exchange sends me back to the dawn of our new understanding. Back to his confession and my unwilling acceptance. Back to, of all places, the snack bar in the Royal Festival Hall.

'There's something I have to tell you,' he said on the footbridge over the Thames, drawing out of our kiss. He hadn't lost his touch for breaking the mood, for stamping out any possibility of burgeoning romance. No 'hello' or 'how are you?', just: 'There's something I have to tell you.'

He let me go and took a step back. Suddenly the only thing between us was the breeze coming off the river. 'Let's get something to eat.' I thought we'd be going to a restaurant — the sort of candlelit dinner we'd never had — but he led me back over the bridge and into the Royal Festival Hall. He asked after my journey, what the children were doing today, how Robert was, not listening to the answers, and led the way to a snack bar and ordered a pot of tea and some scones. As he paid for them he turned to me, as an afterthought. 'I take it you've no objection to tea and scones?'

He carried the tray outside and we sat at a table overlooking the river. He cut his scone in half in silence and I poured the tea.

'What's this amazing thing you have to tell me?' Deprived of the dinner I'd been anticipating, I felt sour and antagonistic. He stirred in some milk thoughtfully.

'It isn't amazing at all, it's just something you ought to know.' He paused. 'About me.' Two boys, about Simon's age, came spinning past on skateboards, the noise on the paving stones almost drowning him out. 'I treated you very badly, I've admitted that. But I haven't told you why.' I wanted to register my astonishment that he had a reason — I'd thought it was just a callous bloody-mindedness — but the scone had turned to a heavy dough in my mouth and I was always taught not to speak with my mouth full. I toyed with the idea of spitting the scone into a napkin while Max was gazing into his cup, but the risk of him catching me in mid spew was too great. 'Angelique wasn't Angelique at all. She was Alex.'

I can't see what he's getting at. I didn't know any girl called Alex at college, and even if I had being two-timed for one is pretty much like being two-timed for another. I swallowed the glutinous scone with a mouthful of tea and said so.

Max looked amused. 'Alex wasn't a girl, and you did know him. He was doing music.'

'Like Angelique?'

'Well, yes, he did everything that I said Angelique did. It was simpler to keep to the truth that way.'

'The truth? Since when did you worry about the truth?'

He put his hand over mine. 'Calm down, Ellie, people are looking.' I was calm, but this was nonsense. If the two couples at distant tables could hear us over the skateboarders then they had more acute hearing than Superman. 'Do you understand what I'm telling you?'

I didn't really, but I sensed I'd been made an even greater fool of than I realised. The memory of past desolation sat like a weight in my stomach, though that could just have been the scone. It reminded me of the Pandora's box of pain I used to carry about, the myriad unkindnesses trapped in it beating their evil wings.

Max refilled our cups, determined to be civilized. 'I didn't understand my own sexuality, that was the problem. These days it's all out in the open, anything goes, but I'd had some bad experiences at school and I wasn't sure what

I felt. There was you and there was Alex. I liked you both. I was attracted to you both.'

I didn't know what to do with my hands. If I smoked I could have got a cigarette out, tapped it to settle the tobacco, fiddled in my bag for a lighter and then sat back regarding him coolly. That's what they do in movies. To my annoyance this is what Max now did.

'So do you mean,' I said, needing to ask but still hoping wildly that I'd misunderstood completely, 'that while you were sleeping with me you were also sleeping with him?'

'Well not "while" exactly. Let's say, "before and after".' He laughed at that.

'I could have caught something.'

'Oh, there weren't the things to catch then that there are now. And anyway, as far as I remember Alex was more likely to catch something off you.'

It's lucky I don't smoke because I'd have stubbed my cigarette out on his ugly self-satisfied face. Instead, I did the only thing I could. I swept my handbag from the table and strode off back towards the station. Pandora's box was all he would ever be to me; why couldn't I remember that?

He caught me as I reached the bust of Nelson Mandela and blocked my path. It was ironic that he should stop me here, where I'd stood with such brave optimism less than an hour earlier.

'I'm sorry, I'm handling this really badly. Come and sit down again.' I didn't want to sit down but if I went home now what reason could I give to Robert? I wouldn't go back to the table (people were looking) but I allowed myself to be propelled along by the river. We walked in silence, broken only by Max's occasional pointing out of a famous landmark, and ended up leaning against the wall overlooking the river.

'This is a waste of time, Max. I don't know why you wanted us to meet again, but you've had me trail half way across London for nothing. I'm going home.' I could buy myself a book at the station and get something to eat there. An hour's quiet reading would settle me down and use up the time until I could reasonably go back to Robert.

'Home to Robert?' he said with what was almost a sneer. 'I don't know what your relationship is with him,' he began, 'but I've drawn a few conclusions just from the fact you're here today.' I decided to buy some cigarettes the next chance I got. 'And there's something going on with that young boy, isn't there? So maybe you're not as tied in to your marriage as you'd have me believe.' He raised his tone at the end of the sentence, turning it into a question, but I kept my eyes directed ahead. 'I just wanted you to understand the reasons things had gone wrong between us, so if you were ready to try again . . .' He'd turned it into another question but I still didn't answer.

As we walked back he began telling me about an exhibition he had been to that day at the Hayward Gallery. So that was why I had had to cross London in the rush hour — because it was convenient for Max coming out of an art exhibition.

'You said you wanted to tell me something. Is that it then? Some nonsense that you two-timed me for a boy when I'd thought it was a girl, and that you've had a good time at some old exhibition?'

'It wasn't some old exhibition.' Strange that this should be the part of my complaint that he felt offended about. I marched ahead but he caught my arm again. 'I haven't made you understand.'

IMMACULATE MISCONCEPTIONS

'You've made me understand you're as much of a bastard as I always thought.' I hadn't had time yet to consider how I felt about being thrown over in favour of a boy, but I was certain I wasn't going to like it when I did.

He took me by the shoulders and held me still. The skateboarders came shooting past, so that I flinched, thinking they were going to run into us, and in the sudden scraping noise along the pavement I almost missed his next words. But not quite.

'I thought I was gay, Ellie.' His face was full of the pain of confession. Gone the supercilious smile, the confident raising of the chin. And he was meeting my eyes, not letting them slide away in his usual manner. 'I couldn't make any sort of commitment because I didn't know what I wanted. I was terrified of getting too involved. Do you know when I found out I wasn't gay?' I didn't want to hear any of this, but you can't just walk off when someone is baring their soul. Besides, I was just a bit curious. 'When I knew you were getting married.' He pinched the bridge of his nose with his fingertips and turned away but I didn't go to him. I felt oddly unmoved. Maybe it was satisfying to be able to pay him out, or perhaps it was because this new emotional Max was a stranger.

When he turned back he wore a rueful smile. 'Whatever you think I did to you, I've paid for it. I got married and I've had more girlfriends than I can remember, but you're the one I always wanted.' His face wore the expression I used to long for. 'I want to give you everything I never did.' He waved his arm in the direction of the Festival Hall. 'Take you to concerts, buy you presents, show you places you've never been before. There, tell me somewhere you've never been.'

I think he meant somewhere like the Hayward Gallery

or to the Proms, so I punished him by requesting the impossible. He needn't think a few cheap presents would make things right after all these years. Two students passed us on my left. One was tall and olive-skinned with a thick mop of greasy curls, and he was speaking in French to his female companion who was laughing and gazing up at him. 'Paris,' I said. 'I've never been to Paris.'

He laughed, delighted, as though I'd committed myself to something. 'Okay, Paris it is! When do you want to go?'

That was obviously too easy so I added an obstacle. 'Thursday. It has to be next Thursday.'

'Okay! I'll book up tomorrow.' He threw his head back with laughter, and then his arms came round me, pressing me tight against him. I tried to pull away because I was just stringing him along — I wasn't about to go away with someone who'd dumped me on the off-chance he was gay, who had lied and connived, someone I'd never really known. For more than a decade I'd been pining after someone who had never existed.

In the strength of the embrace my arms were pinned, and as I stopped struggling and relaxed against him I caught the scent of his old familiar smell. Woody and smoky and indisputably male. Long afterwards, when I wondered why I'd agreed, I realised this was what had changed my mind: the old smell that brought back oddly not the pain, but all the hope and optimism I used to feel. I couldn't turn down the chance to see the past put right.

In the end, of course, there was no way I could get away so soon, but the problem was mine not Max's. He was prepared to be as good as his word, which was a novelty in itself.

He said something else too: 'I want to make love to you. Real love, not what we used to do.'

* * *

And now he has done so, in the magical Hotel Florence, crying hot tears against my neck in the afterglow, while I thanked God for Max, for that moment, and for the quilted bed-head which surely is all that prevented him from getting concussion.

I reach across the table for his hand, causing the waiter – who, close up, doesn't resemble the one from the Festival Hall at all – to wait before he can put down our bowls of onion soup.

'I love you,' I say. And now, in this public place where people might see or overhear and the waiter definitely will, he leans across the table and kisses me. 'And I love you too,' he says.

The lid of Pandora's Box flies off, but everything in it has turned to flower petals.

'So what do you think of it?'

The many times I've seen the Eiffel Tower on television, in pictures and in gift shops in statuette form, have not prepared me for its grandeur, or the strange peacefulness of its setting amidst the row of lawns and fountains. We've approached it from the Trocadero and I had no idea, as we rounded the corner, of the imposing scene I was about to witness. It seems entirely appropriate to be seeing this modern wonder of the world – this cold, hard, metallic phallic symbol – in the company of my cold, hard, first love.

'I hadn't expected it to be so big.' I realise my Freudian slip too late and wait, embarrassed, for the inevitable joke. But Max has no truck with the predictable.

'Yes, it is rather majestic isn't it, with that sweep of the sides? Look at the arch at the bottom with its deep curve, and those horizontal platforms.' He recites a few facts about its construction, the opposition to it when it was built, the numbers of visitors who go up it each year. I watch the fountains and the arc the jets of water make as they fall, and think of Max's reflection in the wardrobe mirrors.

'Would you like to go up it?'

'You can't come to Paris and not climb the Eiffel Tower, can you?'

'Why ever not?' But he leads me to the throng of jeans-clad tourists underneath the mesh of metal girders and we stand looking up. 'There's quite a queue,' Max murmurs doubtfully as we line up behind a family with five children, two of whom are crying. 'You're sure you want to do this?'

I do, I want to gaze out across the most romantic city in the world, hand in hand with my lover. I want to kiss him as the breeze strokes our cheeks and he whispers '*je t'aime*'. I want to gaze down on the city that is the centre of art and culture for the whole of Europe and know that I am on the threshold of a new phase in my life. I want most of all to go up to the top, as high as we can get, and have sex. But Max is already glancing around, checking his watch, riffling through some brochures we picked up at the hotel.

'There's not really that much to see. And it's so crowded today, I think you'll be disappointed.'

He squeezes my shoulder while I try to maintain an even expression, but perhaps my disappointment shows. 'I'd hate you to miss anything because we spent too long in a queue here,' he says. 'And there's plenty of time; we can come back tomorrow.' His closeness is persuasive. He takes my elbow and leads me away.

The steps at Notre Dame are steep and winding, and

Max goes first, holding my hand to guide me.

'You are clumsy, aren't you?' he says, hauling me up for the fourth time, just the smallest hint of irritation behind the smile; but he's helping me out of kindness, and it would be cruel to point out that it would be easier if he just left me to it. When we step outside he has recovered his charm. It's cooler up here, and a sudden gust of wind makes me shiver. Up close the gargoyles seem imbued with power, and one with a long neck and the face of a dog fixes me with a disconcerting stare. Max sees me looking at it and embarks on the history of the gargoyle, what it represented, when it first appeared, but nothing he says explains why it seems to have the hurt and accusing eyes of Robert. I stare it out, and gradually the fearsome face is diminished, turning back into nothing more than fashioned stone. We start to laugh at the distorted faces and Max points out one which has its lips turned back in a snarl, which reminds him of his old professor from college. As I lean over the edge, gazing down on to the heads of the people, Max presses up behind me. Well, having sex half-way up Notre Dame is a reasonable substitute for having it at the top of the Eiffel, if a touch sacrilegious, and there's no one around just now. I wait for his arms to come round me, feeling for my breasts, the way Robert or even Steven would, but he keeps his hands in his pockets. He's just teasing me and thinks if he doesn't touch me, no one will notice him pushing his rigid self against my bottom.

As we turn to continue the climb to the next level I notice that the gargoyle dog is still staring at me.

After lunch it starts to rain so we head for The Louvre. The Pyramid, which looked so incongruous among the old buildings when seen on television, is rather fine when you're inside but I don't say I think so until I've heard Max exclaim on its uncompromising style; I haven't the same vocabulary to support my opinions that he has. Max scoffs at joining the crowd admiring the Mona Lisa but we linger at Delacroix's *Dante and Virgil*, where he tells me of how the painter came by his models, and the scandal this painting caused when it was exhibited in 1822. Some saw in it, he says, the first seeds of Romanticism. I say I can't see what's romantic about it, it being just a lot of half-naked people falling out of a boat, and he chucks me under the chin and calls me a philistine.

Actually, Delacroix is one of the few painters I know anything about — I did a project on him at school instead of spending a term on life drawing — but when I offer a small insight I see it is unwelcome. Max is the perennial teacher; I, the eternal student. Our roles were cast long since; it's too late to change them now. Maybe I don't even want to. What I adore about being with Max is the mental stimulation, his knowledge and breadth of interest in all the arts, the sense of being at the cutting edge. I'm proud of the commanding way he expresses himself, and to note other tourists craning to listen to his informed opinion.

In bed later, flicking through the catalogue he bought for me on our arrival, I'm amused to see that much of his apparent extensive knowledge was repeated verbatim from the guide, but that doesn't diminish my admiration — in fact, it adds to it. Although he carried the catalogue throughout I barely saw him glance at it; if he remembers chunks of it by heart from his many visits then that is surely a feat in itself.

By the time we leave the Louvre my mind is a mêlée of who painted what and when, but my time hasn't been

IMMACULATE MISCONCEPTIONS

wasted. While I listened with rapt attention to the varied and learned discourse, my eyes were sliding sideways. If I can observe French women long enough, some of their effortless style might rub off.

Later, riding back to the hotel on the Metro, while Max is telling me the plot of the play he's writing, I notice a thin gangly man in the seat across the aisle. His eyes are rimmed red and he's hunched over in a position that looks awkward and uncomfortable. As I watch he takes something from his pocket; at first I think it's a small black box, but he moves the fingers of one bony hand and the black box becomes a gun. I look away from the man, thinking I was surely mistaken, but when I glance back he's still holding it, and it's definitely a gun. He pulls down part of the handle and inserts something. He's loading it. I nudge Max's arm and hiss in his ear. 'The man opposite us. Don't look.'

'What's the point of telling me not to look—'

He hasn't even lowered his voice, so I grip his arm until I can feel my fingernails bending back. 'He's got a gun. Let's get off.'

Max laughs and puts his arm round my shoulder. 'You're such an idiot.'

'He's got a gun!'

'Oh don't be ridiculous—' but now he can see it too and he shuts up. The man sees us watching him and twists his back round towards us, still hunching over the gun. At any moment he could start spraying bullets, and I can see tomorrow's headline in the *Evening Standard*: 'BRITONS KILLED IN METRO MASSACRE. *Young mother of two Eleanor Cope was last night fatally shot while on holiday with a man reported to be her . . .*' I hope it would be fatal too. It'd be terrible to be wounded and have to explain everything to my mother. I get up from my seat and wait near the doors, hiding behind the broad back of a fat Parisian. Max follows at a slower pace. The train slows and we get off.

'Weird,' says Max, nonchalant but watching to see if the man has got off behind us. Max is checking his watch as the train pulls out and thus doesn't see the man stand up and, aiming two fingers at us, shoot us stone dead. As he disappears from sight he's still laughing. I try to imagine Robert and Steven weeping at my graveside, but they only say, 'She had it coming to her.'

It's nothing to worry about really, just one of those inexplicable things that happens, but it upsets me. The malevolence in the man's red-rimmed eyes was the same as the gargoyle at Notre Dame. I feel as though a curse has been put on us.

Back at the hotel, Max unlocks the door and pushes me in, slamming the door with his foot.

'I've been wanting you all day.' The embers which have been smouldering since Notre Dame flicker into life and I unbutton his shirt in a frenzy.

'Oh, by the way,' he says, 'this isn't a gun in my pocket, I'm just pleased to see you.'

Lying next to Max afterwards, while he gazes at the ceiling and smokes a cigarette, it occurs to me that, in some respects, all men resemble each other when making love but in the afterplay they're all entirely different. With Robert, our *après-sex* is distinguished by my efforts to hide my irritation with him, though he takes my silence as the sweet companionable lingering it used to be. When we first dated, we would spend entire days in bed, doing the crossword, reading, listening to music. Any time we weren't naked and entwined beneath the covers was time wasted. But now he isn't concerned that I turn over and go to sleep, while he pads off to the bathroom, sets his alarm for the morning, reads another chapter of his book. Robert thinks routine and acceptance is what married sex is all about, and that's its strength. For Steven, on the other hand, sex is all novelty, and he wants as much as he can get; our afterplay has consisted not so much of a winding down from sex as a gearing up to have it again. There's been no time for lingering and longing. If I've done that it's been on my own after he's gone home. But I don't want to think about Steven.

With Max, what I feel is a sense of wonder. He makes love with the enthusiasm of youth and the control of experience. And he knows what to do. After the monotony of Robert, and having to show Steven almost everything, this has to count as best-ever sex. Added to which, rolling away from me with a satisfied sigh, he said he loves me. Oh I know what they say, that the sex is bound to be good with anyone you fancy desperately, the implication being that that level of fancying can't last. But why not? I've stayed hot for this man for almost twenty years, why shouldn't it last another decade or two?

I poke my finger into the centres of the smoke rings he's blowing. For some reason Max says he finds this erotic. He stubs his fag out and rolls me on to my stomach.

Later his mood turns playful.

'Your mascara's run. You look like you've got two black eyes.' (He can still say the sweetest things.) 'So tell me,' he traces the line of my collarbone thoughtfully and bends to kiss my breast. 'What did I do that you liked best?' I wish the light was out; I don't like to be looked at while

I'm talking about sex. It's different with Steven, but then I'm the tutor, he's the one most liable to blush.

'Oh, all of it really.' A line from a Webster play drifts into my mind, something about women fearing to name that which they do not fear to handle.

'You're blushing!'

I hit him in the chest and say 'I'm not!,' feeling my face go redder.

He laughs and takes hold of my wrist, opening the palm and holding it against his cheek. 'Oral. Okay, we've seen that.' I'm smiling foolishly as though I expect a mark out of ten. 'But what else? Have you tried anything different, or wasn't Robert game?' I wish he wouldn't mention Robert. And I thought oral sex *was* different. 'Do you like to experiment?' Of course I do. My most recent experiment has been to see how quick I can make Robert come to get it all over with.

I try to remember the pictures from *The Joy of Sex*, which has lain under our bed undisturbed since we got it as a special offer from a book club — but that was before Simon was born.

'What sort of things are you thinking of?'

'Oh, dressing up, role playing. Master and servant, have you tried that?' I've spent my adult life acting as Robert's servant — cooking, cleaning, being strumpet of the boudoir — and when I get into bed I don't do anything that means getting out again. (I don't say this, wishing Max to believe I've led the existence of an independent career woman who doesn't cook and clean for anybody.)

'I always think that sounds a bit juvenile,' I say, deciding to trash what I don't understand.

'Okay, well what about sex toys?'

I shake my head.

Immaculate Misconceptions

'S & M?'

'Aren't they those chocolate sweets with the crisp candy coating?' He looks puzzled. 'Oh no, that's M & M's.'

It's a pathetic attempt at a joke but he smiles and continues it. 'Oh, I thought you meant Treets. It can be quite a treat too, with the right partner.' At least, I hope he's joking.

I always used to wonder what Max saw in me but I think I begin to understand now. He is actually attracted by my gaucheness and naïvety, enjoys putting me in situations where he is better able to demonstrate it. That way I act as a constant boost to his ego; the dimmer I seem, the brighter he shines. Fortunately, seeming dim in his presence has never been difficult.

Max swings his legs out of bed and goes into the bathroom. The canals of Venice wobble alarmingly as he closes the door.

'I thought we'd do something different tomorrow,' Max says as we climb the steps out of the Metro on the way to the fish restaurant that a friend of his has recommended. For the briefest moment the word 'different' rings alarm bells, in case it's a veiled reference to another area of sexuality I will have to busk my way through, but Max continues: 'I've hired a car for the day; we can drive out somewhere. I've got a little surprise for you.'

I can't resist a glance round at the other diners to see if they realise I'm with the sort of man who troubles to surprise me. And I think I know what it will be. I've always longed to visit Versailles, ever since my history master told me that the palace there was so cold that the wine froze in the glasses. Max said the story was just a tale (by which he means he hasn't heard it himself;

I'm beginning to find cracks in the wide body of Max's knowledge), and anyway a weekend break wouldn't give us time to go. I'd been disappointed at the time, but now it seems that that was just a ruse to make it more special. When Max starts mentioning something about French homes, I'm sure of it. French stately homes is what he's getting at. Versailles! I squeeze his arm in appreciation without mentioning I've guessed his secret, but I show the depth of my gratitude when we get back to our room.

I don't want to think about Steven, but everywhere we go I see him. He was the youth selling tickets for the boat ride we took along the Seine, the bookseller on the riverside from whom Max bought a secondhand Victor Hugo, the waiter who brought our pastries in the café near our hotel. I should have spoken to him before I came, but there was so much to think about and I couldn't face dealing with that too. There'll be plenty of time when I get home. He might have met someone else himself by now.

When we've been driving for two hours and no matter which way I twist the map I still can't make it look like we're doubling back to go to Versailles, I finally give in to disappointment.

'So where *are* we going?' I take out my exasperation on a chocolate bar, snapping off a chunk with my teeth. Pain shoots up my jaw making my eyes water.

'I told you you wouldn't guess!'

'So why don't you just tell me?'

'You'll find out soon. We're nearly there.' He's excited about his surprise and glances at me with unaccustomed fondness.

We leave the main road and drive for some miles

through villages of scattered houses until we turn off, then turn off again, and now we're on what is little more than a farm track. We pass through a gate and Max pulls up outside a wide stone-built cottage. To the left stands an outbuilding, in the process of renovation.

Max grins at me broadly as he steps out of the car. 'What do you think?'

'What do I think of what?' If he has brought me to meet some of his arty pals I wish he'd warned me. I'm dressed in jeans and trainers as befits a hard day's sight-seeing. But he did say this was to be a surprise and perhaps these people are among his media contacts: famous writers and intellectuals, actors or artists, people I'll be thrilled to meet. I hope they speak English.

A tall man in his mid forties looks out of the door, and comes out to meet us, wiping his hands on his jeans. Max goes to him and they shake hands, as another man, almost as tall but slim and boyish with close-cropped blond hair, comes out and stands diffidently in the doorway.

As I approach, Max turns to introduce me. 'Laurence, this is Ellie, my . . .' his hesitation is so slight I doubt he notices it, '. . . friend. Ellie, this is Laurence Travers. I'm buying his house.' Max looks me full in the face to observe the extent of my astonishment. Laurence laughs as though he's in on the joke. 'I wanted to take another look before we finalise details. Just one or two things I want to clarify,' Max says, for the benefit of us both. And then to Laurence, 'And I particularly wanted Ellie to see it. I'm hoping she's going to live in it with me.'

When I went to Rebecca's first sports day at infants school she announced, on my arrival, that she'd put me down for the Mothers' Race. I felt the same sense of bewilderment and 'What the hell put that in her head?' that I feel now.

Laurence raises one eyebrow at Max and then turns his warm smile on me, grasping my hand as though this news gives him the greatest personal satisfaction. 'I hope you'll be as happy here as I've been,' he says. His fingers suddenly come in contact with my wedding ring and he glances down but doesn't comment.

Laurence has prepared lunch for us; cheeses, and salads grown from his own garden, and while we eat he tells us about the house and its locality. I want to know where the nearest town is with proper shops but Laurence tells me I don't want to spend all my time in a town with all these fields and woods to roam around in, and embarks on a fascinating and detailed description of the drainage system and damp-proof course.

He's an attractive man, balding, but with his remaining hair cut close, like Sean Connery's, and some of the same easy charm if you can get him off the subject of house renovating. Ricky, the boy with short blond hair, has the gaunt, angular features of an adolescent although on closer inspection he must be in his mid-twenties. He eats in silence, avoiding our eyes.

Laurence tells us that seven acres of land come with the house but only the small plot nearest the house has been cultivated, the rest is just grass with one area incorporating a few scattered trees they call the orchard.

'What do you want all this land for?' I whisper to Max while Laurence goes to fetch more wine. 'I bet you've never kept so much as a window box.'

He laughs. 'It's to keep the neighbours at a distance. Can't bear people dropping in all the time.'

'Have your neighbours ever dropped in?' I can't imagine they'd dare.

'No, but you never know when they might start.' His face is all smiles, he's lord of the manor and loving it. He tells me that Laurence has lived in this house for two years and has restored it from a state of utter dereliction. When we finish eating and before I can escape outside, Laurence produces 'Before and After' photographs. He has put in a new roof, floors, walls, stairs, and outside there is a patio and swimming pool which he invites us to swim in later. The external walls are all that remain of the original structure. In the kitchen where we eat the floor is of Italian tiles of terracotta, and the white walls are hung with copper cooking pots and utensils, and Laurence's paintings. Apparently he still exhibits occasionally. The few *objets d'art* on display around the house are carefully placed, as though this is a show home that no real people live in. There are no abandoned coffee cups or magazines on view. The house resembles an art gallery more than an artist's studio.

I comment on the beauty and orderliness of our surroundings.

'It's like living in a bloody museum,' says Ricky. It's almost the first time he has spoken.

Although Laurence still paints, it emerges that he makes a better living by doing up houses like this and selling at a profit, '. . . though there's been rather less profit in this one than most,' he adds hurriedly. It may be the truth, because it has been on the market for a year and he is accepting considerably less than the asking price.

'Have you looked at many houses?' I ask Max, sipping my coffee, and wondering if there were any placed nearer a cinema.

'A few, but only for a comparison. Laurence does excellent workmanship, so I knew I wouldn't want to look much further.'

'Did you know Laurence already then?' This would explain why the vendor is treating us so royally. I thought he was just keen to sell his house.

Both Laurence and Max laugh. 'Good Lord, yes,' says Max. 'We were at school together. Lost touch down the years but I bumped into him a few years ago when he was renovating the flat next door to mine.'

'He gave me tickets for the opening night of his play,' Laurence chipped in. 'I'd seen the posters already but I hadn't thought it would be *this* Max'.

'Then when I started looking for properties, someone told me Laurence was selling. It was just what I'd been looking for. Somewhere quiet, in the heart of the countryside, where I can come to work.'

'Don't sell your London flat until I do it up for you,' says Laurence, but Max says he's too late and they both laugh again. Laurence, it appears, had quite a reputation for his interior design. Before he moved here, flats he renovated were in some demand.

I see Max looking at Ricky. Ricky has a hint of the surly about him, like a pop star who knows he's looked at and lusted after and can afford to show his ill temper. I get the feeling he has taken a dislike to Max but maybe he's just feeling excluded. I decide to bring him into the conversation.

'Are you keen on decorating too, Ricky?' Laurence and Max hoot, though I'm unsure whether that's because I've reduced the extensive renovation and design work down to 'decorating', or at the idea of Ricky doing anything that might ruin his hands.

'Waste of bloody time. I'd rather move into a furnished flat and get on with it than mess about with all this.'

'That's because you're an idle little jerk,' says Laurence, suddenly hostile, starting to clear away.

'Chance'd be a fine thing.'

In the pause that follows Max takes out a packet of cigarettes and offers one to Ricky. A sour smile crosses Ricky's face.

'You'd better put those away,' he says, 'Laurence doesn't let anyone smoke in here.'

'Not "anyone", Ricky, only you.' He pours more coffee into Max's cup. 'Make yourself at home — I mean, it'll soon be your home. Do what you want.'

Ricky gets up, scraping his chair loudly against the tiles, and lopes off into the garden.

'Sorry about that,' says Laurence, studying his fingernails, 'we had a bit of a tiff before you arrived.'

Laurence and Max begin to reminisce about their school days and I take the opportunity to consider what's uppermost in my mind. What did he mean, 'hope she's going to live here with me'? It's just ridiculous. What about my kids, what about my job (with a pang I remember I no longer have a job), what about my family and all my friends? (I can feel Robert whispering, 'and what about me?' but I ignore it.) I can't just abandon my house, all my commitments, drop everything and take flight.

By the time Laurence rises to take me on a tour of the house I've confirmed what I was never in any doubt about; not really — that it's impossible. Which makes it strange that a part of my brain keeps asking me, 'Why not?'

'You will stay to supper, won't you?' asks Laurence as we admire the master bedroom with en suite whirlpool bath. 'I've asked a few people over for you to meet.'

'You mean neighbours?' I try not to smile.

'Well, only loosely. They live about twelve miles away, but they're the nearest Brits around and sometimes it is a relief to talk in your own language. They don't actually live in France but they stay for a month in the summer and they're often over at weekends. *She*'s a bit of a harridan but *he* is very good value. Bit of a coincidence really — I was at school with him. You might remember him, Max.'

I go on ahead to see the second bedroom. I'm a bit sick of all the people Max seems to have been at school with. When they catch me up, Laurence is trying to jog Max's memory. 'Podgy with glasses, but a bit of a wag. Three or four years above us, made deputy head boy. You must remember him. Hugo Barker. Quite a decent bloke. Rick describes him as all Bollinger and bonhomie.'

Max still can't place him, but I can.

'His wife's called Eileen.'

'Jesus, how did you know that?' Laurence is looking impressed, he thinks I'm psychic; I'd noticed a carefully placed book on the paranormal on the coffee table.

'They've got three grown up boys,' I add, enjoying the limelight while it lasts.

'Yes, I believe they may have. Never met them though; Hugo and Eileen always come by themselves.'

I explain why we won't be staying for supper after all. Well I can't risk word getting back to Robert before I have, and I don't want to get drummed out of the second-hand clothes sale sorority ('Why not?' says the same voice as before).

While Max and Laurence finalise a few details I seek out Ricky on the patio. He stubs out a cigarette guiltily as I round the corner as though he's expecting someone else. He glances at me sideways but doesn't speak. His silence is intriguing and I try to bring him out.

'We've heard what Laurence thinks about living here,' I say, 'but what do you think?'

He's silent for a few moments and I think he isn't going to answer, but then he leans back in his chair and thrusts his legs out in front of him. He's wearing khaki shorts and the hairs on his legs glint gold.

'I look at it like this. You want flowers, you go to a florist. You want grass, you go to a park. There's better things to do than mending fences and mowing meadows.'

'Max says he'll get someone in to do that.'

'Oh yeah, like who? We're ten miles out of the village remember.' He snorts. 'The village! You know where I used to live? In a flat overlooking Hyde Park.' He lets his gaze roam across the pool to the orchard as though it were city slums.

'Can't you go back?'

'To Hyde Park?' He turns to look at me as though he's surprised at the question. 'Not really. He threw me out.'

'Laurence?'

He looks as though he's about to tell me something but then changes his mind. 'No, this was before Laurence.'

I'm curious to hear his history but he doesn't offer any more. 'Where are you both moving to?'

He shrugs. 'Laurence is buying another dump over here. I can't see why though – no clubs, no shops, no one to talk to, I don't see the point. I might go back to England, I don't know.'

Max appears round the corner looking for me. Before he's near enough to overhear, Ricky whispers, 'You live in London?'

I nod. 'On the outskirts.'

'Then stay there. It's okay here now, but wait till February when you're snowed in, the lane's impassable and you've no water because the pipes are frozen.'

He stands as he finishes this speech and extends his hand to Max. Ricky seems more relaxed with Max now. He says something and Max laughs, slapping him on the shoulder, but before I can find out what they're talking about Laurence comes over and kisses me briefly on the cheek.

'You'll love it here,' he says. 'And Max tells me you have children. There's a school in the village, I see the kids coming home in their little overalls. It'll be perfect.'

I try to imagine Simon in a little overall but fail.

'Ricky's attractive, isn't he?' I say as we drive back.

'Is he? I didn't notice.'

'So you don't look at boys any more? Since Alex, I mean.'

He pulls up on to the side of the road and stops, taking my hands between his.

'Darling, I was just a kid then. Not only do I not look at boys any more, since I got you back I don't even look at other women.' He leans across to kiss me, a kiss which turns into a deeper, more serious exchange than he first intended. He draws out of it abruptly and gets out of the car. 'Come on.'

We're parked on the edge of a wood and he leads me in just far enough to be out of sight of the road, where a carpet of leaves covers the uneven ground. But the leaves are too damp to sit or kneel on and he says we must use the services of a nearby tree. I don't care – my sexual pilot light seems to be always burning these days. I tear my jeans off and lean back against the wide trunk of an oak. The bark is sharp on my buttocks but the sensation isn't unpleasant.

IMMACULATE MISCONCEPTIONS

'You look ridiculous,' I say to Max who has his jeans pulled down to his knees. But as he takes my face between his palms and kisses me, he isn't ridiculous at all. The soft pressure of his thighs against mine is almost unbearable; he produces an ache in me that even he can't entirely satisfy, and which his husky whispered obscenities only exacerbate. His fingers make me come before he does, but it isn't enough, I want more of him, want to touch him, suck him, to do not just be done to. I want to bring him to the peak of ecstasy until I have to smother his cries with kisses. I want to be back in our hotel room, making love between starched cotton sheets, or outside, high above the traffic, bending backwards over the balcony.

What I also want is a box of Kleenex.

'You did bring the tissues out of the car?' Max asks accusingly, as we stand unsteadily against the tree trunk. I'm developing an allergy to the bark, which has chafed my skin with help from Max's thrusting. I have a desperate desire to scratch but I can't get my hand behind me, even if social convention allowed it. I think I may have a tissue in my handbag so we shuffle, still joined, across to where it lies on a fallen tree trunk near our feet. We reach it with the utmost effort and from its deepest recesses I produce two screwed up and dubious looking tissues, suspiciously crisp and minus all powers of absorbency.

'Ah, the pleasures of country life,' I say, as the tissue scratches against my skin.

'Absolutely,' Max answers, purposely ignoring my sarcasm. 'You couldn't do this at the Barbican, could you?'

When we're both dressed again I try to conceal the screwed-up balls of paper among the leaves, but Max says we must on no account litter the French countryside and must take them home to be disposed of. I throw one at him and we have a snowball fight racing back to the car.

Later, as we approach the hotel, he says, 'You will move in with me, won't you?'

'Oh Max, I can't.' *You can, you can.*

'It doesn't have to be next week, it needn't even be next month, but it will happen — I know it.'

Max persuading me into a commitment. I can't believe it.

'And just think about it,' he goes on. 'Unlimited peace and serenity. Time to do whatever you want. You could try writing a book.'

'I don't want to write a book.'

'Write a play then; offer one of your magazines a diary-type piece on country living; write short stories.'

'The sort of work I do, it's all about contacts. I have to be at the end of a phone line.'

'You will be, won't you? They just dial a few extra digits. Where's the problem in that? And I'll be coming back every few weeks for the bookshop; it's not far you know, especially now we've got the Channel Tunnel. It'll be wonderful fun for Rebecca and Simon.'

'So you are including them in all this?' Despite Laurence's comments about the school I hadn't imagined Max to be serious.

'Of course they're included. It's a dream come true, a ready-made family but without the shitty nappy stage. I think your children are delightful.'

'You haven't even met Rebecca.'

'Women love me,' he says, smiling sideways.

It isn't possible, I know, and yet . . . The children could swim, take up riding (Rebecca is scared of horses so I don't dwell on that), there'd be no worrying about traffic. They could lead the kind of rural existence they had so envied at Carol's. And it would be a huge advantage to them to be fluent in a second language. ('What about me?' says Robert). And what about the incidental advantages — such as Josie's look of astonishment and envy, or the chance to shock the other mothers I've seen congregating at the school gates and who look askance at me because I'm not part of their clique. ('Just cleared off to France, never a word to anyone.') What about me? says Steven.

'Where would we live when we're in England?'

'At my flat. Or I could sell it and get a bigger place. Money isn't a problem, you know. We can do what we want to do.'

Money may start to be a problem if I don't start earning and he has to support his new family single-handed, but for now, as we speed through the golden dusk of the French countryside, that doesn't seem important.

'It's just a dream, isn't it?' I say regretfully, slamming the door of the car outside the hotel.

Max stops with the key in the lock. 'What's holding you back? It's over between you and Robert. Time to move on. And we belong together.'

We eat at the hotel, for quickness, and go to bed early to discuss plans. Making love later, I realise I'm perched on all fours on top and that Max is watching my backside in the mirror. I wiggle it and we both laugh.

Chapter 26

'Think about it,' Max says as we kiss goodbye at Gatwick, but I know that leaving Robert is impossible, know it so clearly that the little voice inside isn't even trying any more to tell me that it is. Max has been inspiring – he's opened the door to a new kind of happiness, and I want more of it. It's been like eating just one crisp when you want the whole packet. On the other hand, Robert may be boring old ready salted compared to Max's salt and vinegar, but he's kind and good and, most of all, he's part of my life. I'm not sure I'm ready for such major change; besides which, there are the kids to think of – I can't just tear the home apart on the strength of a weekend, however salty and addictive.

On the other hand, it's because the weekend has been so passionate, filling in all the gaps of our earlier relationship to such good effect, that I can't tell any of this to Max. 'I'll ring you,' is all I say.

Squeezing Max's hand goodbye my eyes brim and suddenly I'm in a movie, turning my back on Trevor Howard, striding away, Doing The Right Thing. Once out of Max's sight I duck into the loo, lock myself in and cry properly. I've been telling myself we can still meet but in my heart I know we can't. I love him and I want him, but it's over. Delving into the recesses of my handbag I draw out a screwed up tissue. It reminds me of our episode in the woods and I cry even harder.

It takes me longer to recover myself than I expect and, by the time I board the train which is to deliver me back to the station where I'm to meet Josie, I'm nearly forty minutes late. Greg is dropping her somewhere *en route*, and as I get off the train my first thought is that Josie will be having kittens in case I'm not coming. She isn't there, but that probably means her journey has been delayed as was mine. I get out the paperback I bought on the outward journey and never got round to opening and try to read. I can't settle though, and after a few minutes I walk up the platform and check the ladies. Later I ask a rail employee sweeping the platform, but he hasn't seen her either. When half an hour has passed I ring her home. Maybe she got the time wrong/thought she'd missed me/had to get back in a hurry. No reply. I wait a further half an hour and ring again. David answers and I hang up guiltily. I wait ten minutes, then another ten minutes, then I get a taxi. If David should see me I'll say that Josie met an old school friend — why not? Max seems to meet them everywhere — at the airport and went for a coffee but I was in a hurry to get home so I didn't wait for her. Not a brilliant piece of invention, I know, but it'll do, as long as Josie goes along with it.

I pay the taxi, watching Josie's house all the while, but David's car isn't there so maybe he's gone out now.

I open the front door and kick it shut so that it slams loudly. It's strange to be home, to find everything so much the same when so much has changed for me.

'I'm home!' I've bought a costume doll for Rebecca and

a model of the Eiffel Tower for Simon. The Eiffel Tower acts as a reminder of Max and I wish I'd chosen a less phallic present for my son. Besides, seeing as he can't eat it or shoot someone with it, it was never going to be the ideal present.

I wait on the threshold for the children to fling themselves into my arms, but there is no thunder of footsteps from upstairs, or voices in the garden; the house is strangely quiet. They're probably hiding, ready to spring out on me. I creep into the lounge and peer round the door. Then the kitchen door opens.

'Where've you been?' says Robert. His hair is hanging down into his eyes making him seem to glower. He's got a heavy cold, from the look of him.

'You know where I've been. Where is everyone?'

'The kids are at Cathy's. I wanted them out of the way. I said, where have you been?'

There's something not right here, but I'm not about to put myself in the wrong without a reason and attack is the best line of defence.

'Why aren't they here? You knew I was coming home!'

'Why weren't you with Josie?' Oh *is that* all it is.

'It was quite a coincidence really. We were waiting for our luggage to come through and she saw this old friend—'

'When did you last see her? Yesterday? Day before?'

Ah. Play dumb. 'Robert, I don't know what—'

'Ellie!' He takes a step towards me and raises his arm and I flinch, expecting him to hit me. But he brings it up to his face and shrinks into a chair with his head in his hands.

'Josie's in intensive care. She was in a car crash coming

back from somewhere in the west country – with some shit of a bloke. He was drunk.'

'Is she all right?'

'She's in intensive care; of course she's not all right!'

'What about—?' How would Josie take it if anything happened to Greg?

'So you know him, do you? All in on this together, I suppose.'

'No, I never met—'

'It doesn't matter what you say, I can't believe any of it, can I?'

'Oh Robert . . .' I perch on the arm of the chair and put my arm round him but he shrugs me off.

'Who were you with?'

He looks little and old. He resembles the photos of his father that his mother keeps on her sideboard. It'll just compound things to tell him.

'No one you know,' I say.

'Bitch!' He stands up and pushes me aside with such force that I slide off the arm of the chair on to the floor with a bump. 'It was Max, you lying bitch! David told me. That swine of Josie's hasn't kept anything back.'

Sitting on the floor, feeling pain surge through my coccyx, I want to cry and I feel ashamed that I can only produce tears for my own pain, not Robert's, or Josie's. God – Josie, what's happened to her? But Robert ignores my question, striding up and down, kicking at the table, the sofa, at Ginge who has chosen that moment to walk by, and tells me what I am.

'I'm sorry.'

'Sorry? What good is sorry? What made you do it? Haven't we been happy? What do you want that I haven't given you?' The things I wanted were never in his gift

– the exhilaration of the new, the chance to take a few risks – the thrill of falling in love again. But that wasn't his fault, and I couldn't say so even if it were, so I just shrug which only enrages him further. 'Was he better in bed than me? Because that isn't what you used to say. You used to say what a crap lover he was.' Did I say that?

'It wasn't about sex.'

'Oh really? You mean it was about money, then? He has more to spend on you, is that it? He could take you to Paris and I can't. He's a predator, a manipulator. He takes what he wants and moves on. Do you really imagine he's any different than he used to be?' Robert on the attack is a new phenomenon to me; I don't know how to handle him. I start to speak but he leaps in, 'Don't tell me his wife doesn't understand him, because I can read him like a book.'

'This wasn't about you or him. It was about me.'

'What's that supposed to mean?'

Hell, I don't know. It made perfect sense when someone on *The Archers* said it. That's the trouble with real life, it's always shooting off at tangents you're not expecting. 'If it was about you then of course it was about me,' says Robert angrily. 'Anything else is like saying your right leg getting broken doesn't affect the other one. Of course it does.'

Robert's choice of metaphor makes me think of Josie and suddenly I start to cry, my throat swelling with a dry ache. I can't stop the tears but I'm relieved they've come at last; tears have always been the quickest route to Robert's sympathies, as Rebecca would testify.

'And don't think crying will get you anywhere.' I draw my knees up to my chest and bury my face but he just keeps on. 'Don't you love me? Is that it? Are you bored with me?' Through my fingers, I glimpse him raking his hands through his hair in frustration. The lock of hair falls back as it always does. 'You're always complaining about how we've had to keep moving house for my job, but haven't you ever asked yourself why I had to do that?'

At last, a chance to put myself back in the right. 'Because you always wanted the next promotion, and you're selfish, self-centred—' It isn't true but I get it in first before he can say it to me.

'To get you everything you wanted, that's why. Did you really think I wanted to move that last time? I liked my old job, I liked everyone there, a damn sight better than I do here, but do you care about that? Do you ever even ask?' He pauses long enough for me to start to answer but then sets off again without listening. 'You've wanted a nice house, your own car — to stay at home with the kids—'

'I didn't want to stay at home!'

'. . . so I've done what I had to do to get it all for you. And this is the thanks I get.'

'I always wanted—'

'And don't give me any crap about your job, because that's just your hobby. If you'd been serious about a career, you'd have taken a training course, knocked on a few editors' doors. But no, you'd rather play at it — and screw around in your spare time like that slut Josie.'

Sometimes a person can say a thing, maybe only a small thing, that completely alters your perspective. But it isn't the hugely unfair things he is saying about my work, but the hugely unfair idea that Josie is a slut which is affecting me most. As if she ever could be! She's only had one lover and even I've had two.

He isn't right about my job either. Of course it's not just a hobby, and he knows very well that I had to stay at home with the kids because I couldn't earn enough to cover the cost of childcare. But even though he's so obviously wrong, the idea eats at me. Why didn't I ever take a course, even just a correspondence course? Even the editor on my humble paper might have helped me off the women's page if I'd asked. I'm curled up smaller now, trying to hide myself behind my knees, but I can't get away from the sound of his voice. He's putting me in the wrong, a place I'm not used to being.

'We've trusted you, all of us. Me, the kids, my mother. Whatever you told us, we've believed it. Even David next door. You know what he said? He said he'd always had his suspicions about Josie — but he just couldn't believe it about you. It's the kids I feel sorry for. You've let us all down.'

Suddenly I'm back in school: 'You've let us all down, Eleanor. Worst of all you've let yourself down.' I was unjustly accused at the time and now, even though he has a point, all my old indignation comes surging back. Anger makes me fight.

'Oh really? And what about you with your—'

I've no idea what I'm going to say next but he rides straight over me anyway. 'And Steven.'

I stop speaking, stop crying; I almost stop breathing. 'Steven?' Robert knowing about Max is just about bearable for him: this is old ground really; the revival of a past enemy maybe, but one Robert has beaten before and can again. But Steven is new ground. Home ground. Robert thought he was his friend. Please God, please God, don't let Robert suffer any more; don't let him know about Steven and me and what's gone on here, in this house — in every room in this house. 'Even Steve,' he says.

A car hoots outside and there's a squeal of brakes and

then more hooting. 'What made you do it?' His face looks tortured, different from how I've ever seen it before. He sits down with his head in his hands while I listen to my heart beating, frightened at how rapidly events have moved out of my control. The car roars off with much revving of its engine.

Robert steps to the window and looks out with his back to me. It seems an age before he picks up the thread.

'Even Steve. He's just a kid, but he's crazy about you. Giving him work, helping with his studying. To hear him, you'd think you were Mother bloody Teresa.' There's an ugly sneer in Robert's voice but when he turns round his eyes are puffy and red. 'He'll probably kick himself because he didn't try it on with you himself.'

Oh thank you God, thank you God; he doesn't know. I'm so busy throwing up prayers that I scarcely realise that Robert is still talking. 'I know you've always wanted to work, I've tried to understand, be supportive, tried to take an interest. Do you remember that article I helped you with?' Last summer he came with me to all the local attractions, helping me collect information for 'Fifteen Places to Visit for Under a Fiver' — what they cost, when they were open, which ages they most suited. So he didn't mean what he said about my work, or not all of it. 'But he's always been there in the background, hasn't he? That bastard, I've always known he'd come back.'

'Robert—' I unfold my stiffening legs and shake my tear-sodden skirt away from my knees. Perhaps this is an opportunity for us to cry together and make up. And I do want to make up. I want to put everything back how it was. It hasn't been my fault, not really. I've been the victim of a mid-life crisis, but now the crisis is past and my temperature is coming back to normal. Maybe I've had to go through all this to find out that it's Robert I wanted all along. But when I try to put my arm round his shoulders he thrusts me aside and stands up abruptly. At the door he pauses for a moment.

'Did you used to think of him when I was making love to you?'

I start to deny it but he's already striding out, Ginge at his heels. I grab at Ginge, wanting to hold his soft fur against my face, but he follows Robert, narrowly missing being caught in the door as it slams shut.

When Cathy brings the children back it's getting dark but I'm still sitting there. There's no sign of Robert.

Rebecca is delighted to see me and angry with Daddy for not letting her wait at home to meet me but I explain that Auntie Josie is poorly in hospital and Daddy thought I might be upset as we'd been travelling together.

'What's the matter with her?' Rebecca looks aghast. She has a horror of death and illness. I explain that Josie will be fully recovered and come back home any day. I hope I'm right. Rebecca looks not entirely convinced, but is eventually distracted by the costume doll. Even before the presentation of the Eiffel Tower, Simon has taken the news of Josie on the chin, asking if there's time to watch a video before bed.

It's only when the children are occupied that I'm able to find out what has really happened to Josie. Robert has told Cathy that Josie has head injuries and two broken legs. The car went into a spin before turning over. David is remaining optimistic although it's really too soon to know. It's worse than I'd thought. In my heart I've been hoping that Robert was exaggerating about her being in intensive care just to punish me. Ironically, Greg was barely scratched.

I must look faint because Cathy sits me back down and rushes to the kitchen to make a cup of tea.

When I go upstairs later to put the children to bed I see that Robert has taken the nightdress I've taken to wearing, my dressing gown and my jars of moisturiser and cleanser, which are normally left on the dressing table, and dumped them all in the spare room, that repository of household junk that no one wants and which doesn't seem to belong anywhere else. The symbolism is not lost on me.

The next morning I stay in bed until I know Robert will already have left for work. I'm at a loss for what to say to him, and in the early morning fug my powers of diplomacy or invention are at their weakest. Seeing David's car parked in his drive, I ring to see if there's news of Josie but he puts the phone down when he hears my voice.

It's disconcerting to find that your place in the world has shifted. I've never been *persona non grata* before; people have always been glad when I phone, touched to be remembered, impressed with my thoughtfulness. I seem to have moved into a parallel time zone where everyone looks the same but behaves in a way with which I'm totally unfamiliar.

Ironically, the one person who would really love to hear from me I can't face at all. I didn't tell Max it was over when I should have done, and now I haven't the strength. I still mean to do it, because Robert and I have a life together (he's surprisingly forceful and determined when galvanised to action, can be strangely appealing). We won't really collapse over this, however it may look. But I can't speak to Max right now, not today. And he won't be sympathetic about Josie. He'll blame her for choosing a man who drinks and drives, or me for planning our liaison via a woman foolish enough to be driven by one. If I tell him I can't see him again he'll be cutting and acerbic which I won't be able to cope with in my present state. Not that I'd feel guilty whatever he'd said. I mean, just because I talked Josie into deceiving her husband and coming away for the weekend, it doesn't make me responsible for the fact that she had a car crash and was nearly killed. Of course it doesn't . . . I start to cry again.

I want sympathy and understanding but, of the only two people who could give it, one is lying in intensive care and the other has stormed off as though he never wants to see me again.

Two days ago, an entirely different scenario had seemed possible. Sitting over cappuccinos and wafer biscuits in a pavement café we'd decided how easy it would all be. I would explain to Robert that our marriage had gone stale and we'd be better apart, and after a week or two of gentle insistence he would agree and we'd part amicably. He would understand that it was far easier for me to take the children and would be content that he would see plenty of them. On our frequent trips to England the children could stay with him; I might even stay here myself, *that's* how friendly it would all be. And that way the break would be gradual and less traumatic. I'd had a clear picture of him nodding his understanding, agreeing that this was a solution that would suit all parties, and that living in France was an opportunity for the children not to be missed. Of course, he said he would miss me, but then I said I would miss him too, we had been very happy when the children were small (at this point in the café I had become tearful, causing Max concern, but I'd secretly thought that it would be no bad thing if these same tears were to start up when I spoke to Robert; he'd know then how genuinely regretful I was.) Phrases such as 'You bitch!' and 'You scheming cow!' had never entered the scenario at all.

By an extraordinary and atypical stroke of luck Rebecca and Simon have both been invited out today, so by ten-thirty I have the house to myself. Once they've gone, and silence surrounds me like a black cloud, the luck element seems to diminish. I stare at the phone and try to will it into ringing. I could do with some gentle conversation, perhaps with Cathy, or even better any of the mothers of the children's friends, someone who knows nothing about our circumstances and would offer me unbridled sympathy for the tragedy that has befallen my friend and therefore me. I'm still staring at the handset when, eerily, it rings. I close my eyes and wish for it to be Theresa. It's Max.

'Can't speak now,' I lie, 'Robert's here,' and put the phone down.

I'm carrying an armful of sweaters into the spare room from my wardrobe, and have just decided that I should let my clothes stay put and stake my claim to my own bedroom, when I happen to glance out of the window. He's there: Steven, the other problem I've been pushing to the back of my mind. He's bending down, dead-heading roses in Josie's garden. I didn't realise they'd taken him on too. He's wearing jeans cut off above the knee and a denim shirt which hangs open, and as I watch he straightens up and wipes his nose on his sleeve. Simon used to do that, but even he knows now that sleeves are for arms not noses. His hair needs cutting; it's pulled into a pony-tail at the back but the sides are ragged and untidy and maybe it needs washing too, you can't tell under that damned cap. I don't know what's been happening to me. I must have been under a spell, like Titania. I woke up and was bewitched into falling in love with the first man I came into contact with. I feel ashamed. And stupid. I wish I hadn't told anyone.

I'm collecting Lego pieces up from the floor in Simon's room when the doorbell rings and, looking down through the landing window, I see the crown of a red cap and a ponytail. I toy with the idea of standing still until he goes away but I've opened the bedroom windows so he will know someone is in.

I open the door with a smile while trying to project rays that signal: 'Go away'. It's chastening, to see your lovers the way others must have seen them. I should have broken off with him while I could still remember what had attracted me; now shame and embarrassment make me brutal. Steven's waiting smile fades when he sees my expression.

'Ellie? Are you all right?'

'Yes, of course I am.'

He sways a little at my snappishness. 'You look ill, that's all.' I don't respond so he continues. 'You've been away ages. Can I come in?'

Yes, you can come in, and we can sit over coffee, as we used to, while I tell you that I no longer love you, never did, probably, and that I would like you to go far away so I won't be reminded of my own foolishness and those awful embarrassing things we did.

But I'm not quite up to telling him all that just now. Instead I glance back over my shoulder as though I might find a reason there for why he can't come in. As it happens

I do. 'I've just hoovered the hall carpet.' He blinks and I realise this isn't as good a reason as I'd thought. 'I'm going to shampoo it now so it mustn't be walked on.'

'Oh. Okay. Shall I come round the back through the kitchen then?'

Now it's my turn to blink. My brain is sluggish today but an answer comes eventually. 'I've just cleaned the floor in there too.'

The animation leaves his face and his jaw clenches as he tries to work out what has changed. Then he draws himself up a little, as though to suggest if I can tough it out then so can he.

'While you was away Robert said would I come and mow the lawn once a week. I'll have to do it today because I've got another painting job – off that friend of yours, Max.'

For a moment a knot forms in my stomach and I think he's telling me he knows something, but he goes on, 'I give him a quote last week and he says go ahead. I'm going round tomorrow.' ('Tomorrer' he says, causing a second knot in my stomach.)

'Yes, that'll be fine.'

'It'll have to be won't it? Will you get the mower out then?'

I hold his gaze for a moment. It's the first time he's ever expected me to lift anything heavier than my own sweater. 'I'll unlock the shed door and you can get it yourself.'

He looks hard at me as I start to close the door, but he puts his hand on the doorframe to stop me.

'Had enough of me then, have you?'

It's embarrassing when someone goes straight to the heart of the ugly problem instead of politely skirting round it.

'It isn't like that—'

'Then what is it like?'

It comes to me that I've enjoyed feeling he's dimmer than me; that I've shone the brighter next to his dull light. But that was just a silly phrase I thought up about Max, I'm not like that at all.

'Of course I'm still fond of you—'

'Oh, it's fond now is it?'

'But it was never going to work out, was it? I'm older than you, and the kids are always around—'

'Have you got someone else?'

I say no but can't tell whether or not he believes me.

'My mates said you was using me. Wanting a bit of rough.'

'You've discussed me with your friends?'

Don't some of them work on the checkout in Tesco's? They could all be sniggering at me, contemplating my sexual technique as they're ringing up my frozen peas. What kind of a person is he? I would never have discussed the things we did together with anyone. I mean, you can't count Josie. Or Carol.

The phone rings and I leave him standing there while I go to answer it. A few minutes later I hear the sound of the mower.

The phone call is from one of the magazines I submitted an article to ages ago. They've only just got round to reading it, but they want to buy it and for me to go in and discuss some more ideas with them. The features editor is about to go on holiday so we agree a date for three weeks' time. Putting the phone down I consider how thrilled I would have been to get this news in any week but this.

* * *

Of course, that wasn't the end of it with Steven. When I looked out of the kitchen window and saw his red baseball cap on the greenhouse shelf I thought he'd just left it behind. It was only when I went outside to bring the washing in that I saw it wasn't on the shelf at all, he was wearing it, crouched down on the floor with his knees drawn up in front of him and his face buried in his arms. It was the same position I'd sat in while Robert had railed at me, and a wave of nausea passed over me at the memory. When I touched Steven's shoulder he jerked away as though I'd stung him.

'Fuck off, cow.' This was the first time I'd heard him swear (unless you count occasional obscenities when making love, but they were more by way of direct instruction than any kind of oath).

I'd handled this all wrong, but it's so hard to know: if you're soft and gentle they think you don't mean it; if you're hard and cruel it's, well, hard and cruel. Better to let them see how you feel from your actions and draw their own conclusions.

If I'd thought things through I might have realised that this is the approach Max always used on me. It hadn't worked then either.

I told Steven I was sorry but that these things happen, my feelings had changed, it was no reflection on him. I said I would still help him with his English, we would always be friends and I would always love him though not in that way (as if there were any other way that counted). I said we'd had wonderful times together and he would always have a special place in my heart. I said a lot of other things too, and the more I said the more insincere it sounded and the less inclined he seemed to say anything at all. He didn't even move except to flinch the way Robert had when I tried to put my arm round him.

Eventually he raised his face, looking straight ahead. Such sad, hurt eyes looked at me, the fight all gone out of them. He stood up, rubbing his hands down his shorts, and walked past me out of the greenhouse.

'If Robert wants me to finish off the patio he better ring me,' was all he said.

The hospital looks subtly different now I'm entering it as a visitor rather than a patient. Walls that had seemed dark with menace are now just dark through poor lighting. Josie's ward is on a different floor from the one I was in, but is otherwise identical. (She is waiting to have a private room allocated but is having to slum it until one falls vacant.) The nurse points out her bed but I hesitate at the foot of it. The figure that can't possibly be Josie shifts slightly in the bed and raises a wrist weakly. The face is as pale as the starched pillowcase but with a greyer hue. The white lips attempt a smile.

'Ellie!'

I try not to look as shocked as I feel. Her head is bandaged and her face is cut and bruised. Her legs are raised into a position that looks disconcertingly similar to something I saw reflected in the mirrored hotel room.

'How are you?'

'Fine.' She bears as much resemblance to 'fine' as Arnold Schwarzenegger does to a seven-stone weakling. Her voice is a husky rasp, but somehow she is smiling. 'I'm not too bad really. They thought I might have brain damage, you know.'

'How could they tell?' I don't normally crack jokes against Josie, in fact I wouldn't normally crack a sick one like this at all, but embarrassment has taken control of my tongue.

Fortunately she smiles. 'Did David tell you?'

'He's not speaking to me. No, it was Robert.'

'I didn't think he'd be speaking to you either.'

'It was the last thing he said before he stopped.' I force a smile I don't feel.

Robert and I have been communicating in single sentences if at all. 'Where have you put the iron?' 'Don't use up all the bread.' 'Piss off.'

Josie nods with difficulty against the pillow. 'David says he wants me better first and then we'll talk about everything, but I think he's hoping that this will mean it's over with Greg. He's been so sweet I've had to let him think that.'

Looking at her, my eyes start to fill up and she squeezes my hand.

'I was hoping you'd come, Ellie.' I squeeze hers back, thinking how our relationship has deepened over the past months. But then she spoils it by adding, 'There's just no one else I can ask to ring Greg.' She has tried calling on the 'mobile' phone which they wheel to the bedside, but she can't get a reply. 'I know they said he wasn't hurt, but he could have done something that didn't show up and have collapsed somewhere. I'm really worried about him.'

'Hasn't he phoned here?'

'I don't know. Someone keeps phoning but I think that's been a woman.' It's been me actually, but maybe Greg has phoned as well.

'Give me his number then, and I'll do it as soon as I get back. Shall I ask him to ring you?'

'No, in case David's here. Just find out and let me know.'

I reach into my bag for the grapes, orange juice and magazines I've brought with me, and feel a sense of *déjà vu* as Josie thanks me for the gifts without looking at them. It's so strange to be back here, so familiar and yet so very different. The woman in the next bed even resembles Rita. For the second time I have the sensation of having stepped into a parallel universe. The sunflower drapes that screen Josie from the patient on the other side add to the effect. They're identical to the ones I remember, but faded and wan. Why did I imbue them with such significance?

'I thought you'd enjoy these,' I say, holding up the magazines so Josie can see the covers without turning her head. These will cheer her if anything will. Once I heard Britt Ekland on *Desert Island Discs* rejecting the opportunity to take a book in favour of a pile of magazines. I told Josie, thinking how funny it was, but she thought it was an excellent choice. 'There's always so much to read,' she said, 'you'd never be bored. And you'd have a constant reminder not to neglect your exercise and skincare routine.'

She had grossly exaggerated the comfort that magazines would bring. Now she closes her eyes and sinks deeper into her pillow, even though she can't possibly have seen the current issue of *Hello* yet.

A week after Josie's accident I wake up to hear much banging about from Robert and, when I go to the landing to see what's going on, find him lugging two suitcases downstairs. Behind him Rebecca is struggling with a rucksack in the shape of a koala which seems to be stuffed with teddies.

'What the hell is going on?'

'I'm taking the kids to my mother's for a few days,' he

says, adding when Rebecca has taken her bag out to the car, 'We can't go on like this; we're not getting anywhere and quite honestly I can't bear the sight of you.'

Despite his coolness over the past week, I'm astonished to hear this. I thought he was just punishing me and that once I had suffered enough he would relent and we would go back to normal. I've been very penitent to show that his treatment was having its effect, so I don't deserve this latest development.

'By all means go yourself, if you want a break, but you can't take the kids.' If the kids are here, he will have to call in more often.

'There's not much you can do about it; I don't see any judge taking the side of a mother who deserts them for a dirty weekend. Besides, you've left me no choice. If they stay here what's to say you won't let that bastard call round?'

'I'll give you my word on that; but there's no sense in just walking away, that won't resolve anything.'

'The only thing I want to resolve is how soon you can leave. If there's nothing here for you to stay for, you might go a bit sooner.' He heaves a suitcase into the boot of the car. 'And don't bother giving me your word on anything, I know what that's worth.'

'Robert—'

He lifts a box of the children's toys and arranges it in a corner of the boot so that it won't fall over. I try to get his attention because there's one thing I still haven't said, not in so many words.

'Robert — give me another chance.'

He slams down the lid of the boot and regards me with a cool objectivity. It's alarming to be looked at so coldly by the person you have spent half your life with, and who has always focused on your strengths, not your faults.

'You're in my way,' he says, pushing past me.

I could have caused a scene but that would have gained nothing and only upset the kids. It's the first time they've ever slept at their grandmother's — if they've needed babysitting she has always come to us — so they think it's a great adventure. It is also the first time I haven't been able to get my way about the children.

'Please Robert, you can't go—'

'Too late. I've gone.'

He revs the engine and pulls away. I've never seen him so stubborn before and as the car moves off I consider what a fool he is being. There's no need for us to split up over this — it was an aberration on my part, that's all. Okay, two aberrations, if you count Steven. They were still no more than blips on a graph, nothing signifying a general trend. Other men would have talked things over, tried to understand what had caused those blips, but not Robert, oh no, for him everything is cut and dried. Well if this is how he wants it, fine. Max, in the course of hurried or surreptitious phone calls during the week, has been trying to persuade me to change my mind and move in with him. I've resisted but now, at last, I can see the truth of it. I came home from Paris with every intention of putting Max behind me, but it's Robert's decision and that's fine; it couldn't be working out better. And now I can stop trying to dredge up arguments to persuade Max (as if I could ever persuade Max of anything), that I can't go to him. He's right, as he's always right. This was planned. It's meant. Fate has decreed, I have no choice, and if I go now it makes everyone happy, even Robert — maybe especially Robert. Max and I were meant for each other and only a twist of fate prevented it. Well, now the skein has been unwound and our lives are back on course. I can go to my old love, my first love, and start again with a clear conscience. (That'll make Robert sorry.)

As soon as Robert calms down I'll discuss when I can have the kids back. He's a reasonable man underneath it all; he'll know they need to be with their mother.

I stand at the end of the drive and watch the last vestiges of my old life disappear into the distance.

I'm just jotting down a few ideas for the magazine editor — including 'Contemplating Infidelity', which Theresa had turned down — when the phone rings.

'Is that — Ellie?'

'Yes?'

'You don't know me, but you left a message on my answerphone.'

'Greg!'

'No, sorry. I'm a friend of his; he was staying here for a few weeks while I was away on holiday. He's left now.'

'He is all right, is he? Only his girlfriend has been very worried.'

'Oh yes, he's fine.' I wonder why he doesn't just give me Greg's new number and get off the phone. When I ask, he hesitates. He's really only ringing because he thinks someone should let Josie know and it doesn't seem that Greg is going to. At last he blurts it out.

'He's gone back to his wife.' He rings off before I can offer any observations on Greg's parentage.

I'm so angry with Greg, with his friend, with every man in the history of mankind, that I throw the phone at him with such force that the handset comes apart and a piece of wood the size of a fifty-pence piece flies off the door frame. I kick Greg as he lies there, defenceless, sending a sharp pain through my right foot as it comes in contact with the skirting board.

Chapter 27

Max carries my luggage in, then busies himself in the kitchen while I look around. It's exhilarating to be here, in my lover's home. The soft rugs and strategically placed lamps arranged for love and seduction send a frisson through me. The bathroom is hung with black and white erotic prints. The pop of a champagne cork sounds and Max comes back carrying two glasses. He smiles a little shamefacedly.

'A bit of a cliché, champagne. But it does rather hit the spot for a special occasion.' Yes, I think as I take a sip, it's hitting my G-spot.

I perch on the edge of the leather Chesterfield, pressing my thighs together and feeling awkward in these unfamiliar surroundings, but Max is oblivious.

'I can't believe this has all come true,' he says, leaning back and stretching his legs out; I'm not used to seeing him so relaxed. 'And so quickly. I was prepared to wait, you know.'

Such an admission from Max is like a politician admitting he's only in politics for the power and the glory. Even though you've always known it to be so you never expect to hear one say so.

I wonder how long it will take before I stop being astonished by Max's new devotion, stop feeling the rush of heat to the loins whenever I see him. Hopefully never. I get a thrill of pleasure, not to mention wonder, every time he says something like this.

The flat is larger than I'd expected, with a lounge equal in size to ours at home, though it looks bigger without the array of kids' abandoned shoes, jackets, toys, sweet papers and board games (unless you include the expensive chess set laid out under the window). The smell of fresh paint in the air seems entirely appropriate for our new beginning.

'I can only stay until Friday,' I explain. 'I want to be there when the children come home, but I'll be back when they go back to Robert's mother's.'

Max nods, quite prepared to accept these arrangements. 'And it won't be long,' he says, 'before we can move into our new house. Laurence is leaving at the end of the month.' If we move in soon, we'll be able to use the pool before the summer is over. It's ironic that I was so upset at having to cancel the holiday in France with Robert and now I'm going there to live. If we hadn't cancelled it, I'd be there right now cooking fried eggs on a two-ring gas cooker in a poky little caravan — instead of being here, about to christen the pine four-poster of my wild and exquisitely talented lover.

'Time for bed I think,' he says, standing up and picking up the bottle from the table. He's right, it's already three o'clock in the afternoon so we've wasted half an hour already.

We sleep after making love and when I open my eyes again it's growing dark outside. It's disorientating, waking for the first time in a strange room, and though it's only eight o'clock I have the sense of unease you get when you wake at two-thirty on a winter's night, when everyone else is still and sleeping, and your troubles come crowding in, snapping at your heels. It's all been so sudden and there are so many things to be resolved: the kids, the house, my finances, which side of the bed to sleep on (in Paris I was magnanimous but now I want to sleep on the side which gives me the shortest walk to the loo).

But when I get in Max's shower and finally work out how to operate the controls I start to feel better. The hot jets are therapeutic and send my anxieties scuttling down the drain. When Max wakes and gets in with me, lifting me up so that my legs curl round his waist, I think: Ellie, you worry too much. After a few minutes of this I don't think of anything at all.

'What are we going to have for dinner?' I ask as I stand on one leg and Max dries my toes.

'I'm having smoked salmon down at the wine bar. I don't know what you're having.' I'm about to say that that sounds good to me (smoked salmon isn't something I've had too much of recently – which is to say, ever) when he adds, 'I'm meeting the producer of my new play at nine. But you can come if you want.' The offhand manner is too much like the old Max, but unlike the old Max he is giving me an option, however grudging. I'm looking forward to appearing with him in company as his partner, but there will be time for that and tonight I'm seduced by his flat. I want to spread out and bask in the atmosphere of my new home. Soon to be just one of my new homes: I can't believe I'm the sort of person who has two residences (two and a half really, if you count the one I still share with Robert).

When Max has gone I make a sandwich and stand at

the lounge window looking out. From here I can look down on to the tops of buses and taxis, from one of which emerges an elegant woman in a cream suit. She runs inside our block while a man in a suit pays the cab. It's a strange vantage point but I'm fascinated, having always been used to seeing passers by at my own eye level, especially if we ever forget to close the curtains in the evening. You'd have to be King Kong to gaze in at these windows. In fact I almost expect to see him; I feel feminine and desirable, like Fay Wray. Across the road lies parkland beyond which rise the roofs and buildings of the metropolis. I think of Carol's country home and wish she could see me now.

Max has left a wardrobe empty for me but he hasn't left enough hangers, so I go along the racks in the other cupboards looking for spares. His clothes hold the shape of him and I can't resist lying my face against the cuff of a beige cotton jacket and caressing the collar of a pale silk shirt. He has beautiful shoes too, lined up in the bottom of the wardrobe. I kneel down and trace the familiar crease that forms where his toes join his foot. His sweaters are folded neatly on shelves; he obviously favours the Benetton method of storage rather than the mode I generally use (church hall jumble sale). I run my finger along the rough wool of a heavy Arran. He'll look wonderful in that on evening strolls through the local French villages or reclining on a rug sipping hot chocolate in front of the fire on a winter's night. (Out of habit I look at the label to see whether it's hand-wash only.)

Max stores his suitcases on top of the wardrobes and, when mine are empty, I pull up a chair and climb up to heave mine up there with them.

I don't know what makes me look inside the carrier bag. I hear it rather than see it. As I slide my case along it meets an obstruction and pushes it sideways. It's a large bag holding what could be just a pile of papers. It's probably just the overflow from his filing system (we keep ours under the bed). I'm not nosy or anything obviously, but it's only sensible to know where he keeps all his belongings. As I bring it towards me I have a sense of foreboding: is it something to do with his ex-wife perhaps? But surely he wouldn't have left anything lying about that he didn't want me to see?

The bag is heavy and as I heave it forward it slides from my grip and some of its contents fall out. It's full of magazines. But not the ones Robert reads — *What Car, Which Car, What the Hell for Car* — these are of the type I've noticed, or mostly not even noticed, on the top shelves of newsagents, of women with bare bottoms, plunging bras and pouting lips. Except that Max's magazines are of men, almost all of them. Fat men, thin men, men in varying stages of excitement and exposure. Men kneeling before other men, being tied up or tied down, wearing straps, chains, handcuffs, wearing boots, wielding whips. As I gather them up hurriedly and shove them back in the bag, one of the magazines which has been folded inside out takes my notice. The half closed eyes look familiar, but it must just be coincidence — surely I'd have remembered that long blond hair. And then I do remember, but of course the hair isn't that length any more, and checking the date of the magazine I find it's four years old, which explains why he looks so much younger. The naked young man, licking his lips and glaring contemptuously at the camera, is Ricky.

Of course, it doesn't mean anything. People read all sorts of things and it doesn't mean they want to do them; often that's *why* they read about them. I mean, Robert would like a Porsche but he still drives the same old company Ford he's had for years. And Carol had told me about some of the astonishing things that perfectly ordinary women fantasise about. According to some book she had read, if you don't dream of being gang-banged by a nun, a navvy and an Alsatian dog then you're practically abnormal.

But gazing out across London I recall the pavement café in Paris and watching Max's eyes follow the trim backside of a waiter from table to table. I remember being quizzed, and more than once, on what 'different' kinds of sex I liked, and I remember seeing him bidding his farewell to Ricky, clasping his hand for longer than seemed necessary and talking of something I strained to overhear. Not that it means anything, of course.

The traffic moves silently below me, a stream of moving fairy lights with Hyde Park forming an inky backcloth. Which is where Ricky used to live. In a flat overlooking Hyde Park.

When I've put the carrier bag back where I found it, I haul one of my cases back down and repack. I don't know why really, I'm not planning to leave; you don't run away just because you don't share someone's taste in reading matter but I do it all the same. I leave the second case unpacked as though I've only had time to get half done. Then I get undressed and go to bed. When Max comes home at one-thirty he thinks I'm asleep.

Afterwards you think, 'Why didn't I just say something at the time?' I could have said, 'You're a dark horse! When I was putting my case away on the wardrobe I found some very strange bedtime reading!' Or how about, 'Your magazines fell down off the wardrobe; one of the guys in there was the spitting image of Ricky!' Or I could just have come out with it and said, 'Look, as far as I'm concerned that's all kinky stuff, right? So just don't try any of it on me.' But I don't say anything at all, not even next morning after Max has gone to a rehearsal and, searching more rigorously than is strictly necessary for a new loo roll, I find a toilet bag at the back of the cupboard under the bath. It contains several of the sex toys that were advertised in the back of the magazine Ricky was adorning, as well as strawberry flavoured barrier cream, handcuffs and a pair of eyelash curlers. I can't guess what the eyelash curlers are doing in there but I doubt they're for curling eyelashes. Folded underneath is a black hood that fastens at the neck and two silk scarves. I'd rather not speculate on them at all.

I switch the radio on and wonder what to do. It's just as though I've discovered there's no Santa, or rather there is but he's really the dirty old tramp who swears and tries to feel you up when you pass him in the street. But it isn't just the presence of the sex toys *per se* which is so troubling, rather the feeling that I've stumbled on the residue of past affairs, old lovers . . . old boyfriends; and the possibility that they're not all as far in the past as he'd led me to believe. I begin to wonder why he broke up with his wife.

The radio is tuned to a talk show and the closing item is on safe sex — how safe is it? — and how middle-aged people are less diligent than those younger. I'm nowhere near middle age obviously, but I switch it off anyway.

'Cheer up, Ellie,' Max says when he gets back. 'It might never happen.' One of the many things I don't say is that it already has.

*   *   *

After lunch Max makes some revisions to his play and I read the *Guardian*, which is to say I have it open in front of me.

'Are you missing your children?' says Max, looking concerned. I've been trying to control my expression but looking bright and cheerful is something I can't manage just now. Perhaps I am missing them, but what I'm missing more is my own bed, my own home and my old life. I want to crawl into my bed, the king-size, pull the old familiar duvet over my head, and stay there. I want to be having coffee with Josie, telling her that I don't want to have an affair and become a new woman; I liked the woman I was. I want to be back in hospital where all I had to worry about was whether I was going to die.

'Would you like to see a film tonight? Or go to the theatre?' I shake my head again. 'If something's wrong, darling, you ought to tell me.' He calls me 'darling' now instead of 'stupid'. I look at him and I'm so proud of him, his skills and talents, the way he can make me feel. How can this be happening to us? I take a deep breath.

'I love you, Max,' I say, 'whoever you are.'

'You know who I am,' he says, looking puzzled.

But I say no, I don't. Tell me – let me in on your secrets – and I will understand and stay by you, even though I'm frightened because if you go with men that's a dangerous thing, you could catch things, diseases too terrible to name, and you could give them to me which is worse, and, what is worse still, perhaps you will find a man and love him more than you love me. It has happened before.

'I love you,' he says, 'and only you. Before you there was Sophie, my wife, but I didn't love her as I love you; and before her, long, long before, there was Alex and I didn't love him at all.'

I go to him and we kiss and he opens another bottle of champagne. We drink it in bed.

Of course, it doesn't come out quite like this. When Max asks me if something is wrong I say no, everything's fine.

'Maybe I'm just feeling guilty that I haven't got a job and I'm not working on my magazine ideas. I think I'll drive home and pick up my word processor.' I smile and see by Max's expression that it must look genuine and sincere.

Max says I can set up a little office on the kitchen table, and looks relaxed and happy with the prospect of our future working lives. I feel such a traitor for pretending everything is the same as it was yesterday.

My suitcases are already in the car, but I've left a few items about so it doesn't look too obvious. I give him a quick kiss, the kind you give to a man you expect to be seeing again in the next hour, and close the door behind me.

Chapter 28

The weather has turned already although the children have only been back at school a week, and I've started to switch the central heating on in the evenings. It's unfortunate, because it's easier to sell a house when the sun is shining; the only buyers who have viewed so far have brought with them a grey drizzle. It's a nuisance Robert not being here too, because he could tell them things I can't, such as when the cavity insulation was put in and how much the patio will cost to finish, but he won't stay at the house if I'm here. At weekends he comes back to the children and I leave to stay with my mother. The irony is that now when I see him his mere presence thrills as it used to, and the way he stands with his hands thrust in his pockets and his head on one side can make me feel positively weak. But I, of all people, should respect his wish to maintain his distance. If anyone knows that you can't go back, it's me. ('But we can still go forward, Robert,' I tell him when he telephones to speak to the children. He doesn't answer.)

Parting from Max was the hardest thing, harder even than when he parted with me all those years ago. Oh, leaving the flat was easy by comparison, but when I didn't return he phoned of course, and he was inconsolable, just couldn't imagine what had gone wrong. I said I had come to realise that it would be too much of an upheaval for the children (which he didn't buy) and that after all I didn't love him as much as I'd thought (which he did). It wasn't true; perhaps what was true was that I couldn't give up as much for him as I'd thought. Peace of mind, trust, whether I was going to contract something life-threatening, they weren't issues I'd had to think much about with Robert.

On the third day, when I'd stopped answering the phone in case it was him, he came to the house. I wouldn't let him in and he stood on the doorstep with his face pressed against the glass and cried the way Simon does when he has grazed his knee and I'm not quick enough coming to the door. I went upstairs and put Capital Radio on very loud but I could still hear him. That was the hardest thing of all, but what could I do? If I'd held him I would have said yes, okay, we'll try again, I'm sorry. But I would only have had to run away again and hide. He says I'm punishing him for something he can't help; but isn't that what he is doing to me?

When I make my usual visit to Josie I find her looking quite her old self, sitting up in bed with her make-up on. She has her eye on the registrar.

'I did love Greg, but these things don't last forever, do they? He had this irritating habit of sniffing before he said anything he thought was important.'

'Poor you.'

'No, poor you. Twenty years in love with the same guy and then to find you've made a terrible mistake.' That's as much as I've told Josie. And I told her I discovered my mistake in Paris not in Max's London flat, and nothing at all about what the mistake actually was.

'Will you be able to manage on your own?'

'Oh yes, I'm enjoying it.' I am too, though I could wish that independence didn't have to imply having no man around to fix the dishwasher or get the top off a pickle jar.

You expect, don't you, that when something momentous is about to happen in your life that you'll have some sense of foreboding. I think I did too, before I came upon Max's magazine collection. But when the door bell rings I have no premonition at all about what is coming.

It's Max, holding a carrier bag. For one terrible moment I think he's about to present me with the evidence.

'I brought these back,' he says, handing it to me. I hesitate to look inside but after all it's only a few washing items and some make-up I left behind.

'Thank you.' I wait, expecting more beseeching or else to be cut down with an acerbic remark. My make-up is just the excuse that has brought him here.

'You didn't have to just walk out, you know. If you didn't want to stay you had only to say so.' We've been over all this already.

'Thanks for bringing my things back. I could have collected them.' We both know I never would have and my lack of encouragement makes him angry.

'Yes, well, I'm going away today and I wanted all your stuff out.' He cuts the air with his hand: finis. 'I've got someone else moving in.' So this is what he has come to say.

'That didn't take long.'

'No, it never does.' A slight sneer crosses his face.

'Who is it? Ricky?'

He smiles, surprised. 'Well done. So you worked it out about Ricky.'

'He was living with you before you met your wife, wasn't he?'

'After I met my wife, actually. I left Sophie when I met him. It only lasted a year or so, that's when he and Laurence got together. But he's a sly little shit, Laurence has found that out already.' So he'd passed his wife over for Ricky just as he had me for Alex. I want him to go but he doesn't move.

'Actually you know the new incumbent.'

'Oh?'

'And quite intimately, from what he tells me.'

I look at him blankly, not following.

'He needs a father figure, doesn't he? Someone to look up to.' He nods behind him to where his car is parked at the end of the drive. The hedge is partly blocking my view but I'd know that baseball cap anywhere.

'Steven!' I race down the path but Max gets to the car first and blocks my way. Steven is looking straight ahead and blushing scarlet, like someone whose car is blocking a junction with everyone glaring at him. A muscle in his cheek twitches.

'Steven, get out of there—'

Max is enjoying this. 'He's old enough to know what he wants. And what he wants right now is to work as my assistant in France. There'll be plenty on the estate to keep him busy.'

'Steven, what about your mother?'

'Rita? She's delighted, isn't she Steve? Thinks he's really fallen on his feet. And she's very grateful to you, Ellie, for providing the introduction.'

I don't want to cry in front of Max but I can't help it.

'And the irony is,' says Max, 'that you're responsible. He was painting my flat when you gave him the old heave-ho. He was very upset about it, weren't you Steve? I was going to take over the tutoring for his GCSEs. Of course that won't be necessary now.' Max places his hand on the car door but then leans forward to me conspiratorially and, in a low voice, so that Steven won't hear, 'And I'm planning to take over a few of the other areas you schooled him in too. It'll give me quite a buzz, going where you've been before me.' Steven continues to stare ahead. Max opens the car door and eases in. 'I suppose we should be grateful to her, shouldn't we, Steve? She's opened out a whole new life for you.' Steven doesn't answer and Max pulls away with a roar.

Sandra, the aromatherapist, takes my right foot and massages oil in between my toes. I begin to drift off and as I float away I see them all, on the furthest shore, my past loves: Steven, Max, poor Robert, and all the others before them, and I know I have learned nothing. Only the faces change, the circumstances, the words, the pain and the justifications go round and round forever like television repeats. I wonder why I thought Rita was so foolish continuously getting pregnant by the same dissolute man. Isn't it better to make your mistakes with the same man than always the same mistakes with a different one?

Rita. If only we hadn't shared the same ward, the same fears. Because what Max did to me at eighteen I have also done to Steven, leaving him with all the unresolved hurts that he will spend his life trying to resolve. And whatever

I have done, Max will surely redouble. A terrible sob rises in my throat and I bury my face in the pillow.

'Just relax,' says Sandra, kneading my calf muscle.

I'm just crossing the road on my way home from Sandra's when I hear a voice behind me.

'Weren't we at school together?' (And I'd thought it was only Max who was always running into people he had been at school with.) The man has thick hair, very dark and cut neatly about the ears. He's broader than the slim youth I remember but even with glasses I'd know him anywhere. It's Eddie, friend of Neil who I went to Annette's fifteenth birthday party with. We reminisce about our old schools, which friends we have kept in touch with (in my case, none), what paths we have followed since school (I don't mention my recent detours), and then he tells me he's divorced and asks me to go for a drink.

He's still good looking, seems like fun, and I can sense the old feelings beginning to stir. But I can also sense where those old feelings lead and when he sways forward a little into my space it feels like a warning. We'll only break up in the end anyway, we might as well do it now and save all the expense and aggravation (the wine and the whining, so to speak). 'Another time,' I say, airily, 'I'm not free just now.' I leave him standing there and hurry back to my car.

It occurs to me, as I pull away from the lights ahead of a young executive in his company car (winning a race he didn't know he was in), that independence is liberating — it frees you to look at your life, see where you are and where you want to get to. I feel empowered. I can do anything (even get the lid off a pickle jar. You just have to grip it tight with a rubber glove), be anything (such as a cool and sophisticated career woman who doesn't fall gratefully into the arms of the first man who asks her, and who can beat a young executive away from the lights). And most of all, I can get anything. (At the next set of lights the young executive cuts me up. I catch his victorious gleam in his driving mirror.) And what I want most is to get Robert back, the new dynamic Robert who I see roaring off in his new company car (he just got a promotion), his hair restyled so that it no longer flops into his eyes, a steely glint in his new contact lenses. I can get him back too, though I haven't worked out quite how to do it, and it will mean competing with his new girlfriend. (She's something big in product development at Ann Summers. But how many edible panties can one man eat?) I'll get him, too, I'll do it. I've made my mind up.

The meeting with the magazine editor goes very well and as we're hitting it off I ask about editorial vacancies. She asks me where I work and gradually it all comes out, everything that has happened to me over the past six months. She gets very excited at the news of all my bad luck and immediately commissions a second piece; working title, 'Having an Affair: Is it Worth the Risk?' I come away feeling more optimistic about my career than I have in years (and with a new insight on what it takes to get ahead). It's true what they say: one door closes, another door slams in your face. But there's no law that says the doors can't be opened again.

As soon as I get home from the magazine editor's office I sit down, ready to brainstorm the article but when I start to write, the words that flow from my biro aren't on the risks of having an affair at all. Or at least, only in a manner of speaking.

'When I was fourteen,' I write, 'my friend wrote "Having Sex: An Instruction Manual". It had one page with two matchstick people . . .'